THE COST OF forgetting YOU

HANNAH BIRD

Also by Hannah Bird

Loveless series

The End and Then (Book 1)

What's Left of Me (Book 2)

Standalones

Promise Me This

Novellas

That Christmas Kind of Feeling

Author's Note

Dear Reader,

Thank you, as always, for picking up a story of mine. When I set out to write *The Cost of Forgetting You,* it was my dream to create a love letter to the caretaker, a role so often overlooked in our society. I wanted to show the struggles and joys of loving someone with dementia, and to explore the reality that our loved ones are not just their illness, but all the very real fears, dreams, and experiences they had prior to their diagnosis. It is my hope that I have handled these topics with the utmost care and sensitivity, and shown the respect that is due all those who work and care for patients in this space.

Henry's story represents only one example of living with dementia, of which there are millions. As a result, his reality may look very different from what you've experienced. To best prepare you, I've listed possible triggers below that may come up in this book. I hope that you will take care of yourself above all else when considering whether this is the right read for you.

Throughout this novel, there are mentions of: *death of a parent (on page and past), cancer in a parent, frontotemporal dementia in a parent (described in detail), emotionally abusive parents and spouses, grief, bullying, and teen pregnancy (past)* in various degrees of depth.

If you are caring for a loved one with dementia of any kind, I highly recommend following @creativeconnectionsdementia on Instagram for Montessori-based and trauma-informed care tips for living with this condition.

With love,

HB

For all the women who had to raise themselves.
Who hold the world on their shoulders and their hearts in their
hands.
This love story is yours.

Chapter One

Delilah

Henry Ridgefield has left you a voicemail.

I STARE AT THE NOTIFICATION. For a moment I'm convinced I'm imagining things. But even after I reach for my glass of water and swallow enough to drench the Sahara my mouth has become, the words still read the same.

Unbelievable. My father hasn't left me a voicemail since my eighteenth birthday.

The memory pulses through my mind. It'd been a year since the affair. A year since Mom and I packed up and moved to South Carolina to live with her parents. My phone rang as the smoke from the candles on my cake was still dissipating. I hadn't picked up, of course. I never answered any of his calls. That didn't stop him from making them, though.

Until the letter.

The letter that pulled the wayward string on our already threadbare relationship. I'd written it as a therapy exercise. Filled it with the anger and betrayal previously sealed up in the mausoleum of my heart. After all, I never allowed myself to be angry. *Mom* was angry. She had every right to be. It was my job to be calm. Levelheaded. I was a lifeboat in tumultuous waters. It was all I could do to keep us both afloat.

I poured my whole heart onto those pages. Questions I never allowed myself to ask came tumbling out. Line after line of *Why did you do this?* and *Why did I have to be the one to pick up the pieces when you did?*

The letter sat on my dresser for months, addressed but not stamped. I didn't know if I even wanted to send it. My therapist, the one my grandparents paid for after Mom and I moved in with them, said mailing it wasn't the point. It was just about getting it out. About setting a little bit of the weight down.

It was Mom who made that decision for me. Mom, who liked to borrow my clothes. We wore the same size in everything, right down to our tiny size 6 shoes. I suppose she saw the letter on one of her routine closet raids. Or during one of her late-night venting sessions. It wasn't even the letter I realized was missing, but his voicemails.

"Dad hasn't called in three weeks," I'd mused over dinner. I was separating the peas from my pot pie with one of Grandma's real silver forks. Everything in their house was fancier than it needed to be. Certainly fancier than the things we'd left behind in Alabama.

Mom hadn't even looked up. *"I guess he got your letter."*

"My letter?" Panic like a lightning strike hit my chest.

"Oh, honey," she sighed, finally glancing my way. *"I knew you'd never do it yourself, and I wanted to help. Now you see what I've been telling you all along. He never really cared about either of us. He was waiting to be let off the hook—and he finally has been."* She deposited a large piece of beef into her mouth. It was only partially chewed when she added, *"We're on our own, Delilah. Just you and me. But it's good, because we're free to have whatever life we want. He can't hold us back anymore."*

The truth was, I didn't know that I wanted a life outside of the one we'd had with Dad, but I knew better than to say as much. I couldn't even find it in me to be angry with her for mailing it, since the lack of notifications had already proven her right about one thing. I was on my own.

He didn't call again. Not until today.

My thumb hovers over the *PLAY* button. *Do I want to know? Do I even care what he has to say after so many years of silence?*

Later, I decide. There's no time limit on it. He's given me nothing all these years. The least I deserve is a few hours to process.

"Who are you texting?" Mom asks.

Anxiety bursts like a bubble in my chest. I quickly swipe up and swap back to the screen I was on when his phone call came through. I stared at his name—I'd long since swapped out *Dad* with *Henry*—while it rang and rang and rang, finally disappearing, just for the voicemail notification to pop up in its place.

"I'm not." I unravel my legs and stretch them out under the dining table. The thin gingham tablecloth brushes my thighs. I do my best to look nonchalant when I feel anything but.

Just as I knew she would, Mom kicks her ballet flats off to the left of the archway and pads across the tile to stand behind me. She peers over my shoulder, her breath tickling my neck. "Apartments? Why are you looking at apartments?"

I glance at the Zillow listings on my screen and pinch a sigh off with my lips. Uncertainty takes root in my stomach. I had a laundry list of good reasons for this potential move before Dad's phone call derailed my train of thought. Now I'm grasping at straws.

"I don't know, Mom…maybe because I'm twenty-six years old?" I clear my throat. "I make enough money, and with me working from home, it might be easier—"

"But we have so much space here." She steps back and gestures broadly to my grandparents' house. "*I'm* here. And you don't make *that* much money. You really wanna waste it on an apartment and leave me all alone?"

Her voice enters familiar territory—wary and a little bit desperate. It's the same tone she used with the letter. With my college applications. With anything and everything that's ever threatened to put more than an inch of space between us since we left Dad.

Before that, she hardly wanted to be around me. I guess having our lives upended really put things into perspective for her. And since my grandparents passed, I'm all she has left. Me and her wayward sister, Helen, whose whereabouts volley between *Who the fuck knows?* and *Who the fuck wants to know?* on the regular.

There's a soft *click* as I lock my phone. "It's not that."

Her hands find the curve of her hips. "Then what is it?"

"It's nothing at all, Mom." The sigh is halfway out of my lungs before I can think better of it. Her penciled-in eyebrows lift. The shade is a bit dark for her blonde hair but perfect for my own mouse-brown waves. She must've swiped it from my makeup bag this morning while I was still sleeping.

We stare at each other, twin hazel gazes communicating in a language only years spent up each other's asses can forge. Deep down I'm sure she at least has an inkling why I want space. I also know that she'll never be ready for it.

And we *both* know who'll win the battle today.

Her already thin lips pinch together. I rise from the wooden dining chair my grandfather carved by hand, my back muscles screaming in protest.

"I've got another meeting in five minutes." I scoop my half-eaten sandwich from the table and start toward the staircase. Its grandiose presence dominates the foyer at the front of the house, which is separated from the kitchen by an arched threshold. I have the entire upstairs level to myself, in this house which has always been too big and yet not big enough.

"But I thought we'd have lunch together." She joins me in the archway, the in-between, and points to a white paper bag with her favorite sub shop's logo sitting on the console table in the foyer. "I came home on my break just to spend time with you. We haven't seen each other much this week."

That was intentional, I want to say. But like so much else, I keep it to myself. Lately I find my patience with her wearing so thin, the artificially rose-colored veil over my eyes when it comes to her all but disappearing. But I'm not ready for an all-out war, which is what I'd have on my hands if I ever told her how I'm feeling.

Her down-turned eyes only serve to emphasize the pout she's sporting. Mine may be colored the same as hers, but they're shaped like Dad's, early onset crow's feet and all. Something she's always suggesting a new cream to fix.

"I'm sorry, but I can't skip this meeting. Maybe dinner instead?"

She drops the pity party, realizing it's not working out the way she'd like. Suddenly her pinkie nail becomes the most interesting thing in the room, demanding her full attention. "I'm actually going out for margaritas with some of the ladies from work."

"Well." I glance over her shoulder at the clock on the wall. Two minutes to get upstairs and logged in. "Have fun with that."

"You'll pick me up, right?"

My gaze flickers back to her. The eyebrow pencil really isn't doing her any favors. "Yep. Have an extra margarita for me."

She winks, oblivious to my tone. "I have the best daughter."

I offer a tight-lipped smile and return to my tower.

My phone taunts me the entire afternoon.

By my third meeting, I've lost all ability to focus. The clients I'm supposed to be training are having to repeat their questions twice for me to finally register what they're asking. There's a tension headache building at my temples. When my vision goes blurry, I block off the last hour of the day and close my laptop.

My gaze catches on my thumb as I do it. The cuticle is angry and bleeding where I've chewed it raw.

I glance at my phone again, and anxiety bubbles to the surface once more. No one calls after eight years to chat about the economy. Whatever my dad has to say to me, it's bad. I don't know how I know, but I do. It's the kind of sixth sense you only develop after the rug's been pulled from beneath you once before. The knowledge that it can, and most likely will, happen again.

Just rip the Band-Aid off. I tap on the notification.

"Hi, sweet pea, it's Dad."

I hit pause so hard the phone flies off my desk and falls screen first on the beige carpet. Guilt slaps me across the face. What would Mom think if she knew about this? Even listening to his voice feels like betrayal.

My heart lodges in my throat. The tip of my nose burns. I need *air.*

The window groans in protest as I pry it open for the first time in months. It may be spring everywhere else in the country, but in South Carolina it's already sweltering. Living on the outskirts of Charleston, we're close enough to the marshes that a salty breeze pushes that warm air against my face. I drink it in like water.

All the while I'm wishing for a different breeze, carrying the heady scent of a river and magnolia blooms and the Parkers' farm in the distance. I haven't allowed myself this yearning in so long. It's all I can do not to stumble beneath the weight of it.

Sweet pea.

I was eighteen the last time he called me that, and suddenly I am eighteen again. Hot tears streak my cheeks; sticky snot fills the hollow above my upper lip. I feel so incredibly small. I feel like somebody's child, and I can't remember the last time I felt that way.

A deep, shuddering breath. An exhale that lasts five seconds. Rinse and repeat.

I glance over my shoulder. The fading sunlight reflects off the back of my phone. I want to know what he has to say, and yet I'm so ashamed to want it.

Because Mom was right. He never called again. How do you give up so easily on your child? The words in that letter were harsh, yes, but they were never meant to be read. I was angry and confused, living in a world that had been turned upside down on a dime. A world where the one person I thought I knew best became someone I didn't even recognize.

Even so, he could've tried. He could've reached out. But he didn't. So why, after all this time, should I care what he has to say?

Another deep breath. This time when I exhale, I send all my expectations out with the air. If you don't want anything, it can't be taken away. Without hope, there's no disappointment.

I kneel by the desk and flip my phone over. The screen lights up. The voicemail is still paused where I left it. I sink my teeth into my lower lip and press play.

"I'm sorry to call after all this time. I wanted to give you space like you asked. I wanted... Well, it doesn't matter now, does it? I'm just sorry. I wish...I wish I had some better news, but the doctors... Things are getting worse. Not better. And you're my next of kin, sweet pea, so I needed to let you know that I'm sick—"

I hit pause again. The phone screen blurs. What started as simple tears dissolves into full-blown sobbing. Sick? How could he be sick? He's forty-five years old, for Christ's sake.

I was supposed to have more time.

More time to be angry. To be resentful if I feel like it. To actually figure out what the fuck I want without Mom's opinions overshadowing any of my own. Time to start over.

When I press play again, my finger trembles.

"It's called fronto...fron...ah, hell." There's the sound of papers shuffling in the background, followed by a distant voice. My dad mutters something to the person before speaking into the receiver. *"I can't remember what it's called, and that's the whole problem. I have what Nana had. I've just got a head start, I guess."*

My mind finishes what he couldn't. *Frontotemporal dementia.* My heart stops, and it's all I can do to hold on to the phone with my shaking hand.

Nana, my dad's mother, passed away when I was eight years old. She lived with us at first, but most of my memories of her come after, when she had already moved to a memory care facility. By that time she no longer knew who we were. She was young to have dementia, they told me. But she was still in her sixties. Ancient to a little kid.

Not like my dad.

"I just wanted to tell you I love you. And that I'm sorry for... for so much. That's all. You don't have to do anything for me. I'm getting it all figured out. Well, me and that Parker boy...Truett. You remember him?"

Truett's face flashes in my mind. A million iterations. All the ways I've known him. He's six and gap-toothed and dressed like a superhero for the school trunk-or-treat. He's twelve and skinning his knee from attempting a jump on his bike. He's just shy of seventeen and kissing me beneath a willow tree. Then two weeks later, he's turning his head, pretending not to see me crying in a field of cruel teenagers.

That movement—my oldest friend, my first love, refusing to even bear witness. It cut deeper than the others ever could.

My cheeks heat. Why is Truett Parker of all people helping out *my* dad?

"Anyway, I love you. I always have, Delilah. And I... I'd love to see you. But if I don't hear from you, I'll understand. Just wanted to be the one to tell you. Be good, sweet pea. Always be good."

A stilted, robotic voice lets me know I can press one to play the message again or press two to delete it. I choose neither. I just stare at the phone until the screen goes dark, mind racing yet staying stock-still all at once.

I don't know how much time passes with me kneeling on the floor. Enough that my tears dry and the carpet permanently imprints on my knees. Enough that my phone lights up once more, this time with my mom's face plastered across the screen.

"Hello," I croak, my voice fractured from disuse.

"Delilah, can you come get us?" A fit of giggles fills my ear. I jerk the phone away to spare my hearing. "Debbie and I are a bit tipsy."

That knot in my throat grows larger. I peel myself off the ground and swallow hard. *This is real life.* I'm not in a dream. I have to act normal when nothing feels normal anymore.

I can do this. I can take care of my mom when my whole world has just fallen apart beneath me. After all, it wouldn't be the first time.

"On my way."

"Thank you!" she singsongs. I hang up as they dissolve into laughter once more.

Debbie lives on the opposite side of town, so thirty minutes pass before my mother and I are alone in the car together. She adjusts my right air vent to face her, adding to the two already on her side. "Good Lord, it's already so hot out and it's only May."

Sweat beads at my temples. Collects in the bends of my arms.

I think about making small talk. I really do. But the minute I open my mouth to comment on the weather, out slips, "Dad's sick."

Her hand pauses over the temperature dial. I feel her gaze land on my face, but keep mine trained on the asphalt ahead.

"Well." She wets her lips audibly. "I didn't know you were in contact with Henry."

"I wasn't," I say too quickly. I shift in my seat. "I'm not. He left me a voicemail today."

Silence grows taut between us. It takes three stoplights before she replies with simply, "Oh."

"He's *really* sick." I turn on the blinker for our street. It's more of a gravel path than anything, with only my grandparents' house at the end of it. "It sounds like he has what Nana did." I can't bring myself to say the word *dementia.* It feels too raw. Too real.

I expect her to ask anyway. To want that clarification. Part of me even thinks she'll burst into tears the way I did. After all, they were married for seventeen years. How it ended doesn't change the fact that for a time he was the center of our world.

"You know you don't have to go, right?"

My head snaps toward her. I blink twice, not quite comprehending.

"Don't look at me like that. After everything he did to us—"

"To you," I interject without thinking. My fingertips land on my lips, not quite believing they actually formed those words.

"What did you say?"

She's giving me a chance to course correct. I could lie right now, and we'd both go on pretending the words never slipped out of me in the first place. But I'm so tired all of a sudden. Tired of being angry for both of us.

"After what he did *to you.* He cheated on *you,* Mom." *Not me,* I want to add. But this much I can hold back.

We're parked in front of the house. My headlights illuminate the colonial-style home that's older than both of us combined. It looks more like a museum than a place where two women live. It feels like one, too.

"How could you say something like that to me?" Her voice pitches up, then warbles at the end. She's going to start crying. And I'm going to end up cleaning up the mess.

A heavy sigh passes over my lips. It's not worth it to argue with her. "I'm sorry. I wasn't thinking."

Her lips thin. She's studying my face, searching for something. I smile, weary as I am, and she returns it. Content to believe the fragile facade I've presented.

She reaches out and strokes my cheek with the back of her hand. Her knuckles are cold. The ornate gold ring she inherited when her mother passed scrapes my skin lightly.

I wince, but she's already turning to open her door.

"Glad that's settled." She retrieves her purse from the floorboard and steps out into the night. She doesn't wait for a response before closing the door. She's never had to wonder if I'll do as she asks.

But as I watch her foot land on the first step of the wide staircase leading up to the porch, I feel something shift within myself. For the first time in so long, I imagine my dad sitting on a different front porch. His Converse scuff against the wooden floorboards, kicking him into motion on the swing he put in for my mom the year his mother moved into the nursing home. I hear cows in the distance. Sweat beads on my forehead. When I step in front of him, he turns, but his gaze shows no sign of recognition.

"I'm going," I whisper, surprising myself. Because deep down, I know I mean it, even if it's the one thing my mother could never understand. The one thing she could never forgive.

Because if I stay, I may never forgive myself. And shouldn't that matter more?

Chapter Two

Delilah

Fly Hollow has a population of 3,112 according to the newly minted sign at the edge of town, but even that number seems a bit of a stretch. With not much more than a small grocery store, a school that you attend from kindergarten all the way to graduation, a church, and copious amounts of farmland, I'm not sure where all those people are hiding. I'd be willing to bet they included cattle in the tally, just to beef up the numbers.

A half-hearted giggle bubbles over my lips. The cluster of cows near the fence line to my right moo as I drive past, as though disapproving of my joke, but I ignore them with a tired smile.

Leaves rustle overhead. A familiar canopy of live oaks blots out the pale blue sky. Birds perched in the sprawling branches call to one another. In the distance a tractor starts up. I turn down the volume on my road-trip playlist and unfurl my arm out the open car window, capturing the hot breeze in my clammy palm.

Homesickness stirs in my chest, adding to the already long list of complicated emotions I have to sort through. It's all the same. It's all so hard.

The scent of azaleas blooming along the road filters in, light and sweet, while the words dancing in my mind are anything but.

"He doesn't deserve your pity."

A middle-aged man wearing a faded ball cap stands on the weather-beaten deck behind the post office, loading mail into a beat-to-shit Jeep for delivery.

"You're all that I have; you can't go."

The only grocery store and gas station in town, Sunshine Grocery—where Dad and I would grab breakfast sandwiches from the deli on our way to school each morning—appears up ahead on the right.

"How could you do this to me?"

I veer into the cracked asphalt lot and throw the car into park. Here, the sound of cicadas and people chitchatting over the gas pumps nearly drowns out the memory of my mother's voice in my head.

Nearly.

As if on cue, my phone vibrates with another text from her. This time I swipe to delete it without sparing her words a glance. It's my version of boundary setting. Something else my former therapist tried to teach me.

The music, a quiet rhythm under the cacophony of small-town life, cuts out with an incoming call.

Mom's picture pops up on the screen. My skull thuds against the headrest. Maybe things like private letters and boundaries work for other people, but I'm beginning to think that therapist was out of her depth with a woman like my mother. If my grandparents weren't already gone, I'd recommend they get their money back.

Finally the call drops. Before the music can resume, though, I cut the engine.

Heat in south Alabama is a living thing. When I step onto the pavement, it embraces me. I stretch my legs out in front of me, leaning against the wheel well for support. Nine hours of driving has my whole body spent. My mind, however, is wired.

I'm ten minutes away from my father. My father, whom I haven't seen since junior year of high school. My *sick* father, whom I didn't even warn I was coming. Goose bumps prickle on my forearms despite the relentless sunshine overhead. My mom was right; this was a terrible fucking idea.

I push my hands through my hair and shake it out. When they drop back to my sides, they're trembling. Being here, in this town that holds so much of my hurt as well as my joy, is too much. The sprawling fields and undulating curves of the river, which seemed endless to me as a child, now feel impossibly small. I'm suffocating, but I'm surrounded by open space.

A bell jingles, drawing my attention. The front door of Sunshine Grocery swings open. The man who steps through it is about my age, with shaggy blond hair cut in a grown-out mullet. Harsh sunlight illuminates his five-o'clock shadow–ridden face as he glances in my direction, and my breath stalls in my lungs.

Time folds in on itself. Suddenly I'm seventeen again, walking through the tall grass of a field.

Trucks are parked in a loose semicircle ahead, their head-lights illuminating a cluster of kids from school who stand around a bonfire, sipping from plastic cups. Their shouts and laughter carry over to me on the breeze. I rub my forearm, regretting the decision to wear short sleeves. It's colder than I thought it would be.

Kyle Miller glances over his shoulder at me, pausing mid-laugh to scan my body as I approach. I wore this shirt because of the deep V-neck, hoping it would be sexy enough for someone with his experience. Heat fills my cheeks. I've never tried to be sexy before. The only guy I ever cared about impressing has seen me traipsing through fields of cow manure in boots and loose-

fitting jeans. Dressing up for Truett was never going to change how he saw me.

Of course, after everything that's happened these last few weeks, impressing him is no longer an option. Speaking to him is no longer an option. He made sure of that.

Kyle, on the other hand, has never been on my radar. He's good-looking enough, with tightly cropped blond hair and brown eyes that are approximately 70 percent cacao. As our school's star tight end, he's certainly sought after by the other girls. I've been so busy pining after my best friend, though, that Kyle never managed to make it out of my peripheral. Not until yesterday, when he invited me to this party.

When he sought me out during the loneliest period of my life.

Which is how I find myself here, trying to impress him with no idea how to do it. I tug at the hem of my shirt and hope this V-neck and what little bit of makeup I have on are enough to make me something more than the unremarkable person I've always been.

Kyle's lips stretch into a wide smile. "There you are, Delilah."

"Here I am." I shift my weight and glance around at the crowd, noting the familiar faces. In a town as small as Fly Hollow, it's impossible not to know everyone. It's also impossible to keep your business to yourself. Especially when your dad decides to conduct that business on school grounds.

So when I catch Emily and her best friend, Katelyn, casting sidelong glances my way before closing ranks with their shoulders and dissolving into laughter, I suddenly wish I were anywhere but here.

"You look beautiful," Kyle says.

My gaze cuts back to him. Despite my anxiety, I find myself preening at his compliment. Have I ever been called beautiful?

Not by anyone but my dad, I realize. Pathetic.

Perhaps that's why I lean into Kyle when he opens his arms for me. Aligning my body to his, I can feel every muscle, every contour. I lace my arm around his waist like I know how to do this. Like my experience goes beyond a few stolen kisses in the shade of a willow tree with my best friend.

Like said best friend didn't just arrive and grab a beer from a group of guys ten feet away, without ever bothering to acknowledge my presence.

Ignoring him takes every ounce of my strength. When I finally pry my gaze from the back of Truett's head, Kyle's friends are looking at me expectantly. I realize I've missed what was just said.

I clear my throat and fix my face into the friendliest expression I can. The least nervous. "I'm sorry, what did you say?"

Kyle's hand slips an inch down my waist. Tension crawls into my spine, but moving away from his touch only brings me closer to his side. He takes it as a good sign, hooking his thumb through my belt loop and squeezing.

"I asked how things are going," his friend Noah clarifies. Noah's the quarterback and the basketball captain and class president all in one. Perks of a small school and outgoing personality, I guess.

"You know," Kyle adds, glancing down at me, "with your parents."

I shrug, not really interested in this line of questioning. "Hell if I know."

"That's so wild Mrs. Parker and your dad fucked at school. The man's got balls; that's for sure!" Noah howls with laughter.

Their other friend, Asher, slaps his shoulder. "That's what Mrs. Parker said."

Noah's laughing too hard to respond.

I, on the other hand, bristle. "Dad said they didn't have sex."

I don't know if I believe him. Mom certainly doesn't. But it feels wrong to let these idiots shit talk him in front of me without even trying to come to his defense.

The look everyone gives me screams, Oh, you sweet, summer child.

I huff a breath, clouding the night air with vapor. "I'm getting a drink," I mutter. But when I try to slip away from Kyle's embrace, he simply walks with me toward the tailgate where luke-warm beer lies in wait, never releasing his hold from my waist.

It's something couples at school do all the time, which drives me absolutely nuts. No amount of infatuation justifies needing to be literally attached at the hip, taking up all the space in the hallway.

My mind, and my gaze, flash to Truett. Even from this distance, I can see exactly what his eyes are locked on.

Kyle's hand. On my waist.

"Sorry about those guys," Kyle says as he passes me a can of Natural Light. "They don't have a lot of couth."

I try not to show my surprise that he even knows the meaning of the word couth. *My eyebrows shoot up anyway.*

"It's whatever." I do my best to sound unaffected. The slight warble in my tone would give me away, but Kyle's staring at my chest. The chances he heard, or cared even if he did, are minimal. Not when he's practically salivating.

V-neck saves the day. Who knew?

He finally tears his gaze away from what, if I'm honest, is barely a B-cup on a good day. "How come you're never at these parties?"

Because I'm not usually invited. Because even if I were, I have volleyball practice to fill most nights and, lately, Mom's tantrums to fill the others. Because I'm newly motivated to study hard to get into a great college so I can leave this place, and my parents' issues, behind.

The reasons threaten to roll off my tongue. Luckily I'm well-trained in the art of biting it.

I shrug. "I'm usually busy."

In one smooth motion, he plucks the beer I've barely taken two sips of from my hand, deposits it on the tailgate, and folds me into him so we're chest to chest. The sour scent of beer breath mixes with his Axe cologne, hitting me in the back of the throat.

"I'm glad you weren't too busy for me tonight." His lips curl in a half smile, stretching like a lazy cat. "I've got the most beautiful date here."

I'm not blind. I've seen my competition. Emily and Katelyn are both bombshell brunettes who lost all their childhood chub in middle school and never gained an ounce back. Every other girl at this party has a million traits I could pick out as more desirable than the sum of mine. I know I'm not the most beautiful. Not by a mile.

But when he says it, some small part of me rises up from the depths and latches on to it. Believes in it with all she's got.

I've only ever kissed Truett Parker. Kisses that were slow and sweet, secret and all the better for it. So when Kyle's lips land on mine in a flurry of movement, when his tongue immediately demands access to my mouth, I'm unprepared. I'd stumble backward if he wasn't holding me so tightly. His tongue darts from side to side, searching for God knows what. A courageous hand slips from my waist to my ass and pinches, eliciting a yelp that crashes into his lips and falls silent in the onslaught.

His other hand, which had been lazily stroking my cheek, slowly moves to my throat. Down, down, down, until his palm presses against my breast and squeezes. Hard.

"That's enough," I say against his mouth. Somehow I manage to fit my hands between us and flatten them against his chest, pushing him back. "What the fuck?"

"Aw, come on." Kyle smirks and pats the tailgate beside him.

"I know it's not a piano, but I bet I can fuck better than your dad did."

Hoots and hollers sound behind us. I jerk toward the sound, suddenly confronted with a row of people holding their phones up in our direction. Recording. They're recording this.

I stumble backward. Kyle reaches for my elbow, but I skirt his grasp. "What is going on?"

Kyle's eyes, already brown as the mud beneath my boots, darken. "Don't act like you aren't easy, Delilah. The apple can't fall that far from the tree."

Laughter. More shouts, calls for him to give it to me. Give what to me, I don't know, but I'm not sticking around to find out.

I shove through the line of my classmates, kids I've known since kindergarten. On the other side, I'm met with the rest of the party attendees. People who didn't care enough to film but also didn't care enough to stop it from happening.

Among them is Truett. He won't even look in my direction. In fact, he turns his back on me and walks away, toward the wood line. Probably has to take a piss or something. Anything is more important than his best friend of, I don't know, our entire lives?

The tears come, hot and prickly. I blink them away, determined not to add to my humiliation by letting these people see me cry. I take off toward the road, in the opposite direction of Tru. Through the mud and the tall grass I charge, ignoring the catcalls behind me. When I finally get to Dad's car, which he let me borrow without so much as a question as to my destination, I kick out of my muck-covered shoes and toss them into the trunk.

I drive home barefoot, blinded by tears.

The benefit of a small town, I suppose, is that you could drive the roads blindfolded. Or sobbing your eyes out.

When I park in front of the house, there's no movement inside. There hasn't been movement for weeks. Not since the night when everything fell apart.

Now my parents just haunt opposite sides of the house, my dad silent and sulking and my mother hell-bent on letting us both know how badly he hurt her. No one's there when I drop my boots by the front door, walk inside, and collapse onto the bench in the breakfast nook.

It's always been my favorite place in the house. A three-sided bench seat situated just off the kitchen, surrounded by windows overlooking our yard and the Parkers' pasture beyond it. The best view in the house, until now. Until my dad had to go and sleep with Truett's mom, effectively ruining everything.

Footsteps on the hardwood draw my attention from the moonlit field. Mom shuffles to the fridge, removes a bottle of wine, and uncorks it. She doesn't bother with a glass. I'm tempted to ask her for a swig. With the way things have been going lately, she'd probably hand it over.

But I don't. Instead I clear my throat, startling her.

"Oh, Delilah"—she flattens a palm over her heart—"I didn't know you were home."

I run a finger along the familiar wood grain of the table. A table I've done all my homework at, eaten every dinner. Something that used to bring me comfort but now feels like another reminder of everything that's been tainted. "Are you still planning on moving to Grandma and Grandpa's?"

Her shoulders droop. Behind her, my baby pictures stare back at me from their place on the yellow-white fridge. They didn't make it into the boxes she packed, I guess. The ones lining our living room wall, awaiting pickup on Tuesday by the moving truck my grandparents hired.

"Yes, it's what's best for me. With everything that's happened, I can't stay here." She sits on the bench opposite me. The wine bottle rattles against the wood when she sets it down. "I know you don't want to leave your dad." Venom leaks into her voice. She takes a sip, like wine might wash it away. "But I really wish you'd

come with me. He doesn't need you like I do. Besides, you'd love Charleston. Lots more to do there."

My hand, which was still tracing that grain, is swallowed by hers. Cold and damp from the perspiration on the bottle.

She catches my gaze, a smile slowly stretching her lips. "We'd have so much fun together."

The old house groans as if in mourning. "I'll come with you," I whisper.

Her eyes go wide, alertness sparking in them for the first time in weeks. "You will? Oh, that's fantastic."

I expect her to hug me. To ask me why the change of heart, maybe. But instead she abandons me and her wine bottle, taking off for the study where my dad has been sleeping since he was caught cheating with Lucy Parker.

Of course she'd want to rub it in his face. I've just handed her something precious, and her first thought is to hone it into a weapon and hurl it at my dad.

The wine is bitter but better than warm, cheap beer. I take a swig and hope it washes away the fear that I'm making a mistake.

<hr>

Kyle doesn't recognize me. At least, from the way his gaze travels over me and then flickers away without so much as a reaction, I can assume he doesn't. Why would he? After all, one of the worst nights of my life was probably just another Friday for him.

Fucking small towns. You can't go anywhere without running into someone.

He walks past me without a word and climbs into the same red pickup truck he was driving in high school, where an older and softer version of Katelyn Phillips sits waiting for him. Her hand—lined with braided, multicolored bracelets—hangs out the window. She takes the bottle of Sprite he offers, the receipt it's wrapped in crackling when she grabs it. He quickly deposits a wad of dip into his lower lip and starts the truck, reversing without another glance my way.

This place never changes.

Perhaps it's why I thought I had more time. That I could leave and come back when I was finally ready, and like a time capsule, it'd all be sealed here, waiting for me. No dust. No aging.

No forgetting.

I duck into my car and start the engine back up. The leather of the steering wheel sears my palms, but my hands no longer shake. *My dad is sick*, I remind myself. I'm here to take care of him. To get some answers if I can. I know how to do this. To be the responsible one, the voice of reason. The life raft. I can't drown if I'm focused on saving someone else.

Those words cycle through my mind over and over for the next ten minutes. A steady heartbeat as I drive down more familiar roads, past homes of girls I used to have sleepovers with but haven't heard from since I left town, and finally turn by an overgrown magnolia tree whose blooms blot out its leaves like full moons.

Nestled amid a grove of live oaks, my childhood home appears. The white paint is faded in some places. My rope swing and the branch it hung from are missing from the tree out front, a large oak with a trunk the size of a grain silo. Probably rotted or blown away in a hurricane. Or maybe Dad cut it down so he didn't have to look at it every day and remember me.

My heart lurches at the thought. It took me a week to gather the courage to tell Mom I was leaving. Another to actually get my ass in the car. How much could things have changed in those two weeks? Will he recognize me? Will he remember who I am?

I shake my head. Everything I've seen online says that's not how this disease works. I've got time. I've got to have time.

Time for what, I don't know. Time for answers? An apology?

From him or from me? I swallow back bile and put the car in park.

Cows call out from the fields beyond the house. I don't glance in their direction. Truett may have been helping Dad in my absence, but I'm here now. And I've got this. He can go back to his farm and his mother and leave my family the hell alone.

I park behind Dad's silver Altima. As I get out of my car and amble closer, I realize it looks like it's been in an accident. The hood and front bumper are caved in. Angry black streaks peel back the paint along the driver's side doors. I scrape a shaking hand through my hair, blowing out a whistle as I take in the extent of the damage. I'd be shocked if it even runs.

Beside it, there's a baby-blue pickup truck. Newer, by the looks of it, or restored to look new. A replacement for the totaled car?

The floorboards of the porch creak underfoot. Several pairs of shoes, including mud-stained Converse, sit discarded by the door. Mom's swing sways gently in the hot breeze. It brings with it the scent of magnolias and river water, as well as cattle from the Parkers' farm.

I drop my backpack to the ground and school my face into a neutral expression before knocking on the door.

It swings away from my fist in a rush. Suddenly Dad is standing right in front of me for the first time in so long. My heart seizes and my eyes burn with unshed tears, but I force it all down. Because it's not about me right now. It can't be.

When his gaze lands on me, I brace myself for the look of confusion that filled Nana's eyes in those final years. Logically I know it takes time to get there. But fear knows no logic. And right now I'm a little girl, afraid her dad has already forgotten her. That he did long before he got sick.

The crow's feet around his eyes have deepened. Gray has started to appear, dense at his temples and sporadic in the rest of his brown hair. He's handsome; I've always thought so. My class-mates used to tease me about it. He smiles, and that same front tooth of his is still crooked. Still familiar, when so much of his life is foreign to me now.

Tears well in his blue eyes. "Delilah, you came."

I exhale. My clenched fists unfurl. *Be calm*, I tell myself. *You don't want to overwhelm him.*

"Of course I did," I whisper. Though I suspect, behind Mom, he was second most sure that I wouldn't.

When he opens his arms, expression hesitant but hopeful, I crack. A single tear. It might as well be a torrent. For a moment all the anger and hurt dissipates like morning fog burned off by the sun. All I feel is relief that he remembers.

Because as long as he remembers, there's still time.

We embrace in the threshold with my backpack at our feet.

Chapter Three

Delilah

"COME INSIDE, COME INSIDE." Dad steps back and waves me in. "You must be tired! What's that drive, nine hours or so?"

I pause mid shoe removal and blink at him. "You know how far it is?"

He winces, hooks his hand on the nape of his neck. "I've been to Nancy and Greg's house a time or two. It's a long drive, but at least it's scenic."

The bruise on my heart aches as though he's pressed a finger right into it. *Why didn't you come to see me, then?* I want to ask. But I don't, because what difference would it make?

I finish removing my white sneakers and leave them next to his black Converse, a little yin and yang there on the porch. When I step over the threshold, the honey-colored floor creaks under my weight. Same board as always. You can't come or go in this house without being announced.

"I see you haven't fixed the floorboard," I tease.

"I'll get to it next week."

We both turn toward that voice. One whose drawl, despite the years since I last heard it, I'd recognize anywhere.

"No one's touching the floor." Dad's hand, warm and familiar, cups my bicep. "Delilah, you remember Truett Parker?"

Remember Truett Parker? How could I fucking forget.

He's seated in my spot at the breakfast nook, gaze trained on me with an intensity that makes my skin crawl. He was always tan from weekends and afternoons spent helping his dad around the farm, but he's especially tawny now. It makes his dirty blond hair seem so light by comparison, his blue-gray eyes bright. The youthful wiriness is gone from his body, replaced by taut muscles that strain the shoulders of his T-shirt, the seams of his Wranglers. He stretches his long legs out like he sees me studying them and wants to give me a better angle.

I blush, drawing my gaze back up to his. He's clean-shaven, leaving the strong angles of his jaw on full display. His lip twitches toward a knowing smile, causing the dimples in his cheeks to pop.

"Hello, Temptress."

The nickname, born from the misfortune of having the name Delilah while growing up in the rural South—where they take their Bible stories very seriously—grates on me. Though with my dad watching, who always found it amusing, I swallow my retort.

Instead I say, "Surprised to see you here."

He lifts an incredulous brow. "Suppose I could say the same to you."

It's a barb that I don't want to admit has hit its mark. I turn and grab my bag from the porch. Clear my throat.

"Welp." Truett slaps his knees, pushing on them to lift himself. As much as I wish I were immune, his forearms—sun-kissed and corded—draw my attention. "Guess I'll give you two time to catch up." He saunters toward us in no hurry, like my presence doesn't affect him at all. It's that apathy more than anything that boils my blood. "Henry, Roberta will start on

Monday. It's all taken care of, so no need to do anything but be your charming self."

He offers my father a genuine smile that falters when he turns to me. "Are you planning on sticking around that long?"

I narrow my eyes at him. "Excuse me?"

He acknowledges my glare with a nod but doesn't flinch. Instead he shrugs and retrieves a folded leather wallet from the back pocket of his too-snug Wranglers. "Here's her card in case you need it."

"Who's Roberta?"

He offers the small white business card to me. Our skin brushes—his hot, mine cold—as I pluck it from his hand. His gaze catches mine and holds it.

"Your dad's new in-home nurse," he says matter-of-factly.

My heart twists in on itself. I crumple the card into my front pocket, earning a glare of my own from Truett.

"Sure you don't wanna stay for dinner? I can make—ah…" Dad's voice trails off. He smacks his lips once, twice, like whatever he's trying to say might manifest that way.

Finally, with a subtle shake of his head meant only for me, Truett looks back at my dad. Softens. "No, sir, I've got cows to feed. You two have fun though. I'll be back tomorrow to check on you."

Truett moves toward the door, my dad and I parting like the Red Sea to let him through. He slips into a pair of boots in the pile outside the door; then he's across the porch and down the steps in a few strides of his long, muscular legs. The thin fabric of his white T-shirt gathers and relaxes between his shoulder blades with each swing of his arms. I watch it, that movement, for a beat too long before my brain remembers how to do its thing.

"One second, Dad."

My sock feet thud against the porch, drawing Truett's attention. He spins on the heel of one boot but continues putting distance between us, walking backward. "What do you need, Temptress?"

"Stop calling me that." I slip into my Keds and bound down the steps. A glance back at my father, who's staring hard into the kitchen, tells me he's not paying us any attention. The front door remains open, though, so I reach for Truett's hand and pull him toward my car. "Help me get the rest of my things, would you?"

His brows furrow, but he doesn't resist.

Once we're out of my father's earshot, I release his hand like I've been burned. "Why does he need an in-home nurse?"

"He has dementia." The *duh* is unspoken but very much present.

"Don't be a smart-ass. How bad is it, really? He seems fine to me." I glance over my shoulder as if to confirm this with a cursory scan of Dad's profile. When at last I turn back to Tru, pity is waiting for me in his eyes.

He shifts his weight, then crosses his arms over his chest and rolls his bottom lip between his teeth. "He crashed his car two weeks ago. Nearly took out the sign for the First Baptist Church. So things aren't great, per se."

I open my mouth to speak, but nothing comes out. My heart is lodged in my throat, blocking all flow of air.

Things are getting worse. Not better.

He studies me as this information takes hold, searching my face for a reaction. Whatever he finds, his expression softens. "He's still himself, aside from the occasional outburst when he's having a bad day. But he gets confused with things like showering and cooking. Remembering certain words can be hard for him. I try to help out as much as I can but have to work during the day, so Roberta seemed like the logical next step. She'll come for five hours a few days a week."

I don't know what to say. How to ingest all that at once. So I choose silence instead, reaching for the latch of the trunk to busy my trembling hands.

Tru rests his hip against the side of the car. A muscle in his jaw ticks when he sees my large suitcase and laptop bag. "How long are you planning on staying?"

I pause, hands resting on top of my luggage. *How long* am *I staying?* The truth is, I have no clue. I didn't even know how I'd feel when I saw Dad until he opened the door, let alone if I'd be welcomed across the threshold. There are so many feelings, good and bad and in between, swirling around in my gut. All I know is that Dad is sick, and it's my job to take care of him. Not some stranger Truett hired, and not Truett. Me. Considering how I feel about any of it is a luxury time didn't afford.

Hooking my hands through the loops of the suitcase, I drag it from the trunk and deposit it against Truett's chest. "As long as I'm needed. You can call off the nurse. And you don't need to stop by anymore to check on him. I've got it from here."

He scoffs and drops my suitcase in the dirt.

"Hey—"

"With all due respect, Delilah," he interjects, "you have no idea what he needs."

I bite down hard on the inside of my cheek. "I know he needs help. That's why I'm here."

Truett steps around my discarded luggage till he's so close I can smell the same mixture of sweat and fresh air that always coated his skin after a long day working the farm. "He may seem fine because you've only said five words to him, but trust me when I tell you it's already hard. It's only going to get worse. You won't be able to do it on your own. So let Roberta help. Let *me* help."

Rich, considering how much he helped me when everything fell apart. Which is to say, not at all.

Doesn't he know I've only ever had myself to depend on? Even when I thought I could count on him, he proved me wrong.

"You have no idea what I'm capable of handling." What I've *been* handling since the day we left. If I can manage my mom, Dad will be a walk in the park. "You've done enough, Truett. Thanks for everything, but I'm here now. Just leave us be."

The slam of the trunk echoes through the trees. Somewhere a hawk screeches, offended by the disturbance. I move to go around Tru and retrieve my suitcase, but he blocks my path.

"Can you move." It's not a question.

"You haven't been here." He jabs a finger in my direction, nearly touching me before he apparently thinks better of it. Still, I sense the heat of his hand hovering a few inches from my collarbone. "I have. You stayed away all these years."

"He wasn't exactly beating down my door, either."

"Because you told him not to!"

The fact that he knows this, that my dad told him about the letter—or worse, let him read it—hits me like a blow to the chest, that private, aching piece of my story now everyone's business to discuss and judge me over.

What else is new?

I glare up at Truett. His jaw is taut; I swear he's grinding his teeth. His lips—normally a soft, perfect pout—are pinched in frustration. Everything about him is hardened, accusatory.

Except his eyes. Those are wide, desperate for an explanation. Realizing this, I step backward. Put a foot and then another between us.

He doesn't get to look at me like that. Like I hurt him by staying away. Not when he did it first.

"Our relationship"—I gesture between myself and the doorway, where Dad is no longer visible—"is none of your concern. I will handle this like I've handled everything else—*on my own.* You made sure of that."

This time when I step around him, he doesn't move. I lift my luggage with an embarrassing *hmph*, laptop bag tucked under my armpit, and start walking.

"Delilah, wai—"

"Goodbye, Truett."

I don't look back, and he doesn't make another move to stop me. Instead I hear a door open, and then the truck engine rumbles to life. It slowly grows quieter as he drives down the long dirt road that leads to the Parkers' farmhouse. Eventually I can't hear it at all.

I suck in a breath as I step onto the porch. In my mind, brick after solid brick goes up around thoughts of Truett and everything that he said. I need control if I'm going to get through this. If *we're* going to get through this, I think as I step through the doorway.

"Sorry about that." I deposit my bags to the left of the door and shut it behind me. Dad, who's opening and closing each kitchen cabinet in turn, doesn't glance up. "Can I help you find something?"

"Just looking for the cat food." He stands, strokes his chin with one hand, and rests the other against the base of his spine. "Skittles will be hungry soon."

My breath hitches. I replay his words in my mind, hoping I simply misheard him, but no. I did not.

Dad's gaze cuts to me. His features relax, and the fog that seemed to fill his gaze clears. "You hungry? We could go to the Grille. You always liked their shrimp sandwiches."

There's a ringing in my ears as my racing pulse calms, leaving quiet in its wake. I nod, tugging this bit of normalcy around my shoulders like a blanket against the cold. "Yeah, Dad. I'd like that." I point at my bags. "Can I change first? If that's okay. I've been sweating in these clothes all day."

He smiles, flashing that crooked tooth. "Sure. Your room's

still the same."

Of course it is. I smile weakly and gather my bags. "Be back in a second."

The hallway is dim, but when I flick the switch to illuminate my path, nothing happens. Typical. Whenever another light in the house went out, the first bulb we'd steal was from the hall. This, like so much else, has not changed. It makes me acutely aware of the distance between myself and this place, and all the things that have shifted within me as a result. It's like running on a treadmill. You do all this work just to end up right where you started.

My room, the last on the left, appears untouched at first glance. There are my pictures, tucked into the white frame of my vanity mirror. Heavy curtains to block out the light so my teenage self could sleep in well past noon. Even the bedspread, a purple, floral thing, remains. But the room smells of cleaner. There's not a speck of dust on any surface.

He may not have known I would come, but I recognize it in this room. The hope. It fills a gap somewhere in my heart, like concrete in a pothole you'd grown so accustomed to giving a wide berth.

I set my things at the foot of my bed, except for my laptop, which I place on the vanity. For the time being, this will make do as a desk. The blinds slap shut when I pull the cord. I strip my tank top from my body. Reapply deodorant that I retrieve from the outer pocket of my backpack. The first T-shirt my hands touch gets tugged over my head. A few pieces of hair have fallen from my ponytail, so I remove the band and redo it, using my hands as a hairbrush to smooth it out.

Dad's standing by the table when I return to the kitchen. His gaze is lost somewhere on the other side of the breakfast nook windows, on the pasture and the Parkers' house beyond it.

Do he and Lucy still see each other? Is that why Truett is so determined to be involved? The thought makes my chest physically ache. My eyes burn. In my absence, I imagine another family forming. One with no space for me.

I swipe at my eyes, twin streaks of mascara lining my fingers. When I wipe them on my cutoffs, Dad glances over at me.

"You ready?"

I press my lips together. For the first time since walking through the door, I really take him in. Nine years without seeing him. Eight without hearing his voice. While living them, it felt like an eternity. But looking at my dad, it's hard to believe so much time has passed. A few extra wrinkles, that peppering of gray hair. But he's still my father. His fingertips are calloused from plucking guitar strings. There's a barbecue stain on the pocket of his Fly Hollow Marching Band T-shirt. It stings the back of my throat, the way I missed him. The shame of not having been here, even though being here fills me with guilt.

"Dad," I whimper, "is it really okay that I came?"

I want permission, I realize. Reassurance. To know that I haven't ruined my relationship with one parent for another who doesn't even want me.

His face crumples, eyes filling with unshed tears. "It's more than okay. It's everything."

I want to run to him and cry and cry and cry. To be small and comforted by my father's embrace. But I don't. I can't. Not when he needs me to be strong, to take care of him. Not when there's still so much hurt festering inside me.

Instead I suck in a deep breath and let it out through my teeth. Wipe my eyes once more and clean them off on my shorts. Something crinkles in my pocket. Pinching it between two fingers, I remove the crumpled business card Truett handed me.

Roberta Dunn is a certified nurse practitioner with over fifteen years of home care experience, according to her business card. She sounds qualified. She also sounds expensive.

I walk over to Dad with every intention of tossing her card in the trash can beside him, but then I notice the kitchen cabinets, still swung open from his earlier search.

I smooth the card out on the counter. Just in case.

Roberta's name grows blurry as I finally summon the strength to say, "I'm really sorry about the letter."

"What letter?" Dad asks.

My gaze jolts to his, which is twinkling with mischief.

I swallow and nod, the relief so overwhelming that for a moment I can't formulate a response. Finally a smile pulls my lips tight. "Ready for shrimp sandwiches?"

He slings an arm around my shoulder and guides me out. "Born ready, sweet pea."

The door slams shut behind us as he steps into his Converse. I pause, waiting for him to lock it, but he doesn't. Just starts toward my car while tossing, "You're driving!" over his shoulder.

Typical small-town mindset. I'll bet the locking mechanism is rusted over from lack of use. "I figured as much," I say, chuckling. Even without looking, the image of his mangled car flits across my mind. I shake my head, slip into my shoes, and follow my dad.

Chapter Four

Delilah

AT FIRST THINGS are awkward between Dad and me. Stilted. I know this house but not his life in it. Not since I went away, at least. The floorboard still creaks, but we don't talk about my nine-year-long absence. The pots are still in the same place, but I don't know how to ask if Lucy's going to drop by any minute. Don't know if I even have the right to. Instead I glean little pieces of information as he drops them, hoping soon they'll add up to something resembling the truth.

I gather that he no longer works outside the home, whether by choice or by necessity, I'm not sure. On Saturday he gives a makeshift piano lesson using the keyboard in his study. The poor kid has an Alfalfa-style cowlick and can't play "Mary Had a Little Lamb" for the life of him. Nevertheless, each time I pass the cracked-open door, I find my dad smiling ear to ear.

The kid's mom waits in our kitchen, smiling at me piteously each time we make eye contact. *"Such a shame,"* she murmurs. Enough times to make my blood boil, but I try to ignore it. It's only when she shifts to questions about me, saying she didn't realize Henry had a daughter, that I retreat to my room permanently.

That afternoon Dad stands at the door, watching the woman drive away with her son.

"I'm going back," he says, shaking his head. "Lessons at home work for now, but when I'm better, I'm going back."

Neither of us point out the obvious. That there is no getting better from dementia. As Truett so kindly pointed out, it's only going to get worse. But if Dad is willing to ignore that fact, then so am I. For now.

It's hard to believe he's sick. Not just because I don't want it to be true, though I'm sure that's part of it, but also because so much of him seems the same. Same dry sense of humor. Same long, rambling stories about students' antics. It's only when I'm going over his pill bottles, learning each med and the times when he has to take them, that the severity really slips in. Truett's familiar scrawl blurs when a tear falls from my cheek onto his written instructions, meant to help Dad keep track of his medications. Dad stood over the instructions, squinting at them for several slow minutes, before finally glancing up at me with fear in his eyes and asking for help.

I see the cracks in his facade in the way he trails off midsentence and then forgets the topic entirely. Or trips over words like they taste foreign on his tongue. Last night he stood in front of the bathroom door for so long that I passed him on my way to my room to change and again ten minutes later when I emerged to watch TV in the living room. The second time, I touched his shoulder to ask if he needed help, and he sucked in a breath. When he glanced at me, his blue eyes were frantic.

Then he flushed, muttered something unintelligible, and retreated to his bedroom.

I turned on an episode of *Schitt's Creek* and cried softly into the scratchy burlap throw pillow Mom bought sophomore year, with black lettering on the front declaring us the Ridgefield Family.

Some family.

Sunday night I find him sitting in the driver's seat of his mangled car, staring blankly through the windshield at the house. Panic lances through me, but I force in small breaths, climbing into the passenger side but leaving the door open to let cool evening air in.

"I came out of the bathroom and couldn't find you." I tuck a damp strand of hair behind my ear and frown. "You had me worried there for a second."

"I thought I had a concert to get to, but now I'm not so sure."

I'm ashamed to say I glance toward Truett's house, momentarily wishing I could ask him what to do. It's a weakness, depending on him. One I thought I kicked long ago.

Dad tears his gaze from the windshield, landing on me with a spark of clarity that I sense more than see. "I'm so glad you're here, sweet pea."

I don't know what it is about sitting in the cab of a car with another person that makes confessing your fears seem so much less daunting, but in the dull twilight of the late summer evening I find myself whispering, "I didn't think you'd want to see me."

His brow furrows. "Why not?"

Because I left. Because of my letter. Because I wasn't here when you needed me to be.

All the anger at him has leaked out of me in the face of his illness, and it turns out sadness was the layer beneath, with guilt not far behind.

"It's been nine years," I say instead, unable to give voice to those other vulnerabilities, yet summing them up in four short words all the same.

"It's never too late." His voice grows thick, swelling with emotion.

I feel a responding thud in my heart, where no beat should

exist, and rub a hand against my chest to dull it. "What happens now?"

He blinks. Runs his teeth across his bottom lip. In the evening light, the silver strands in his hair glimmer brightly, reflecting the shimmer of the moon. He looks so young still, and so other-worldly, that I can hardly believe he's sick.

"Nana remembered us for a very long time." His speech slips on some words. Drags out others. But it's subtle. For now. "Talking… that was hard for her. More so at the end." He laughs softly at a memory playing out in his mind even as a tear pricks the corner of his eye. "She thought we were all stealing from her. Constantly accusing us of taking things she misplaced."

"So I need to maintain a good alibi, is what you're saying?"

He snorts. The light catches on his crooked front tooth. "Exactly."

"It doesn't sound so bad," I say honestly. "I can handle that."

A shadow crosses his face. Something mournful that I do not recognize. "It's hard. It was so hard with Nana. I don't want it to be like that for you."

"Guess you should've thought of that before you got sick." Humor, no matter how dark, always worked between us. I pray it still does. That we have this, even if we've lost so much else.

He chuckles heartily. Grabs my hand and squeezes. "Believe me, I did."

Silence falls as I consider his words. As he considers mine. I feel like I could burst into tears, but I work to hold it in. No crying in front of Dad. I have to prove to him I can do this.

"Tru helped me…prepare things. Make decisions. When things get bad, I'll go into a home. Sell the house to cover it, then Medicaid after that. You won't have to worry about me, I promise."

My eyes widen in shock. "I'm not putting you in a home, Dad. No way. I'll take care of you. No matter what."

He doesn't disagree, but his gaze remains set. The blue is so bright, so hard it could be an aquamarine. Set it in gold and it'd be beautiful.

In his eyes, though, it chills me straight through.

"Come on," I say, desperate to change the subject. "Let's go in and order pizza. Does Hungry Howie's still deliver out here?"

He smiles, though it doesn't reach his eyes. "Domino's, too."

"You guys got Domino's?" I whistle brightly. "Fly Hollow is moving up in the world."

He allows me to guide him inside without incident. Waits patiently in the breakfast nook, watching the moonlight play over the swells and valleys of the Parkers' land, as I order the pizza. Neither of us brings up the conversation in the car, and for once I pray he's forgotten.

Truett doesn't return the entire weekend. I swallow my disappointment like bile. Its presence doesn't even make sense to me. I should be grateful that he heeded my warning, that I don't have to worry about seeing him. About the complicated feelings that come up when he's around. Without the reminder, I can almost go back to forgetting about him.

Almost.

Besides, I have enough to worry about without adding him to the mix. Enough to grieve. With Dad's and my conversation playing on a loop in my mind throughout the night, it's a miracle I can think of anything else.

But, as has always been the case with Truett, he somehow wiggles his way in through the madness.

Monday morning starts with the steady roar of a lawn mower. I blink awake, eyes burning from lack of sleep. Once, I knew each noise this house made in the night. Now I wake for every groaning pipe, each whistle of the air conditioner ramping up. I dream that Truett's eyes are the sky, and so I cannot escape them. I'm tired, but going back to sleep knowing that's what awaits me? Not worth the risk.

I roll away from the wall and any thoughts about Tru to study my room in the early morning light. Twin streaks of milky sunbeams leak through the outer edges of the blackout curtains. Those streaks illuminate my volleyball trophies, perched high on a shelf on the opposite wall. There are photos, too, sitting between each one. My dad and me at the state championship, the practices, the awards ceremonies. Mom appears in only one, taken that final year when the edges of our family were starting to fray. Before that, it was always just Dad and me. Mom didn't like the noise or the crowds.

The mower passes by my window, causing that fragmented source of light to flicker. I smile, untangle my legs from the sheets, and sit up on the edge of my bed. So many summer mornings started this way. Dad would mow the lawn, something he was always precious about, never allowing me to help. Then he'd come in sweat-slicked and smelling like fresh-cut grass, the beginnings of a sunglasses tan line etched into his face. I'd cook pancakes with fresh blueberries from the bushes outside, and Mom would complain they were making her fat but devour three before heading to work. Dad would happily eat a whole stack, then shower off his hard work while I washed dishes.

I blink away tears forming at the edges of my eyes, my smile faltering. His face last night flashes through my mind. Firmly set with determination, even as he nodded along when I told him I'd take care of him. He didn't believe me. And why would he? I'm the one who left and never came back. But I'll prove to him that I'm capable of caring for him. That a nursing home isn't something he'll ever have to consider.

With the lawn mower rumbling and my ceiling fan rocking

overhead and the plush shag carpet scrubbing softly against my toes, I can almost pretend things are normal. Can almost pretend I feel certain I'm right.

I'm inviting heartache, the way I'm clinging to all these *almosts.*

I try not to focus on it as I slip out of my pajama shorts and into denim cutoffs. My sleep shirt, an oversize faded graphic tee from some ex-boyfriend or other, pools on the floor. I catch sight of myself in the vanity mirror—small boobs, soft stomach, bland brown hair sticking out in every direction—before turning away to dig a bra and shirt out of my bag. It remains packed despite an empty closet and chest of drawers waiting to be filled.

For a long, heavy moment I stare at the suitcase, biting my lip. Then, before my mother's voice spouting all the reasons this was a terrible mistake can get too loud, I escape the time capsule of my room to repeat history.

I pad around the empty kitchen, gathering the ingredients from memory. Blueberries. Flour. Milk. Butter. Some sugar. One hand is perched on the refrigerator door as I survey its contents, searching for a carton of eggs to complete my pancake batter, when a door opening behind me sends my heart into my throat.

I whip around, clutching a whisk against my chest, to see Dad standing in front of his bedroom door. His hair is standing up on one side, cheek red with sheet wrinkles. He blinks at me, confused. "What the fuck are you doing?"

My jaw slackens. Dad never cusses. Mom? Sure. But Dad?

"Excuse me?"

He blinks. The edges of his eyes crinkle, and he shakes his head. "What did you say?"

"You cussed at me."

He starts, reeling back. "No I didn't."

I'm about to argue when the sounds of the morning come

rushing back in. I glance from him to the door and back as the lawn mower's engine cuts off. "I thought you were…?"

"You're gonna be late for school."

"I— What?" My pulse kicks up a notch. Then I say the first thing that comes to my frantic mind. "It's summer, Dad."

"Oh, right." A trembling hand scratches at his temple. "I knew that."

I'm pointing the whisk at the door, confusion mottling my features, when footsteps thud up the front porch steps and the door swings open, groaning on its hinges.

Truett kicks his shoes off outside and lets himself in, smelling like cut grass and sweat. There's a hint of fresh air, too, coming off his skin, but I wrinkle my nose at him anyway.

"Good morning, Ridgefield family." He grins at my dad, pearlescent teeth popping against his tan skin and a thin layer of dark blond stubble. When his gaze drifts to meet mine, the smile falters. Slightly, but enough. There's a memory in his eyes, and I find myself wondering which one. "You look lovely this morning, Delilah."

The whisk drops to my side. Some part of me knows he's making fun of me. He can't mean it, not when I've just rolled out of bed. Or ever, for that matter. But the moment with my dad still lingers, tipping me off-kilter, so I let his comment slide.

"Why are you mowing the lawn?" I narrow my gaze at him. There are pieces of grass glued to his skin with sweat, forming constellations with the freckles on his sun-kissed forearms. One eyebrow perks at my tone, but he's otherwise unaffected. As he's always been when it comes to me, while I remain painfully affected by him.

He shrugs. "Can't a guy just help out 'cause he wants to?" His gaze, a pale blue-gray like the early summer sky outside, travels over my shoulder to the cluster of supplies on the counter. "Are you making pancakes? For little ole me?"

I want to snap at him. To tell him I'm too old for his taunting, that I've put enough distance between myself and this place that he can't touch me anymore. I want to scream that there's no Ridgefield family, there's just me and my sick dad and Tru's nosy ass that has shown up despite clear instructions otherwise. But I can't deny the relief at his presence that unfurls in my body, softening my bones. And one look at Dad, who's smiling at Truett like he's something special, has my teeth clamping down on my tongue.

"Yes," I grit out. "But I'm only making enough for two."

"Three, you mean." He straightens his ball cap and rolls his shoulders. I'm about to make a smart remark when he adds, "Roberta will be here soon."

Dad shuffles over to the breakfast nook and settles into his usual spot, content to watch the banter with an amused, slightly distant look on his face, our confusing conversation all but forgotten. Tru leans his dirty elbows on the kitchen island and perches his chin on folded hands, waiting for me to make a move.

I won't play his games, though. If I've learned anything in my smattering of relationships, it's that the best way to discourage behavior you don't want is to ignore it.

It also works on dogs, which is telling.

He snorts when I turn without comment, but falls quiet behind me when I bend over to retrieve a pan from the cabinet to the right of the stove. I don't read into it. Not really. But I do stand a bit straighter when I right myself and begin assembling the batter.

"How are you feeling this morning, Henry?"

"Oh, you know," Dad replies, drumming his fingers against the wooden table. "Same old, same old. My brain is just broken."

The egg in my hand splinters against the edge of a metal mixing bowl. I stare at the fault lines that spread from the site of impact. My hands tremble. When I suck in my next breath, it's through my teeth.

The sink turns on behind me, but I can't force myself to look over my shoulder. My nose burns and my vision blurs, those tiny cracks losing focus until I can almost believe the egg is whole again. That we've gone back in time and the damage is undone.

Warmth like an aura fills the space behind me. A tan, strong hand comes alongside my own pale and fragile-looking one. There are water droplets still freckling Tru's knuckles as he encapsulates the egg—my hand with it—and splits it into the bowl. He lingers there, holding me while I cling to the empty shell, and whispers into my hair, "It's okay. It's just how he processes it sometimes."

It's the intimacy in that sentence, the way he knows how my dad deals with his diagnosis because he's been here while I've been states away, that causes jealousy to bloom in my chest. I cling to it, because it's better than the hurt it replaced. The aching. The regret.

"I know," I quip, although I didn't. "It caught me by surprise, that's all."

I drop the eggshell into his hand, suck in a breath, and force myself to turn and face him. He's so close, his features so defined that I waver. But only for a moment.

"Can you take that to the trash?" I jerk my chin in the general direction.

Sarcasm is what I expect, or perhaps indifference. The kind he gave me all those years ago when I needed him most. But instead his cheeks hollow and his slate-colored eyes soften with something akin to sorrow. His gaze flickers over my face, and I remember I'm not wearing a lick of makeup. All he's seeing is plain, unremarkable me. Good enough in practice, but never for real.

I break the stare first.

Butter sizzles in the pan. I finish mixing the batter and fill a ladle with it, then pour it over the bubbling liquid. The lid of the trash can slaps against the side of the cabinets when Truett steps on the pedal to dispose of the eggshell. Instead of returning to his place at the island, I hear his footsteps retreat to the nook.

A breath comes whooshing out of me, releasing some of the ache with it.

"Roberta ought to be here shortly," Truett says. "It'll be good to see her."

"It will be. How's she doing since…" Dad smacks his lips once, twice, then pauses. I make three more pancakes before he starts over. "How's Lucy?"

My heartbeat stutters, then kicks into high gear. Since I arrived, we've managed to avoid this subject at all costs. Now, whether I'm ready or not, I'm going to get the answers I've been dreading.

Surely they aren't dating or she'd be here instead of her son. Truett's dad, Waylon, left town the week after everything happened, once he'd blasted her name to whomever would listen, but did he come back? Did they get a divorce? Does my dad still love her?

A wave of nausea rolls through me.

Dad whispered that confession to me through tears as Mom ransacked the house that night, tearing frames off the walls—from photos of her and Dad to shots of the three of us to pictures of Truett and me as children—and shouting loud enough to make my ears ring. I can still see him when I close my eyes, which I do now as I wait for Tru's answer. Dad's gaze is bright blue and red-rimmed, tears streaking down gaunt cheeks. His hand is splayed over his heart, a gold wedding ring still glinting on his finger as he whispers, *"I love her, Delilah. I'm so sorry, but I've always loved her."*

How? I wanted to ask but didn't. I was a child still, only seventeen, and watching my parents' relationship crumble to the ground right in front of me. But my dad, the one I told all my secrets to, was giving me his own confession. One I couldn't possibly understand.

How could this man whom I viewed as the picture of perfection, of dedication, do something like that? Hurt us like that?

I've turned to watch without realizing it. Truett glances at me, Adam's apple bobbing, before smiling at my dad. The expression doesn't reach his eyes.

"She's good, Henry." He traces the same wood grain I did the night I decided to leave. "Up on the hill, you know. Enjoying the nice morning."

"She loves it there," Dad whispers, gazing out the window at the hill in question. It rises up in the distance beyond the Parkers' farm, shrouded in trees with spring-green leaves that shake and sway in the breeze.

Truett nods, lips pressed together. He looks at my dad with sorrow etched into his face that I don't understand.

Before I can ask, though, the acrid scent of a pancake burning in the pan hits me. I spin around, grumble, *"Shit,"* under my breath, and flip it onto a waiting paper towel where the first, ugly pancake also waits. The discard pile.

Dad and Truett wait in silence while I finish the pancakes. True to my word, I only make enough for two—a short stack of three pancakes landing on each plate. I set one plate in front of my dad, who digs in right away, and cover the other with a paper towel.

"You're not eating?" Truett asks.

I'm already at the mouth of the hallway. I glance over my shoulder at him. "No, I've got a meeting. Tell Roberta those are for her."

There's a warning in there, too. *Don't eat them.*

The truth is, my stomach is tied in too many knots to even consider eating a pancake. Whatever semblance of peace I felt this morning has gone out the window. I've spent the weekend in a bubble of almost-normalcy, pretending that night didn't happen. For my sake and my dad's. It's easy to shove away the anger and hurt when the reason for it isn't glaring at me right in the face.

But I can't sit here and listen to them talk about Lucy without feeling like I'm going to throw up. Because she isn't just some woman my dad fell for and had an affair with, though that would be bad enough. She's Truett's mom, for Christ's sake. The one who helped me put makeup on him when we were eight years old and hosed us off when we played too hard in the pasture. I can't count the number of times I sat on a barstool pulled up to their kitchen counter and listened to her tell stories while she baked, all the while wishing she were my mom instead of the one I got. She was at every volleyball game, cheering me on with Truett in the stands. She held me when I cried because the boy I had a crush on asked someone else to homecoming, though I couldn't tell her then it was her son. I hated her for taking herself away from me just as much as I hated her for tearing apart my family.

It's why I couldn't blame my dad for his tearful confession, even as it shredded my heart into pieces. Because I loved Lucy Parker, too.

"Hey," Truett says, that strong hand landing on my shoulder. I pause with my back to him, soaking in his touch for a beat before shrugging away from it. A tiny indulgence I allow myself.

Maybe I'm more like my dad than I'd care to admit.

"I told you; I've got a meeting."

I swing open the door to my bedroom but hold tight to the knob, fully prepared to slam it in his face. But he moves too quickly, slipping in behind me before I can turn around.

The silent treatment, then. If he won't go away, I'll ice him out.

I pull out the chair in front of my vanity and take a seat, plucking open my laptop. Truett stands with his hands on his hips, scanning my childhood bedroom. He's seen it a thousand times.

Still, there's a shiver down my spine, that sensation of having all my secrets exposed, as he spins in a slow circle.

My nails click against the keyboard as I log into my computer and load my email. I try to ignore the large man behind me, but his overwhelming scent makes it nearly impossible. I'll be smelling fresh air and Truett's sweat tonight when I go to sleep, I just know it.

The responding pulse between my legs at the thought of that causes me to flush. I cross my legs and squeeze, hoping to quell the ache.

"What do you do for work?"

My fingers pause, hovering over the keys. It's such a mundane question that swinging my brain in that direction after trudging through the pain of my memories gives me whiplash.

Truett sits on the edge of my bed, the mattress creaking under his weight. I squeeze my thighs tighter.

I can see him in my peripheral, staring at me expectantly. Even if I couldn't, I feel his gaze on me like a spotlight. Or a target.

So not the silent treatment, then. I sigh. Maybe the only way out is through.

I shift in my seat, rest my left forearm across the back of it, and level him with a pointed stare. "I'm a Client Relationship Manager."

A wrinkle forms between his eyebrows. "A what?"

My finger twitches, desperate to smooth it out. I curl my hand into a fist. "I work for a company that sells a product called a CRM, or customer relationship management tool, and it's my job to teach the people who buy that product how to use it."

He stares at me blankly.

"I hold training calls, answer questions, send tips via email, help reset passwords…"

"Oh, so you're like customer service."

I bite the inside of my cheek, but I can feel the heat blanketing my face. "Sure, Tru. If that's all your Neanderthal brain can understand, then I'm customer service. Now can you leave so I can service this customer?"

As soon as I say it, his eyes go wide. Embarrassment knots my throat.

"That's not what I meant—"

He removes his hat, his sweat-darkened locks sticking out in every direction, and presses it to his chest, which is shaking with laughter. "Well if it isn't our temptress, living up to her name after all."

I bristle. Suddenly all the pent-up frustration I've been biting back comes rushing to the surface. And not all of it may be related to him or remotely his fault, but a lot of it is. That's my defense for losing my carefully managed cool and surging out of my chair, finger pointed at the door.

"Get out."

"Aw, come on, Delilah, you know I was just joking." He sighs out the remainder of his laughter, his face falling to a more serious, thoughtful expression. His gaze makes a pass over me, and he sits up, folding his hands together on his lap. Whatever he sees in my face dulls his amusement. He shakes his head softly, his gaze dropping to his hands. "I'm sorry if it struck a nerve. What Kyle did—"

"Get the fuck out of my room, Truett." The prickling anger has turned to full-blown rage. "I understand you and my dad have a close relationship, and for his sake, I'll put up with it, but we don't have to talk. In fact, *don't* talk to me unless it's about my dad's condition and care. Got it?"

He stands and takes a step toward me. "I said I was sorry, Delilah, and I meant it. Just let me explain—"

"No," I interject. My tone is firm, my shoulders squared. I may be a solid six inches shorter than him, but I'm not backing down. "We don't need to talk about it because we aren't friends. Not anymore. You're just the son of some woman my dad had an affair with. That's it."

Pain ripples across his face. "Actually, about my mom…"

"I don't want to talk about Lucy."

He presses his lips together, holding back whatever retort he had planned. Good. I didn't want to hear it anyway.

"Now, as I said, I have a meeting. So go."

His lips part like he's going to speak, to defend himself, to do whatever people like him do. But then he thinks better of it or decides I'm not worth the fight, I'm not sure which, and turns on his heel to face the hall. In two strides he's through the door, one hand on the knob as he lets his gaze fall to mine a final time. He winces when our eyes meet, but he doesn't look away.

Instead it's me who ends it. Who turns, cutting him off. He shuts the door softly without another word.

Chapter Five

Henry

October 1st, 1996

LUCY BARLOW IS the most beautiful girl I've ever seen.

I've also said a grand total of five words to her in the years I've been attending this church with my parents. She's Pastor Timothy's kid, and I've never been too keen to draw his attention my way by telling his daughter that the light from the chandeliers makes her hair look like spun golden thread. Or that listening to her sing hymns takes me far away, to a room with only the two of us in it, her grayish-blue eyes chilling me even as the curves of her body send a rush of blood to somewhere that's definitely not appropriate for church.

I shift on the piano bench. Images of my grandma standing stark naked in the bathtub while Mom washes her play like the world's worst slideshow in my mind. Anything to keep from getting a boner while my parents chat with the pastor in the next room over.

It's our own little Sunday tradition. I allow myself to be dragged from my bed and shoved into a pew for two long hours, and in exchange, they commandeer a moment of Pastor Timothy's time after services have ended. For those glorious minutes each Sunday morning, I take advantage of the petite grand piano to the left of the green-carpeted stage. The nicest thing this small-town church owns, it was donated by a parishioner who came from old money and passed with no one to inherit it. Now it's used to bang out choppy hymns that Lucy somehow turns into music with her angelic voice, and for me to spin notes and melodies into songs that will never be heard outside these four walls.

They could be though. Sometimes I allow myself to wish for as much. I've got pamphlets for music schools tucked away under my schoolbooks at home. In the dark of night, I convince myself I could make a go of it. Really give this music thing a shot. My parents wouldn't sign up to go into debt over a career that may never make money, but Nashville isn't too far away. Perhaps I could skip college altogether and just move there when I graduate. Play in the bars after nightfall and get discovered by some unsuspecting agent…

"What is that you're playing, Henry?"

I jolt, my fingers seizing on a glaringly loud minor key. When I look up, blinking the imagined cigarette smoke of some faraway bar out of my eyes, there's Lucy, perched on the other side of the piano. Her delicate elbow is balanced to the right of the lid prop, cheek cupped in her petite hand. There's a silver purity ring twinkling on her third finger, a reminder to herself and everyone else of her promise to wait.

I'd wait forever for Lucy Barlow.

Anxiety bubbles in my abdomen. She's staring at me expectantly, but I've forgotten every word in the English language except *beautiful, beautiful, beautiful.*

Her gaze takes its time roaming over my face. Suddenly I'm certain all my secrets, the hours I've spent sitting in the pews rapt as she sings to the congregation, are written plainly for her to read. I flush crimson, glancing back at the keys and my trembling hands resting atop them.

"Is it an original?"

"What?" I croak.

"The song." She moves around the piano and gestures with the flick of a hand for me to scoot, which I oblige. When she sits down beside me, the scent of honeysuckle fills my lungs. "I've never heard it before. Did you write it?"

"I—" My mouth opens and closes like a fish gasping for air. I'm floundering. Even so, her rosebud lips turn up at the corners. The softness in her features, so unlike the fire and brimstone of her father, relaxes something in me. I exhale slowly and smile in return. "It's just something I like to play around with."

"Can I play too?"

"Yeah—yes." I smile, this time so hard my cheeks ache. "I don't really know where I'm going with it."

"That's okay." She spreads her hands over the keys, trilling a little melody as a warmup. "We can find out together."

And we do. When we start to play, music flows from me in a way it never has. Like it's a language I'm speaking that only Lucy knows, and she answers with a gusto that hits me hard in the chest. It stretches and splinters, embeds itself in every piece of me. Sweat beads at my brow. A lump forms in my throat. The harmony we have found unfurls and bellows through the cavernous sanctuary. It dances between the pews. Creates shadows behind the stained glass. An entire story—an entire *world*—is born beneath our fingertips. It's birth and death; it's the beginning of the end.

I don't know how long we play, only that I'd do it until my lungs give out. Until my muscles melt away from my bones and I am nothing but a memory. But eventually the song finds its way to the end. Lucy's long, thin fingers trill that same melody she used to warm up, and it's the perfect ending. I wonder how she could've possibly known.

"You're magic," I whisper. Completely unintentionally.

She hears, though, and it's her turn to blush. It colors the apples of her cheeks and dusts the tops of her ears. Her hands fall to her lap, spreading her yellow cotton dress flat over her thighs. I let my gaze trail across their swells and valleys. My fingers flex. I've never touched a girl, but I instinctively know what Lucy would feel like. How soft, how warm she would be.

A throat being cleared throws a bucket of cold water on my thoughts.

"Lucy, what are you doing?"

She glances up at her dad, and the spark our playing ignited in her gaze morphs. The one before melted her eyes into pools of the brightest blue. This one turns them glacial.

"We were playing some music, Daddy." She stands up, back ramrod straight, and steps away from the bench. Every inch of distance she puts between us tightens the noose around my heart until I'm certain it's going to stop beating.

Pastor Timothy folds one hand over the other, a Bible clutched in his grasp, and presses them against his protruding belly. Waylon Parker, a kiss up who follows the pastor everywhere since leaving the military a year ago, echoes the movement. Part of me wants to ask if he does it on purpose, or if he's just that far up Pastor Timothy's ass. The other part of me—one with a bit more self-preservation skills—decides to refrain. For now.

"You know our son, Henry," Mom says, extending a hand with nails painted ruby red in my direction. Her other clutches the string of my grandmother's pearls around her neck. "He's always had a knack for music. Hasn't he, David?"

Dad is zoned out, probably thinking about the football game he's missing at home, when Mom's elbow connects with his rib.

"Huh? Oh, yes. Loves his music." He rubs a hand over the

affronted rib. "Can't hardly get him to focus on anything else these days."

Pastor Timothy is watching me with one bushy black eyebrow cocked. Lucy got her blonde hair from her mom—a quiet woman who works in the nursery each Sunday and stays there with Lucy's younger brother and sister until it's finally time to return home to the parsonage. There is no darkness in Lucy. Not like her father.

He opens his mouth to speak, but it's Waylon whose voice comes out. "Lucy, we were going over the plan for that special Wednesday night service you and I discussed." His eyes, dark and guarded, bounce off my face like I'm nothing to think twice about. Asshole. "We thought it'd be nice if you sang while I played guitar."

"You play guitar?" I don't mean for the snide tone to leak into my voice, but it's there. I can tell by the way Waylon and the pastor bristle. And by the tiny smirk Lucy hides behind a cough.

"He does," Pastor Timothy grits out. He throws an arm around Waylon's shoulders and squeezes. "Mr. Parker here has not only paid a great service to our country, he also delights in music— mostly for the benefit of the church—and studies agriculture at the local college." There's pride in his smile, more than he's ever shown for Lucy. An ache forms behind my sternum. "You'd do well to follow in the footsteps of a man like him, Son. I know you're not currently in any small groups—perhaps joining Waylon's would be a step in the right direction."

I'm tempted to mention that the now-pious Waylon left a less than stellar reputation behind at our school for beating up freshmen for sport. I learned early on to steer clear in case he started branching out to the middle schoolers. He also loved to tell the whole student body about the things he'd force his girlfriends to do underneath the bleachers, but I doubt Pastor Timothy wants to hear about that.

Uncomfortable silence settles around us, seeping into the green carpet. With our song still buzzing beneath my fingertips, it feels glaring by comparison. I glance at Lucy, willing her to look at me, to acknowledge that she feels it too. But her eyes are trained on that puke-colored carpet. And her dad's, when I check, are still glaring at me.

If he doesn't stop, it's going to be puke *covered* soon.

"We'd better be going," Mom says, injecting a bit of her perpetual sunshine into this awkward moment. She's good at that. Always looking at the bright side of things. I, like my dad, tend to not be so upbeat. "This one has some chores to attend to."

She reaches out a hand for mine. I stand but don't take it. Not in front of Waylon. Not in front of Lucy.

I swallow, summoning all the bravery I have in my wiry teenage body, and turn to Lucy. "We should do that again sometime."

She tilts her head gently, a sad smile tugging at her lips. Before she can answer, her dad interjects. "Come on and look at the music for Wednesday with Waylon, dear, and then your mama will need your help with the baby." He beckons her, and she jolts forward as if tugged by a leading rope. When his hand meets the place between her shoulder blades and she winces, my hands curl into fists.

One day, I vow, *I'll touch that same place, and it will be everything. With my fingertips, my lips. One day I'll be able to hold her and replace all that fear with something sweeter. Something right.*

Because everything about this, about making music with Lucy, felt absolutely and completely right. And now that I've tasted it, I'll be chasing it forever.

She follows Waylon's lead out of the room, head hung low, while her father continues to watch me. My mom smiles at him politely and loops her arm through my father's. "We'll see you next Sunday, Tim."

My parents walk together down the aisle. The midday sun illuminates the double glass doors at the other end of the room, and they make their way toward it with heads tilted together, discussing something in hushed voices.

I close the lid over the keys and take a step in their direction, but the pastor captures my bicep in a firm grasp. I tip my chin up to look at him while tugging my arm away.

His hand drops to his side, but his gaze hardens. "Boy, I know my daughter is pretty. She gets that from her mother. But she's not allowed to date anyone I don't approve of, you hear me?" I try to speak, but he holds up the hand clasping the brown leather Bible to stop me. "I was young once. I know what goes through a kid's brain. Just say you and me have an understanding, all right?"

I swallow, my Adam's apple bobbing. "Yes, sir."

He smiles—an awkward, bitter thing—and claps that Bible against my shoulder. "Good. Now go on and have a blessed Sunday."

I nod. He turns away without another thought spared in my direction, and strolls after Waylon and Lucy, whistling to the tune of "Amazing Grace." My feet beg to scurry after my parents. That part of me—my fear—is still very much a child. But my heart yearns for the girl in the next room with golden hair and a yellow sundress. My hands itch to roam over her thighs, spread them open, explore what's underneath.

Perhaps Pastor Timothy was right about my intentions.

It's not purely physical, though. How could it be? Before today, I knew Lucy Barlow was beautiful. But now I know what her mind can create. The music that lives just beneath her skin. And with everything I have, I want to let it out. To set her free.

One day, Lucy. I promise we'll make music again.

Chapter Six

Delilah

AN HOUR later I finally log out of a call that takes at least two years off my life. The man needing training would've been better suited to a Computers 101 course before ever trying to operate our system, but who am I to judge? Just the one who has to repeatedly remind him to use his mouse to click on things instead of poking his monitor with a fat, greasy finger.

I close my laptop with a sigh and turn toward my bedroom door, steeling myself. Facing Truett shouldn't rattle me the way it does. Not after all this time, in the face of so many more important challenges. But when he's in front of me... my body reacts on my behalf. My mouth runs twenty paces ahead of my poor brain. I'm always playing catch-up with him, and I can't afford to be.

The only way I'm going to get through this whole ordeal is by holding my wants and needs at arm's length. When I find myself halfway down the hall, I'm still not sure which category he falls under.

The scent of coffee hits me first, followed by the soft trill of a feminine voice and my father's responding tenor. When I emerge from the hallway, the fist around my heart relaxes a bit. Truett is nowhere in sight.

Instead, seated at the table with my father is a woman in her early fifties. Roberta, I deduce. Her brown hair is streaked with gray and flows in soft waves around a heart-shaped face. When she smiles, her whole face gives over to the expression. And she smiles easily. In response to every word out of my dad's mouth, though he's simply talking about various music lessons he's given through the years. It can't be that interesting to her, but she watches him intently, giving him another warm grin.

Comfort relaxes my limbs just from entering her orbit. She's exactly who you'd want in a nurse. A caretaker. Hell, even a mom. She looks kind. Like she gives the best hugs. A small part of me knows Truett made a good choice, even if I hate to admit it. Even if I can't afford it.

I pad over to the coffeepot, remove a mug from the cupboard, and pour myself a hefty serving.

"You must be Henry's daughter!"

I glance over my shoulder to see Roberta watching me, another award-winning smile on her face. Her nose comes neatly to a point, which on anyone else would be a flaw, but with so much softness in her features, it somehow serves her well.

"Yes, sorry." I finish shoveling a few spoonfuls of sugar into my mug and turn to face them, resting my butt against the counter. "Sorry to be rude, but I didn't want to interrupt." *And I've never had to fire anyone before, so I'm biding my time.*

"Nonsense." Dad sweeps a hand in Roberta's direction. "This is Roberta. She's gonna be hanging out with me during the day so you don't get sick of your old man." There's a glassiness to his gaze that belies his chuckle. He watches her thoughtfully, the corners of his eyes crinkling.

I press my lips together, heart aching, and shake my head softly. "I'd never get sick of you, Dad."

Roberta smiles, but this time it doesn't touch her eyes. A rare occasion for her, it seems. "Henry and I will be more like coworkers." She pats his hand where it lies trembling on the table. "Isn't that right?"

"That's right." His voice is full of gravel and grit. It hurts my throat just to hear it.

I tilt my head, studying him. I can't imagine being sick enough to need help, but aware enough to be ashamed of that fact. All the more reason to keep his care between us. Roberta's presence, while calming to me, seems to trigger a sad type of shame in him that I itch to soothe away.

"Besides, we're old pros by now," Roberta muses. The words drip with melancholy.

I take a sip of my coffee. "How so?"

She glances at my dad as if prompting him to answer. His gaze drifts out the window instead, to that far-off hilltop, as a tear slips silently over his cheek.

There's a distinct shift in the atmosphere of the room, like how the air turns thick and irritable right before a storm rolls in. Instinct has me checking the cloudless sky on the other side of the windows, but all I find is endless sunshine.

Sunshine that pours in and sets Roberta's gray streaks alight. She nods, accepting my dad's nonanswer, and rolls her bottom lip beneath her teeth. "I was Lucy's caretaker, too."

The coffee sours in my stomach. "Pardon me?"

Dad winces, his gaze transfixed. Roberta rubs his knuckles gently. "Is everything okay, Henry?"

I forget to inhale. My lungs scream for oxygen, but I can't bring myself to do this basic bodily function. I'm watching my dad. Waiting, hoping for the punch line to this awful joke. Willing him to make the world sensible again.

For a moment the distant bellowing of cows is the only sound in the room. And then he whispers, "I'd like to see her. Lucy. Will you take me today?"

Without missing a beat, Roberta says, "Lucy's busy today. Maybe tomorrow?"

Relief courses through me, right up until I check Roberta's gaze. It's then that I see the hesitation. The sadness. That relief turns to ice in my veins.

"You bitch!" Dad slams his hand on the table. "Don't lie to me! She's not busy!" The corners of his eyes fold, pain wrenching his features. "Why doesn't she want to see me?"

My hands are trembling. I set my coffee mug down for fear I'll shatter it. This isn't my dad. Not any version of him that I knew, at least.

"Where is she?" he asks again. "Don't lie to me."

She rubs at her pert nose with her free hand. Compassion softens her expression as she says, "Lucy passed away, Henry."

He looks almost relieved at this news, like she confirmed what he knew in his heart. Still, he whispers, "She's gone?"

"That's right. Lucy's gone." Roberta nods. Her voice is silken, and yet it shreds me to pieces. She turns to me, a crescent-moon frown fitting ill on her face. "When her cancer got bad, Truett hired me to help so she could pass comfortably at home."

The words hit me square in the chest. When I finally inhale, it's like I've swallowed a thousand bees. My throat stings and throbs, lungs much the same.

It's inconceivable, a world without Lucy Parker.

"I miss her," Dad whimpers. Quiet tears slowly morph into sobs that rack his entire body. He tugs his navy-blue sleep shirt up to wipe his nose and sucks in a deep breath, only to let out the most heartbreaking wail I've ever heard. My stomach hits the floor, cemented there with my feet, as I watch my dad shatter into a million pieces while I'm helpless to stop it.

I've seen my mother lose control lots of times. From an early age I learned she was volatile, a volcano waiting to erupt if anything shifted. So I never shifted. I remained the constant in our lives: always dependable, always the same. "*Henry is so prone to whimsy, with his music and wild dreams. But my Delilah has her head on her shoulders straight. She's solid as a rock,*" she'd proudly tell her family each time they'd visit, and I'd grin and bear it, all the while swallowing my heart back down when it surged to defend Dad and his dreams. Dreams a part of me understood, if not shared.

Solid as a rock. Over the years Dad learned to do the same. This dance we both knew despite never being taught the choreography. Behave as expected. Don't disagree. Keep your true feelings buried deep down, and everything will be all right.

We spent so much time avoiding her breakdowns that neither of us got to have any. I've only ever seen my dad cry once, that night on his knees as he begged forgiveness. I didn't know what to do then, and I certainly don't now.

Even as panic rises like a tide in my chest, Roberta remains peaceful, although her face is etched with grief. She continues rubbing my dad's hand. His sobs dissolve into hiccups, then into deep, uneven breaths. Finally he tears his eyes away from that distant hill and looks at Roberta and then me, face turning a mottled red.

"I've got— I've got to…" He rubs his lips together. I lurch forward like I can tug the words out of him. This I can do, assisting with a problem. It's the raw, unfixable emotions I don't know how to handle.

But he stands, shaking his head, and walks toward his room. Once inside, he slams the door behind him, and quiet descends in his wake.

It feels like one. A wake. Like we've buried Lucy right here in this room.

Roberta's gaze remains locked on his door. "Sometimes it's like it happened yesterday, even for me."

I plant my hands on the kitchen island, desperately needing to anchor myself to something. Anything.

Lucy Parker is dead. Truett's mom is *dead.*

"Delilah, do you want to talk about it?"

Yeah, I want to talk about it. I turn to Roberta, blinking her into focus. Tears stream down my cheeks and pool in the hollow of my collarbones. I'd wipe them away, but I'm pretty sure my hands on the countertop are the only thing holding me upright.

"How could you do that?" The words spew out of me, but they lack any venom. I don't have it in me. I'm barely standing as it is.

Roberta hardly reacts. Her gaze remains soft. She crosses one leg over the other and folds her hands, resting them on her knee. "Do what?"

"'*Do what?*' Do that!" I point to my dad's door. "He clearly didn't remember! When he and Truett—" *My God, Truett.* I press the heel of my hand against my chest. "You broke his heart all over again."

Her head tilts, lips pressed into a frown. "He may not have remembered outright that she died, but he knew something was wrong. He cried when I first arrived, too, because he remembers how he felt around me last, even if he couldn't put it into words right at that moment. Sometimes people with dementia benefit from avoiding the subject, but sometimes they know something is off and they need to be allowed to grieve just like we do. Since he asked me directly if she was gone, it would've upset him more to lie."

"But Tru lied." Every word is an effort. I focus on each syllable, forcing them out through the driest throat I've ever experienced. "Earlier, when they were talking, he said… he said she was on the hilltop, just enjoying the day. Why would he do that?"

Something flashes in her eyes. One of many stories I missed out on by being away. "He didn't know any better. And maybe he needed to pretend for himself, too."

"H-how do I know? How do I know what to do?" My face crumples. Roberta stands and crosses the room, offering her open arms to me. I collapse into her. My forehead rests against the soft skin of her neck. My tears soak into the rough fabric of her polo shirt. Her hand moves in steady, slow circles over my back. I suck in a breath, bracing myself to tell her a truth I haven't even admitted to myself. "I'm so out of my depth, Roberta. I have no clue what I'm doing here."

Somehow it's easier giving it to a stranger. Someone who doesn't know me well enough to hold it against me.

She pulls back and places a warm palm on each of my cheeks. "You're here for your dad. It's as simple and as complicated as that." Her gaze levels with mine, two big, brown eyes brimming with empathy. "Have you ever been around someone with any form of dementia?"

I nod my head in her hands. "My nana had it. She died when I was a kid." That fact feels too fragile, too close to home. It's easier to think of Dad's condition as a change in circumstances than the beginning of an ending. A semicolon rather than a period. Saying it aloud, even in reference to my grandmother, feels like I'm jinxing us all. "She didn't remember any of us, though. Dad's isn't that bad."

Roberta's lips flatten. I glance away as best I can so I don't see the pity in her gaze.

"He's been fine for the most part all weekend. I don't know what's wrong with him today. He's not an angry person, I promise." I open my mouth to continue but stop short. My gaze cuts to the pill organizer on the counter, and the heat drains from my face. "I forgot his meds. Oh my God, what the fuck is wrong with me?"

"It'll be all right." She rubs my shoulder, then reaches for the pills. "These things happen. You're only human, Delilah."

I can't afford to be.

"The meds will help. He also might just be having a bad day. That's how things go with dementia. Things change by the day, by the hour even." She wipes a tear from my cheek with her thumb. "I'll be here with you every step, Delilah. I have some resources I'll give you to study up on. Everything it means to have his diagnosis, to be a caretaker. And you can call or text me whenever you want."

It all sounds so comforting. And so *expensive.* I choke on the knot rising in my throat. We've delved too far into our emotions; I've lost sight of what I came out here to say. I need to get back to stable ground. Back to the task at hand.

"How much are we paying you?"

She balks. It was probably the last thing she expected me to say, but I can't help it. Her knowledge, her experience, the resources… all that comes at a cost. And Mom made it clear I was on my own coming here, for however long I stay.

"I'm sorry—I don't mean to be rude. But I don't know if we —*if I*—can afford all this. Dad's doing a few lessons here and there, but who knows how long that'll last. I'll need to help him apply for disability, and I make decent money but not stellar—"

"Truett's paying for it."

I clamp my mouth shut. A cow somewhere lets out a surprised bellow. *Same.*

"What do you mean, he's paying for it?"

"Exactly that." Her hands come together at her waist. The thick gold band on her pinky shimmers in the fluorescent kitchen lighting as she fidgets with it. "He told me not to tell you, but I'm not sure how he thought we'd avoid a conversation exactly like this one."

Heat catches at the back of my neck, spreading until my cheeks are engulfed.

My gaze flicks to the bay window and the farmland beyond it. In the distance, a lone figure is hunched over the old part of the Parkers' fence with a cluster of cows standing watch nearby. His face when he saw the suitcase in my trunk flashes in my mind. "Because he never thought I'd stay."

I watch him working for a heartbeat too long, recounting every interaction we've had since I arrived. Suddenly the shadows in his eyes make all the sense in the world. The weight that sits on his shoulders. It's grief. And grief can make you do crazy things.

Before I realize it's happening, I'm moving. Opening the door. Jamming my feet into my Keds. Pounding down the steps and hitting grass.

Roberta braces a hand on the doorway. "Where are you going?"

"To talk to Truett."

Her response is lost to the summer breeze.

The Parkers' farm spans 100 acres, most of it sprawling across the hills behind the little farmhouse, but enough between our homes that I'm out of breath from running the distance. The dirt road cuts a winding path through the fields, so I opt for the more direct route: straight through the pasture. Truett is still bent over a fence post to the left of the house. The few cows standing around are observing his progress with disinterest, their tails swatting back and forth to keep flies away. When they finally catch wind of my approach, their large heads swing in my direction. One grunts, drawing Truett's attention. He turns to see what the fuss is about, removing his ball cap when he lays eyes on me.

"If it isn't Delilah Ridgefield." His brow furrows. As I close the distance between us, I can see the wheels in his brain turning. "Didn't expect you to come calling after you kicked me out of your room earlier."

"Truett, I—"

He immediately cuts me off, a wry grin catching the corner of his mouth. "You may want to watch—"

"Can you just let me speak for—" I start, but then my foot lands in something squidgy and hot, and the words die on my lips. If I weren't already bright red from crying, I'd certainly be turning that color now. I don't even have to look, but I do. My once-white shoe is now coated in a thick layer of cow manure.

He wipes a hand over his mouth, hiding a laugh. "That's unfortunate."

"Son of a bitch." I kick the shoe off, putting my bare foot down on a clear patch of grass a safe distance from the patty.

"Rookie mistake." He clicks his tongue. "You never take your eye off the ground when cattle are nearby."

I roll my eyes. The grass tickles the soft underside of my foot. Shifting my weight to balance my bare foot on the remaining unsoiled shoe relieves the uncomfortable sensation, but it also further proves Truett's point. I've forgotten basic farm protocol.

"Haven't been barefoot in a while?" he asks, smirking.

None of the responses I have for that are particularly helpful. Mostly a lot of pathetic, *You'd know if you hadn't abandoned me when I needed you most,* and other similar quips. Letting him know how much he hurt me after all this time is decidedly not high on my list of secrets to share, so I swallow back the words as quickly as they rise. I'm here for a reason.

It's not about me.

"Truett, I know about your mom."

He scrubs a hand through his hair, so long on top that his natural waves are peeking through. It makes him handsome in a charming, boyish way. Not that I'll be telling him as much. His face goes soft at the edges, like he heard the compliment anyway. He swipes his tongue over his bottom lip. "Guess Roberta told you, huh."

I suck in a deep breath. I don't want to cry, not in front of Truett.

"Yes. She told me." My voice cracks. I'm looking at my bare toes. The cows over his shoulder. Anywhere but at him. "And I think you were trying to tell me earlier. I'm sorry I didn't let you speak."

He clears his throat. My gaze drifts to his against my better judgment. He's watching me with an expression I can't even put a name to, but it guts me. Despite everything that has or hasn't happened between us, it's muscle memory to step into his orbit.

My arms come around him. We embrace gingerly at first, and then so tightly I could map the topography of his muscular back. He collapses over me, his tall frame sloping to meet mine. His chin tucks into my neck, and I feel his damp eyelashes brushing the sensitive skin of my ear. He smells like sweat and sky and home. Like a memory I've been pretending not to have.

My lips move against the fabric of his T-shirt, along the hollow beneath his collarbone underneath. "I'm so sorry, Truett. I can't imagine."

When he pulls back, a sad smile tugs at his lips, exposing the places he's chewed them raw. "Part of me thinks you can."

I don't want my mind to go there, but it does. Imagining this same conversation a year from now, maybe five, in which I'm the one mourning someone who cannot be replaced. Reality snaps back into place like a rubber band. I step away, praying all the while that the memory of his skin against mine will fade quickly.

"I can't." My head shakes back and forth of its own volition. The tears are there, pressing against my eyes. I fight hard to blink them back. "But I loved your mom. I wish you'd told me."

"Kinda hard to do when you blocked my number."

I grit my teeth. "You could've found a way if you'd wanted to."

We stand there watching one another. I wonder if he feels as exposed as I do, with all these secrets flying between us. Because now I know he tried to call. He had to, to realize he was blocked. Was it after the party that night? Or once I moved?

But I also showed my hand to him. And I can see in his eyes that he knows it. There was want in my words. Need. The two things I'm supposed to be keeping at a distance.

The standoff lasts a beat too long, with each of us willing the other to rip their confession wide open. But I'm not doing it. And apparently neither is he.

I finally let out a sigh, releasing the tension between us. "I came to talk to you about Roberta."

His eyes are the pale gray of a rain cloud. That ball cap taps against his thigh. "Listen, I meant what I said before. Things are manageable right now, but they're going to get hard. You'll need her."

I hear the unspoken *and me* that he wants to add. For both our sakes, I'm glad he didn't.

Bile that tastes suspiciously like shame gets stuck in the back of my throat. I swallow it. "Roberta told me you're the one who was going to pay for her. But that was before you knew I was coming back, and I can't... I can't afford her."

"What"—a cocky smile brightens his face—"not *servicing* enough customers?"

"Don't deflect with humor." I plant my bare foot firmly on the ground. Grass be damned, I need to feel it. To anchor myself to something when I feel so beyond control. "I'm serious, Tru. We— I—will find another way. A more affordable option. But me owing you isn't it."

Hurt flashes in his eyes, that impish grin faltering.

My lungs ache with a deep inhale. The scent of his farm and the river and the magnolia blooms—it's home. But it's also pain. Something I'm realizing Tru knows more about than I thought.

"Listen, I know you're doing this for your mom, but you've

paid your debt, okay?" I swipe my arms, palms out. "You're free."

I half expect him to argue. To quip something smart. But he just stands there, stoic as his grandfather behind the pulpit, watching me. Sunlight hollows his tanned cheeks, casting shadows over his angular features. It touches him reverently, like it's in on the secret. Truett Parker is someone who's easy to adore.

I should know. It only makes it that much harder when he lets you down.

When he doesn't object, doesn't comment, I hum my agreement for both of us. Scooping up my soiled shoe, I give that patty a wide berth and start the long trek back to the house. I'm a good twenty feet away when I pause and turn, finding Tru exactly where I left him.

"One last thing." I jab a thumb over my shoulder. "You don't need to mow the lawn anymore."

His gaze lifts from the hat in his hands. "Let me guess. You can do it on your own?"

I nod. A curt, jerky motion. "That's right."

A cow saunters over to the fence, swings her head over the top, and nuzzles his shoulder. Her dark black fur turns almost brown where the sun hits her flank. She's petite compared to the others, with eyes like saucers of chocolate. Without releasing my gaze, Truett reaches back to scratch her neck. "I tell you what, Delilah. Roberta stays. I'm paying for her. There's no getting around it."

"Tru—"

He makes a noise low in his throat, two degrees shy of a growl, to let me know he wasn't finished. "You won't owe me a dime. I'm doing it for him. Not my mom, and not you." The deep melody of his voice breaks. "I love Henry."

My mouth snaps shut. A solemn hush falls over the field, as if even the wind is holding its breath for what comes next.

One strong, dusty hand combs back his hair before he replaces the cap on his head. "As far as the mowing goes, I'd love to see you try." Warmth returns to his gaze as he scans my body, measuring me up but also lingering too long on the curve of my hips, the swell of my chest. When he finally meets my own stare, there's a spark there that fills me with a delicious warmth, even from this distance. "Always nice to have some new entertainment around here."

He takes a step in my direction, then another. Faster than I ever could, he closes the distance between us until he's a breath away. A heartbreak within reach.

His chin dips, gaze darkening. "If you really want to pay me back, spend some time with me." A grin curves those perfect lips, framed by a day's worth of stubble. "We can play in the river like when we were kids." One eyebrow quirks on the word *play,* sending all the heat in my cheeks due south. "Or I could cook you dinner."

I'm breathless. My lungs are lodged somewhere between my stomach and my toes, though closer to the latter. When he's this close to me, I can see every detail on his face. As familiar as my own and yet wholly new. Unexplored. Tantalizing.

A dangerous thought. Warning alarms go off in my brain. No matter how tempting, I can't go down this road. He showed me who he was once; I can't afford to forget.

I stumble backward, narrowly avoiding another patty. The sun is showing off, throwing rainbows in arcs across the river in the valley behind his house. Cattle dot the landscape in every direction. And this man stands in the midst of it all, looking a lot like a temptation I can't afford. I'm here for my dad. For as long as he needs me, I realize. I can't be distracted by pieces of my past—no matter how good they look in Wranglers and cowboy boots.

"No." I shake my head, stepping even farther away. "In case you haven't noticed, we're *not* kids anymore. Our parents are gone or going… or something just as bad. We've gotta be the responsible ones." I bite my lip. It's not lost on me that his eyes are there the moment it happens. That they linger long after it's over. "It's time to grow up, Tru."

Before he can argue, or I fall back into his embrace like I so desperately want to, or both, I slip out of my unsoiled shoe, collect it alongside the other in my fist, and take off running barefoot toward the house.

Chapter Seven

Delilah

MY SHOES THUD against the bottom of my dad's garbage can. Waste Management, which is really just a guy named Frank who drives a pickup truck with a caged-in trailer hitched to the back, already came by this morning, so I haul the bin up the dirt drive-way. I make a mental note to also write an apology letter to Frank for next Monday when he has to pick up this stinking mess.

I deposit the bin around the side of the house and make my way barefoot up the steps, hoping beyond hope to avoid a splinter. The wood is warm underfoot and worn smooth from years of traf-fic, but I've had enough of the prickly bastards in my life to know it's still possible. One time a particularly bad splinter wedged itself in the sensitive bend of my big toe. Dad heard me screech on the porch, and it only took one look at me crying with my foot in my hand for him to retrieve a sewing needle and a bottle of hydrogen peroxide and sit down beside me, pulling my foot into his lap.

He told me a story about the worst splinter he ever got, right in his butt cheek from a rope swing down by the river, and I was laughing so hard I didn't even feel him pluck out my own.

I've been trying to hold it together. To be stable and in control so my dad and everyone else could trust that I'm capable of handling this. That I can take care of him. To prove to my mom that I made the right decision. But as I lean against a porch post and stare at that top step where Dad held me through my hurt, not only in that moment but countless others, I can feel my heart crack open. Within seconds, I'm broken and bleeding without a single wound to show for it.

My spine bows, and I cross my arms over my chest, clinging to my shoulders. If I can just hold myself tight enough, I can keep it all in. The frustration of not knowing what to do or how to fix this. The agony of knowing it can't be fixed, only endured.

Hot, sticky tears dampen my cheeks. The air has turned humid as the sun rises high into the sky, bleaching the world with its light. I take quick, gasping breaths, willing my heart to slow down. I can't be in this state when I walk inside. My dad can't take the splinters out anymore.

It's my turn to take care of him.

It's my turn, and I'm not ready.

Through the haze of tears, I stare at the weathered porch swing. At the towering live oaks. Even, against my better judgment, at the fields beyond our property where a distant Truett finishes patching the fence and mounts his four-wheeler to move on to the next task, our conversation seemingly easily brushed aside.

The world, practical and unbiased, goes on spinning. And I have to find a way to be ready.

I tug my shirt up to wipe away the evidence of my breakdown as best I can. Deep breaths, one after the other, slow my heartbeat to a pace one bracket shy of a racehorse. I can do this. I grew up a long fucking time ago. Being the one in charge, the parent for all intents and purposes, is nothing new.

My hand lands on the doorknob, slick with condensation, and I push my way inside.

Dad is sitting in his recliner in the living room, that burlap pillow squished against his chest. Roberta is cleaning up the dishes in the sink, aside from my half-drunk coffee, which sits chilled on the kitchen island. Once I've closed the door behind me, Dad's gaze catches mine, bright blue with the faintest rim of red to remind me of his breakdown. He smiles, and I let loose a relieved exhale.

"You're home early!" His grin widens. "How was school, sweetheart?"

Roberta turns off the water and dries her hands. When she turns to face me, her lips are forming a smile, but her eyes are apologetic. She nods once, a gesture meant only for me.

Suddenly I'm grateful for the breakdown on the porch. As it stands, I'm fresh out of tears. Instead I steel myself against all the ways this moment hurts, and focus instead on Roberta. Following her cue, I reply, "It was fine, Dad. Great."

"Delilah here is a very promising volleyball player." He hops from his seat, shuffling over to me in a fresh set of clothes. His jeans are dark and well-worn, and he wears a faded T-shirt that says *Nothing but* with a treble clef underneath.

It makes me smile—a real, genuine expression—as his arm comes around me and squeezes.

"But her real secret," he adds, and my gaze shoots to his, "is that she's a hell of a piano player, too."

"Is that so?" Roberta tilts her head, scanning me in light of this new information. Because it is new, to her and everyone else. Mom and Dad are the only ones who've ever heard me play. Mom made sure of it.

He plants a kiss against my temple. His breath is sour, like he hasn't brushed in days, but I ignore it. I'm just grateful he's here. Grateful to pretend, if only for a moment, that we've gone back in time. That I can make my choices differently this time. And so can he.

"Yes, ma'am, she's really got a talent for it. It's too bad…" His voice trails off, a frown tugging at his lips. Our eyes meet, and he blinks, shaking his head ever so slightly. "Well, it's just too bad."

Too bad, indeed.

He smacks his lips, willing new words to fill the void. When they don't, his hand moves from my shoulder to the back of his neck, which he rubs like it's sore. The tips of his ears go red, and a grimace distorts his face. "My damn brain, you know?"

He's looking at me, but it's Roberta who answers, "We know, Henry."

"It's okay," I whisper, wrapping an arm around his middle and squeezing.

His chin finds purchase on the crown of my head as his arms encircle me again, and for a moment I'm held, like all those years ago on the porch. And for that reason I know I have to do this. Despite the catastrophic way he let me down, for all the times he held me up, I can do the same for him now.

He squeezes my side and then releases me, taking a step back. "What are you up to, sweet pea?"

I shift my weight, unsure if he's here with me now, or if he still sees me as the kid who just got home from school. Will it confuse him if I say I have meetings? Or does he think I need to head to practice soon?

"Um, I…" I glance over my shoulder at Roberta, who's politely organizing hand-dried dishes into their spots in the cabinets.

She must've been watching me in her peripheral, though, because the moment I look to her for help, she intervenes. "You have work, right, Delilah?"

"Y-yes, but…"

"Henry and I are going to the store to pick up some groceries. Do you need anything?"

"Oh." I nod my head, feeling a blush creeping up my cheeks. "Actually, yes. I could use a pair of flip-flops if you don't mind."

Roberta's eyebrows scrunch together, but before she can speak, I hold up a hand. "It's a long story."

"Noted." Her laughter—a light, lilting thing—eases some of the tightness in my chest. "We'll be back in a little while then. Do you have my number if you think of anything else?"

I point to her card where it still sits smoothed flat on the counter.

Her gaze flicks in that direction, along with my dad's, who laughs so loud I startle. "Would you look at that!"

"Okay, well, don't hesitate to call." She smiles again, the warmth returning to her face. For someone who's spent years in stressful environments, it's amazing that it doesn't show in her skin. The only wrinkles she has are happy ones, from smiling too hard, laughing too much.

I absent-mindedly reach up to smooth the skin between my eyebrows, knowing my skin will tell a very different story when the time comes. I've spent my whole life worrying about something.

The thought makes me frown.

"Bye, sweet pea." Dad tugs the door open, plucking his Converse from the porch and sliding into them.

"Have fun, you two." I wave over my shoulder as I head for the hallway, not missing Roberta's watchful gaze tracing my steps.

From my makeshift desk, I hear the engine of a car start up and retreat, leaving me in the stillness of an empty house.

My calendar is blessedly empty of meetings until three o'clock. I take the time to catch up on emails and shoot my boss a quick reply letting him know I am, in fact, alive. Luckily Cameron and the rest of my team are incredibly understanding. Without a single question digging for details, I was told to go take care of what I need to down here. Any slowness to respond or sudden appointments thrown on my calendar were totally okay, so long as I let them know if I needed them—for work or otherwise.

I won't, I assured them. *I've got it all under control.*

I glance at my closed door, imagining the living room and kitchen beyond it, and all the ways in which I utterly did not have things under control today. For all that I want Truett to be wrong, he's right about one thing. I need Roberta.

My resulting sigh is so heavy it blows a photo off the mirror. It falls against my foot, and when I pick it up, I see that it's a shot of Truett and me in Halloween costumes when we were maybe eight or nine years old. I'm dressed as Hermione from Harry Potter, and he's supposed to be Harry. He drew the scar on his cheek instead of his forehead, though. I was the one obsessed with the books; he only played along to amuse me.

It's so hard to reconcile that boy with the one who turned away at the party when I needed him most. Even harder to hold the two up next to the man in the field this morning, one affected by grief and something deeper that I don't understand.

I touch the curve of my ear, where I can still feel the featherlight brush of his lashes. My breath catches. How can I still want him this badly, after so much time? Haven't I been hurt enough?

I know one thing for sure. I absolutely cannot take him up on his offer. Indebted or not, any time spent alone with Truett will be bad for my health.

The small drawer in my vanity resists at first but finally relents to my tugging. It's full of old makeup brushes and bobby pins, busted compacts and a hairbrush missing half its bristles. I set the photo on top of it all and push the drawer shut. Out of sight, out of mind. I've got more important things to worry about than a childhood crush.

Before I can chicken out, I open a new tab to a search engine on my computer and type in *frontotemporal dementia*. My hands tremble as it loads. Every bone in my body aches to slam the laptop shut. To hide from the results that unravel before me. I gave the articles a cursory glance before coming here, but part of growing up means knowing all the hard details, even the ones you wish you didn't. So I force myself to do a deep dive into it all.

The symptoms. The timelines. The fact that it's genetic—something I suspected but for the very first time hits me square in the chest and steals my breath. One day it could be me. In an instant the years I've spent in limbo, waiting for my life to start, all to spare my mom's feelings—they feel wasted. And now? How could I subject someone to loving me, knowing what could possibly lie dormant in my DNA?

All the more reason to keep everyone at a distance. Less to forget, less to grieve when the time finally comes.

Hours later, as the sound of tires turning over our driveway reaches my ears, I'm numb. But not in a bad way. In a way that makes me feel powerful. I've pushed the fear deep down inside and replaced it with knowledge. With a plan. I know what's coming, as much as anyone can when it comes to this kind of diagnosis, and I'm going to do everything in my power to take care of my dad, the way I'd want someone to care for me.

But first I have to call my mom.

Unsurprisingly it goes straight to voicemail. It's not the first time she's given me the silent treatment, and it certainly won't be the last.

"Hi, Mom. I know you're probably still upset… and I get it. I do." Dad's voice drifts down the hall, followed by Roberta's laughter. I bite the inside of my cheek. "I'm going to have to stay for… well, for a while. I don't know exactly how long. Dad needs me. I don't expect you to understand, but just know that I'd do it for you, too. I have to push the past aside. I hope you can, too. For me."

I close my eyes. Empty my thoughts. It's the only way to function. The only way to get through.

"I need you to mail me my extra monitor and a few other things. I'll send you the list and transfer some money for shipping. I hope—I hope you can forgive me. I love you."

I end the call and fire off a quick text with the list of things I need to make a life here for the foreseeable future. Then I set my phone aside and stand. Knowledge is heavy. It's up to me whether I crumble beneath it or get strong enough to bear it.

Aimless pain is useless, but this I can work with. I have direction. A plan. It's more than I had this morning when I woke up, that's for sure.

I hear the rustling of bags as I round the corner. Roberta unloads the groceries while my dad directs her. She's chattering away about her granddaughter who recently started playing soccer. When Dad tells her to put the sugar in the cabinet with the cups, she course-corrects to the pantry without missing a beat.

"She made her first goal and she was so proud, but"—Roberta bites her bottom lip, holding back tears—"it was for the other team!"

Dad lets out a belly laugh, head thrown back, and I pause to take it in. It doesn't matter what happened between him and Mom. How badly it hurt me. What's done is done. All that matters is making sure I have this version of him for as long as possible. If that means owing Truett Parker, then my pride be damned.

"Hey, Dad?"

He sucks in a deep breath and turns to me, eyes bright with amusement. "Yes, sweet pea?"

I hold up a jump drive, the result of my hours of research and a subscription to a Montessori-based dementia care podcast. "Do you have a printer I could use? And a laminator?"

Roberta runs the printer, humming her approval with every

sheet, while my dad and I spend thirty minutes digging through his office. He only gets frustrated once, but this time when he lets out a slew of insults, I barely flinch. Eventually we find the laminator and, beside it, several unopened packages of laminating sheets. I carry both into my room along with the stack of papers and clear a space on the top of the dresser. With some effort, my suitcase is moved to the center of the floor, and the plug it was blocking is free to use.

While the first sheet runs through the laminator, I turn to my luggage and begin unpacking.

Chapter Eight

Henry

January 10th, 1997

IT WASN'T my idea for Lucy to sneak out in the dead of winter. Not that winter means much more than a slight chill in the air around here, but still. Lying low in the holly bushes outside the parsonage, shrouded in darkness, I see a flash of golden hair reflecting the full moon's light. She moves across the ground like a dancer, barely touching the earth. The sigh of her footsteps against the dead leaves could just as easily be the wind. Or the breath that escapes my lips when I see her creep past the last window at the edge of the house, then step fully into view.

Lucy Barlow isn't just beautiful; she's brave, too.

I heeded her dad's warning. As much as I wanted Lucy for myself, more than anything I wanted her happy. And if leaving her alone kept Pastor Timothy off her back, then leave her alone I would.

That didn't stop me from looking. And after that day at the piano, Lucy looked back.

Stolen glances at first. Eye contact that could've been mistaken as accidental had she not flushed red and glanced down at her toes the first dozen times it happened. Then one morning, while serenading the congregation with yet another of her father's favorite old hymns, her gaze found mine and held it. By the end of the song, I was sure she'd meant it only for me.

Then came the notes. Slipped between the slats in my locker door at school, she addressed them to "The next Mozart" and signed each one "Love, your co-composer."

I thumbed the word *love* so many times on that very first note that it became a blur of ink. It didn't matter, though. By seventh period, the words were impressed upon my heart.

Most of the time we talked about music. Her secret love for TLC and my weird obsession with classical composers and Phil Collins, a combination she could never quite wrap her head around. Occasionally she'd ask about things I was doing on the weekends with my friends. She never seemed to have any plans with hers, a group of girls who were daughters of the deacons at church. Rarely did I mention my parents. Even more rarely did she mention hers.

I thought nothing of it when I wrote to her this morning letting her know we'd be going to the field tonight to hang out. All day I checked my locker between classes and found nothing. I tried to tamp down my disappointment, reassuring myself she was simply busy. The new semester was ramping up, and things were bound to get in the way. Still, sadness plagued me.

When the final bell rang, signaling the end of the day, I shoved my books into my locker without a second glance.

"You've been in a shitty mood all day, you know that?"

The glare I fired Derell's way was enough to silence him but not to wipe the smirk off his face.

"Dude—"

"I don't wanna hear it, Jed." I elbowed our other friend, a heavyset brute with unfortunate teeth but a killer sense of humor. "Let's just go."

"You might wanna listen to him." Derell pointed over my shoulder. "Pastor's daughter incoming."

I followed my friends' stares, and when I saw Lucy approaching, it was all I could do not to shove them into the opposing locker room just to get them away from her.

"Hi, Henry." Lucy's hair was braided into a single spindle down her back. Her gaze flickered from Jed on my one side to Derell on the other before settling on me, one delicate hand tugging that braid over her shoulder and twirling it around her fingers. "I was wondering, er, if I could come with you tonight. You know. To the bonfire."

I've swallowed my own spit a million times in my life, but I swear to God in that moment I completely forgot how to do it. Instead a thick glob of it knotted my throat, rendering me speechless.

"He'd love that." Derell's arm came around my shoulder with a slap.

Her lashes, fair but long, dusted her cheeks as she blinked, waiting for me to be the one to answer. The one to say I would, in fact, love that.

"Will your dad let you?"

Jesus Christ. As soon as the words were out of my mouth, I regretted them. I wanted her there with every bone in my body, so why on earth was I saying anything to suggest otherwise?

Her lips, the perfect shade of pink, curved into a mischievous grin. "No, but that's why we aren't going to tell him."

So no, sneaking out wouldn't have been my first choice, but I'd do it all over again for the look on her face as she darts across her yard to me. Moonlight turns the blue-gray of her eyes to liquid silver, wide and unabashed. She's all teeth with the way she smiles. I've never been one for art, but my fingertips itch to paint the flush of her skin, turned rosy in the cold.

She's also wearing jeans that snap just below her navel, which is exposed by the sweater she's tied up in a knot. The sight of her smooth abdomen sends a shiver down my spine that has nothing to do with the fact that it's forty degrees out.

"Henry, are you there?" She wraps her denim jacket tight around her middle, hunching over to peer into the bush where I'm crouched.

"I'm here!"

I pop up a little too suddenly, and she startles, her hand flying to her heart. "Shit, you scared me!"

Nervous laughter bubbles up in my chest, escaping in low, choppy breaths. "Did you just curse?"

Her eyes widen, then dart to the ground. "Sorry, I just wanted to try it."

Our breaths are merging into puffs of smoke in the air. Even though I know I shouldn't, I reach for her arm and squeeze. "Hey, look at me."

It takes a few seconds, but she obliges.

"You can try anything with me." I use my other hand to cross my heart. "Promise."

Her smile returns, and it's like day breaking in the middle of the night. This close, I can hear the ragged pace of her breaths, but I don't understand. Is she cold? Is she nervous? My hand slips down her arm to her wrist, taking in the rapid thrum of her pulse. Mine echoes hers, a resounding snare drum in my ears. "Lucy—"

She shoves her hands into her pockets, huffing out another cloud. "So, are we going to this party or what?"

I nod, taking an unsteady step backward and then another until there's enough space between us that I can inhale without the scent of honeysuckle accompanying the breath. "Right, yes. I parked up the street a ways so your dad couldn't hear the truck. Are you okay to walk?"

Her lips form a thin smile, and she nods, gesturing for me to lead the way.

When we arrive at the field on the outskirts of town, there are already several trucks forming a semicircle around a bonfire housed in a cinder-block ring. I back in next to Derell's beat-up Ford, several discarded beer cans crunching under my tires. Derell and Jed are leaning against his tailgate, ogling the object of Jed's desire since third grade: Talia Winters.

She's tall with a dark, slicked-back ponytail and a perpetual pout coated in her signature plum lipstick. She's also a bit into herself for my taste, but she's given a blow job to at least two guys in our grade, and Jed is desperate to be next. I roll my eyes, snickering as I shut off the engine.

"What's so funny?" Lucy clicks the release on her seat belt, and as it retracts, her exposed midsection comes back into view.

My dick strains against the seam of my jeans. I shake my head. *I have no room to judge my friends.* Reaching for the door, all I can do is hope the dark is enough to hide my reaction to her. "Nothing. Come on, let's go catch up with the guys."

Jed whistles as we approach. "Well I'll be damned. You actually made it!" He punches Lucy's shoulder gently when she comes within reach. "Didn't know you had it in you."

My stomach flips over. I open my mouth to jump to her defense and tell my friend to shut the fuck up, but then my gaze finds Lucy's, and I'm speechless.

Her chest has puffed up with pride, another wide smile gracing her soft features. Her eyes reflect the firelight like a stone warmed by the sun. "I didn't either. But I owe it all to my getaway driver."

My answering smile only brightens hers more, and it sends a twinge of hope down my spine. *Maybe she likes me, too.*

"D'you want a beer?" Derell asks, leaning around Jed with a can in hand. He shakes it a little. "Got 'em from my dad's stash."

"Oh, um." She worries at her bottom lip, staring at the drink intently.

I step closer, touching my fingertips to her elbow. "You don't have to, you know."

Her teeth sink into her bottom lip. When her tongue flicks out to soothe her own bite, every thought I've ever had empties from my useless head. The fire cracks and pops to my left, warming that side of my body. Our classmates laugh and shout and chatter, but all that falls away till there's only Lucy. And her lips. And her tongue.

"I want to," she says, breaking the spell. Derell plops the can into her outstretched hand, and it hisses to life beneath her fingers. When the first sip hits her tongue, she turns to me with her nose scrunched up. "Wow, that is disgusting. How do you drink that stuff?"

"He doesn't," Jed and Derell quip in sync.

I keep my eyes on her. "I don't."

"You don't?" Another sip. The wince is bigger this time, and so cute my heart seizes. "Why not?"

I shrug. "Not my thing."

This time when she takes a swig, it results in a whole-body shiver. She holds the beer out to Derell. "I don't think it's my thing either."

He laughs, his white teeth flashing. "No judgment." Jed offers his can for a toast, and Derell knocks the discarded beer against it. "More for us."

"More for you," Lucy chimes, and she doesn't sound sad about it. When she looks up at me, several strands of blonde hair cling to her cheeks. "Thank you for bringing me."

I decide for once in my life to be a little brave. With a gingerly brush of my hand, I sweep the tresses off her face, all the while committing the softness of her skin to memory. "Anytime."

We don't stay long at the party. It's late, and the cold gets more unbearable the longer you're in it. There's also an underlying frenetic energy zapping my nerves as time stretches on, putting us at more and more risk of Lucy's parents discovering her absence. After ensuring Jed's good enough to drive (he stopped after two beers) and that Derell is keeping an eye on our lovestruck friend (he blearily assures me he is), I usher Lucy to the passenger door of my truck. She takes my hand as she climbs in, and I commit the feeling to memory.

My tires crunch back over those discarded cans, announcing my exit. I follow the well-worn path through the tall grass back to the highway, glancing both ways before turning left toward town.

"Thank you again for tonight," Lucy says, her normally melodic voice raspy from the cold. She shifts in her seat, hugging herself tighter. "I never thought I'd get to go to a real party."

Sadness pings in my heart. Sure, no parent loves the idea of their kid getting drunk somewhere in a field. But mine have always given me the freedom to go out and make those choices for myself, trusting that I'd do right by them when the time came. And I have. I always have.

But Lucy has never even had the chance. She dutifully serves at church, gets better grades than most of our class, and spends her weekends taking care of her younger siblings. And yet, in all that, she still dreams. In our notes she tells me about the places she'd like to visit when she's finally able to move out. She says she'll come to Nashville and watch me play. Maybe even sing along to my music.

Suddenly my throat is thick with yearning, though I don't have that word for it yet. Instead, in some corner of my mind, I file it away under Lucy's name, because it's an emotion I'll always associate with her.

"Can you pull over real quick?"

"Huh?" I ask, startled from my reverie.

Lucy points to the shoulder. "Pull over there, by those trees."

I do as she asks, shifting into park as soon as we're stopped. "Are you okay?" My hand finds hers in the dark, and our gazes do the same. "You're not gonna be sick, are you?"

Her head shakes. Slowly my eyes adjust, and I see that her bottom lip is trembling. The air around us grows heavy and electric, pricking my skin in a thousand places. She's looking at me— I mean really *looking*—the way I did that day in the sanctuary when I realized just how much she was capable of. My spine straightens and I swallow, unsure if my voice will be there when I reach for it to speak.

"What's wrong, Lucy?"

She wets her lips, leaving them glistening in the moonlight. "You know how you said I could try anything with you?"

My dick twitches. In what I hope is a subtle movement, I rest one hand on my lap as a shield. "Yes."

"Could we…I mean could I…"

A car passes by outside, rocking the truck gently in its wake. Her cheek hollows like she's biting it. Hesitantly she turns over our hands in the seat between us, using her other to trace the lines in my palm as best she can.

"Could we what, Lucy?" Because suddenly I need to know. *Have* to know.

"I've never been kissed." Her voice cracks and she swallows. Licks her lips again. "And I was wondering if you could change that."

My heart pounds so loudly in my chest I'm convinced she can hear it. The moment I nod, all the oxygen leaves the cab of the truck. It's now a vacuum, a black hole, and the middle seat is the center point drawing us in. I unclip my seat belt at the same time she does, and we move toward one another in sync, our hips, thighs, knees meeting in one deliciously warm greeting.

It's second only to the feeling when our lips collide.

Lacing one hand through the silken threads of her hair, I move my mouth over hers. Gently at first, then with more courage. Her lips part, one gasping breath coating my cheeks, and then I'm right there, brushing my tongue in tandem with hers. A soft whimper escapes the kiss, barely audible over my racing pulse, but I'll remember it for the rest of my life, that sound. I know it. I just do.

I'm not sure how much time passes before we part, lips swollen and cheeks flushed. It could be seconds or hours. All I know is my whole life begins and ends with that kiss. With Lucy and her soft skin, and her beautiful eyes with pupils so blown I can barely make out her irises. But they're there. Miraculous and striking as always.

"Does it always feel like that?" she whispers. Two fingers find her bottom lip, and she traces that swollen skin like she too can't believe the sensations originating there.

I don't tell her that unless you count the peck on the lips Rebecca Hornstead gave me in kindergarten, then this is my first kiss, too.

I shake my head. I don't have to kiss other girls to know this was special. "No, no it doesn't."

Our foreheads meet. Her scent envelops me like a blanket against the cold. She laughs and I feel it down in my core.

Her gaze drops to my lips. "Can we do it again?"

I have every intention of obliging, but the second I try to, the cab is lit up with red and blue.

Chapter Nine

Delilah

It rains every day for a week straight, which is not unusual for summertime in the South. But it does mean the grass is up to mid-shin come the following Monday morning, so I roll out of bed just as the sky is turning a pale shade of peach, and slip into a pair of jeans and a loose T-shirt. I'm going to prove Truett wrong.

I'm just going to do it before he has a chance to wake up and watch me.

My skin flushes. As I walk over to the shed behind the house, I force myself not to check the fields for his presence. Still, the memory of his threat has me feeling his eyes all over me. A sensation I'm ashamed to admit leaves me aching.

The right door is hanging slanted on its hinges. It's held in place by an open padlock that's looped through the two door handles. When I slip the lock off, the right door swings open and slaps against the siding of the shed, startling a few birds in the tree to my right. They scatter, blotting out little pieces of sky in their escape. I open the other side carefully, guiding it all the way till it rests against the opposite side.

Dad's push mower sits in the same place it has for twenty years. Beside it, stacks of discarded bags of gardening soil and a few cracked plastic pots lie gathering dust. There's a gas can with questionably aged liquid inside on the shelf above it. On first examination, the lawn mower itself doesn't seem too difficult to operate. My lack of green thumb shouldn't stop me from pulling a chain to start an engine. Pushing it around is just a matter of exercise. Two whole acres worth.

I drag the mower down the ramp of the shed and park it in the grass, then return to the shed to retrieve the gas can. I uncap it and sniff. My nose wrinkles. The fuel smells like, well, fuel. Not that I know what it'd smell like if it had gone off. *It's probably fine, right?* I pour it into the tank and hope for the best.

My hands find my hips as I survey the lawn. Besides dodging the live oaks and a smattering of bushes around the perimeter of the house, there's not much to maneuver. Truett was just trying to psych me out. Surely it can't be that hard.

I grab the handle of the pull starter and yank hard like I've seen my dad do a thousand times, but nothing happens. I yank a second time, but still no dice. Then a third and fourth. My breath comes in abbreviated huffs. Sweat beads at my hairline. Even this early, the air is thick with humidity. It clings to my skin like a damp sheet. I stand, fist my hands against my hips, and blow out a breath. "This can't be that fucking difficult."

The sound of an engine reaches my ears. I narrow my gaze on the mower, wondering if it's spontaneously decided to get with the program. Then the realization hits me. I pivot on my heel as Truett tops the last hill that separates our properties, looking smug as ever on his riding lawn mower. Suddenly I regret not having given the farm a once-over this morning. Maybe if I'd known he was definitely watching, I could've been a little more stealthy. Or, at the very least, prepared.

He comes to a stop in front of me. Leaving the engine idling, he pulls apart the handles and jumps off the mower. He's wearing a brown T-shirt and stained jeans that cover his equally dirty boots. Even with a tan cowboy hat casting a shadow over his features, the spark of amusement in his eyes is visible. "You're determined; I'll give you that."

I tear my gaze off the swell of his biceps as he crosses his arms over his chest. "Why are you *up* this early?"

"Couldn't sleep." He winks. "I had an idea you might try to mow this morning, and the anticipation kept me up all night."

This time it's me who crosses my arms. "I'm perfectly capable."

"Never said you weren't. Just that I wanted to watch."

A thousand needle points prick my skin at once, followed by a hot flash of self-admonishment. Truett Parker may be a flirt, but that doesn't mean he's flirting with me. Nor should I want him to be.

A tiny, indulgent part of me revels in it anyway.

I drop my arms and sweep one hand in the direction of the mower. "It won't start."

"I saw that." He scans me from head to toe, the brim of his hat shielding his face from my view for a long, merciful moment that helps me get my bearings. "And you were planning to mow in flip-flops? Do you know how dangerous that is?"

I glance down at my feet, where his gaze has settled, and wiggle my exposed toes. "They're all I have. Kinda ruined my other ones last week, remember?"

We look up at the same time, our gazes meeting in the middle.

"You only brought two pairs of shoes?"

"One. Roberta got these for me afterward." I shrug. "I've got a few more coming in the mail from home, though."

He removes his hat and runs a hand through his dirty blond hair, then over his face, before dropping his hand. "You're never gonna get that mower to start. It doesn't work."

I kick the tire, frowning. "Why not?"

He goes on as though he didn't hear me. "And besides, it'd

take you forever to mow this lawn with that thing. Do you remember how long your dad would be out here?"

"A few hours."

"Exactly." He replaces his hat and points to his riding mower. "I'll teach you to use the zero-turn if you want. It'll make your life a lot easier."

I quirk a brow. "You'd do that?"

"Sure I would. I said I wanted to watch, not that I had all day to do it." He turns and climbs onto the mower. Once seated, he pats his lap. "Come on. I'll take you for a spin."

An uncomfortable feeling settles in my gut. Gratitude alongside wariness. The knowledge that I need to keep him at a distance, as well as the desire to get closer. *Remnants of an old crush,* I reason. I'm an adult now. I can be around him—can even be attracted to him—without mistakenly believing it's more than that.

Right?

"Unless you wanna cut it by hand?" He narrows his gaze. "In which case, I'm sure Henry's got a pair of scissors that should work."

I scowl but step forward, taking his offered hand to climb on board.

He grabs my hips to situate me farther back on his lap. When my gaze darts to his, he raises his eyebrows. "I have to have space for the handlebars to close." He grabs the bars and pulls them together in front of us, demonstrating his point. "Is this okay?"

I nod because I don't trust myself to speak.

"Great. I'm just gonna take you for a quick tutorial today, because I can't in good conscience let you mow in open-toed shoes. But this way you'll know how to do it, and next week I can drop the mower off for you to use whenever you want it. Deal?"

It takes more effort than I'd like to admit to say, "Deal."

"Great." He flashes a wide smile. "So you have to have the

handlebars closed to go anywhere. They're currently in a neutral position, which is why we're standing still. To move, you push them forward." He retrieves my hands from my lap and places them in the right position, then covers them with his own. "Like this."

We lurch forward, which throws me against him. I can already feel his strong thighs beneath my own, the firm plane of his abdomen against my lower back. But now I'm flush against his chest. My hands are covered by his. Every nerve ending in my body is standing at attention, desperate for the sensation of Truett's touch.

It was hard enough to remain focused when we were two innocent teenagers and my greatest fantasy was running my fingers through his hair. Turns out, with a little more knowledge under my belt, I'm having a very hard time watching his hands flex over mine without picturing them slipping beneath my waistband, down, down until they are buried inside me…

"Did you hear me, Delilah?"

I jerk my head around. "Hm?"

He lets the handlebars come back to a neutral position, bringing us to a stop. One eyebrow lifts. "If you're going to operate the thing safely, you've got to pay attention." Releasing one of my hands, he delicately taps my temple. "Where is your head at?"

I'm hoping he writes my resulting blush off as a symptom of the early morning heat.

I clear my throat. "What did I miss?"

"I *said*"—he places his hand back on mine and pushes us forward—"you want to run at full throttle for the best cut. It's easier on the engine and keeps it consistent."

I nod like I understand, but I'm still struggling to pull my mind out of the gutter. I'm dizzy from the pendulum of my thoughts. One second I'm reminding myself how badly he hurt me all those years ago. The next I'm thinking about the fact that his dick is pressed against my ass.

And either his cell phone is in his front pocket, or he's at least a *little* happy to have me on his lap. Though the thick ridge pressing into me feels anything but little.

I cough abruptly, choking on my own inappropriate thoughts.

We're approaching one of the live oaks dead-on. The engine rumbles loudly, drowning out the next words out of his mouth.

"What?" I say loudly, my voice hoarse.

He leans forward till his lips brush the shell of my ear. "To turn, you have to pull the handlebar toward you for the direction you want to go. So to turn right"—he tugs at my right hand and, subsequently, the handlebar—"you pull on the right. And the same with the left."

We carve a wide arc around the tree. I suspect we could cut closer, but he's erring on the side of caution with me on board. Or he doesn't trust me not to crash what is likely a very expensive piece of equipment into the tree. Unclear.

He guides me through a few passes of the front yard. We leave clean lines in the grass, far nicer than any I could've done on my own. Not that I'll ever admit it.

I find my heart squeezing tight in my chest despite myself. If he wanted, he could've come over here and commandeered the whole thing. But he knew I wanted to do it myself. So instead he's giving me the tools to do so. Once I get the proper footwear.

I glance at my feet where they rest between his much larger ones as we come to a stop back where we started.

"And that"—he opens the handlebars—"is lawn mowing 101."

The fact that I don't want to get up is exactly why I have to. And *fast.*

I put a healthy three feet between us before turning back to him, one hand cupping my other elbow. "Thanks. You didn't have to do that."

"I wanted to."

His smile is genuine, and genuinely confusing.

I close my eyes and breathe deep, willing my nerves to settle. And my hormones. The more I try to figure Truett out, the less I understand anything between us. Why help me now, if he hated me enough to abandon me back then? Why abandon me back then, when the look in his eyes betrays thoughts that feel like anything but disinterest?

Why help my dad, if not for his mom?

I could sit here and let my thoughts run in circles all day, or I could go inside and get some actual work done. After a long, cold shower. And a few blueberry pancakes.

When I open my eyes again, Truett's watching me. And I can tell that he's not just looking but really *seeing*. And that, more than anything else, gets my butt into gear.

"Dad'll be up soon, so I better go." I grab the handlebar of the push mower and start rolling it back into the shed. "Thanks again."

"Anytime, Delilah."

I lock the shed back and turn to leave, giving the mower—and Truett—a wide berth. He reaches out for me as I pass, though, and with his long, muscular arms, makes purchase. I glance at his hand where it encircles my forearm. Even after he releases me, I feel it there, warm as the sunshine on my skin.

"I wasn't kidding about spending time with you, by the way." He bites his bottom lip, releasing it slowly. "There's so much I don't know, so much that's happened..." His gaze levels with mine. "There's just so much. But I'd like to make it less."

I shake my head. With some space between us, I'm coming back to my senses, albeit slowly. And my senses remind me of all the reasons spending time with Truett is a very bad idea.

"Thanks for the lesson, Tru." I take a step away from him, letting my gaze drop to avoid the disappointment there. "See you later."

Before he can protest, I disappear around the corner of the house.

Chapter Ten

Delilah

I DROP my toothbrush into the porcelain cup by the sink and spit. The faucet handle squeaks as I turn it. Toothpaste swirls down toward the drain, around and around, and I try to let it mesmerize me. Numb me. Mom's words can cut if you let them. So you just have to be determined not to.

The rough fabric of a decades-old towel scratches my face dry. I catch a glimpse of myself in the mirror above the sink. My hair is dull and frizzy from the humidity, so I tie it back in a low bun. I stand tall, shoulders braced. *No sense crying over spilled milk,* my mom always insisted. I wonder sometimes if she knew she'd be the one tipping the carton over ninety percent of the time.

I gaze at the laminated chart I hung up by the mirror. A step-by-step guide to brushing your teeth with pictures, not words, so Dad can follow it even when reading becomes too difficult. It strikes me that my parents put up something similar when I was a child, new to caring for my body. Now here I am, putting little charts and graphs up around the house for my father. To preserve his dignity, so he doesn't have to tell me when he's forgotten the steps to things that were once second nature.

Gentle strums of the guitar fill the hall with music. No song in particular; it's a melodic blend of so many I've heard my dad play through the years. Pieces of the chorus from "Heaven" by Los Lonely Boys. A random run from "In the Air Tonight" by Phil Collins. Finally it fades into the rhythmic tune of "Can't Help Falling in Love." Tears prick my eyes.

"Delilah?"

I pause in front of the gapped door to Dad's study. "Yeah?"

"Can you come in?"

He's sitting on the window seat, still playing the song absent-mindedly. The disorder from last week's search for the laminator has been rectified. Bookshelves line the far wall from floor to ceiling. Trinkets and trophies decorate the space in front of the spines. To my right, various instruments are displayed on their respective stands. While Dad prefers piano most of all, he's dabbled in so many other fields. There's a violin case leaning against a filing cabinet full of music sheets from years teaching band classes. His keyboard is tucked against the wall behind his desk to my left, which separates the entry from the window.

He turns toward me, taking me in with a clouded gaze. "Come play with me."

My chest tightens. Those tears are still present, threatening to fall. I shake my head slowly. "I can't right now. Mom mailed some of my things. I've gotta go pick them up."

"How is Kimberly?"

Hearing my mom's name is always jarring. So often I forget that she has an identity outside of her relationship to me. She doesn't date much, and I haven't brought someone home in over a year. My circle of friends and my coworkers overlap perfectly, so I talk to them online but never in person. It's just my mother and me in that big old house, an echo chamber that makes our reality feel like the only one.

"She's very much the same."

He frowns like he knows that's not a ringing endorsement. Still, the next words out of his mouth are laced with nostalgia. "Did you know we danced to this song at our wedding?"

"I did." A weak smile pulls at my lips. Every year on their anniversary, Dad would slip an Elvis CD into the living room stereo and press play. Then he'd ask my mom to dance. It's one of the few times it looked like their love was on purpose rather than something they stumbled into. Then they'd fold me into their embrace, and we'd sway in circles around the living room. A complete family, albeit an imperfect one.

I want to ask him about it. About how he could give that up for Lucy. But upsetting him hardly seems worth answers that will do nothing to change what's already happened.

"You will play with me sometime, though? On another day?"

He comes back into focus. His hands move nimbly over the chords. Years of practice and a whole lot of God-given talent are evident in the movement. He's watching me with barely contained hope and something else. I recognize it, though I wish I didn't. He'd wear the same expression when we walked into Nana's room at the memory care facility when I was a child. The safely guarded expectation that the person in front of him might not be quite the same as he remembered.

It strikes me that I should be looking at him like that, not the other way around. But my decision to leave with Mom all those years ago—to stay away after my letter opened the chasm between us—has brought us here. A fact that lodges my reply in my throat.

I nod instead. His shoulders slump beneath the weight of his relief.

Affection used to flow freely between my dad and me. We were the huggers. The teasing pinchers. The elbow nudgers and hip bumpers. The awkwardness I've felt since returning has made that piece of our relationship so dim. A shadow of what it once was. Despite this, or maybe because of it, I find myself wandering over to him and looping my arm around his neck. Placing a kiss on his forehead. His breath, now fresh with the scent of tooth-paste, flows over me. He leans into me, humming his apprecia-tion, while the heartbreaking melody fades away.

He moves on to a song I don't recognize. Something equal parts mournful and joyous. I back out of the room, leaving it cracked so he can fill the entire house with music.

My flip-flops slap against the hot asphalt, the plastic melting slightly on the scalding parking lot. The post office is a brown, squatty building with a metal roof and a faded American flag flut-tering high on the pole outside. A bell chimes when I open the door, and a blast of cool air makes my eyes water. It's a single room, with PO boxes lining one wall and a framed-in desk with a door on the left separating the customer area from the mailroom. Behind the counter, Odette Love is fanning her face with a news-paper, a thin sheen of sweat coating her brown skin.

"Delilah Ridgefield, as I live and breathe!" She shimmies off her stool, drops the newspaper on the register, and reaches for me over the counter.

I take her outstretched hands, littered with wrinkles and sunspots, and smile awkwardly.

"I saw your package come in and thought it must be some kind of mistake." She squeezes so hard the bones in my hands grind together. "How long has it been? You're so grown. And *beautiful*." She releases me, then does a twirl with her finger. "You know, you look just like your grandmother. She sure was a stunner."

My shoes stick to the floor when I try to spin for her. The whole movement is clumsy and unfamiliar. I'm not used to being observed from one direction, let alone all 360 degrees. The compliment tucks itself behind my sternum, making my chest tight. The version of Nana I knew was a shadow of what faded photographs tell me she once was. To be compared to a woman I've heard nothing but praises for, even if it's hard to believe Odette's words, fills me with warmth.

I place my fingertips on the counter to steady myself, though my world goes on spinning for a few seconds. "So you got my package?"

"Yes, ma'am." She shuffles down an aisle of shelves behind the desk, gaze combing the stack of boxes. She notes what I assume is mine with a harrumph and turns to me. "I've got a bad shoulder. Can you come grab it, sugar? Leonard is out doing deliveries, or I'd trouble him."

"Sure."

"Just reach over that little partition and grab the latch." She swats a hand. "No, other side. There you go."

The top half of the Dutch door is already open and resting against the wall of PO boxes. I open the bottom partition gingerly and step through. She points out which one is mine, a large

Amazon box that my mother has repurposed. I hoist it from the bottom shelf with a grunt. "I see why you didn't want to lift it."

Odette scoffs. "Apparently your mother shipped a box of weights."

I snicker. My walk back to the front is more of a waddle as I work to find a comfortable position for the heavy package.

"How is she doing anyway? Your mother."

That question again. Odette locks eyes with me, barely guarding the curiosity in her expression. No one loves gossip more than the postmaster, and she gets plenty of it in her position. I'm convinced it's why she hasn't retired. She sits here all day, waiting for someone like me to walk in. A fresh story. If anyone didn't know I was in town before, by the end of today they will.

A wrinkle forms between my brows. No matter how complicated my feelings toward my mother are, I still remember how it felt to have our family's worst moment on display for the whole town to dissect. Horrible. Invasive. The whispers about her, about my dad, from the kids in the hallways and people behind me in line at Sunshine Grocery alike, still haunt me. And though Odette has never been anything but kind to me, I can't help but feel defensive. I couldn't protect my parents from themselves, but I can protect them from this.

"She's fine." I plaster a glittering smile on my face. "Better than ever."

Odette licks her lips, which in turn spread into a jovial smile. "Well, that's good to hear."

I nod. "Take care, Miss Odette."

"You too, sugar." She retrieves the newspaper from the register and starts fanning herself again. "Don't be a stranger."

A chiming bell announces my exit and drowns out my half-hearted reply.

Mom picks up before the phone has finished its first ring. "I was beginning to think you'd forgotten about me."

I stop at the only blinking red light in town, waving a tractor on. Once he clears the intersection, I pull forward.

"I got your package. Thank you for sending it."

"You're welcome." Her tone is clipped. She may allow me to gloss over her comment, but she's not going to forget it either. She sighs dramatically. "I meant to return your call, but it's been such a busy week. I've picked up a few extra shifts since I've got no one at home to spend time with."

"At least you'll have some extra spending money."

We both know she doesn't need it. Just like we both know what she's trying to imply.

I turn down the dirt road that leads to our house. In the distance, Truett's four-wheeler zips across the pasture. There's a calf splayed over his lap, and what I presume is the calf's mama trotting close behind as they head for the barn in the shallow valley behind his house.

A mixture of anxiety and yearning clenches my gut. I find myself craving his arms around me. Our embrace in the field, his tutorial on the mower… it unlocked something I'd have preferred to keep hidden away. I was perfectly happy wanting nothing from him. This, I don't know how to navigate. This, I don't know how to quell.

Mom clears her throat. "So, how are things?"

I shake my head. From one impossible situation to another.

"As good as they can be." Acorns crunch under my tires as I pull into our driveway. "He's mostly himself. There are some things he needs help with here and there. Reminders." I think of him weeping over Lucy. Of the brightness in his face when he thought I was still in high school. I wonder absently if his brain just patched up the wounds of the last nine years by wiping them clean, and can't help but feel a pang of envy. "Today is a good day."

"You're staying there to give him reminders?" She snorts.

"Seems like something Lucy Parker is perfectly capable of handling on her own."

I swallow the bile that rises in my throat. *She doesn't know,* I remind myself. She doesn't know that the person who hurt her most in the world is gone. I try to let her animosity roll off my skin, but it leaves a few abrasions behind.

"Yeah, Mom. I am." I watch the porch swing sway in a breeze. Let the motion lull me. There's a bag on the front door-mat, next to Dad's Converse. A delivery, maybe? "Lucy… she died. A couple years ago, from the sound of it."

It still feels so difficult to say. I half expect that if I walked into Tru's kitchen right this second, she'd be standing there by the sink, teeth sinking into a peach. Juice dribbling down her pointed chin. She'd wipe it away and smile at me. Ask me where I've been.

Mom sighs heavily. "Well, what's that her daddy used to say? The Lord works in mysterious ways."

My heartbeat stills. The world tilts like I'm about to be sick. I step out of the car, sucking in a breath of humid air. *She's hurting,* I reason. *She doesn't mean it.*

"I have to go, Mom," I manage to squeak out. "I'll talk to you later."

Before she can reply, I end the call, slipping my phone back into my pocket.

There are so many types of hurt in the world, and no two of them the same. My gaze drifts toward the Parkers' farm. I try to remind myself that I'll never understand what my mother went through. Just like I'll never understand why my dad did it in the first place.

I kick off my flip-flops beside my dad's shoes and pick up the bag. The thick, white plastic sports the logo from the shoe store in the city mall. Curious, I reach inside and remove the box. I tuck the bag under my arm and turn the box over, which is how I see the note taped to the bottom.

Temptress,

These ought to fit your tiny feet, but if they don't, let me know and I'll exchange them. Can't have you mowing with those cute toes hanging out.

And before you even think it, you don't owe me a dime. But if you're inclined to repay me, the offer for dinner still stands.

Or skinny-dipping in the river. You pick.

Sincerely,
Tru

Inside lies a pair of white Keds, just like the ones I destroyed last week in his field. I remove them from the box and discard it beside me, tucking the bag inside. Before I even slip one on, I know, but I do it just to confirm.

Size 6. A perfect fit.

Chapter Eleven

Henry

January 10th, 1997

WE LURCH APART, Lucy and I, landing in our respective seats on opposite sides of the cab just as the officer raps his knuckles on my window. My hands tremble against the crank as I wind it down. A gust of cold air flows in through the gap I create. Out of the corner of my eye, I see Lucy tighten her jacket around herself. She's shivering. Whether from the cold or nerves, I'm not sure. Despite the fear violently twisting my gut, I wish I could comfort her. Make her warm.

"Good evening, Officer." I keep my head down, avoiding eye contact. Hope beyond hope that he doesn't see the beautiful blonde in my passenger seat who most definitely shouldn't be out this late. In a town as small as Fly Hollow, and with her father being a well-known member of the community, this guy's bound to recognize Lucy.

"Henry Ridgefield?"

I glance up, startled, and nod. The first thing I notice is the hat he's wearing. One of those cold-weather things with the flaps that cover the ears. The second is his expression. I haven't had a run-in with the cops before, but I'd never have guessed that they feel particularly bad about pulling people over. This man, however, has eyes pinched at the corners and lips flatlined. The lights from his cruiser reflect in a fresh coat of tears over his irises, hiding their color.

From the cold, I'm sure.

When he speaks, it brushes through a thick, white broom of a mustache and dissipates like fog in the air.

"Your mama's looking for you." He clears his throat. "You need to go to South Baldwin Regional. She's waiting for you there."

My gaze cuts to Lucy, still huddled in her corner of the cab. Our eyes meet, twin expressions of fear. I hear rustling behind me, and when I turn back, the officer is bent over and peering into my truck. He catches sight of Lucy, and his expression softens.

"Miss Barlow, I better take you on home." He glances between the two of us. "I doubt the pastor knows you're out this late, huh?"

Tears well in her eyes. They're different from the ones the officer was fighting back a moment ago. She's afraid. And in this moment, terror ripples through me. My mom is at the hospital. Lucy is about to get brought home by a policeman. I want to split myself in two and send each half in a different direction—one to take care of my mother; the other to protect Lucy from the consequences of my own terrible decisions.

The officer—Langston, according to the gold badge pinned to his pocket—shakes his head gently. "I'll get her home safe. Your mama… Well, she needs you, son. Better go."

He pats the roof of my truck and offers a solemn nod, then turns back toward his cruiser.

A hand, featherlight and impossibly soft, lands on my fore-arm. Lucy tilts her head toward the policeman's retreating form. "This is going to be so bad."

"I'm sorry." I grab that hand. Hold it tight. "I never should've gotten you into this."

Her eyes are wide and glossy. "What do you think happened? With your mom?"

"I don't know." That fist around my heart tightens. Wrings me out. A thought reaches me, almost against my will. "My dad…"

"He didn't mention your dad."

We stare at each other, both realizing what that could mean. A laundry list of things I don't want to inspect.

A quick blip sounds from the cruiser. I squint against the bright lights to see the officer nod.

"You have to go."

"Henry," she whispers.

When I look back at her, her teeth are buried in her bottom lip. The blue and red dance over her blonde hair, distorting its color. I reach out to touch it. To remind myself this was real, if only for a moment. Because deep in the cavern of my heart, I know that everything is about to change.

"My dad… he'll be so upset." A tear slips from the precipice of her lashes. I swipe it away with the back of my index finger. "He already doesn't like you." She sniffles. "He won't be able to forget this."

"I know." And I do. The moment the officer laid eyes on Lucy, there was only one outcome for all of us. "I'm sorry, Lucy. But I have to go. I'll find a way to apologize. I'll make your dad understand it wasn't your choice; it was mine."

"Henry—"

I cover her mouth with mine. For long moments after I release her, the feel of her tearstained cheeks against my palms remains. Eventually her eyelids flutter open.

"Be safe." She finds the handle and pulls.

"You too."

I watch her walk toward the cruiser like she's approaching the gallows. In a way, she is. After the warning I've already received from the pastor, this night will not be easily forgiven. But I meant what I told her. I'll make it up to her father somehow. I can't lose her. Not now that I've finally had her.

I wait until the cop pulls away, then I flip a U-turn and head toward the hospital.

* * *

January 13th, 1997

"It was a massive heart attack." My mom's lips warble over the words. "A widow-maker, they called it. I suppose that's apt."

She folds in on herself, arms wrapped over her center, as sobs send shock waves through her body. A woman I've never seen as anything but invincible is slowly fracturing in front of me, and I'm useless to stop it. Pastor Timothy, face arranged in some hollow semblance of empathy, clicks his tongue. He reaches over the back of the pew he's sitting in and settles his hand on my mother's bouncing knee.

"Loretta, I know it hurts."

Does he? Does he know that it feels like the entire world has been remade around us? That in the course of a night, our reality was completely distorted, no longer recognizable to either of us? Does he know that I held my mother in the sterile hallway of South Baldwin Regional as she wailed so loud the nurses even shed a few tears? Does he know that I had to be the one to hold my father's hand as they removed him from life support, because my mother couldn't force herself into that room?

Does he know what a body feels like when the life goes out of it? How that person takes a piece of you with them, rips out a section of your soul and drags it from your flesh when they go.

Because I do. I do, and I wish so badly I didn't.

115

"But David has gone on to Glory and is resting in Heaven alongside Jesus. He is in no pain. He is laughing and rejoicing with those he loves, and you will see him again someday."

"I want to see him *now,*" she wails. It echoes around the sanctuary. Reverberates in my ears. For as long as I live, I'll never forget it. The specific note of losing the love of your life. The saddest song ever written.

A member of the choir, Odette, steps through the door by the stage, hands folded at her waist. Her hair frames her face in a shock of curls, the darkest shade of velvet. She approaches us slowly, steps light on the green carpet, like we're animals she might spook with any sudden movement. She's a bit younger than my parents, but she and my mother have always bonded over a shared love of pearl jewelry and the dessert table at any church potluck.

"Loretta, do you wanna come with me for a bit? I'm sure the funeral plans can wait."

Mom glances between myself and the pastor. Her features are twisted around the agony she feels inside. I feel it, too, along with a roiling ocean of rage and disbelief and absolute helplessness. But for my mother, I push that all away. Lock it up in a corner of my heart to come back to later, alone in my room where she cannot see. My mother, who has always wanted to fix things for me, cannot fix this. But I can make the burden easier, and so I will.

"Go, Mom." I pat her shoulder. "I can handle this."

Her face crumples as another sob ripples through her. Her palm, clammy and trembling, cups my cheek. "You're just a child, Henry. You shouldn't have to handle this."

I let the words roll off me. If I dwell on the unfairness of it all for too long, I'll find myself in a pit I can't dig myself out of. *Later,* I reason. When I'm alone.

I force a smile onto my face. It's a lopsided, incomplete thing.

But it's the best I've got. I'm not sure if my mother is blinded by grief or simply desperate, but she takes the expression at surface value. She rises from her seat, nods to Pastor Timothy, and then shimmies her way around my knees and out of the pew. Taking Odette's outstretched hand, she allows herself to be escorted away. Even after they retreat through the door Odette first appeared from, I swear I can hear the echo of my mother's cry. That impossibly somber melody.

"Now, son."

I turn to Pastor Timothy, truly focusing on him for the first time this morning. The whole world feels like it's held at a distance, though it's not me who's holding it up anymore. Not even God. Something else. Something that doesn't care if two good people like my parents love each other enough to grow old together. Doesn't give a rip that now a son will miss out on a lifetime of knowing his father. Making him proud. Giving him grandchildren. Caring for him in his old age.

The pastor's gaze is hard and pointed. It pierces through that fog and grounds me, though the motion is nausea-inducing.

"I know you are going through it right now, but don't think we're gonna gloss over the fact that you snuck my daughter out. Gave her alcohol. Don't lie to me, either, because I smelled it on her breath." A wrinkle forms between his thick brows as he narrows his eyes. "You're lucky Joe Langston talked me out of pressing charges in light of the circumstances, because I most certainly would've."

I shake my head, though not at him in particular. At this situation. At my life. Losing my father, the magnitude of my mother's grief, putting Lucy in such an impossible position… It's all too much. And I'm only one person.

One task. I can focus on exactly one task, and then another. Step by step until I make it through. It's the only way.

My eyes drift closed, head tilted back. A sigh escapes my lips, releasing some of the tightness in my chest. When I inhale again, my lungs are full of pins and needles, but I drink down the oxygen as a lifeline.

"Everyone has to wear jerseys."

"Excuse me?"

I open my eyes. The chandeliers sway in the flow of air from the heating vents. Back and forth, their golden light shimmering.

"We'll need a few days for my grandparents to get here. They live in South Florida. He wouldn't care about flowers, but Mom likes lilies, so we'll do those." The thousands of times I sat beside my dad in Sunday service, watching these very lights cast an angelic glow around Lucy's head, flit through my mind. "And magnolia blooms, from the tree on our street."

Never mind that they aren't in season and likely won't bloom for months. I'm mostly musing aloud at this point. None of this is Pastor Timothy's concern anyway, but I continue as if it is.

"You can tell the choir to sing whatever they like. Write the sermon however you please."

None of it matters. All of it does. Somehow, both these things are true.

"But everyone has to wear jerseys. Even if they're an Auburn fan." At this, a tear streaks down my face. I ignore it. Along with the expression of barely contained contempt on the pastor's face. "It's what Dad would have wanted. He hated wearing suits. I won't make him wear one forever."

I rise from the pew. Pastor Timothy echoes the movement, meeting me in the aisle when I step out. He buttons his suit jacket over his protruding stomach and smiles. A look only meant to placate, never to convey any real joy.

He offers his hand, and I take it. His other claps against my forearm, pinning my hand in his iron grasp. "You take good care of your mama, Henry." An eyebrow lifts. "And remember, *no temptation has overtaken you that is not common to man. God is faithful, and he will not let you be tempted beyond your ability."*

That fog is taking over my brain. I shake my head, hoping the words will shift into some kind of sense, but no luck. "What?"

My question falls on deaf ears. Instead of explaining, he uses my arm to yank me closer, until his spearmint- and tobacco-scented breath wafts over my face. "If you let that temptation bring you near my daughter again, I will not be so forgiving."

He releases me with one final shake. When he turns to stride toward the exit, I see Waylon waiting in the foyer of the church, silhouetted against the glass doors. Outside, a winter rainstorm has rolled in, painting the sky a slate gray. The two men clap each other's backs by way of greeting. Waylon lifts an umbrella from the bucket by the door, expands it through an open door, then leads the way for Pastor Timothy. They disappear in the driving rain, turning left toward the parsonage.

I watch them go, all the while wondering if I'm the first person to ever feel this hopeless in a house of worship. And so impossibly alone.

January 17th, 1997

The day we bury my father, a freak snowstorm coats Fly Hollow in a thin dusting of white. The ground is hard beneath my feet. An impossible cold penetrates the layers of my jacket, jersey, and undershirt. It's one of Dad's, so it fits loosely over my slim frame. It smells like his aftershave. As I walk away from the casket—which sits poised over a gaping hole that feels impossibly small to hold such a large piece of my life—I dodge headstone after headstone. Each a testament to someone loved and lost.

It still feels inconceivable that my dad is among them.

My mother stays behind to talk to the pastor. Odette and my grandmother support each of Mom's elbows, like she may collapse if not held up. And perhaps she would. It's been a week since I held her in that hospital hallway, but the scent of antiseptic still burns my nose. Each night when I close my eyes, I feel the weight of my father's hand in mine. Then the absence of it. It's almost more than I can bear.

I round the old oak tree at the edge of the church cemetery, prepared to wait for my mom in the truck, and walk right into Lucy.

"*Oof,*" I grunt, stepping back with hands braced on her shoulders.

Her gray eyes mirror the snowy sky. They sweep over me as though checking me for injuries. Satisfied, she returns her gaze to mine. I blink against the shock of it. The difference from that night in my truck, the hopeful spark in her eyes when she gifted me her very first kiss, to the slicing sympathy that spills from them now. I want to erase it. Go back to that memory. Redo it all again and get a different result.

"Are you okay?" She touches her hand to my heart. "Who am I kidding? Of course you're not okay. That was so stupid." She steps closer till our exhales mingle in a cloud of condensation. "I've been so worried. Daddy was so angry, but I thought about what you said and you're right. You can talk to him. *We* can talk to him, together. He'll snap out of it. He has to. When the dust has settled a little bit, we can explain—"

I throw my arms around her and pull her to me, crushing her small frame against my own larger one. She melts into me, safe in the knowledge that the large oak shields us from view of the funeral goers. And, more importantly, her father.

For the first time since this all happened, I allow myself to weep. Wholeheartedly, with total abandon. Sobs wrench through my chest, crack open my ribs. My stomach turns over like I'm going to be sick. Tears freeze on my cheeks. Through it all, Lucy holds me tightly. Strokes her hand over my back. Up and down, up and down. The way my mother did when I was small.

I don't know how long we remain like that. But eventually the tears dry up and I right myself. I step away from Lucy, using my father's jersey to clear my face. It's only a matter of time till her father and my mother make their way out of the cemetery. I may not be able to help myself, but I can do this one thing for her. I won't be the reason for any more pain in Lucy's life.

"You have to go," I whisper. "Your dad can't see us together."

She nods, casting a glance behind me. "We can talk at school. By summertime he'll soften up. I'll tell him this is what I want—"

"We can't."

The crease between her eyebrows deepens. "What?"

How do I explain what's happened in the past week? What's changed within me? I've taken over for my mother. Grown up in the blink of an eye. I have to get a job, help pay the bills. I couldn't give Lucy what she deserves even in the best of circumstances, but now? And with her father's hatred weighing on top of it all? It will only hurt her in the end, and I'm not willing to let that happen.

I shake my head. "The two of us… It won't work. It'll never work." *Your dad will never accept me. I'm an absolute wreck. I have to take care of my mom when I'm not even sure how to take care of myself. Help me. Please.* "I'm sorry, Lucy."

All those unspoken words turn and tumble in my gut. They eat me alive. But I won't let them out. Won't make my problems hers to deal with. I can't.

"I don't understand." She reaches for my hand, which hangs limply where she holds it. "I know you're upset. I'm sorry for what happened. For getting you in trouble. For your dad…" Her voice trails off as she sucks in a wavering breath. "But you said we'd get through this. That you'd make Dad understand—"

"That was before." It rushes out of me unbidden. And from the way she flinches, I know it causes damage that I'll never be able to repair.

She blinks back a fresh pool of tears. "I can be there for you. You just have to let me."

Snow has gathered in her golden hair. A few flakes are caught in her lashes. I let my gaze sweep over her face. I gather the details—her flushed cheeks, her silken skin, those rosebud lips and the memory of their warmth against mine—and I stow them away for safekeeping. It's the closest I'll ever get again. For her sake, even if it kills me inside.

"I have to go." I place a kiss on her forehead. And perhaps it's a mistake, but it's the only weakness I'll allow myself in all of this. I swear it on my father's grave. The proximity of which presses in on my lungs, making it hard to take my next breath. Next step. Each of which takes me farther away from Lucy and the life I wish I could have if circumstances were different.

"Henry?" Lucy cries.

I don't turn back. I don't let myself react. I just keep moving, head down, toward the truck.

Chapter Twelve

Delilah

So I hate to even ask this, but Dad is convinced someone stole his wallet. You wouldn't happen to know where it is? (I promise I'm not accusing you, I've just looked everywhere for it)

ROBERTA

I told you to text me with any questions ;) I'm not offended, don't worry.

ROBERTA

Check the flowerpot on the front porch. That's where we found it on Wednesday.

ME

Ding, ding, ding! Flowerpot was the correct answer.

ROBERTA

Yay! What do I win?

ME

...the pride of knowing you were right?

ROBERTA

I'll take it!

"WHAT DO YOU MEAN, you don't have shrimp sandwiches? We always get shrimp sandwiches."

The waitress—a girl of about sixteen with glitter eyeshadow and braided hair—shifts her weight uncomfortably. "We do normally, but we ran out." Her gaze cuts to me, flaring wide, then back to Dad again. "I'm real sorry, sir."

I bite my lip. Dad's cheeks are flushed. His hands shake where they grip the menu. His gaze dances over the words but doesn't register on any one thing. He reaches for his glass, but a particularly harsh tremor knocks it sideways. The table floods with water. Our napkins, the bread plate, and even my lap get soaked. Tears fill the wrinkles at the corners of my dad's eyes.

"You know what, why don't we get burgers, Dad? You love their burgers."

I do my best to keep the panic out of my voice, but my nerves are frayed. I don't know how to make this better, and people are starting to stare, including Kyle Miller, who sits at a booth across the aisle from us. Recognition flares in his eyes, because of course it would in this moment when I wish most to slip under the radar. The waitress grabs extra napkins from a nearby table and starts patting up the spill. Dad's mouth parts and then closes. It's too much. And I'm not enough.

"I want to go home," he whimpers.

My throat seizes around a breath, lodging it in my lungs. A burning sensation fills my chest, the base of my neck, the pit of my stomach. I want to fix this, but I don't know how.

I exchange a desperate look with the waitress. She's so young and just as confused as I am, but I could plant a kiss on her forehead when she offers, "I can get some burgers to-go for you?"

My responding nod is only halfway done when she pivots on her heel and makes a break for the kitchen.

"It's all right, Dad." I stand, ignoring the whispers Kyle exchanges with the other guys at his table. People from high school that I've all but managed to forget. "We're going home."

Dad won't look me in the eye. His gaze remains locked on the ratty gray carpet as we make our way to the hostess podium. In my peripheral, I notice his chin wobbling, and it shatters a piece of my heart.

I cup his elbow, calling his attention to me. He pauses but doesn't look up.

"We're gonna wait here for our food, okay?"

He glances at the podium, brow furrowing. "Shrimp sandwiches?"

"No, Dad. They're out of shrimp. I got us burgers."

"Out of shrimp."

"Yes, sir." I slide my hand up his bicep in a soothing motion. "But you like their burgers."

He smacks his lips and drops his gaze back to the floor. The toe of his shoe scuffs against the carpet. "I like their burgers?"

"You do. And so do I."

He shakes his head. "What's wrong with me, sweet pea?"

I study my father. The gray at his temples that makes him look so distinguished. The slight bend to his nose. His lips part, exposing that crooked front tooth. It's the most jarring part of this whole thing. That he can look so much the same and internally be wasting away.

At his appointment today, he told the doctor I was taking care of him for now, but that he will eventually go into a care facility. He's been agitated the past few days, and every time, as soon as the moment passes, he either begs me for forgiveness or has forgotten it happened altogether. When he does remember, he explains this is exactly why he can't stay home. Why he won't.

I assured the doctor this was incorrect, that I'd be caring for Dad till the very end. But when he handed me a prescription sheet for a new medication to add to Dad's regime, there were a handful of pamphlets beneath it. Brochures for facilities in the surrounding area. It took everything in me not to dump the stack in the garbage on the way out.

I clear my throat. "Nothing's wrong with you, Dad. Just a rough day, that's all."

Dad fiddles with the toothpick dispenser but doesn't comment.

Images of Nana in her room at her facility flit through my mind. The cold, sterile walls with generic hotel art and the floral love seat where she'd always be sitting when we arrived. I try to imagine my dad in a place like that, and a shiver runs down my spine. Sure, she had nurses on call and someone there to remind her to eat and bathe. Dad and Mom were busy raising me, working full-time. They couldn't do that for her. But with my job's flexibility and Roberta's help…

I square my shoulders against the mental onslaught of fears. Insecurities. Too many damn questions to count. At the end of the day, he's my father. No matter what, it's my job to take care of him. To do what's right. After everything, I owe him that much.

"Here you go." The waitress offers a tight-lipped smile as she places the to-go containers on the hostess stand. "That'll be $24.15."

I fish a few bills out of my wallet and place them in her open hand. "Keep the change. And thanks so much."

We lock gazes, and she gives me an empathetic nod. I look away so she won't see the fresh tears welling up in my eyes.

While Dad picks at his dinner, I busy myself with small chores in between encouraging him to keep eating. I straighten up the living room. Do a load of laundry. Divvy his new meds into the pill organizer and add a note to Truett's handwritten instructions. Anything to keep my mind occupied. Between the doctor's visit, the episode at dinner, and my own unrelenting brain, it's all too much. Since I got here, I've done everything to convince myself that Dad's diagnosis is mild. Maybe even a mistake. But the more time that passes, the more it becomes clear. And that clarity is cutting me straight through.

As I clean up the remnants of our dinner—which took two hours to complete as Dad went back and forth over whether he did, in fact, like burgers—he opens and closes each kitchen cabinet in turn. I sweep the last of my stodgy, half-eaten burger into the garbage (it's hard to have an appetite when you're focused on getting someone else to eat) and suck in a breath.

"Can I help you find anything?"

He scratches the back of his head. "Did you feed Skittles?"

I close my eyes, chest deflating, and nod.

A low grumble of understanding, and then he turns toward the hall. "Guess I better shower."

He shuffles past the bathroom, then retraces his steps, head hung low. I wait with bated breath for the water to start running. For the charts to do their job. For the tension to eek out of my spine at last.

After a beat, the hot water screams to life. I let myself exhale.

Then there's a clatter, followed by mumbled cursing. I take a nervous step forward, and then another. Something else falls. A shampoo bottle, by the sounds of it. Anxiety ripples through me. What if he's fallen? What if he's hurt?

I jump as something solid hits the other side of the door. My hand closes around the doorknob. It's locked. "Dad? Do you need me?"

More mumbling. I rap my fist against the hardwood.

"Dad!"

"Get the fuck away from me!"

I jump backward, my back slamming into the wall opposite the bathroom. A searing pain reverberates through my shoulder, but it's nothing compared to the one in my heart.

I don't know if you ever get used to your normally gentle, encouraging parent screaming at you like this. There's so much vitriol in his voice that it disturbs my sense of equilibrium. I feel like I'm falling, though I'm safely braced against the wall. Trembling, I step forward and flatten my palms over the door, ignoring the erratic breaths forcing their way out of my lungs.

"I can help, Dad." My voice is softer now. I'm just as afraid to be let in as I am not to. "But you've gotta unlock the door."

"I don't want you!" His voice is desperate, like the cries of a trapped animal.

Tears spring forth, dripping down my cheeks in slow rivulets. I let my forehead fall against the hardwood. "I'm all you've got." *I'm sorry,* I want to add. *I wish I was more.* The loneliness grips me. Swallows me whole. "You've got to let me in."

Something else hits the door. Steam from the shower billows out from the crack at my feet. I watch it curl around my legs, then dissolve entirely. I can barely hear my dad's heavy breathing over the rush of water. Then, a keening like I've never heard before. Worse than Roberta reminding him of Lucy, though at the time, I couldn't have imagined it possible.

Roberta. *Fuck.* I find my purse where I discarded it on the island. My phone lights up, and I click on our conversation from this morning. I don't even bother typing it all out. With trembling fingers, I select her contact image and press call.

It goes straight to voicemail. Before I've gotten a single word out, a message comes through. One of those automated ones that lets me know the person I'm trying to reach is driving, but they'll get back to me soon. I drop the phone on the counter without leaving a message. Dad's sobbing grows louder. I want to plug my ears. I want to be let inside. I don't have a fucking clue what to do.

My head falls into my hands. I lift my gaze, scrubbing my face as I do. In the distance the windows of the farmhouse glow like beacons on the hilltop. I suck in a breath.

Dad's phone lies abandoned on the kitchen table. I grab it, grateful he's trusting enough not to password protect it, and select Truett's name from his speed-dial list.

"Henry? Is everything all right?"

A small whimper escapes my lips even as I clamp down on it.

"Delilah?" Something clinks in the background, like he's setting down a glass. "What's going on?"

"It's Dad." I hate how weak I sound. How out of control. But I am. And it makes me desperate. "He's locked himself in the bathroom and won't let me in."

"I'm on my way."

I see the door open and a figure bound down the front steps, silhouetted by the porch light. There's a covered shed behind the house, and moments later the headlights of a four-wheeler appear from around the corner. They bounce and shift as he traverses the land between our two homes. He never hangs up. I hear the rip of the engine and his steady breathing. I align mine to it on instinct, and it calms my racing heart.

From inside the bathroom, the distinct sound of a curtain rod falling brings me back to the chaos.

"Dad! Truett is coming." I press my ear to the door. The sobbing has slowed, but the muttered cursing has returned. "He'll be here any—"

"I'm here," Truett calls from behind me. The front door remains wide open, his shoes on, as he crosses the space between us. His hand falls to the base of my spine, the other to the doorknob. "Henry, it's Tru. You've gotta let me in, ya hear? Delilah's real worried."

A shadow interrupts the light under the door. I inhale sharply and point, drawing Truett's gaze downward.

He nods. Taps lightly on the door. "Open up, Henry. Let me help you."

"I don't want her to see me like this," Dad whisper-shouts, his earlier anger all gone. These words are comprised entirely of desperation. Stitched together with utter shame.

Tru's gaze meets mine and softens. The hand that was resting against my spine now lifts to my cheek, wiping away a fresh flood of tears. "I've got this, Delilah. Just wait for me out here?"

Despite everything inside me that screams it's my responsibility, I relent. If my dad doesn't want me, I can't force it. It'll only cause more pain for us both.

I step out of Truett's orbit, feeling cold to the bone the second I do. Halfway to the living room, I hear the lock disengage and the door ease open. A glance over my shoulder catches Truett disappearing inside. Soft voices join the flow of water and the sound of my breaking heart.

Chapter Thirteen

Delilah

TRU LEANS BACK against Dad's bedroom door once it's shut, exhaustion heavy on his shoulders. "He's fast asleep. All that fussing really tuckered him out."

I pull the throw pillow tighter to my chest, like I can brand the words *Ridgefield Family* into my sternum if I squeeze hard enough. My body sinks into the couch cushions. I stare straight at Tru, straight *through* him, without blinking.

Truett sighs, a heavy, bone-weary sound. Then he rounds the side table and kneels in front of me, hands braced on my knees. "It's just a bad day, Delilah. They happen every now and then."

My gaze lands on his hands. On the steady circles his thumbs impress upon my skin. "The doctor upped his meds. It feels like things are progressing. Aggressively."

I've heard that word used to describe a multitude of diseases throughout my life. Things like cancer. Heart failure. Kidney disease. "An aggressive form," they'd call it. I never understood how accurate a word it was until now.

It feels like an attack. Not only on my dad, but on me too. It feels malicious. Hateful. Like the universe itself has a bone to pick with my family.

Truett's thumbs pause. I glance up, fully allowing myself to absorb his gaze for once.

Perhaps it does, I muse.

He claps my knees. "You're coming with me."

"What?" My gaze shoots to Dad's door. "I can't. What if he wakes up and needs me?" *What if he doesn't want me and instead needs you?* My pride is barely holding together as it is, but I'm not above begging Truett to stay. Anything to keep my dad from hurting like he was earlier.

He couldn't figure out the shower. Truett told me once he'd helped Dad bathe, given him a fresh set of clothes, and left him to dress himself. Dad had gotten confused trying to remember how the faucet works, and if he needed to take off his socks or shorts first. When his clothes got soaked with blazing hot water, he started throwing things out of fear. "*It's no big deal,*" Truett said, shrugging. But it was the biggest deal to me.

The corners of Truett's gaze soften. He's dressed casually, in jeans and a faded T-shirt. No hat this time. His hair looks so impossibly soft. I clench my fists against the pillow, trapping desire in my grasp.

"He took some melatonin to help him sleep. He'll be out all night. Besides, we aren't going far." As if he senses the war that rages inside me, Truett reaches for one of my hands. His touch is gentle, palms calloused. I'm too tired to fight. Not tonight, after the day I've had. I let myself be pulled from the couch, guided to the door, and escorted out into the humid night. Crickets and frogs cry out to one another, filling my head with the cacophony of summer. My focus never leaves our woven hands.

"Where are we going?"

Truett releases me to straddle his four-wheeler. He leaves enough space between him and the handles that I know I'm meant to fill it, but I hesitate. Glance over my shoulder. Between my worry over Dad and the waking wet dreams about riding the lawn mower with Truett that have been popping into my head all week, I'm certain this is a terrible idea.

He pats the seat, smirking up at me. "Come on, Temptress. I don't bite."

"Hate it when you call me that," I mutter. I do my best to mount the vehicle without sliding my ass against Truett's hips. I'm only partially successful.

He shifts, and something hard presses against my ass. I swallow thickly, tilting my hips forward ever so slightly to relieve myself of that particular temptation.

"Do you really or are you just saying that to be contentious?"

I stiffen against my urge to shiver as his words tickle the back of my ear. "I didn't realize you knew what that word meant."

He starts the engine and steers us toward his house. "I'm not some dumb cowboy, despite what you may think."

I've never thought that, I want to say. But we're going faster now, veering left around the base of the hill behind his house. Warm summer air slices at my cheeks. Roars in my ears. If I spoke, I'm afraid my reply would be lost to the wind. So I keep it to myself, nestled in the hollow of my heart with everything I've never been able to confess to Truett.

We roll to a stop in front of a rusted iron gate at the edge of the open pasture. We're in the farthest field from the house, the one they use as a feeder lot. Here at the perimeter, the shade trees huddle close, blocking out all but a few silvery streams of moonlight. He dismounts, approaches one side of the gate, and makes quick work of the chain link holding it in place. It swings open with a groan that a nearby steer echoes.

"Can you drive it on through?"

In another lifetime, this was second nature to me. But I find myself grateful for the cover of darkness when my first attempt at pulling forward results in a lurch that sends a blush straight to my cheeks.

"It's okay; just try again. Slower this time."

I do as he says, easing forward at a snail's pace.

"Well, not that slow."

A scowl he can't see distorts my face. "Do you mind?"

He cocks his head. The moonlight turns his blond hair to silver, like a spider's silk. "I like it when you're testy."

I ignore him, but something like a growl rumbles in my throat.

He closes off the gate as soon as I clear the opening. When he settles back into the space behind me and his arms come around mine to grab the handles, he huffs, "Don't want any tagalongs."

I glance back at him. "To where exactly?"

An eyebrow lifts. "I'm shocked you don't remember this place." Something like disappointment ripples across his features, but it could just be a trick of the light.

He nods toward a break in the trees ahead, and I follow his gaze as we pull forward.

The shaded path spits us out into a small meadow along the edge of the river that flows through his pasture. A sandy shoreline is framed by knee-height switchgrass. In the center of the meadow, the thick tendrils of a willow tree brush the ground, creating a whispered song all their own. Fireflies weave in and out of the branches. The bench Truett built in shop class freshman year sits at its base, weathered but otherwise unchanged.

Recognition washes over me. Here, upstream from the farm, we spent countless days splashing in the water. Climbing the eroded bank on the opposite side of the river and swinging out on a frayed rope that gave my mother a conniption. We'd lounge in the shade of the willow tree and do homework or talk about life.

The memory of the last time we were here, of the kiss that we shared, flushes my skin.

I'm a grown woman. I realize that feeling this way about a childhood crush is absolutely ridiculous. I've had better kisses, some amazing sex, since then. Well, standard sex. But standard sex is still more amazing than an innocent kiss, right?

So there's no reason I should feel like this. But my stomach turns to liquid and my face grows hot and my hands leech of all warmth. Truett, meanwhile, drives us to the perimeter of the tree's swaying branches without so much as an ease of the throttle to let me know he, too, remembers what we shared here.

Because for him, it was just practice. But for me it was everything.

Once the engine is cut off, the chorus of a country night looms close. Those frogs and crickets are accompanied by flowing water and the whisper of willow branches tangling together on the breeze. I close my eyes and draw the air deep into my lungs. A familiar comfort seeps into my skin. My taut spine relaxes. The headache that was forming disappears.

I hear the rustling of clothing. My eyes split open.

"What are you doing?"

Truett, whose shirt is already off, stops fiddling with his fly. "What do you think?"

Without hesitation, he strips his Wranglers off and leaves them discarded beside his boots. His body is toned and painted with a farmer's tan from days spent working in the fields. My gaze flits over his broad shoulders. The defined slopes of his biceps. The sinful V-shaped dip that disappears beneath the waistband of his boxer briefs.

His thumbs hook there, and I hold up a finger. "Don't you dare."

The corner of his mouth twitches. "A little skinny-dipping never hurt anyone."

"Except for the person who has to witness it." I cross my arms. "I'd like to keep some things about you to the imagination, thanks."

"So you're saying you've imagined what I look like naked?"

"No!" *Yes.* The heat in my cheeks is unbearable. "I'm saying — You know what I'm saying. Just keep your underwear on."

"As you wish." He bows, then turns and takes a running leap into the dark, swirling river. The current carries him a few feet down. He comes up hollering, his cheerful cries mingling with the melody of the forest around us. His arms sweep outward, drawing him toward me until he finds purchase in the soft sand of the river bottom. He plants his feet and rises, silver rivulets of water spilling down his chest beneath the light of the full moon. There's a dark spot on his ribs, a tattoo of some kind, that I can't make out in the shadows. "You coming?"

I scoff. "I am *not* getting naked in front of you."

"It's nothing I haven't seen before."

My feet cement to the ground. Any oxygen left in my brain drains completely, leaving me dizzy. "Excuse me? What the hell are you talking about?"

He crosses his arms over his chest and uses one hand to scratch his chin thoughtfully. "Let's see, would've been early 2000s. You were knee-high to a grasshopper, and hell, so was I." He laughs, his teeth flashing. "We got into some mud where the river cuts through the north pasture, and Mama hosed us off in the backyard. She was so pissed at me." His chuckle dissolves into soft hiccups as his arms drop to his sides. The water parts around his fingertips where he swirls them along the surface, the reflection of the night sky rippling apart. "You've forgotten so much since being away."

The words gut me as thoroughly as if he'd used a blade.

I stagger forward, through tall patches of switchgrass that tickle my exposed calves. There's a smooth expanse of sugar-soft sand near the water's edge, and I collapse onto it with my legs stretched out before me. The water laps at the shore, nearly brushing the toes of my new Keds. I draw them close, wrap my arms around my shins, and rest my chin on my knees.

"So that's a no on skinny-dipping?"

I stare straight ahead, to the far riverbank. "Dad brought up memory care facilities today." *Again,* I almost add. Though it feels like admitting to some sort of failure to do so.

"Like the one your nana was in?"

I nod, blinking slowly. I've been away so long I'd forgotten how it feels for someone to know your history as thoroughly as you do. To not have to fill in the blanks.

He wades into my line of vision, face solemn, and for once he reminds me of his dad. The hollows of his cheeks, the slight cleft of his chin. Waylon wasn't around much when I'd come over. He'd be out working the cattle with their farmhands or in town doing God knows what, but the few times he came to dinner with my family or passed by me in their kitchen on his way to retrieve a beer from the fridge, his expression was always stern. It made the chiseled lines of his face seem so harsh.

Paired with the gentle slope of Lucy's nose and her soft gray eyes, however, it makes Truett look like a man lovingly carved from stone. Like artwork set free from a column of marble.

"If you need money for it, I can help. I've got enough set aside—"

I stiffen. "I'm not putting my dad in a home."

"No one said you had to, yet. I'm just saying, when the time comes—"

"The time won't come!" Sand flies in every direction as I shoot to my feet. "How could you think I would do that? Would you have put Lucy in a home when she was dying?"

My words echo through the meadow, reverberating back to me in harsh staccatos. Tru's eyes are too dark for me to read, but the muscle in his jaw ticks. It's enough.

I stumble backward, lungs aching. "I'm sorry, Tru. I didn't mean to… I know it was different. But I can't do that. Not to my dad. I can't abandon him again."

There it is. My thoroughly guarded secret, laid bare for him to dissect. I'm tempted to cave in on myself, to reel in the words I've already spoken, but I force myself to stand still. Not strong, but strong-acting.

Water falls off him in streams as he wades forward, rising from the dark river like some sort of aquatic god. He strides toward me, closing the distance in the time it takes my heart to remember to keep beating. He's close now. So close I can make out the small bundle of flowers tattooed onto his rib cage, begging my fingers to trace it.

"There wasn't time for Mom to need a home. Pancreatic cancer moves too quickly. By the time we knew she had it, it was everywhere."

My hand covers my heart, a pathetic balm that doesn't begin to soothe the ache. For a moment I forget my confession. I'm too busy drowning in grief.

"You're right; it's different with your dad. It may be moving fast, but we'll still have *years* with him. Years that won't always be pleasant." He grimaces like he's seeing something I can't possibly imagine. "At some point he may need care that even Roberta can't provide. And that's okay. It doesn't make you a bad daughter to get him the kind of help he needs. In fact, it makes you the *best* daughter."

My chin wobbles. I clamp down on my lip, hopeful to stop the trembling. Truett's gaze drops to that place. He reaches for me and I flinch. His hand pauses midair, and then his fingertips find my bottom lip, which he tugs from the grasp of my teeth.

His hand drops. "Did you know he was diagnosed a year ago?"

A sharp gasp stings my lungs. "What? W-why? Why would he wait?" *So much time lost,* I think. Not just the year, but those that preceded it, too.

"He wanted to take care of things first."

Dad's words in the voicemail filter through my mind. *"I'm getting it all figured out. Well, me and that Parker boy...Truett. You remember him?"*

I blink up at that Parker boy. The one I could never forget.

"What kind of things?"

Truett lowers himself to the sandy bank. Once seated, he reaches up for the hem of my shirt and tugs. I allow myself to be pulled down, mostly because my feet are unsteady beneath me. We sit thigh to thigh, shoulder to shoulder, staring out at the brimming river.

"The first thing he said when he got the diagnosis was your name."

I close my eyes, steeling myself. A sharp, quick breath breaks the barrier of my pinched lips.

"His biggest fear was that you'd give up your life trying to care for him. He wanted to make sure everything was in order so that you didn't have to be stuck here working things out like..." His voice trails off. When I glance over at him, his mouth is a firm line.

I nudge his shoulder. "Like what?"

He fills his cheeks with air and releases it. "Like *you* were the parent."

I briefly forget how to breathe. Awareness brushes over my skin in the form of goose bumps. How often have I thought of myself like that? The parent to two people who had me too young, who made mistakes that I suffered the consequences of. I always assumed Dad didn't see how his affair affected me, how it forced me to grow up overnight. That he wasn't thinking of me at all. Mom, I was used to managing. But suddenly both of them were falling apart, and who did that leave to take care of things?

Me. Always me.

"He'd already pulled back at the music school after Mama died. Once he got the diagnosis, he switched entirely to at-home lessons. But even those petered out eventually." He clears his throat. Swipes his hand under his nose. "I helped him get the tests. Figure out his meds. Filled out the disability application. Made a list of homes to look at when the time came. We made a plan for how this would all end, how he'd afford it. Hell, we even picked out a headstone."

Tears spill over my cheeks. Disability I thought of, but headstones? Funerals? I never even considered the possibility. My chest feels impossibly tight. "Where does he want to be buried?"

"Remember the little cemetery on top of the hill? It's where we buried Mama. Your dad asked to be next to her."

A half-bitten sob passes through my parted lips. I shove my fist against my mouth to cover it, but he hears. Of course he hears. To my surprise, I feel his arms come around me, and one hand presses my head into his chest. He cradles me there, chin tucked against the crown of my head, breath rustling stray strands of my hair. He smells like fresh air and vetiver-scented soap. I drink it in with each gulping sob, desperate for something light in all this darkness.

"He didn't want to tell you until everything was squared away, so that if you decided to respond at all, to be involved in any way… Well, he wanted you to be able to focus on whatever it is you're feeling, instead of letting obligation get in the way. Grief. Or relief." His chin rolls against the crown of my head as he shakes his. "None of the fucking logistics of dying."

I flinch away from him. Run a hand through my mussed hair. "Relief? Why the fuck would I be relieved?"

He finds my gaze and holds it. "He hadn't seen you in nine years, Delilah. Neither of us knew what you'd think. Or want." Each word is clearly articulated, a blade perfectly honed.

"You don't get to judge me for how I handled things." I shake my head. "You weren't there, Tru. You couldn't possibly understand."

His brows rise. "It happened to me, too. Did you forget about that?"

"I didn't see people cornering you in the hallways. Passing you notes with horrible things about your parents written on them." I study his face. The ripple of regret. "No one tricked you into coming to a party so they could film you being sexually assaulted, did they?"

He reels backward as though I've hit him. And I hope I have, right where it hurts. Because I've been bearing the brunt of it for far too long. All by myself.

Just like Dad thought I would. *Knew* I would.

"I didn't know that part until you were already gone, Delilah, I swear. I—I wanted to say something the minute you showed up at that party. And then when he kissed you, and you seemed so into it… I—"

"You walked away."

He winces. "What?"

"You walked away when I needed you." I stand, putting as much distance between us as possible. Hating the desperate plea in my words when all I want is to show this man I'm strong enough to do this alone. I didn't *need* him back then. Not really. I've never needed anyone. I'm practically an expert at handling myself.

I correct myself with my next words, hoping to convince us both. "My world was falling apart and the only person I *wanted* was my best friend, but you shut me out."

His mouth parts, but I cut him off.

"You became yet another person who left me to deal with everything on my own. How am I supposed to forget that, Truett?"

His gaze searches my face. For what, I don't know. But I stopped waiting for a response from Tru nine years ago.

"Take me back to the house." I turn toward the four-wheeler, leaving him standing among the switchgrass. "It's been a really awful day."

I don't watch as he gathers his clothes and tugs them back onto his damp body. This time I'm not even tempted.

We ride in silence. Or as silent as the engine and the insects and the animals can all get, which is still magnificently noisy. But we do not speak. I sit behind him instead of in front, hands braced on the rack behind me so I don't have to hold on to his waist. I ignore the way his T-shirt clings to the damp ridges of muscles cording his shoulders. I also ignore his hand reaching for me as I dismount and walk away, leaving him as alone in my front yard as I was all those years ago.

My phone lights up the moment I drop it on the dresser. I glance at it, fully prepared to delete whatever message he's sent me before I remember he's blocked. Instead I see my mother's contact photo.

MOM

Miss you. Can't wait for you to be home.

Guilt blooms in my chest, right along with all the raw pain this night has brought forth. I collapse into my bed, sand-covered shorts and all, and close my eyes. I pray for sleep and enough good sense to stay the hell away from Truett Parker.

Chapter Fourteen

Henry

May 17th, 1997

MONTHS PASS like scenes on a movie reel. Shadows of the world unfolding on the screen. I become something of a silhouette in my daily life. Still taking up space, but I'm empty inside.

I go to school. Get good enough grades for Mom not to worry. Not that she's checking. Saturdays and Sundays are filled with shifts at the factory where my dad worked, scraping in extra cash to help Mom with the bills. She picks up a job waitressing at the local diner. We remain in constant motion, never slowing enough for the grief to catch us. On the rare occasion we're both home, we're less like a family and more like two ghosts haunting the same old house. Neither of us know how to move on.

I start to forget the way football games filled our home with background noise on the weekends. The sound of my father's larger-than-life sneezes. The sight of the two of them dancing in the living room while Etta James crooned through the boom box speakers. At some point I even forget exactly which song has the skip in it, the result of a small scratch on the CD—my fault from dropping it a few years back.

The idea of running off to Nashville falls by the wayside. Instead I'll go full-time at the factory after I graduate next month. Save up some money. Make sure Mom's all right. Then, in a few years, I can follow my dreams. It's just a pit stop, not a complete derailment. At least, that's what I tell myself.

Part of me wants to ask Lucy to wait for me. A bigger part insists I have no right.

We stop going to church. Mom, because she can't walk into that sanctuary without seeing Dad's casket at the base of the stage steps. Me, because I can't be near Lucy without wanting to hold her. Touch her. Make music with her. Passing her in the hallway is miserable enough. I can't sit through two hours of her dad's rambling sermons while feeling her presence like a heartbeat outside my body three pews ahead.

It's a season of wanting everything I can't have, and despising everything that I do.

Derell and Jed do their best to support me. They still invite me out every Friday, despite the fact that I haven't stepped foot in that field since that night. They try. Really, they do. But I feel too far gone to be reached. Come fall, Derell will be off to the University of Alabama and Jed will leave to work on an oil rig offshore. Their lives will move forward, while mine feels impossibly stuck.

Just a pit stop, not a derailment, I remind myself. But the words feel hollow.

Perhaps it's the thought of them leaving, the realization that the last few pieces of my life that remain unchanged are about to morph into something I don't recognize, that convinces me to let my friends drag me to prom. It certainly wasn't the thought of seeing Lucy, even from a distance, dressed in a beautiful gown. I'm no masochist.

My gaze flits past face after face in the gymnasium, but none of them are hers. Disappointment settles like a stone in my gut.

Okay, so I'm a *little bit* of a masochist.

Jed elbows me in the ribs. "Dude, look at Talia."

I halt my search of the room and follow his gaze. Through the mess of writhing bodies, I spot Talia Winters doing a shimmy against one of her friends. Her lashes are lowered, purple pout perfectly in place. She points to Jed, then does a come-hither curl of her finger.

"Is this really happening?" Jed tugs at the stiff collar of his button-down.

Derell lets out a sharp whistle from my other side. "I don't fucking believe it. But yes, I think it is. Go get 'em, Tiger!"

I chuckle. It's a loose, breathy thing. I could blame it on a lack of practice and a parched throat. More likely it's the result of spotting Lucy the second she walks through the gymnasium doors, looking like a dream.

Her dress is made of dark blue velvet that drapes over the swells and valleys of her body like flowing water. It ties at the nape of her neck, covering her chest in a modest way that I'm sure the pastor approves of, but her delicate shoulders are exposed. I've never gotten hard at the sight of shoulders before, but suddenly all those dress code rules make a little more sense.

Golden strands fall in soft curls around her heart-shaped face. The rest of her hair is swept up high on her head, with small bits and bobs pinned throughout that twinkle in the flashing lights. A thin shawl comes around her shoulders, placed by familiar hands.

Attached to a familiar body.

Belonging to a familiar face.

Jed finally snaps out of whatever trance he was in, abandoning us for the possibility of a post-prom blow job from Talia. I grind down on my molars.

"Who is that?" Derell throws a half-hearted punch against my bicep, as though I'm not already locked in on the scene unfolding fifteen feet away. "He looks too old to be at prom, right?"

Waylon Parker squeezes Lucy's now-covered shoulders. He leans in to whisper something in her ear. Her lips pinch together and she nods. When he walks away, bound for the table of snacks and punch on the far side of the basketball court, I swear she looses a breath. That shawl drops from her shoulders ever so slightly.

"Definitely too old," Derell says, confirming his own statement. "The guy's, like, twenty-two or something."

"Twenty-three." My fists clench and release at my sides. I'll never understand how her dad could have a problem with me, but he'll send her off with someone like Waylon without an issue. There's no way he's changed all that much in the short time since he was a student here. Does the pastor truly believe Waylon's wannabe pious persona? Kissing ass must really work wonders.

Anger and hurt tighten my sternum. I suck in a breath to loosen it, but it's no use. My lungs don't want the air. They just want her.

Her honeysuckle scent. Her sweet breath flowing over my lips. The feel of her body crushed against mine behind the oak tree. Even though it was the worst day of my life, it's a sacred memory. Maybe especially so, for that exact reason.

"What happened with you two?" Derell's eyebrows rise, his dark eyes locking with mine. "You seemed to be getting cozy leading up to that night when your dad…" His voice trails off, Adam's apple visibly bobbing beneath tawny skin as he swallows. "Well, you know."

I shake my head, letting my gaze fall away from his. "Nothing happened."

Lucy's eyes find mine in the crowd. Her lips part, and I imagine the sharp intake of her breath. Not unlike the one when our mouths collided in the cab of my truck. The shawl drops farther, and I notice a dark birthmark in the hollow where her right collarbone meets the shoulder. I wet my lips. Watch her track the movement. Just as she takes a step forward, Waylon returns with two glasses of punch in hand, a lazy smile pulling at one side of his mouth.

His gaze follows hers, brow furrowed, until at last landing on me. That smile becomes a scowl. He passes one cup to her, then uses his free arm to take her other hand, guiding her into the crowd and away from me.

"Nothing will ever happen," I add.

Derell glances between me and the place where Waylon and Lucy disappeared, lips folded into a flat line. I suck in a breath like it's the last one I'll get.

"Is there any place to get a drink around here?"

"Excuse me? Like *alcohol?*" Derell's eyes widen. "You. *Drinking?*" He licks a finger and holds it up in the air. "No, it doesn't feel like this hellhole has frozen over. What gives?"

I shake my head. "I just want a drink. You drink all the time, dude."

"Yeah, but you don't. That's, like, one of the few constants in our lives. Tractors will always end up in front of you when you're in a hurry, and Henry doesn't drink."

"Fine," I grumble. "I'll find it myself."

I stalk toward the back set of doors, opposite the way Lucy came in. Derell stays behind. I only glance back once, but even in the sporadic light cast by flashing strobes, I can read the disappointment written plainly on his face. *Who is he to judge?* I pass a tangle of bodies that turns out to be Jed and Talia locked in a make-out inferno. My friend glances up when I brush against his back. Purple lipstick is smeared on his crooked teeth. His gaze narrows on me briefly before a hand sporting long, sparkly nails comes around his neck and pulls him back into his waking wet dream.

Damp evening air blasts me in the face, cool by comparison to the sweaty cluster of bodies I escaped. The gym doors clang shut behind me, trapping the roar of music and conversation inside. It's so painfully quiet that my ears ring, desperate to fill the void with any sound.

I sag against the metal doors, letting the facade drop for the first time all night.

"You look like you could use one of these."

My gaze cuts to the base of the steps, where a girl I hadn't noticed sits in the shadows. The floodlight I stand beneath doesn't quite reach her. Even squinting, I can barely make out the orange glow of a cigarette and shimmering silver eyeshadow around kohl-smudged eyes.

"I don't bite," she says, lifting something from her equally sparkly purse and offering it in an outstretched hand. A pack of cigarettes moves into the circle of light. "You want one?"

Normally the answer would be, *Hell no.* But nothing about these last few months has been normal.

My oxfords scuff against the concrete steps. They're a size too big since they belonged to my dad. When I take a seat beside the girl, who I realize now is blonde with wide hazel eyes and a smirk stretching her thin lips, I can't help but wonder if Dad would approve of what I'm doing in his shoes.

"I'm Kimberly." She smiles wider, exposing a flash of white teeth beneath shimmery red lip gloss. She passes the lit cigarette to me, which I take awkwardly between my index and middle finger, the way that I've seen my friends do it. "Just lit that one, so have at it. I'll get myself another."

"We can share," I mumble. I don't want to be responsible for smoking the entire thing. "And I'm Henry."

Something sparks in her gaze, and she leans closer to me. Her lips close around the cigarette in my hand, and she draws a deep breath, then lets a spool of smoke out in front of us. My mouth covers the print of her lip gloss on the wrapper, and I mimic her movements, trying my best not to look like a total amateur. The smoke burns my throat. I sputter and cough it up in rasping, jerky breaths. Kimberly, to her credit, takes another drag without so much as a wince or snort at my reaction. I relax a little. Whether it's because of the cigarette or her presence, I couldn't say.

"Not having fun at prom, I take it?"

I let my gaze fully settle on her, taking in her features as she draws another breath of smoke. She's watching me from the corner of her eye. Her blonde hair is slicked high in an arrangement not unlike Lucy's. There are brightly colored clips gathering the strands across her crown. I squint, realizing they're shaped like butterflies. It makes me smile for some reason. When she returns the expression, I smile wider.

I shrug. "I wasn't."

She exhales a cloud of smoke that blurs our view of the baseball fields, then passes the cigarette back to me. I take another drag. This time I manage to keep the coughing to a minimum. It still burns my lungs like hell.

"Me neither. Came here with my cousin, but she's in there sucking some dude's face off." Her upper lip curls. "He's not even cute."

"Does your cousin happen to be named Talia?"

Her eyes widen as they cut to me. "You know her?"

"Yeah, that not-cute guy is my friend Jed." She opens her mouth to speak, but I cut her off. "He's in there checking something major off his high school bucket list, so try to go easy on him."

Kimberly bites her lip, gaze flickering over my face like she's trying to gauge how upset I am. I'm not. She wasn't being particularly rude, just a little too honest with a stranger. But I'm the only one who gets to call my friends ugly, so of course I'm gonna stick up for the guy. I'd expect the same in return.

"I didn't realize Talia had a cousin." A ladybug lands on her knee, which the split of her shimmery green dress leaves bare. I brush the insect away absent-mindedly. "You're not from here then?"

She stares at the place where the ladybug was as she speaks. "South Carolina, actually. But I'm a freshman at the University of Southern Mississippi over in Hattiesburg. My semester ended this week and my parents are finishing up some renovations on the house, so I came to see my cousin for a bit before heading home for the summer."

"You weren't over prom already? Being in college and all."

"It's always fun to wear a pretty dress." She brushes the split open farther, exposing her long, bare legs to the cool breeze. "Even if this one is trying to give me a heatstroke."

I fan the lapels of my tux jacket. "I get that."

One pencil-thin eyebrow lifts. "You look handsome though."

Heat that has nothing to do with my tux creeps up my neck. I bring the cigarette to my lips and pull. A sharp burning sensation strikes my fingertips, startling me. I drop the cigarette into my lap on instinct, then jolt to my feet and slap at my front to get it off. The butt falls to the ground, a hazy orange flame still winking up at me. Kimberly tosses her head back, laughing. I'm checking my rental tux for burn marks, which I thankfully avoided.

I sigh heavily, shoulders sagging with relief. "Thank God. My mom would've killed me."

"I know this is your first time." She's still giggling, the words coming out like little hiccups. "But it's best practice to actually look at the cigarette before taking a drag just in case you're getting close to the end. And maybe don't hold it that far up either."

"Noted." Though I already know it will be my first and last cigarette. My mind feels loose and relaxed; all the tension from before has seeped out of me. But my lungs are tight, my throat on fire. Not worth it.

"Do you wanna take me somewhere, Henry?" Her eyes are

wide and hopeful as they gaze up at me. Golden flecks in her irises reflect the limited light. They're not striking like Lucy's, but they're warm.

I kick Dad's shoes against the butt, killing the last few sparks. "Like where?"

"Somewhere we can drink?" she asks, a hopeful pitch lifting her voice.

The field flashes through my mind. It'd be empty tonight; the complete opposite of the rowdy crowd inside. There'd be no Lucy and, more importantly, no Waylon. Perfect, essentially. There's just one problem.

Well, two problems. I can't buy alcohol. And I don't want to replace my last memory in that field, with Lucy pressed close to me and my friends gathered around a warm fire. The last normal moment of my life, now miraculous in its simplicity.

Kimberly rises to her feet, her nose even with my chin thanks to a pair of heels. Her head tilts, blanketing her face in moonlight. She's pretty, I realize, with a face that's all sloping lines and features that are wide and theatrical. She pokes her bottom lip out. "Please? Knowing Talia, she won't be done with your friend anytime soon. I wanna have fun tonight." In a bold move, she reaches for my hand. I twine my fingers with hers almost on instinct. I'm surprised to find it feels nice. Great, even. "Don't you want to have fun?"

Fun feels like such a foreign concept after everything that's happened the last few months. But I realize that tonight I *do* want to enjoy myself. I feel like I've been treading water since the day my dad died. It'd be nice to actually enjoy the swim for once.

My gaze drops to our joined hands. I try not to picture a different hand in mine, on a colder night. I want to solely live in this moment without sparing a thought for the past *or* future, even if only for a moment.

"Yeah. Yes." I look up at her, catching the sunrise of her smile just as it breaks across her face. "Do you like beer?"

She gathers her dress in her other hand, which exposes her feet in those tall, tall heels. A shiver runs down my spine.

"I like anything," she says. "Lead the way."

Chapter Fifteen

Delilah

A WAVE of heat courses through my body, ripping me from a dream where I'm submerged in dark, swirling water. I can still sense it as I toss and turn, stumbling my way to awareness. The feeling of the cool water pressing in on me, filling my throat so I can't even speak. Through the glassy surface, I can just make out Truett. His arm is outstretched, but I shake my head at him, moving like molasses in the quick current. I know this river as well as my own heartbeat. I've been swimming in it my whole life. Why would I need his help?

My eyelids peel apart with great effort. I blink blearily into the darkness of my room. No sliver of sunlight peeks through the crack in my curtains. *I'm still below the surface,* I think for a moment, panic squeezing my lungs. I sit up in bed, hands searching the blankets. For what? I don't know. Awareness comes on the tail end of another wave of heat, this time culminating in the pit of my stomach. Saliva floods my mouth. The realization hits me just in time, and I jolt out of bed.

I'm going to be sick.

I fling open the bathroom door, hand clasped over my mouth like that could save me, and kick it shut behind me. In the dim glow of the night-light, I can just make out the way to the toilet. I collapse at its base and heave. There's barely enough time for my hand to move out of the way and grip the seat before I'm vomiting. Bile burns my throat. Tears spill down my cheeks. Quick, sharp breaths are all I can manage between wave after wave of nausea. By the time my abdomen stops clenching, I'm utterly exhausted and my head is spinning. I fumble for the handle and flush away the contents of my stomach, then collapse onto the cool tile floor.

The cold stings the heated flesh on my cheeks and forehead at first, but as my body melts against it, it morphs into the sweet sensation of relief. I draw in a deep breath and hold it, then release it with a moan through pursed lips. I slap one clammy hand against my forehead. There's no doubt in my mind I have a fever, but suddenly the medicine cabinet in our kitchen seems impossibly far. I resign myself to die here on the bathroom floor, because there's no way I'm crawling the necessary fifteen feet to get Advil.

I want my dad, I realize with a muffled whimper. Thoughts that are quickly overrun with worrying about how, exactly, I'm meant to care for him in this state.

My eyelids flutter closed, the lashes sticky with tears. I let my mind wander back to that dark, swirling water. To Truett. This time I'm not afraid of drowning. I'm too desperate to cool down.

Somewhere, a door clatters shut. I'm able to ignore it for the most part. I slip back beneath the waves of consciousness. An immeasurable time passes before a voice drifts close. Footsteps pad down the hall. Distantly I'm aware that someone is knocking on a door. What door? Couldn't tell you. All I know is that my body aches from head to toe. My throat is a desert. And I'm freezing cold.

"Delilah?"

Roberta's voice breaks through the barricade of my fever, but only barely. I blink slowly, grateful that the only light in the bathroom is the night-light and a small sliver creeping through the gap beneath the door. This is by far the most dated room in the house, with a wrap of ivy wallpaper encircling the top of the ceiling that reminds me distinctly of an Olive Garden dining room. I trace the vines slowly with my gaze, hoping if I can focus on something for a moment, it'll quell the nausea stirring in my stomach.

Footsteps thud against the hardwood in the hall, making their way back toward the bathroom from what I assume was my bedroom door. A shadow stills outside; then the doorknob rattles. When she realizes it's unlocked, Roberta calls, "Delilah? Are you in there?"

I moan something unintelligible, but it must be close enough to, "Come in," because she does.

She's backlit by early morning light that leaves her features shrouded in shadow. I can only make out the haze of her silver-streaked hair, the silhouette of her frame, before my eyelids drift closed again.

"Oh, sweetheart."

I hear shoes hit the tile floor, then a cool hand sweeps over my forehead. It reminds me of my mother on mornings when Dad had already gone to work and I was home, sick as a dog from the latest virus scourging my classroom. She'd do the same move, smooth knuckles brushing the sticky skin of my temples, then call my dad to beg him to come home.

"You look like you feel about as good as Henry does."

My eyes fly open and I jerk upright, but I'm instantly informed that was a terrible mistake when the world spins rapidly around me. Roberta catches me as I slump backward. Pulls me into her chest. She holds me the way I always begged Mom to, but Mom was too afraid of germs. I lift my arm weakly, bringing a trembling hand to cover my mouth. "I'm sick. I don't want to breathe on you."

Even speaking sends a wave of nausea up my throat. I pinch my lips tight, desperate not to vomit again. I have nothing left. My stomach is achingly empty.

"After years of working in hospitals, I have an immune system of steel." Her tone holds a thin layer of amusement, like decoration adorning a warm underbelly of empathy. "And I'm masked."

I squint up at her. The light now falls across her face. A blue medical mask hides her ever-present smile, but I can still see it in the crinkles of her eyes.

"Henry was on the couch, pale and moaning over a salad bowl when I walked in. I thought you'd slept through work, so I was going to wake you up once I got him settled in bed."

Guilt, painfully vile, slithers up my spine. "I need to get up. Need to help."

"Respectfully," she says, amusement coloring her tone, "you're not helping anybody in your state."

A groan rumbles in my throat. It's the spark the nausea kindling in my gut needed. I lurch forward, collapsing over the toilet as stomach bile and not much else works its way out of my body. Roberta strokes a steady hand up and down my spine over the thin fabric of my T-shirt. "Let it out, honey. I know that hurts."

I can't flush the toilet this time. My arms are shaking too badly. Roberta does it for me, then braces a hand under my armpit and pulls me away from the toilet.

"Can you stand?"

I roll my head back and forth in some semblance of a shake.

A hum vibrates her lips, the sound muted by her mask. Then

she releases me and stands. I whimper at the abandonment, suddenly reverting to the emotional capacity of a two-year-old in the face of being alone.

"I'm not leaving you, Delilah. Just needed better leverage." Her forearms brace underneath my biceps and lift. I forget how to assist, and my arms fly up, my shoulders meeting my ears. "You're going to have to help me a bit here. I'm strong but not that strong."

I blow out a breath and nod. This time when she hoists, I'm ready. I use every ounce of strength left in my body to brace my feet against the tile and push. With a lot of grunts and a few concerned breaths, I make it to a standing position, though I'm leaning heavily on Roberta.

"Come on. Let's get you to bed."

I allow her to lead me toward my room, but I whine, "What if I need to be sick again?"

"Surely there are multiple salad bowls in this house."

I'd laugh if I weren't certain it'd lead to vomiting.

She opens the door and ushers me inside. I drop onto my mattress with the grace of a two-ton elephant, then curl into the fetal position. Sand from last night's escapades scratches my skin, sending a tinge of regret up my spine. As if I weren't feeling bad enough already.

Did Truett deserve for me to blow up at him? Probably not. After everything he'd just done for my dad, the least I could do was show him a bit of grace. But nothing I said was untrue. He *did* leave me to fend for myself, like everyone else in my life. Surely that entitles me to some anger.

But as sleep tugs me back under, it's not anger that I feel creeping over the barriers surrounding my heart. It's a feeling much more concerning, one that leaves me exposed. Vulnerable. And not only because I'm too sick to thank Roberta when she deposits a bowl beside my bed.

Exhaustion takes me, but not before the word for that feeling drifts through my mind like a wayward breeze.

Need.

I wake to the buzzing of my phone near my ear. It could be minutes since Roberta escorted me to bed, or possibly hours. My concept of time is warped by whatever virus is plaguing my body. My hand weaves through pillows and clumps of bunched-up sheets until it lands on something smooth and cool. My cell.

"Hello?" My voice is all sharp edges and rasp, like I've raked my vocal cords over hot coals. Or vomit. So. Much. Vomit.

"Oh my God, Delilah. Are you okay?" My boss's voice hits my eardrum like a mallet. I wince. Knowing Cameron means well doesn't stop it from hurting like hell. "I've called a few times. You didn't log on, and I thought something might've happened with your dad."

Tears prick my eyes. Even closing them doesn't ease the stinging. I'm weak, tired, and an emotional wreck from the events of the last twenty-four hours. And I *never* miss work. Certainly not without calling first. I meant to earlier, when Roberta brought me back to my room, but sleep came on so fast.

"I'm so"—I gag around the words, then swallow back the rising bile—"sorry. Dad's okay." I crack an eyelid, spying a glass of water on my bedside table that I assume Roberta left for me. I grab it and bring it to my lips, taking a few small sips. The way my throat burns, you'd think I was throwing back a glass of razor blades. "I'm sick. Some kind of stomach flu."

Cameron groans, his normally bright voice turning to a gravel tumbler. "Oh man, Charis had that a few weeks ago. It took her daycare by storm. Must've made its way to Alabama."

"Joy," I bite out. The few sips of water start to creep back up my throat.

"On the bright side, it only lasted about forty-eight hours."

I can't help it; I let out a little whimper.

"Sorry, Delilah." The telltale sound of a Zoom call coming in blares in the background, triggering something instinctual in me. I almost reach for my phantom mouse to accept the call. Cameron grunts. "Gotta take this. It's the Cale Group. Don't worry about your meetings—I'll divvy them up among the team for the rest of the week. Take a few days to recover. Oh, and get some ginger ale. It's the only thing that helped Charis."

I picture his cute little three-year-old feeling as shitty as I do, and sympathy tugs at my heart.

"Thanks, Cam. Sorry"—I have to pause, exhale slowly, and try again—"for not calling."

"Don't sweat it. Just wanted to make sure everything was all right." The ringing ceases. "Shit. Gotta call them back or Liv will be up my ass for not taking care of our *very important client.*"

It sounds exactly like something Liv, the VP of our division, would say. I snort half-heartedly, then wince.

"Take care!" Cameron singsongs.

My response isn't much of one. More of a grunt. I drop the phone back into the sea of blankets as soon as it goes dark, and my head isn't far behind it. This time as I drift off to sleep, I hear that damn ringtone on repeat till at last I slip away.

Roberta's hand is rougher the next time it brushes against my temple. Not in force, but in texture. It's the first thing I think when my brain comes online. *Roberta needs some fucking lotion.*

"She's awfully warm."

Oh. Perhaps I'm not fully online yet after all. Because that was definitely not Roberta's soothing, melodic voice.

"I haven't been able to get any medicine in her. Every time I try to wake her, she groans and rolls away from me."

That's Roberta. So who the hell…?

A snort sounds nearby. The breeze of it cools my cheek.

"Sounds about right. If you'll leave the bottle on her vanity, I'll get her to take some." Truett's voice is warm in the middle but laced with sharp edges. Something like concern, if I didn't know any better.

Truett. Jesus Christ, this bug has taken all my common sense if I couldn't even identify his voice. I jolt upright, having somehow forgotten my lesson from earlier, just as Roberta places a blue pill bottle next to my sunscreen and mascara on the vanity.

"Whoa, Delilah. Go slow," Truett says.

"I'm not a horse," I rasp. But I do pause, letting my equilibrium catch up with the new position.

Tru comes into focus, all sun-kissed skin and soft, golden hair. His smile is turned down at the corners, pinching his dimple. Bronze freckles dot the bridge of his nose, looking boyish compared to the sharp angles of his jaw. His gaze searches my face briefly. Those lips fall and flatten, and his dimple disappears. "You need to take some meds. You've got a hell of a fever."

My brow furrows. "Why are you here?"

Is that sorrow swimming in his gray eyes? They really are slate today. All the crystalline blue that sometimes appears has leaked away, leaving behind solid stone.

"You've slept all day." Roberta peeks around Truett, the nurse side of her checking me over. Even as that persona falls away, her chocolate gaze remains tight with concern. "I've got to pick up my granddaughter, but Tru's gonna take over. Your dad's fine. His fever broke a while ago, and he's feeling quite a bit better. Just watching some TV in the living room. But I couldn't leave you to fend for yourself."

Her voice screams, *You poor, pitiful thing.* And even though I feel that way, I don't want Tru to know it.

"I'm fine." I swallow the spit that rises with those words. Inhale through my nose. Out through my mouth. I'm not gonna be sick in front of Truett Parker.

Never mind that we got the chickenpox one summer as kids and spent a whole week watching *Rugrats* reruns together while Lucy brought us meds and snacks. That was before Dad started teaching, so he was at school and Mom had work. Lucy, however, was home and more than happy to care for me, too.

Or who could forget the time he gave me mono in middle school. We only had each other for company for a *month.* Truett's no stranger to what I'm like when sick. But that doesn't mean I need his help. Especially not after laying myself bare last night.

"Sure you are," Tru says, smiling. "But I'll be here in case that changes."

Roberta's gaze flicks from Tru to me, then back. "Okay, I've gotta go. Call if you need anything."

"Will do," Truett and I reply simultaneously.

It's the vigor with which I reply that does me in. Roberta has barely taken two steps into the hall when I double over, arm sweeping under the bed for my puke bucket. Truett surges forward from my vanity chair, which he'd pulled over in front of my bed. He scoops up the bowl and hands it to me with seconds to spare. What little water I've been able to put down spills from me in violent heaves, while embarrassment heats any place the fever left unscathed.

Truett stands, and I'm certain he's so disgusted that he's second-guessing his promise to Roberta. She's frozen in the hallway, unsure whether to stay or go. My dad's voice carries unintelligibly from the living room. Truett mutters something to Roberta that I can't make out over my gasping breaths. She nods, turns, and walks away. Instead of following her, Truett yanks open a couple drawers on my vanity. When he returns to my side, there's a giant scrunchie around his wrist.

I hold out my hand for it, still too breathless to verbally request the hair tie, but he bypasses my outstretched palm and comes to stand with his knees pressed against my mattress. I turn to look at him, the world tilting as I do, but his hand gently cups my chin and turns me forward, facing away from him.

"Face the bowl; I may owe you an apology, but that doesn't mean you get to puke on me."

His hands sweep through my hair. My greasy, sweaty hair. In all the fantasies I entertained as a teenager about Truett doing this, none of them involved me feverish and gross, with mouse-brown locks sticking to various patches of my neck and forehead. He combs those back, gathering my hair in a knot on top of my head, and ties it off with the scrunchie.

"Better?"

I grunt something that's meant to be gratitude. My gaze drops to the bowl in my lap. Its disgusting contents stare back at me. Before I can dwell on it for too long or get sick again at the sight of it, the bowl is swept away.

"I can clean it," I mumble.

"You're sick. I'll take care of it. A little puke doesn't scare me, Delilah."

I absently wipe at my mouth in case there are any remnants of vomit. "So what's this I hear about an apology?"

The corner of his mouth twitches. "Another time. When you're feeling better." He sets the bowl on my vanity. The small top drawer is still open from his search, and he plucks something from it. When he returns to my side, the photograph of us from Halloween is pinched between two fingers. "We really were thick as thieves back then, huh?"

Tears pool along my lash line. I'm entirely too weak to hold them back for long. Not with him standing so close. "Yeah, we were."

His gaze lifts to mine, clocking the tears within a heartbeat. *Of course.*

His tongue traces the notches he's bitten into his bottom lip. In the delirium of my illness, I wonder what it would feel like to do so myself. To sink my teeth into his full bottom lip, then lick the pain away.

I blink, and so does he, like he too had found himself on a train of thought going in the wrong direction.

He taps the photograph once, a breathy laugh escaping his throat; then he does something peculiar. Instead of returning it to the drawer, he tucks it back into the gap it left on my vanity mirror. Like he somehow remembered that's exactly where it belonged.

The bottle of Advil rattles as he scoops it up and uncaps it, shakes two pills into his palm, and deposits it beside my puke bowl. He holds his hand out, and I open my palm, catching the pills he drops. He hands me the newly refilled glass of water from my bedside table, as though I'd put even a dent in the original contents, and watches intently as I down the meds.

"I'm not tucking them under my tongue, if that's what you think." I stick it out to prove my point, regretting it a heartbeat later when I remember how rancid my breath must smell. My cheeks grow hotter, as if the fever wasn't bad enough.

To his credit, Truett doesn't seem to notice. He studies his hands, then mine. The distance between them. Or is it me who's measuring?

Growing up, we were so close I often wondered where Truett ended and I began. It felt like we'd always been two parts of a whole, a continuation of one another. My thoughts would echo in his brain. I'd answer his homework questions before he had to admit he couldn't work them out. Even now, I find that tether, thin and frayed as it may be, linking my heart to his. Or perhaps I'm imagining it, sick as I am. Wishing it into existence.

"Have you eaten at all?"

I shake my head.

"Thought so. I'll be right back."

He disappears, and though it's what I wished for initially, loneliness crashes around me the moment he does. It's been so long since I've had anyone around to take care of me. I'd almost forgotten how comforting it can be. Mom's version of helping me when I'm sick is isolating me to my floor of the house, then placing a delivery from whatever restaurant she's craving at breakfast, lunch, and dinner on the landing for me to crawl out of bed and retrieve.

When he returns a few minutes later with a box of saltine crackers, I've already used the bedspread to dry my face. He's seen enough of me crying since my return. So much for showing him just how much I don't need him.

I reach for the box of saltines, but he ignores me and plants himself in the chair by my bed. Plastic wrap crinkles around his hand as he retrieves a cracker and holds it out for me. "One at a time. If you eat too fast, you'll be sick again."

I roll my eyes, and thank God for rapid-relief gels because the world doesn't spin too badly when I do.

I pluck the cracker from his fingertips and bring it to my mouth, taking a small nibble of the corner. It's bland as all get out and I'm not exactly excited by the idea of food right now, but the moment I swallow, I realize how ravenous I actually am.

"You're probably super dehydrated. When's the last time you went to the bathroom?"

My jaw slackens. "I'm not answering that." But he's got a point. Was it last night? This morning? I truly can't remember.

He shakes his head softly. "So testy. Why won't you let me take care of you?"

I try to ignore the way that sentence lodges itself into my heart, taking up far more space than is comfortable. Instead I scoff. "We didn't exactly leave off on good terms last night."

"Right." His lips thin, gaze narrowing on the space above my head. "Bringing us back to the aforementioned apology."

"I'm all ears now. Completely healed and ready to talk. Look at me, the picture of health." I gesture to my body, which I'm now realizing is still in the same clothes as last night, bra and all. It's digging into my rib cage something fierce. If it weren't for Truett, I'd rip it right off. I settle for shifting uncomfortably in an attempt to dislodge the underwire from my soft flesh. The blankets are pooled around my waist, and I tug them higher to disguise my wiggling.

One eyebrow arches as his gaze drops to mine. "Bra bothering you?"

I huff. "You have no business being that observant."

"It's a gift." He snickers. "Lean forward. I'll help."

I balk. If I could go any paler, I would. "I'm good, thanks."

"Relax, Temptress. I'm not trying to seduce you while you're sick."

But what about when I'm not sick? The thought rolls unbidden through my brain. I wince, hoping beyond hope that his ability to read me like an open book didn't catch that.

The corner of his mouth quirks. *Fuck.* What is wrong with me? One stomach bug and suddenly I'm stupidly horny for enemy numero uno. Ridiculous.

"I tell you what. I'll turn my back. You try to take it off. If you can't, just let me know, and I'll help."

I scoff again. Cocky bastard. "Fine."

He spins the chair around. True to his gentlemanly word, he doesn't peek. I lean forward, sweeping my weak arms behind me and under my shirt. It's a move as familiar as breathing, but for some reason my fingers can't quite work the clasp. They shake and tremble. My biceps ache. A little grunt escapes me, and I swear Truett's ears perk up.

"Need help?"

"Nope. Almost got it." I finally get the clasp between my fingers. Sweat beads on my forehead with the effort. My arm gives out as I try to slip the hook and eye apart, and I loose a frustrated breath. "Just a new bra, that's all."

"Oh yeah? Do they stick more at the beginning?"

I don't like the way he says it like he knows better. I don't like that I find myself wondering *how* he knows better. Or, more importantly, *who.* I got one kiss, but who got the rest? Is he seeing anyone? The thought sends fire to the base of my neck that has nothing to do with the fever.

Ridiculous, I chastise myself. *I do not care.*

"Time's up." He rises, pivots on his heel, and closes the distance between us before I can protest.

I was just catching my breath, I want to say. *I was gonna get it.* But the words lodge in my throat as his hands—those strong, calloused hands—sweep under my shirt. They brush the soft skin of my sides, his fingertips dancing lightly over my rib cage. I suck in a breath, resisting the urge to unravel for his touch.

He undoes the clasp with practiced ease that only adds to the twisting in my stomach. He doesn't linger beneath my shirt. In and out, with all the precision of a military operation. And just as much desire. I have no reason to be disappointed, but the feeling settles in my chest anyway, along with a painful realization.

I'm completely and utterly fucked.

His fingertips snake up my sleeves now, hooking the bra straps and tugging them off my shoulders. As soon as my arms are free, the torture device falls away from my chest, and I let out a sigh of relief.

He steps back, smiling briefly. It's there and gone in a flash. I miss it so much I forget to breathe.

"Better?"

This time when he asks that, I'm actually able to offer a verbal response. "Yes, thank you." I retrieve the loose bra from where it's fallen to my waist and toss it across the room, not even checking to see where it lands. Truett's eyes widen slightly. His golden cheeks turn a deep russet color. At least, I think that's what happens. My eyes are growing heavy again now that I'm comfortable, and I could be misinterpreting. Or wishing.

The column of his throat tenses as he swallows, his Adam's apple bobbing. A muscle in his jaw ticks. Those hands find purchase on his hips, bracing against the waistband of time-worn Wranglers. A fresh cut mars his forearm, the blood newly crusted over. There's a dirt stain on the front of his faded Budweiser tee. He's clearly worked all day, and yet he's here taking care of me. Despite everything I said last night.

He was wrong about owing me an apology. Or at least only partially correct.

"I'm sorry," I choke out. It's half sleep laden, half sorrow. All broken.

The wrinkle between his eyebrows deepens. "For what?"

"For last night. I—" I swallow. The tears are building again, and I only have so long before I throw up or sob or both. I choose my words carefully, trying my best to be clear and measured. "You helped me, and I attacked you out of nowhere. About shit that doesn't even matter anymore."

Because why should it matter that he abandoned me all those years ago? It's not like we're anything to each other now. There's no need to drag up old wounds, flaying us both open in the process. Especially over a man I only half-tolerate for my dad's sake. And drool over when sick. Or when I see him in these Wranglers, which is all. The. Time.

Ugh.

He grimaces, probably exhausted by my constant yo-yoing

between bitter asshole and remorseful crybaby. I tug the blanket up over my braless breasts, not that he'd even care to look. I feel so small, lying here while he stands over me, face tense with contemplation.

As though he can hear my thoughts, he forgoes the chair and takes a seat on the bed. The mattress dips around his weight, tilting me into him. I try to scoot away, but it's no use. There's only so much bed, and Truett is a big guy. He takes up a good bit of the empty space and way too much of the oxygen in this room.

His hand rests on my thigh, dangerously close to the apex, though he has no way of really knowing. I'm beneath so many layers of blanket, now freezing as the fever breaks. Goose bumps break out across my skin. Because of the fever or his hand, I couldn't say.

"It does matter, Delilah." His voice is gruff. Thick. He clears it and swallows, gaze shifting from mine to where his hand lies. "Okay, partial apology now and then you really need to get some rest. You're turning green." His cheeks hollow. "I'm sorry I shut you out after everything. And I'm sorry about the party. I thought you left that night because… Well, I don't know. I just thought you left. And Kyle was gone when I got back, so honestly? I thought y'all went somewhere together."

I open my mouth to protest, but he squeezes my thigh once to silence me. It does a lot more than that. Heat pools between my legs. I imagine his hand moving higher, pulsing against my hips. My throat constricts. The juxtaposition of my thoughts and the nausea is enough to send my head spinning.

"I didn't find out until the following Monday about the video. About what Kyle did."

I'd be less sobered if he'd thrown ice cubes down the back of my shirt. I reach for my water, my hand shaking as I bring it to my lips. Hopefully Tru will write it off as a product of the illness rather than the aftereffects of a waking fever dream.

"You'd blocked my number by then." His gaze lifts to mine, bright and clear despite the storm that rages inside. "And then I found out you moved with your mom. That you weren't coming back."

I gulp audibly. "I—I didn't realize…"

He nods. "I know. And I'm not telling you as an excuse, because it's a shitty one at best."

I lick my lips. "Then why are you telling me?" I rasp.

His thumb moves over my thigh, dipping low. Even through the layers, I feel it searing me. It'll take a lifetime to forget the sensation.

"You didn't attack me out of nowhere." He shakes his head, more to himself than me, I'd wager. "And it isn't shit that doesn't matter anymore. Where you're concerned, it'll always matter."

My lips part, but he gets to his feet before I can formulate a response. He retrieves the bowl I'd forgotten about from my vanity and turns to leave the room, foot landing on the strip of brass where carpet meets hardwood in the threshold. "I'll fix dinner and bring it back in a bit. Holler if you need anything." He winces like he's thinking better of that statement. "Actually, you might want to consider unblocking me so you can call instead. Yelling might not be the best move till you're feeling better."

I crack a smile. It's stiff as a rusted water hose wheel, but it eventually cranks into position. "Does that mean I can yell all I want when I'm healthy?"

His lip twitches. "Yeah, Temptress. Get better, and then you can yell at me all you want."

The door snicks closed behind him. I hear the thud of his retreating footsteps, followed by the distant tenor of my father's voice. My chest aches. I've been so sick, Roberta had to be the one to take care of him. I couldn't push through enough to be strong for him. What kind of daughter does that make me?

My spine slumps into the stack of pillows. Something hard

presses against my hip. I retrieve my phone from where it jabs me, and I'm about to toss it on the floor when I remember what Truett said. It takes a few minutes, but I finally figure out where my blocked contacts are housed. It's him and that bitch Jessica Mathias, the one who caught Dad and Lucy and spread it all over school in the first place.

I unblock Truett's number, reinstate him as a contact, then shoot him a text.

ME

Hey, this is Delilah. I unblocked your number.

TRUETT

Good. Now get some rest. Your beauty sleep awaits.

ME

You saying I need it?

TRUETT

You're right. Stay awake. You already have an unfair advantage on everyone else in that department.

I lock the phone and flop onto my belly, smiling despite myself. That smile morphs into a yawn, my jaw popping and crackling as it overtakes me. Every muscle relaxes in its wake. All the feelings of inadequacy, of uncertainty where my dad is concerned, the questions about where I stand—or where I *want* to stand—with Truett, will have to wait. I'm too weak to reach for another sip of water, let alone to decipher why the moment I close my eyes, it's Truett that I see. Shirtless in the river, water rippling over his abdomen, as crickets and frogs call out a lullaby that lulls me to sleep.

Chapter Sixteen

Delilah

TRUETT STAYS until almost two in the morning. I know this because he checks on me every couple hours, even going so far as to bring me homemade chicken noodle soup. I don't lift my head when he places it on my bedside table—mostly because I apparently cannot trust myself around him while sick—but the moment I hear my door close, I draw it gingerly into my lap. Each sip is deliciously salty and calming in a way that only his mother's recipe could be. I'd recognize it anywhere.

I lick the last drop that tries to escape down my chin, savoring it. Suddenly I'm second-guessing turning down Tru's offer for dinner. It's possible that I'm simply starving, but it's the most delicious thing I've had since coming back to town. No offense to the Grille. Though after the day I've had, I'll never look at their burgers the same.

By the time his face appears in the gap of my open door at one thirty in the morning, illuminated by the soft glow of my bedside lamp, I feel almost human again.

"Look who's awake." The line between his eyebrows fades. "You've got some color back."

I rub the seam of my sleep shirt between pinched fingers. I

changed when I got up to go to the bathroom a few hours ago, after enough liquid finally made it through my body to justify doing so. Truett and Dad were sitting together on the couch, talking in hushed voices while the light from the TV transformed their faces with every scene change. Neither glanced up, and after seeing my ghastly reflection in the mirror above the sink, I certainly didn't want to draw Truett's attention. I brushed my hair and teeth and washed my face, then slipped back down the hall as quietly as possible.

"Mostly thanks to you"—I point to the empty bowl—"and Lucy."

A nostalgic smile tugs at the corners of his lips. When our eyes meet, his are lost in a memory. "She'd like that she's still taking care of you. Even now."

I swallow past the knot in my throat. "Thank you. You really didn't have to do this. I could've handled it."

"Really?" His eyebrow lifts. "Do we need to recap the bra incident?"

I scowl. "That is not to be spoken of outside these four walls. Do you understand?"

A breathy laugh escapes his quirked lips. He leans a shoulder against my doorframe and crosses his arms over his chest. His biceps strain against the thin fabric of his T-shirt. Each swell and valley of his muscular arms is highlighted by the shadows my lamp casts. I tear my gaze away, but it's too late. That smile is already a smirk by the time I make it back to his face.

"Well, since we're allowed to talk about it here…"

My breath catches. Holds.

His finger jabs in the direction of my discarded bra. "Do you usually toss those things with such abandon at the end of the day?"

I groan, falling back into my propped-up stack of pillows. "You would too if you were chained up in one for *hours*."

"You could always go without."

Blond lashes flutter as his gaze dips to my chest. Only for a heartbeat. A millisecond, really. The responding clinch of my stomach is disproportionately strong. It's been too long since I've gotten laid, and I'm desperate, apparently. My libido has lost all ability to be discerning.

I glance down at myself. My breasts are small but perky, their outline clear in my baby-blue top. My nipples strain for his attention. *Any attention,* I correct. I'm tired, worked up, and suddenly very acutely aware of my dry spell.

The blanket scrapes against my sensitive nipples as I drag it up, cutting them off from Truett's view. I bite my resulting whimper off at the pass, teeth digging into my bottom lip. He sees that too, because of course he does.

He clears his throat, tearing me out of my mental war games. And not a moment too soon.

His broad hand swipes over his face. "Well, I better be going. The guys show up early, and someone's gotta tell 'em what to do. Your dad is doing good. He's just not tired after sleeping all day."

"I can relate," I mumble.

He cocks his head back. "He's hanging out on the couch watching a movie. I'm sure he'd like some company if you're up for it."

Sympathy laces Truett's every word. Our gazes hold as a silent message passes between us. He knows how badly it hurt me that Dad wanted his help instead of mine when he got confused. I suspect Tru even senses how useless it made me feel. What he can't possibly understand is how much I need to be needed. If my parents can get help from someone else, what am I good for? If I'm not taking care of someone, what else do I have to offer?

"Get out of that pretty little head of yours for a second"—his chin dips, eyes darkening—"and go spend some time with your dad, okay?"

Heat flares in my cheeks.

"Okay," I squeak. My throat is so dry. I drink what's left of my water and try again. "Be safe driving back home."

"Oh yeah, I've certainly got a long, dangerous trek ahead." He chuckles. "You need help getting up?"

I shake my head. If I'm going to prove I'm still capable of caring for my father, getting out of bed is probably a great place to start. I swing my legs over the side and rise, swaying a little before catching myself on the headboard.

Tru reaches for me. I hold out a hand to stop him. "I'm good. Just needed a second."

He watches me warily but doesn't intervene again, even as I wobble across the room to my dresser and pull out an oversize sweater, donning it over my thin shirt. Our gazes meet. I can feel him appraising me. My spine stiffens. I jut my chin out. "I'm ready."

After a beat of silence, he nods, then turns to stride down the hall. I don't watch the lazy swing of his hips or study the way his jeans hug the glorious curve of his ass. Not even a little bit out of the corner of my eye.

And no one can prove any differently.

"Night, Henry."

"Good night," Dad replies. "Don't you get sick, too."

"Wouldn't dream of it." Truett tosses a wave in my dad's direction. His hand claps his thigh on the descent; then he hooks a thumb in his pocket as he glances over his shoulder at me. "Delilah."

"Good night, Tru." I bite the inside of my cheek. My gaze flickers between him and Dad. "Thanks again. For everything."

The noisy summer night floods the room, overpowering even the opening credits of whatever movie Dad has queued up. Truett nods, one foot out the door, and calls, "Anytime." Then the door is shut, the chorus of insects and animals once again blocked out, and that tightness in my chest releases.

"How are you feeling, sweet pea?"

My head jerks toward my dad. He's gazing up at me, brows furrowed. His voice is unusually clear, no hesitation or stuttering as he speaks. He sounds like himself. Suddenly it doesn't matter that it's two in the morning. I'd skip sleep forever if it meant getting this version of him again.

I realize I'm still hovering in the middle of the awkward space between our living room and kitchen, body angled toward the door Truett disappeared through. I backtrack, making my way around the chaise portion of the couch, and settle in next to my dad. He's pale like me, with purple bruises blooming beneath his bright blue eyes, but his smile is firm.

"A lot better, Dad. I'm sorry I left you to fend for yourself."

He blows a raspberry, and it seems so *like him* that for a second I forget about the shower incident. About the restaurant. I even forget the doctor's pamphlets, filing it all away somewhere to remember on a different day.

"I was fine. I've been sick lots of times before you came along, kiddo. Besides, Roberta showed up just in time." His expression softens. "I'm sorry I didn't notice you were sick, too. I haven't felt like myself the last couple of days."

I think of my blowup at the river. At the drool practically spilling out of me at Truett's proximity this evening. I huff a laugh. "You and me both."

He chuckles. It's breathy and tense, but I'll take it.

"What are we watching?" I glance at the television. Before he even answers, I know what he's going to say. Jim Carrey's face fills the screen, framed out by an artificially blue sky.

"*The Truman Show,*" we say together. Dad smiles and adds, "This was the first date your mother and I had after you were born, did you know that?"

I nod but don't interrupt. I like when he tells this story.

"You were a few months old when it debuted, and Kimberly's parents came to town to finally meet you." He sighs, shaking his head. "It was so mind-blowing the first time we saw it. That he couldn't realize it was all a make-believe world and everyone knew it but him."

My pulse slows. I roll my lips. Stare at the screen rather than my dad. Because it is mind-blowing, isn't it? Even though Dad is aware a lot of the time, in those moments where he's not... It's like watching him live in a world outside our own. Unlike Truman, none of us locked him inside. Only his mind. The worst kind of betrayal.

I snuggle close to my dad and try to push the thoughts out of my head, but for the rest of the movie, all I can think about is what the doctor said when he pulled me aside after the appointment and tilted his head sympathetically. *"Enjoy the moments of clarity as best you can. They come less and less as we move into the later stages."*

I didn't realize before what a luxury it was to be so unaware of time and the speed at which it passes. Now I can't look away as each grain of sand slips through the hourglass, marking another second closer to the end.

My eyes are heavy by the time the credits roll. The DVD returns to the home screen, with a still image of Jim Carrey projected on a wall of television monitors. I reach for the remote, prepared to eject the disc, when Dad's hand lands on mine.

It's still dark out, but the clock on the oven tells me it won't be for long. I scan Dad's expression. His eyes are distant, like he's seeing me but not really. He smiles softly. "I love this movie. Would you watch it with me, sweet pea?"

I blink. "But we..."

His gaze cuts to the screen expectantly. "You know I saw it

for the first time with your mom. You were a few months old, and Kimberly's parents came to meet you. It was such a good movie."

What a strange disease, that he can remember all of that and not the hours we just spent together watching it on this couch.

Another piece of sand slips through the hourglass. I press play.

Chapter Seventeen

Henry

May 17th, 1997

MY HOUSE IS dark and silent as we enter, save for the one floorboard by the entrance that squeaks every time you step on it. Dad always promised to replace it, and though I certainly could figure out how, doing so now feels like erasing part of his memory. I leave it so he has something to come back to, despite knowing how insane that sounds.

Moonlight filters in through the wide bay windows around our breakfast nook. They overlook a hundred acres of farmland that hasn't been used since the owner got too old to care for cattle. Every morning, Abel Johnson sits out on his front porch and watches the sun rise over his land. Some mornings when I've got extra time before school, I sit at the table and watch him. It's a tradition he doesn't even know he's a part of, but it brings me comfort all the same.

"There's a beer or two in the fridge." I nod toward the yellowing refrigerator littered with magnets from all the casinos my parents used to frequent. The thing looks like a dated advertisement for Biloxi at this point. "Help yourself."

Kimberly's heels click in a harsh staccato. Her dress swishes around her legs, revealing flashes of creamy skin with every step she takes. She opens the fridge and glances back at me, her face a half-moon in the glow of the small lightbulb. "You want one, too?"

First I wore my dad's shoes while smoking a cigarette. Now I'm adding underage drinking to the list. And it's *his* leftover beer, no less.

I slip the oxfords off, hoping it will reduce the guilt when I say, "Sure."

A groan vibrates her full lips. "Ugh, good idea." She carries two cans over and passes me one before taking a seat on the bench and popping one delicate foot in the air. "Could you help? These heels are absolutely killing me."

"Um, yeah. I can do that." I set my beer on the table and kneel. When I take her foot in my hand and rest it on my knee, I'm struck by how soft and warm her skin is. It ignites something in me, a desire I've only felt once before, outside the confines of my bedroom at least.

The straps are intricate and a bit confusing. With a little instruction from Kimberly, though, I manage to free one foot and then the other. "There you go."

She smiles. "My hero."

For some reason those words make my chest tight. I'm still kneeling in front of her. My gaze travels the long, smooth path of her muscular leg from the foot I'm holding to the place where the slit in her dress parts midthigh. I blink slowly. My dick hardens against my fly. It feels wrong to think of anyone else this way when Lucy's all I've ever wanted. But Lucy's not here. And when I finally tear my gaze from the swell of her thigh, Kimberly's looking at me through lowered lashes.

Her teeth dig into her bottom lip. She removes her foot from my grasp and pushes it against my chest, rocking my balance. "You gonna stay down there all night?"

I swallow hard. "Right. Sorry."

She giggles softly. I stand and take the seat opposite her. When I don't immediately reach for my beer, she pops the tab on it with her long, painted fingernails and passes it back, then does the same to her own. We each take a sip. It's the only sound in the room aside from the miscellaneous creaks and groans of the house. I pray she doesn't notice me wincing in response to the bitter taste. Or that I'm shifting uncomfortably in my seat, willing my boner to go down.

"Will your parents be gone all night?"

I nod. "My mom works late." The diner stays open into the early morning hours after prom to give kids a safe place to go for a late-night snack. She volunteered for the shift once I agreed to go to the dance. Briefly I wonder if she'll notice my absence from the post-prom crowd. Knowing her attention to my comings and goings as of late, I doubt it.

"And your dad?"

I let my gaze drift toward the window. "He passed away in January."

"Oh my gosh. I'm so sorry, Henry."

It's been months, and I still don't know how to respond to that. Instinctually I want to say, *It's okay,* but it's not. *Thank you* also feels weird. *I'm sorry, too* is the most accurate, but it tends to bring the mood down. I settle for flattening my lips and nodding, a half-assed grunt rattling my throat.

Kimberly taps a nail against the aluminum can of beer. I get the sense that she's not comfortable with the direction this conversation has taken. She won't be still, and she makes a low humming noise to fill the silence that's settled between us.

"How's the beer?" It's the best lifeline I can offer.

Her nose wrinkles. "A little flat."

I snort, and she tilts her head, one eyebrow quirked. "What's funny?"

"Nothing," I murmur. I highly doubt she'd enjoy knowing it's my dead father's beer that's been sitting in our fridge, untouched, for months. Neither myself nor Mom could bring ourselves to throw it out.

Her foot brushes against mine beneath the table. At first I assume it's on accident. But then it happens again. The third time, she rubs higher up my calf in a slow stroke. Our eyes meet and the corner of her mouth quirks. "Wanna give me the tour?"

"Um, sure."

I stand, and she does, too. She takes my hand in hers, our palms slick with condensation from the cold beer cans. It doesn't take more than a few steps toward the living room for them to grow warm again.

"Mom's room is there." We stand in the awkward liminal space between the kitchen and the living room, and I point to the closed door beside the couch. "Mine is this way." We turn and walk down the hall, passing the only bathroom in the house on the left before coming to my door.

Kimberly juts her chin toward the door opposite mine, which sits partially ajar. "What's that?"

"A guest bedroom-slash-junk room kind of thing? Mom has a sewing machine and she used to make clothes in there, but she doesn't do that much anymore."

Doesn't have the time to, if I'm being honest. I think of the antique Singer sitting there, gathering dust, and my heart seizes.

"Shame," Kimberly hums. She turns back to my door and grabs the knob. "So what should I expect? A bunch of nudie posters?"

My dick twitches. "No."

She smirks. "Uh-huh, sure."

The hinges whine as she pushes inside. I flick on the light, and we glance around simultaneously. I try to see it through her eyes, as someone who hasn't slept in this room their whole life. There's a window by the bed that I keep open at night to let the sound of wind through the live oaks filter in. My bedspread is a plain blue quilt Mom made for me years ago. There's a guitar in the corner. It's a little beat up, since I bought it used at the thrift store in town, but it's functional. My songbook lies open on the desk in front of us. I reach for it, but Kimberly's closer. She snaps it up in one smooth motion and spins away from my outstretched arm.

"'Wish I could forget your long blonde hair. Wish I could do anything but care. If it were up to me, baby, we could go anywhere. As long as we go together.'" She pats the gathering of hair on her crown. "It's like you knew I was coming, Henry!" She flops back onto my bed, her dress pooling on either side of her legs. "What is this?"

I flush crimson. "It's nothing." I pluck it from her hands and close the notebook, returning it to my desk.

Her hazel gaze drifts to the guitar. "Oh, you're a musician! Those are songs? And here I thought you were a wannabe e. e. cummings."

She stretches her arms up and folds them beneath her head. Something about the expanse of skin the movement exposes—the swath of cream from her elbow to her underarm—helps me ignore the disbelief in her tone. I shrug out of my jacket and drape it across the wooden poster of my bed. When I stretch out beside her, the mattress sags, folding our bodies close enough that our sides touch.

"Poetry and music aren't all that different."

"Except people call cummings a literary master. No one says that about the Spice Girls." She laughs. "But it's a cute hobby, anyway. Not like you're trying to make a career out of it or anything."

I rub at my chest, working out the sting that forms there in response to her comment. "Yeah. You're right."

She rolls in toward me, propping herself up on an elbow. Tendrils of blonde hair are falling from her butterfly clips. Without thinking, I reach for one and brush it behind her ear. Her lips part, a small breath escaping. It smells like the beer we drank mixed with cherry lip gloss. An unpleasant scent, if it weren't accompanied by the sensation of her body aligning with mine. The swell of her breasts presses against my ribs. Her soft belly brushes my side. Gentle fingers caress my cheek. Then my neck.

Everywhere they touch, goose bumps erupt. My dick aches. For her, I realize. And it may be insane, but it's the best realization in the world. To be this completely enraptured by someone other than Lucy. To forget about her long enough to want someone else.

"Are you a virgin, Henry?" Her eyes are on my lips as she asks the question. Before I can answer, she closes the short distance between our mouths. Her lips slant over mine. Gentle. Exploratory. When she pulls away just enough to meet my gaze, her pupils are blown.

I debate lying. I'm not exactly eager for another dig akin to the one about my *cute hobby.* But if this goes anywhere, she'll find me out quickly. Better to be honest up front.

"Yes." I clear my throat. I take advantage of her attention on my words and try to adjust myself. "Are you?"

Her hand settles over mine where I was moving my dick to my waistband. And squeezes.

"No." Her lips curve. "Do you want to still be a virgin when you graduate?"

To be honest, I haven't had a lot of time to think about it the last few months. But now that she's mentioning it? "Not really."

She's giggling as our mouths crash into one another. She finds the button of my shirt and tugs. One after another, they come loose, until the last is pulled free and my heart leaps into my chest.

"Idon'thaveacondom," I murmur in a rushed breath.

"I'm on the pill." She kisses my throat. "It'll be fine."

Our clothes are lost in a flurry of movement. Skin brushes naked skin, cool at first and then so, so hot. I melt into it. Into her. There are teeth and gasping breaths and the salt of another person's sweat on my tongue for the very first time. I break loose, and she does, too. Through it all, our limbs remain tightly woven. For the first time in months, I don't feel alone.

And then I'm *not* a virgin anymore. And the world feels a little bit more tolerable, more kind, at least for tonight.

"How's that for fun?" Kimberly mumbles into my neck, when at last our pulses return to some new version of normal.

"Incredible." It's all I can say. All I can think. *Incredible, incredible, incredible.*

"I won't be back in town till the end of summer when I pass through on my way to college." Kimberly has one hand on my truck's door handle and another on my thigh. We're at the diner, where Talia is supposed to be waiting. That was their plan, apparently. Talia would find someone—in this case, Jed—to spend her evening with, and then she'd get whomever it was to bring her here. Kimberly could do whatever she wanted—in this case, me —as long as she met Talia there after.

I can see my mom serving milkshakes to a table of my classmates. She looks so tired, with prominent bags under her eyes that are visible even from where I'm parked outside the entrance. I can't wait to graduate and be able to work full-time, if nothing more than to be able to provide for her so she can drop a few shifts. She works so hard, lately she's been forgetting simple things. Like the day the water bill is due or where exactly to mail the check. I've taken over nearly all bill payment for her since Dad died, just so I don't have to see her struggle to remember.

"Hello? Earth to Henry!"

I tear my gaze away from my mother. "Sorry, what were you saying?"

"I said you can write to me. If you'd like." She opens my glove compartment and digs through its contents. She finds a receipt and a pen. "Or call."

"I'd like that," I say, though the words feel like peanut butter in my mouth. My gaze is locked on the man stepping out of the diner, into the cool night air.

Waylon holds open the door, and before I can look away, I see Lucy slip under the bridge of his outstretched arm. Our eyes meet, then hers cut to where Kimberly sits in my passenger seat. I don't miss the flash of pain mottling her beautiful features. Or the way she stiffens at Waylon's touch when he drapes an arm over her shoulders. They amble past my truck. Waylon's voice hums outside my window. I want to jump out of this truck and go after them. Tear his arm off her. It's such a violent desire that I have to suck in a breath through my nose and release it.

I'm not like this. I'm not like him.

I glance over at Kimberly, who's finished scribbling her information on the receipt and holds it out for me. The moment I take it from her, I realize that actually I'm *exactly* like Waylon. No better than the version of him who took advantage of girls beneath the bleachers. Because there's no way I can call Kimberly. Or write to her. Not when I feel like this for someone else. Shame coats my throat as I tuck the receipt into my pocket. It makes it hard to swallow. Hard to breathe.

"Thanks again for such a fun night," she singsongs. Her lips smack against mine, leaving residue from her fresh coat of lip gloss behind. She winks. "Congrats on losing your virginity!"

She slips from the truck and bounds into the restaurant with more enthusiasm than I'd think those shoes would allow. Talia rises from a booth in the corner when her cousin enters, and they embrace as the man opposite her turns to glance out the window.

Jed and I lock gazes. His eyes widen for a second before his lips stretch into a wide grin and he offers me a thumbs-up. I don't return it. I can't. I throw the truck into reverse and back out of the space, leaving my friend with a puzzled look on his face and my stomach in such intricate knots I could probably get a badge from the Boy Scouts for weaving them.

* * *

June 10th, 1997

"Whoever decided graduation should be held outdoors in the middle of June can kick rocks," Derell grumbles.

Jed, who has sweat pouring down his face in thick rivulets, groans in agreement.

"I'm just ready to get this over with." I swipe at my brow. My gaze travels over the sea of navy-blue graduation gowns, then the crowd of families in the bleachers beyond. I find Mom alone on the very top bleacher, fanning herself with the graduation program, and my stomach drops.

I imagined this day so differently. Dad could make anything a sporting event, no matter how tame. He reined it in for church, but the few band concerts I participated in before dropping the extracurricular to focus more on my own music? He showed up with foam fingers for him and Mom, wearing a T-shirt that had *Band Dad* emblazoned across the chest. One time he even brought a foghorn, but the band director put a stop to that.

186

Seeing Mom sitting all alone, no foam finger in sight, is truly sobering. It's the first of many milestones Dad won't be around to see, and that more than anything makes my lungs squeeze and my eyes burn. I want to fix this pain for both of us, but I don't know how. I'm doing my best, and it doesn't even put a dent in the grief. Hers or mine.

"You okay, man?" Derell follows my line of sight, and his gaze softens. He leaves for college in a couple months. He'll come home sometimes for a weekend here or there, but the man is a genius studying to be an engineer. He'll get a job that takes him far away from this town. It's another ending. Harder in its own way, because I can see it coming.

I swallow. "Yeah. I will be, anyway."

"So will I," Jed sighs, "'cause here comes Talia."

I turn just as Talia elbows past a group of football players who each let out whoops as she passes. I cringe on her behalf. The guys are no better than cavemen, and only slightly worse than Jed. "Maybe stop drooling, dude."

He hasn't gotten over prom night, though until now we definitely thought Talia had. We all kept our secrets about that night, but one thing was clear: Jed was on cloud nine the following Monday in class. And Talia hasn't talked to him since.

It's weird seeing her without her signature purple lipstick. Her makeup is simple, all pale pinks and soft golds. She's wearing pearl earrings that remind me of my mother's favorite pair. I'm so distracted by them that for a moment I miss the fury on her face. Until she's staring up at me, green eyes blazing, with the collar of my dress shirt clenched in her fist.

"Talia, what the—" Jed starts.

"We need to talk, Henry." Her voice is a snapping leather belt. I'm almost certain it'll leave a mark.

My heart surges into my throat. Did Kimberly tell her about us? Would she do that?

Who am I kidding? Of course she would. It's her fucking cousin, for crying out loud.

I suck in a breath and nod to my friends. Talia's hand drops from my collar and seizes my bicep. She drags me toward the gap between the concessions building and the bathrooms with a surprisingly strong grip. By the time we reach a secluded-enough spot, I'm dripping sweat that has nothing to do with the heat.

"Look, Talia, whatever you heard…"

"Whatever I heard?" she grits out. "Are you an idiot, Henry?"

I balk. "Listen, I'm sorry I haven't called her, but life's been so busy and—"

"Shut up. Right now." She wags a finger at me. Despite her size, it has the desired effect. I'm both intimidated and silent. "I know you've had a rough year, Ridgefield, but I can't believe you'd be so stupid. So careless. So—"

"I didn't plan for it, Talia," I interject. "It's not like I was looking for someone to sleep with. It just happened." Surely she knows that?

"Clearly you planned *nothing* out."

I blink down at her, confused. "What's that supposed to mean?"

"She's pregnant, Henry." Her voice is low and tight. "Too grief-stricken to use a condom, huh?"

Behind us, Principal Tiefermann calls for us to get in line. Our classmates cheer now that things are finally getting underway, bringing us one step closer to getting out of this heat. But I barely register any of it. I barely register Talia, glaring up at me with her jaw clenched, cheeks blazing red. It all falls away to the rush of blood leaving my head, draining all the way to my feet.

"Wh-what?" I stammer. "She said she was on the pill."

"Sometimes the pill fails." She shakes her head. "And then you didn't even have the decency to call her, so she had to use me as a messenger. You messed up. Badly."

My throat is so dry I'm not sure the next words are going to make it out, but I try. "What—" I swallow. Try again. "What do I do?"

Her gaze softens at the edges, but only slightly. Still, it's more than I deserve. "I don't know. But you better figure it out. And fast." She licks her lips. "Call her, Henry. She's really scared."

I nod, unable to find words.

"You do have her number, right?"

My voice scrapes like sandpaper. "I do."

"Good. You can still make this right, okay? But you've gotta man the fuck up. Big-time." She holds my gaze, making sure I'm absorbing her words. Satisfied, she glances past me to our classmates. "Let's go before they graduate without us. Can't raise a baby with no degree."

She shoves past me. I turn to watch her stride over to the lineup, where my friends stand staring at me with puzzled looks. I know I should move but I can't. I've lost all feeling. I'm completely numb aside from the roaring fear burning in my mind, telling me I've ruined not one life but two.

My gaze lifts to my mother. Her hand is flattened over her heart as she cranes her neck, trying to spot me in the line of students pouring out onto the field. My feet are rooted to the ground as I watch the last piece of the life I thought I'd have slip away. Somewhere, states away, I imagine Kimberly doing the same thing. The guilt is white-hot and crushing, and so much more than I can bear.

Lucy's blonde hair flashes past, catching my eye. I watch her step from the paved track to the grass of the football field. From an old life into the new. She glances over her shoulder, and I hold her gaze for only a second. It's the last thing I take for myself.

The last thing I'll *ever* take for myself, because from now on, it can no longer be about me. It's about Kimberly. And our baby.

Our *baby.* My heartbeat stumbles over itself. *I'm going to be a father.*

I eventually make it onto the field, but not before emptying my breakfast into a nearby bin.

Chapter Eighteen

Delilah

CAMERON WAS RIGHT. After forty-eight hours I feel mostly back to normal. Aside from painfully sore abs that haven't been put to this much use since I was in high school training for volleyball. I lift the hem of my loose tank top as I study my reflection in the vanity mirror, half expecting to see a six-pack has miraculously formed from all the heaving.

No such luck.

At least the bruises beneath my eyes are mostly gone. My skin looks healthy again, no longer tinged with a sickly green. I sweep my mussed waves into a ponytail while pushing away the memory of Truett's hands doing the same. My scalp tingles at the thought of his fingers in my hair. Like I can still feel it two days later.

What a ridiculous thing to come undone over. But I sense it, somewhere in the tight knot of my heart. A loose thread. An unraveling.

"Delilah?" Three raps follow my name.

I break eye contact with myself. "Yeah, Roberta?"

My door cracks, whining on its hinges. Her hair is pinned back today, leaving her face bright and exposed. Her brown eyes are crinkled at the corners, a half smile playing on her lips. "What are you getting up to today?"

The sound of a nursery rhyme played on the keyboard spills in from the hall. It's echoed by a choppier rendition. Caleb, the little boy I first met the weekend I arrived, is here for another lesson. I wince at a particularly harsh note. Roberta's lips close around a choked-off giggle.

"I thought about taking Dad for a walk by the river." I turn away from her. If we keep making eye contact, I'm going to burst into laughter. I'm not trying to crush the boy's ego. "You know, once the maestro is done with his lesson."

A sound not unlike what would happen if one pressed every single key at once assaults our ears. My bottom lip quivers as I try to smooth ChapStick on. Roberta snorts but covers it up with a cough.

"Is his mother here?" The memory of her overwhelming questions last time is enough to send a spark of discomfort down my spine. I'll grin and bear it if I have to. But if I can avoid it, I will.

"Nope," Roberta says, popping the *p*. "Said she had errands to run."

The sigh of relief is involuntary. Roberta offers an understanding smile in response.

"That's great, Charlie!" Dad's voice drifts across the hall. "Love your enthusiasm!"

"It's Caleb," a small voice replies.

"Your father is overwhelmingly positive," Roberta muses.

I glance at her reflection in my mirror. I nearly smudge my mascara across my eyebrow when I see how tightly pinched her face is in an effort to contain her laughter.

I bite the corner of my bottom lip. "Always has been. I once served the ball into the bleachers in my early days of volleyball practice, and he stood up cheering like it was the best play he'd ever seen."

We both raise our eyebrows as something close enough to "Twinkle, Twinkle Little Star" follows a brief pep talk from my dad.

Our gazes meet and I shrug. "Positive reinforcement. It works wonders."

"I knew it did." She smiles warmly, sweeping a hand in my direction. "Look how you turned out."

My lungs squeeze, choking off my breath. I glance at her over my shoulder and put on my best smile, though inside it feels like she's carved out a piece of my soul with an ice cream scoop. "Thanks, Roberta."

"Anytime, sweet pea." She winks.

I roll my eyes, that tightness releasing enough for a quick intake of breath. "Did you need something?"

"Yes, actually. The school called."

I turn and rest my hip against the vanity. "The music school?"

She shakes her head. "Nope, the *school* school. They're renovating the band and choir classrooms this summer and found some things of your dad's they thought he might want."

My mouth opens, but nothing comes out. I snap it closed.

Why does even the mention of that place fill me with so much anxiety? I'm a grown woman, so far removed from the girl I was in high school. The girl who walked those halls with her head hung low, listening to the hateful things people who'd known her for her entire life had to say about her family. About *her.* It shouldn't hurt like this anymore. It shouldn't matter.

I patched up that wound with the sutures of a few states' distance. So why does it still ache?

"Truett said he'd go if you don't feel up to it," she offers.

I work to keep my expression neutral, but inside a fault line forms. Do I want to step foot in that hellhole? No. But do I want to let Truett take care of one more thing that is supposed to be my responsibility? Absolutely not.

"I'll do it." My voice sounds more confident than I am.

"Perfect," a familiar voice calls from the living room. Truett's sure strides thud down the hall, and he appears over Roberta's shoulder, all smiles. "I'll drive."

I glance up at him and my jaw slackens. I've been so focused on getting mine and Dad's health back to one-hundred percent that I've had no time to think about the conversation Truett and I had in my room, or even at the river. At the apology he never finished. The one I'm not even sure I'm owed. I don't know what I want from him anymore, if anything at all, and that scares me. Going on a field trip with him right now isn't exactly ideal.

My gaze falls from him to Roberta. All attempts at neutrality drop. I know this, because she winces, and her shoulders hit her ears. *Sorry,* she mouths. But the damage is done.

"Let's go, Temptress." He smirks. "We're late for class."

"Did you miss this?"

I snort. It comes out harsher than I intend, mostly because my nerves are eating me alive. I clear my throat and try for humor. "Miss what? Traffic jams that involve a train holding up the main thoroughfare through town?"

"This." His hand sweeps in front of us. The train groans to life at last, moving forward to clear the tracks, letting the long line of waiting vehicles through. "Fly Hollow."

My gaze cuts from the window to Truett's profile. His jaw is taut as he chews on a thumbnail, but the rest of his face is relaxed. He's got a faded Alabama football hat on backward. A tuft of dirty blond hair sticks through the gap on his bronzed forehead. It reminds me of weekends like this, when we'd hop into his truck and ride to the next town over to get a change of scenery. It's a new truck but the same view. The floorboards are still dusted with grass clippings. The cab still smells of hay and fresh dirt. I breathe it in deeply but quietly. No need for him to know just how much I did, in fact, miss *this*.

He turns. Catches me staring. The thumb falls away, and a knowing smile ghosts his lips.

Heat flares in my cheeks. I roll my lips, trying to think of something to say. The first thing I can manage is, "Why would I miss this town? Nothing ever happens here."

His eyes go wide. "Are you kidding?"

I stare at him, unsure of how I earned such a spirited response.

He shakes his head in disbelief. "*Everything* happens here, Delilah."

I cross my arms over my chest, eyebrow arched. "Like what?"

The car in front of us pulls away, signaling our turn to go. Tru tears his eyes away to focus on the road, but I feel it still. The weight of his attention on me.

"Yesterday, a calf was born in my pasture."

I don't know what I expected him to say, but it wasn't *that*. "Isn't it a little late in the season for that?"

"Bull hopped the fence at an inopportune time," he grumbles, swiping a hand over his face. "Got a few more coming thanks to that horny bastard."

"Right. So a calf being born equals *everything?* Talk about a limited worldview."

A muscle in his jaw ticks. "When did you get so uppity?"

My jaw slackens. I was mostly joking, but now irritation courses through me, solidifying my determination to win this weird argument. "I'm not uppity."

"Are too." His hand flexes on the steering wheel, the veins in his forearm popping.

"What are you, a child?"

Suddenly I'm careening into the center console as he yanks

the wheel toward the shoulder and throws us into park there in the gravel. He turns, gaze fiery, as I right myself.

"What the hell, Tru?"

"Last week, Emily down at Sunshine Grocery said her baby took his first steps."

I open my mouth, but he presses a finger to my lips, stopping my words along with my breath.

"Do you hear that?" He pauses and a familiar, low chime reaches my ears. "The church bells are ringing. Trinity Martin and Cole Whitcomb, you remember them? They just got married. Promised to grow old together in that little white church."

I blink. I don't know how we got here, but I'm tipped unsteady. The phrase *poking the bear* flits through my mind. Passion ripples underneath Tru's skin. He's looking at me hard, gaze raking over my flushed cheeks. My wide eyes. My parted lips, which he releases, though the burn of his touch remains.

His chin dips, and when he speaks again, his voice is low and reverent. It reminds me of his grandfather and the few sermons I watched him preach growing up before my mom put a stop to me going with the Parkers to Sunday service.

"People are starting businesses, building new homes, starting families every damn day. My mama lived and died here, and I stood by as they buried her on that hill behind my home. Things are always happening, Delilah. Life goes on here the same as it does in any big city. *In Charleston.* We're just lucky enough to have a hell of a lot more time to slow down and notice."

He's right. And that fact lets the hot air right out of me.

My gaze drops to my hands, folded in the cradle of my lap. The truth is, I've spent the last nine years listening to my mom rant about everything that makes this town miserable. I've clung to those reasons desperately so I could forget all the reasons I grew up loving where I lived. So I'd never feel the need to return. But Tru's laid them bare before me. There's no hiding from it all.

The simplicity. The slow pace. The way everyone knows about the big and small moments in each other's lives. Much as it's miserable when that moment is a shitty one, it's pretty spectacular when it's something you're proud of.

I wasn't like my friends or even my mom, always itching to get away. I would've stayed forever if circumstances had been different. It's painful to remember that. It feels a lot like grief.

But circumstances *are* different, I remind myself. All the things that drove me away from here in the first place still exist, like an infection festering beneath the surface. It's not lost on me that I'm back in a loud, growly truck with the same painfully tempting boy all these years later, on my way to a school I never thought I'd step foot in again.

Only he's all man now. And I'm a woman who can still feel the buzz of his fingertips on her lips.

I clear my throat, breaking the fragile silence that has settled in the cab, save for the rush of vehicles flying past every few minutes.

"We better go," I say, voice guarded. "Someone'll think you've broken down and pull off to check."

"You're making my point *for* me," he mutters, but he puts the truck in drive, sending us on our way.

Some things never change. In fact, in Fly Hollow, very few ever do. The school being a prime example.

The linoleum floor is still a dingy speckled white. The walls are comprised of cement blocks painted with layer after layer of a pale yellow color that makes the hall seem even more dated. As we follow the same ancient office secretary to the wing that houses electives—which, in a school this small, means band, choir, and shop class—my gaze traces over the years of graduating classes framed on the walls. I never got to be in one. The school I graduated from in South Carolina didn't have that kind of tradition, with 400 students in a single year. I didn't think that bothered me until we pass the one with all my classmates pictured, and I'm nowhere to be found.

"Alicia is right in here," Mrs. Pierson croons. Her voice reminds me of wooden wind chimes, hollow but musical. At just shy of five feet tall, she's a stereotypical grandmother. She wears her readers on a beaded chain. It's possible that her cardigan was crocheted from a bunch of leftover doilies. Her lips are framed by deep wrinkles, and they quiver at the corners when she smiles like she is now.

"Thanks, Patty." Truett leans over and kisses the top of her head. I swear the woman blushes.

"Anytime, handsome." Her birdlike gaze dances between the two of us. "Always did think you two would make the cutest couple someday."

I hold up a hand. "Oh no, we're not—"

"Delilah!"

The three of us turn. The heavy double door to my dad's old classroom is propped open, and Alicia Busby stands in the threshold, rag in one hand and bottle of cleaner in the other. Her gaze is locked on me.

"Alicia," I manage to choke out. "What are you doing here?"

Her smile wavers. Mrs. Pierson and Truett exchange a glance.

"Alicia is the new music teacher," Mrs. Pierson offers. "John Davis, the man who took over after your dad…" Mrs. Pierson's expression turns sheepish. "He retired this year. Passed Alicia the gauntlet. Isn't that so special? I remember the two of you girls huddled close in these halls giggling like fools as though it was yesterday."

Alicia's hand crosses over her waist to cup her elbow. "Well," she says, ignoring Mrs. Pierson's last comment, "this fall I will be. Gotta get the room fixed up first."

"Small world!" Truett swings an arm around Mrs. Pierson's shoulders and smiles down at her. "Patty, why don't I walk you back to the office while these two catch up?"

Her excited, "I'd love that!" drowns out my attempts at protesting.

"Be back shortly, Delilah." Truett's gaze is hard as it locks with mine, like a warning. Or a plea. "Alicia." He nods at her, that tuft of hair bobbing on his forehead, then turns with Mrs. Pierson still in his arms. They walk down the hallway attached at the hip, like those couples that annoyed me in high school. Only much slower.

"Now, when are you coming back to mow my lawn, boy?" is the last thing I hear before they turn the corner.

I scoff. "Whose lawn doesn't he mow?"

"Mine," Alicia pipes up, raising one of her hands as my gaze returns to her. "Though my husband is very territorial about the yard, so it's no surprise. Real lawn guy, that one."

My eyebrows lift. "You're married?"

She flips that raised hand around, the cleaning cloth now tucked between her thumb and forefinger, to show me her sparkling oval-cut ring. "Mrs. Alicia Busby-Hughes at your service."

Hyphenated. *Nice.* I don't recognize the name, so I ask, "Where'd you meet him?"

"College. I went to UWF," she says, smiling softly. Alicia has always been smiley. When we became friends in kindergarten, it was because she was the only other kid who didn't cry on the first day of school. I made friends with the teacher right away, since I'd always enjoyed the company of adults more than kids, so I wasn't scared. Alicia is just a happy-go-lucky person, so she took it all in stride with a gap-toothed grin. We bonded to one another, content with our crayons and picture books, while our teacher handled everyone else.

I shift uncomfortably. Nothing could hold a candle to my friendship with Tru, but for most of my life, Alicia and I were incredibly close. We played volleyball together for years. We'd swap stories about our crushes (she's the only person who ever knew mine was my lifelong best friend) and commiserate over period pains. When she iced me out after everything with my parents, it didn't hurt quite as much as Tru, but it still created a gaping hole in my life.

"Delilah, listen—"

"Where's Dad's stuff?" I interject, glancing over her shoulder. "Y'all told his caretaker you found some of his things."

"Caretaker?" Her dark brows furrow. She looks like Snow White, with pale skin and a thick, black bob that's grown out enough to dust her shoulders. Even her lips are bright red today, her makeup perfect despite the fact that from the looks of the classroom, she's knee-deep in dust and debris from the renovations. "I guess I just assumed I was talking to a new wife or something. Is everything okay?"

I think about sugarcoating it, but my conversation with Truett left me wrung out. Seeing Alicia again is the cherry on top. I can't come up with anything but the truth. "He has dementia."

"What, like Alzheimer's?"

"Frontotemporal dementia," I say, my voice a thin monotone. "Different cause than Alzheimer's. Similar result."

Her red mouth forms a perfect little O of shock. "Isn't he too young?"

I swallow hard, my gaze dropping to the floor. Does it ever get easier to say this all aloud? To make it real by making it known?

To my surprise, she drops the cleaning materials and steps forward, her arms wrapping around my shoulders as she pulls me in tight. She smells like vanilla body spray and paint. I stiffen beneath her touch. Alicia is smiley, and a hugger. It's all so familiar and yet so very strange.

"I'm so sorry, Delilah."

I force myself to reach around her and grab on. Lightly at first, and then I'm squeezing her so much tighter than I planned. Because I'm sorry, too.

She leans back, her hands locking on my biceps as our gazes meet. "I'm sorry for a lot more than that. After everything with your parents, and Tru's mom—"

"We really don't have to talk about all that," I mutter. I try to pull away, but her fingers dig into my skin. Not enough to hurt, but enough to hold me in place.

"We do." She licks her lips and swallows. I briefly wonder what lipstick she's wearing, because it doesn't smudge. "You and your dad were like a second family to me. The number of days I spent in this classroom, soaking up any- and everything he could teach me? I'm sure my brain turned half to mush." She shakes her head, her dark locks swaying gently. "I was seventeen and stupid, and I didn't know how to handle everything when the news got out. My parents were freaking out about your family being a bad influence, people were filling my head with so much nonsense…"

She's babbling, which she always did when she was nervous. I snort at the familiar trait, even as tears burn the backs of my eyes. "Is this supposed to make me feel better?"

She slaps an open palm against her forehead. "Sorry." Her chest expands with a deep breath, and a phantom smile tugs at her lips. "Do you know what's so ironic? While I was away at college, my mom ended up having an affair with Jessica's mom." She shakes her head. "What's that saying again about throwing stones in glass houses?"

"Jessica *Mathias?*" *The bitch who made sure the entire school knew all the sordid details?* "That's fucking rich."

Alicia huffs out a laugh. "Anyway, I should've reached out to you then and told you how sorry I was, but I didn't think you'd want to hear from me." Her arms drop to her sides. "Really, I should've stood up for you in the first place. Like a real friend."

The bridge of my nose burns. I blink against the sting of it, and when that's not enough, pinch the source.

She's watching me with her wide brown gaze. Waiting, I assume, for me to accept her apology. Only I don't know if I want to, or how to do so even if I did. I made up my mind about all these people so many years ago. It's disorienting to find so much wasn't as it seemed.

I'm off-kilter, so out of my depth. With my dad. Truett. And now Alicia. I don't know when, if ever, I'll feel steady again.

"My dad's stuff?" I mumble, folding my hands at my waist.

She nods, offering a somber smile. "Right. Come inside. I'll grab it for you really quick."

The classroom is in a state of disarray. All the posters with cheesy musical puns and various awards the band won during my dad's time are gone from the walls and shelves. The doors to the instrument rooms are open, their cubbies bare. The only thing left is the baby grand piano, which I recognize from its shape alone under a protective drop cloth.

My dad's proudest accomplishment was raising enough money to purchase that piano for the classroom. To teach kids on a "real piano" like he'd always dreamed of owning. It makes me think of the little keyboard in his home office, and my throat constricts. He used to talk about buying one for himself when he retired, a music-obsessed man's version of a midlife crisis. The loss of that dream hits me hard in the chest. I look away from the instrument, past the stacks of chairs by the back door, to the glowing light coming from what used to be his office. Alicia appears in the doorway carrying a cardboard box.

"Let me get that!" Truett calls out from behind me. I turn in time to see him stride past. He relieves Alicia of the box with a grunt. "Man, what'd Henry do? Leave his whole life behind?"

His lips flatten the moment the words are out of his mouth. The room collectively holds its breath, waiting for my response. *He did,* I want to say. *We all did.*

"Is that all?" I mumble instead.

They exchange a quick glance. Alicia takes a step toward me. "That's everything, I think. If I find anything else, I can give you a call. Is your number still the same?"

"Yes," I say at the same time Tru grumbles, "If she hasn't blocked you."

Her mouth pops open, but before she can ask, I say, "You're not blocked!" and shoot Truett an exacerbated glare.

He shrugs and offers Alicia a smile. All that heated tension from the ride over is gone from his face. And thank God, because regular Truett is hard enough to be around. Passionate Truett is a new level of danger for my psyche.

"Thanks, Alicia." I give her a wave and start toward the door with Truett hot on my heels. We step into the hallway, disjointedly bright after the dimness of the deconstructed band room. I blink against the glare coming off the yellow walls, feeling a headache forming at my temples.

"Hey, Delilah?"

I turn. Truett shifts to reveal Alicia braced in the doorway, her flowy tunic top still moving against her thighs as she comes to a stop.

"I don't know how long you're in town, but if you ever want to hang out, I'd love to catch up."

My lips thin and I nod. "I'm not sure, but I'll let you know. Thanks again."

I try to look away before the disappointment on her face can lodge in my memory, but it's too late.

Truett hefts the box into the back seat on my side. As he's

slamming the door shut, I step around him to climb in, and he surprises me with an outstretched hand. "Need a lift?"

Surprise ripples through me. That he would offer, when we were in some sort of pseudo-argument a mere half hour ago. I place my palm in his, briefly marveling at his rough hands against my delicate ones, before he passes me into the seat and lets go.

The truck rumbles to life. I yank my seat belt over my shoulder and clip in. Since this man is prone to flying off the road at any moment to lecture me about the benefits of small-town living, I need all the security I can get.

"So you're not sure how long you'll be here?" His voice dips low as we reverse out of our parking space. "What happened to 'as long as Dad needs me'?"

I stare straight ahead, afraid of what I might see if I glance his way. "That's still the plan."

A hum vibrates his throat. "Do you think you'll take Alicia up on her offer?"

The school slowly grows smaller in the side mirror. I roll the window down and brace my elbow on the sun-warmed windowsill, inhaling the fresh scent of azaleas that flows in on the breeze. "I don't know."

Tru scoffs. "Why not? Are you morally opposed to having friends?"

I turn and level him with a hard glare. "Do I really want friends who can't stand up for me when someone is hurting me? Who will abandon me when my life is falling apart?"

It's harsh, but it's the truth. Just because he and I have found some sort of truce doesn't mean that all magically goes away.

His chest deflates, shoulders caving. He flicks on the blinker to pull onto the main road through town. "You've got to allow people to grow, Delilah. You can't spend your whole life seeing people as their worst mistake. I doubt you'd want to be judged by yours."

I blink, momentarily stunned. Exposed, if I'm being honest.

He pins me with a sidelong glance. "Or does the great Delilah Ridgefield never make mistakes?"

I slump against the leather seat, letting its blistering heat seep into my body, but it does nothing to ward off the cold of his statement. I wish I could tell him that's right. That I don't make mistakes. But all I can see when I close my eyes is my dad's face the day Mom and I drove away. Mom's disappointment when I told her I was coming here. Lately it seems like mistakes are all I make.

We ride the rest of the way home in silence. I climb out of the car and retrieve the box of my father's things wordlessly. As Truett pulls away, headed toward town instead of the farmhouse, I can't help but add the look of disapproval on his face to the slideshow that appears when I blink, contemplating his question.

I've never been able to decide if it's the things I *have* done with Truett or those I wish I had, that make him one of my greatest mistakes. Only that he sits at the top of the list.

Chapter Nineteen

Delilah

ME

Dad seems depressed. He was up on and off all night, asking for his mom. I don't know what to do.

ROBERTA

Maybe try an activity to get his mind occupied. He likes card games.

ME

I couldn't find the cards. I tried a puzzle, but a piece was missing, and that made him even more upset

ROBERTA

Get him out for some fresh air. I promise it works wonders. :)

MY EYES BEG to close the entire drive down to the coast. I'm exhausted, but with every mile that passes, Roberta's advice seems more and more sound. The drive is quiet. More peaceful than the last twenty-four hours in their entirety. Dad's gaze remains locked on the scene unfolding outside the window. Rolling hills are replaced by sugar-sand beaches. Sunbathers stand in for Truett's cattle. It's amazing to me how much the landscape of Alabama can change in a forty-five-minute drive. Another point in the *Pro* column, though I'd never admit it to Truett.

Dad comes to life the minute his toes sink into that soft, white sand. We play in the waves, laughing like we did years ago on this same beach. We eat more fried seafood than anyone should in one sitting, then watch the sunset pool on the surface of the water before the horizon swallows it whole. We sing along to Dad's favorite *Greatest Hits of the '90s* CD on our way home, and I think how badly I wish I could hold on to this moment forever. The two of us, suspended in time. Before the worst that life has to offer comes back for another round.

As I park next to Dad's car in the driveway, I note the lights on in Truett's house, and my stomach clenches. I texted him an invite this morning to prove I'm not *morally opposed to friends* but got no response. I don't know why it bothers me so much. It shouldn't. Distance from him is exactly what I need, after so many blurred lines this past week. But I find myself staring up at those lights anyway, wishing I could explain myself in a way that he would understand. Wishing there was nothing to explain in the first place.

Would I love to simply pick up where things left off with Alicia as though nothing ever happened? Absolutely. Because I wish nothing *had* ever happened. But it did. And I don't know how to reconcile all these people—Truett, my dad, Alicia, even Lucy—with the version of them that lives in my head. The version with clear-cut motivations and even clearer consequences. I was comfortable with the slightly pessimistic view I had of the world because I knew my place in it.

But where do I belong in this one? The one where people might have made mistakes because they were human, not because they didn't care enough about me to do the right thing. The one where Truett and I might not actually be on opposite sides of the playing field but on the very same team.

I hover nearby as Dad brushes his teeth and casually hand him pajamas to change into from the load of laundry I'm putting away. He accepts the help better from me when it's not obvious that's what it is. That's what I'm learning, anyway. And it could all just as easily change tomorrow.

I leave Mom a voicemail letting her know that I'm feeling better and that I miss her. That same sense of being ships passing in the night of that big house has followed me here. I get her texts during meetings and can't reply. I call when she's out with Debbie and her other friends from work, so she doesn't pick up. Late at night while I'm sleeping, she'll leave a voicemail letting me know how badly she wishes I'd come home. That I've done enough for my dad after everything he did to us.

I just don't know anymore. And it's the not knowing that keeps me from acknowledging those voicemails. The idea I formed of Dad during all those years when he didn't call is yet another that I can't reconcile. That's not the same man I stayed up all night watching *The Truman Show* with while he ran a hand through my hair, my head on his lap. I don't know how to feel about any of it, so I ignore my feelings entirely and focus on anticipating Dad's needs, toeing the line of ignoring Mom while still letting her know I'm here.

The distance from her has made it clear this ebb and flow of love is a tool of hers, one she wields when she senses me pulling away. I'm so exhausted by it that I can't be bothered to play along.

In the midst of it all, I find that Truett's the one I want to talk to most. No matter how illogical. No matter how dangerous it feels for my heart. I think of the way he looked at me in the truck when I lamented about this small town that we both know I love. Like he could see right to my core, and he couldn't believe I'd deny what was there.

If he'd truly seen past the walls, though, we'd be in much deeper shit. Because he'd know that he's taking up the largest space in my heart. That he always has.

It's more than enough reason to keep my distance. Should be, at least.

But the next morning when I hear the rumble of the lawn mower outside my window, I practically tumble out of bed. I rush to slip into cutoffs and a green flowy tee, shoving my feet into my shiny new Keds as I race to catch him before he leaves.

It's not him who I find walking away from the mower, though. This man is shorter, with thick, dark hair that curls around his ears and a goatee that reminds me of the man Mom dated briefly following the divorce before he got sick of her mood swings. Tony, was it? Hell if I remember.

"You're not Truett."

He glances toward me. "Correct. Just the delivery boy," he grumbles, tipping a brown cowboy hat in my direction. "I'm Ollie. I drew the short stick this morning. Now I get to walk all the way back to the north field."

I cross my arms over my chest. "Is everything all right?"

He nods and arches a brow. "Yep, just having to move some fencing panels to construct a temporary pen for a few of the steers that got too fat on grain. They're going on a diet."

"So he sent you to bring me the lawn mower?"

"Apparently so." Ollie's dark eyes cut from me to the zero-turn. "You know how to drive that thing?"

I grit my teeth. I enjoy people assuming I'm incapable about as much as I enjoy *being* incapable. "Truett gave me a lesson."

Ollie huffs a laugh. "I'll bet he did."

"What's that supposed to mean?"

He turns to walk away, waving a hand over his head as he does. "Oh, nothing. Just that I won a bet with the other guys about why Parker's britches are in a wad this morning. Have fun and watch out for trees."

I narrow my eyes in the direction of the north field, though it's shrouded from view by the rolling hills and dense groves of oak and pine that spread between me and a certain dirty-blond cowboy who's taken a note from my book on avoidance strategies.

Ollie left the mower running, and thank God because Truett never taught me how to start it. I resign myself to at least knock this out, and then I'll find a way to talk to him, even if I have no clue what on earth I want to say.

By the time I finish, sweat slicks my back and my whole body feels like it's vibrating. Grass clippings coat my shins and thighs, and I'm fairly certain my scalp is sunburnt. My fault for forgetting to grab a hat in my mad dash out the door. Roberta's white SUV bounces over the newest pothole in Dad's driveway as I round the last tree trunk in the front yard. I point toward the farm, and she nods in understanding.

"You want a glass of water first?" She slams the door behind her, gaze scanning me as I drive past. "You look hot, and not in the way I think you'd appreciate."

I huff a laugh. "Thanks, Roberta. I'll grab one as soon as I get back."

"Suit yourself. Should I save you some coffee?"

"Throw it in the fridge, please!" I call, moving the bars out of neutral to pull forward.

She throws a thumbs-up, and I echo it, then head for the road.

I debate leaving the mower at the shed behind Truett's house and walking to the north field, but then I remember how far of a trek it is and decide to take the ride while I've got it. Poor Ollie. I crest the last hill in time to see four men on ATVs herding a group of cattle the color of midnight through a narrow opening in a wall of steel fence panels. The steers huff and bellow in annoyance as they're forced to shoot the gap, their large bodies knocking and sliding against one another in a mesh of hooves and hindquarters. The men work in perfect sync, circling the herd and pushing in close from every angle. In a matter of minutes the cattle are sealed into their new home.

Ollie moves the final steel gate into place with a loud *clang.* "Enjoy WeightWatchers, boys!"

The other three men let out a chorus of cheers from their mounts. I spot Truett on the four-wheeler closest to me. He rises up on his long legs, arms rippling as he revs the throttle and angles away from the pen. A straw cowboy hat shields his face from the blistering sunlight, but it doesn't hide the spark in his eyes when he clocks me.

He lays off the engine. "You know I've got cows to keep this grass short. Didn't exactly need you to mow all the way out here."

Ollie walks along the perimeter of the new fence, head down as he pretends to check the links between the already-secure panels. The other two men—one with hair the color of fire and another so bulky I'm shocked the four-wheeler holds him—don't even attempt to hide that they're listening. I can practically see their ears perk the moment I open my mouth.

"I wanted to talk to you, actually." I open the handlebars and dismount the lawn mower. My legs wobble for an unnerving moment. I glance back at the zero-turn. "I also don't know how to turn it off."

The two men closest to us erupt with poorly suppressed laughter. Truett's gaze cuts to theirs, silencing them with a hard look that I can only half see from my position in front of him. One of them chokes on it, and the other grabs a water bottle from a pack strapped to his ATV and takes a swig. Ollie continues staring intently at the same panel he's been inspecting for a beat too long, but I note his shaking shoulders.

"Ollie, that fence gonna run away if your eyes don't hold it up?"

"Huh?" He whips around. "Oh, no. Sorry, man, I must've zoned out."

Truett grimaces. "Like hell. Jason, take the mower back up to the shed, please." The redhead glances up, raises his brow, and points to the center of his chest where sweat has turned his gray shirt black. Tru nods. "Ollie. Emmett. Go do a calf check. Rosie looked about to pop this morning."

"Got it." Ollie climbs back onto his ATV. He jerks his chin toward the bigger guy—Emmett—and the two of them take off toward the field on the west side of the house where the cows and heifers reside.

Jason cuts the engine on his four-wheeler and ambles over to the lawn mower. His skin is embossed with thousands of freckles. They've bled together on his forearms, forming some semblance of a tan. He clicks his tongue. "You owe me lunch."

"How do you figure?" Tru's head tilts, jaw taut.

"Because I did not participate in the bet"—his green eyes cut from me back to Truett—"and I would've won for sure."

"What bet—" Tru starts, but Jason is already pulling on the left handle to whip a U-turn and head back up the hill.

I cross my arms, grimacing as my sweat-slicked skin sticks together. "They bet on why you were in a bad mood today. Apparently I had something to do with it?"

He stares at me, stone-faced, for a few too many heartbeats. It's unnerving to see him so serious. I shift my weight, thighs chafing as I do. My stomach flips. His gaze drifts downward, following the dip of my shirt over my lace bralette before tracing the expanse of my legs. When he settles at my feet, his lip quirks. "Guess I shoulda bought you boots instead of those white tennis shoes."

I follow his gaze and sigh. The toes of my Keds are smudged with a mixture of dirt and grass clippings. "Fantastic."

"You sure are dirty, Temptress." He folds his arms over the handlebars and leans forward, brow raised. "Did you come all this way to ask permission to skinny-dip in the river? Get cleaned off? Because you know I'm not opposed."

My throat dries out as heat flares in my cheeks. "Why do you always do that?"

"Do what?"

I drag my teeth along my bottom lip. It's humiliating to say aloud, but I'm sick of the way it makes me feel for him to tease like this. We both know it's a stupid joke that I happen to be the butt of, but asking him about it is like acknowledging the elephant in the room. Once you do, someone has to pick up the elephant's shit.

His shoulders slacken, and he looks exhausted all of a sudden. Like waiting for me to find my words is the last thing he has time for today. "Just say whatever you've got to say, Delilah."

"Fine." I uncross my arms, letting them fall to my sides. "I don't understand why you insist on making comments like that."

A wry grin stretches his lips. He's the cat that caught the canary. "What comments, exactly?" He wipes a speck of dirt from his jaw, but the smile remains in place. "You're going to have to be more clear."

I blow out a breath, but my chest is still so tight. My skin prickles with awareness of his gaze. I want to crawl into a hole for even having brought this up, but I stand tall. I'm not going to let him see how much it bothers me. "Pretending to flirt with me, Truett."

His eyebrow lifts. "Who said anything about pretending?"

My mouth opens and then closes. Several times. He studies me, noting every attempt at rebuttal, until at last I give up and clamp my lips together.

"I've never understood why you can't see just how remarkable you are, you know that? You were way out of everyone's league here. No wonder you moved away."

I scoff, but my heart triples its pace. "Now I know you're lying. I was never anything special, let alone *remarkable*. There at the end I was practically a social pariah. I wasn't out of anyone's league."

"You were out of mine."

We stare at each other, neither of us blinking, as that statement settles like dust.

He sits up, braces his hands on his hips, and jerks his chin toward the house. "You wanna continue this conversation inside? I am sweating to death while you take your sweet time chewing on that revelation."

I glance over my shoulder, grateful for an excuse to break our intense stare, and then back at Jason's abandoned four-wheeler. "Want me to take that?" I manage to squeak out.

He smiles. It takes over his face easily, like the expression is his natural state. While mine is a nervous scowl, apparently.

"Long as you promise not to go as slow as you did the other night." He waits for me to mount it and turn the key before revving his engine. "Last one to the house is a rotten egg."

"No way, Tru—"

"Giddy up, Delilah!" He takes off, startling a few grazing steer on the other side of the fence.

Forcing myself not to overthink this, I let it rip, hightailing it after him up the hill. The dust his wheels kick up clouds my lungs. I rise up on my feet as we crest the ridge, then flop on my ass hard once the ground levels out. He's fast, but he's cocky, making wide serpentine sweeps over the field in front of me. I find the path of least resistance, a straight shot that cuts right through a swath of mud, and gun it, spraying him with clumps of it as I zip past. The last thing I see is his mouth going wide to yell something *intentionally flirty*, I'm sure—though I hardly believe him—before a sizable splotch of mud hits him square in the chest and he slows, a look of shock rippling over his features.

"Giddy up, Truett," I grumble, a feeling of triumph washing over me.

***

"I cannot believe you did that."

Tru tips one of his mother's amber glasses beneath the faucet and fills it with water. He knocks it back. I try not to stare at his throat working as he swallows, but I fail. It should not be as sexy as it is. I know that. Still, there's a responding pulse between my legs, and I cross them to cut it off at the pass.

He can't just do things like call me remarkable and expect me to act like everything's normal. *Can he?*

I shrug, feeling anything but nonchalant. "Don't start fights you can't finish."

He turns to me, lips stretched wide in a grin that makes his dimple pop. His shirt is splattered with mud, his forearms the same. He tosses his hat onto the counter and runs a hand through his sweat-darkened hair. It's left sticking up in a few directions, but my chuckle dies in my throat when he crosses the distance from the sink to the island where I'm sitting and leans forward on arms braced against the granite's edge. "I never said we were finished."

"You were mad at me, if I recall?"

"Not mad." He shakes his head, gaze narrowed on me like he's taking my measure. "Irked. You irk me."

I choke on a nervous laugh. "What an honor."

"It's hard to hear you talk down on this town when I know you love it." He licks his lips, his gaze dropping to the glass in his hand. "It's hard to hear you talk about leaving when what I really want is for you to stay."

It's impossible to swallow when my throat is this tight. Immediately all I want is to read into those words. To believe them with all I've got. But for the sake of my fragile heart, I can't. I let my gaze drop, scanning the room instead of meeting his intense stare when it finds me. He's updated some things since I was last here, but the stained-glass window above the sink where Lucy would wash dishes while I sat and talked her ear off is still there. I half expect her to walk out of the hallway and ask if I'd like some tea.

Tru must track my thoughts, because he leans back and his voice is softer when he says, "Is it weird being back here?"

"Not weird," I rasp, overcome with an emotion too painful to name.

It's so familiar. There's the pantry that Tru and I would raid after school when his mom pretended not to look. The barstools are the same, solid wood and painted white one summer day when Lucy had had it with all the dark wood in the kitchen. Now the cabinets, once a deep cherry, are painted white, too. I can't help but smile. "Did you do the cabinets before your mom..."

I can't bring myself to say it, and from the way his eyes crinkle at the edges, I think he appreciates it.

"No. I wish I had, though."

"She'd love it."

He smiles softly. Runs a hand over the closest drawer. "Yeah, I think so, too."

"When did you get so handy?" I cross my legs. A question that's been bubbling below the surface overflows. "Did your dad help you?"

I know his dad left, but I've wondered if he ever returned.

Though, guessing by the look on Tru's face, I'd say that's a *Hell no.*

Tru's gaze turns to stone. He bites at a barely healed notch in his lip and grunts in response. My stomach sinks to the floor.

"You were right, you know." My voice quiets. Though I know it needs to be said, it doesn't make it any easier. His eyebrow lifts, inviting me to explain. So I do. "It happened to you, too. Your parents' marriage—your *life*—imploded right alongside mine. I'm sorry I wasn't more sensitive to that."

A guttural sound rips from his throat. He shakes his head. "No, *you* were right. It was different for me, Delilah. And I forget sometimes that the best thing that ever happened to me was the worst thing that happened to you."

I balk. Surely I misheard him. "What do you mean, the best thing?"

He strides around to my side of the island and straddles the stool beside mine. Our knees brush. His are covered by blue jeans, mine grass clippings, making the sensation muted yet familiar. Intimate in a way that shouldn't feel so good.

"My dad was… How do I put this?" He picks at a cuticle, gaze trained on the half-moon of his nail bed. "He was a piece of shit, Delilah. Self-righteous as all hell. You know that much. I don't think I'll ever fully understand just how awful because Mom was too careful to hide the worst of it from me, but he was so angry all the time. And when he wasn't taking that anger out on the animals, he was taking it out on Mom."

I cover his hand with my own. He doesn't look up.

"And when I got big enough, I tried to take her place as best I could."

My lungs are suddenly impossibly tight. "I'm so sorry, Truett. I had no idea."

"Of course you didn't." He sighs softly, the sound damp with unshed tears. "You were my bright spot. I didn't like to bring the clouds out when you were around."

Tears burn my eyes, and they pool in Truett's. He blinks. Glances up at the ceiling. Anything to keep them at bay.

"Sorry, I don't know why it still gets to me like that."

Rage stirs in my gut, but I force myself not to give it the reins. What good would my anger do him now? What he needed was protection that I couldn't give him, and that's a truth that's harder to swallow than any emotion. Our hands pulse against one another, each of us trying to comfort the other. When I finally find my voice, it's laden with sorrow. "Do you ever hear from him? Your dad?"

"No. If there's one thing Waylon Parker can't stand, it's damaged pride. When everything came out about Mom and Henry, he took off. Last I heard he was out in Arizona with a newer, younger wife. Grandpa shared that particular piece of news before he stopped talking to me, too. Good riddance, honestly. To both of them." Pity flashes in his gaze. "I think a lot about her. The new wife. Wonder if she's safe. If she has anybody who looks out for her."

I savor the warmth of his touch. A reminder that he's here. That he's safe. "Like you did for your mom?"

"Not me." He shakes his head gently, measuring my reaction. "Henry."

My brow knits together. "What do you mean?"

He releases my hand but trades it for my knee, squeezing it tight. His knuckles are dirty, but so is my leg. We match in that way. "I don't think Mom ever would've had the courage to leave my father. What happened with Henry…it's the only thing that saved her. Being loved like that gave her hope."

Love. It was there, in my dad's tearful confession that night. But still some part of me couldn't believe it. Refused to. "You think it was more than an affair? You really think they loved each other?"

He raises his brows, his forehead crumpling slightly. "Why don't you ask your dad?"

"Do you think he'd remember?"

An echo of a smile flits across his face. He's watching me so intently that I forget to breathe as I wait for his response. The edge of the barstool digs into my ass. I've moved close, literally to the edge of my seat, to hear what Truett thinks of this mess that is our lives.

"I don't think he could forget."

There's something in his tone, in the glint of his gray-blue eyes, that makes me ask, "Tru, what do you know about our parents that I don't?"

He sighs. "It's not my story to tell."

"But isn't it mine to know?"

"No." Truett moves closer until our legs are interlocked. "It's theirs. We have our own story to worry about."

I remember the glass I abandoned on the table and grab it, taking a sip of water to quench the desert that is my throat. When did it get so hot in here? And why can't I fucking *breathe?*

I can feel him along every inch of my overheated thighs, and I don't hate it. My gaze meets his like I'm seeing him for the first time instead of the millionth. For a moment I let myself imagine what it'd be like if we'd never grown up together. If I hadn't loved him since I was old enough to give that feeling a name. What if we were just two strangers who met in a bar? What if he asked me to dance, then bought me a drink and we sat on a pair of barstools like the ones here in his kitchen, but we were a hundred miles away from the place so deeply tied to our grief? What happens then, between two people who look at each other the way he's looking at me now?

Like I'm *remarkable,* when I've always been anything but.

"Delilah," he breathes, and that breath washes over my lips, which part like it's the most natural thing in the world to do.

And perhaps it is. Wanting Truett has always felt as right as breathing, and equally necessary.

"What are you doing?" I murmur.

A smile touches those eyes, the palest shade of blue. My favorite one. "Oh come on, Temptress. Surely you remember what I look like when I'm about to kiss you?"

He leans in and our noses brush. My stomach hollows out. He's wrong. I don't remember. When he asked to practice kissing beneath the shade of that willow tree, I watched him coming, sure. But in the aftermath? When everything I knew shattered into a million pieces? I forced the memory of that moment into the recesses of my mind, determined to forget how it felt to be wanted by Truett, even for a moment.

Even for practice.

His hand cups my jaw. "Beautiful," he whispers, his lips featherlight against mine.

The front door slams against the wall as it swings open. "Boss?" Ollie asks as he steps into the room. "The bull got out again. He's in with the ladies—Oh, shit. Sorry."

We break apart, scrambling to our feet as the barstools clamber to balance themselves out. Truett smooths a hand through his hair. "I'll be there in a second, man."

Ollie nods. "Right. Meet you there." His gaze cuts to mine. "Sorry again."

As the door shuts behind him and Truett turns back to me, I feel my spine go rigid. What on earth was I about to do? I almost opened the biggest can of worms with the one person who's as entrenched in my dad's care as I am, save for Roberta. So we kiss, then what? What happens when everything implodes between us, and then Dad refuses anyone's help but Truett's again? What happens when Truett decides things have gotten too hard and he ices me out all over again?

How the fuck could I be so stupid?

"Th-that should *not* have happened."

I move for the door, but Truett cuts me off. His hand cups my bare elbow, sending a shiver straight to my core that I hope he misses. I can't look at him to check. Can't meet his gaze after everything that I know. Words he said but couldn't possibly mean.

I flinch away from his touch, and his arm drops. He pops his lips, and against my better judgment, my gaze flits to them.

His jaw flexes. Those eyes, which were so bright a moment ago, are swallowed by blown pupils. Lust. Desperation, I reason. I'm the closest thing to a fresh face he's gotten in this town in God knows how long. Nothing more.

Nothing like what I felt for him back then. What I still feel for him, despite everything. I curse myself silently for having aged nine years but learned nothing at all.

"Well, I'll be." Truett tuts, gaze full of regret. "Delilah Ridge-field *does* make mistakes."

I blink back a fresh wave of tears and skirt past him. He doesn't know how right he is, and I'm not about to tell him. My hand hits the brass doorknob just as his lands on my waist. I pause, only for a moment, and soak in the feeling before turning out of his touch.

He catches the door when it swings open. I feel small compared to him—not belittled but protected. And it's such a dangerous feeling. Depending on other people. It never works out well in the end.

He leans in so close that his lips brush my ear, sending a shiver down my neck. "You know, it's okay to want things just for yourself."

No, it's not, I want to say. Everything I've ever allowed myself to want has ended up hurting me in the end. First Lucy, then him. Even my dad is being taken from me now. Can't he see that? Doesn't he get it?

Instead I say, "Bye, Tru," then hit his porch at a run, jogging down the steps and onto the road that will lead me home.

Rather than boots or Keds, he should've bought me running shoes, because that's all I seem to know how to do.

Chapter Twenty

Henry

July 8th, 1997

THE NEXT TIME I see Kimberly, she's seated between her parents at my kitchen table. Her hazel eyes are overcast, like the forest floor when a storm blots out the sun. She thumbs the corner of the sonogram prints. To my untrained eye, it looks as though someone printed off a snowy television screen, but they tell me that dark spot is a fetus. A baby. *Our* baby.

Kimberly's hair falls in loose blonde waves over her shoulders. She's not wearing a lick of makeup. Compared to prom night, she seems so much younger. Less confident.

I know how that feels. That night, I felt on the verge of becoming a grown man. Faced with this? I'm suddenly no more than a scared child.

"Can I get y'all coffee? Tea?" Mom wrings her hands together. Her gaze darts from Kimberly's mom, whose mouth is pinched tight, to Kimberly's dad. His jaw is taut, the clean-shaven skin there twitching as he grinds his teeth audibly. Neither responds to my mother. She flattens her palms on the table, fingertips an inch from the sonogram, and sighs.

In the corner of the black photograph, I see *Anderson, Kimberly* printed. I realize I never even asked her last name. Part of me assumed it was Winters like her cousin. I fixate on this fact, reshaping her in my mind. Kimberly Anderson. The mother of my child.

It's a distraction from the shitstorm brewing in her father's eyes.

"What were you thinking?"

"We weren't—" Kimberly murmurs.

"I wasn't asking you," her father bites. Her mother winces. He lifts a fat finger and aims it at me. "You took advantage of my daughter. Now you've ruined her life. She was gonna be an accountant, you know that? Make good money for herself. Now she's gotta quit college to raise your baby."

I wince but don't reply. Because what could I possibly say? He's right on all counts.

"Well?" He practically snarls. "What do you have to say for yourself?"

I glance at Kimberly, but her gaze is trained on the tabletop. After… Well, after we finished that night, she laid in my bed with her leg slung over mine and told me how she actually wanted to be a flight attendant, but her dad thought accounting was a more respectable position. Probably because it's what he does. "*It was a dumb dream anyway,*" she whispered, and suddenly her dismissal of my music stung a little less.

My chest aches, realizing I'm yet another person taking a dream away from her.

"You don't have to quit," I say, directing my voice to her. She gazes up at me from beneath damp lashes, her lower lip trembling. "I make enough at the factory. I can put you through school at the community college—"

Her father scoffs. "And who's gonna raise this baby while you're working and she's at school? You can't do both."

"I'll watch the baby," Mom says. All eyes shift to her. She braces her shoulders, her signature pearls glinting in her ears. "I raised Henry. I can take care of my grandchild."

His hard stare shifts from my mother to me. "And what a fine job you did there."

"*Greg,*" her mother warns.

"Excuse me, but Henry is a good kid." Mom swallows hard. She drops one hand beneath the table to grab ahold of mine and squeeze. "Accidents happen. And last I checked it takes two people to make a baby. At least he's trying to make things right."

Greg—what a friendly name for such an unfriendly guy—looks about to boil. His face is simmering red. I sense more than see his blood pressure rising. He sucks in his lips. My breath catches. I don't know where we go from here. But like Mom said, I'm trying to make this right. As right as I can.

"So you'll marry her, then?"

"*What?*" Kimberly and my mother say in sync.

Her mom lets her eyes drift closed. A tear falls silently over her cheek. She brushes it away with the hand that's not draped over Kimberly's, smudging her nearly perfect eye makeup.

In the few minutes I've sat across from Mrs. Anderson, I've realized she's a proper lady. Quiet, and not one to disagree with her husband openly. But she carries herself with grace and poise, not unlike my mother. I get the sense she and Mom would make good friends if circumstances were different.

"If you two are gonna act like adults, then you're gonna do what adults do." Greg glances at the sonogram. At the shadow that my whole world has now shifted to revolve around. "That baby needs two committed parents. So you're gonna do the right thing and marry Kimberly. *Before* she brings your child into the world a bastard."

"And what if I don't want to?" Kimberly says.

She avoids my gaze. Instead she's staring out the bay

windows at Abel Johnson's sprawling farmland. The simple view that's been the background of my life. I wonder what it looks like to her. If it all seems too small compared to the skies she once imagined flying. Compared to a big university in Mississippi and a career and *fun.* I wonder which of those things she's already missing, based on the devastation crumpling her features. She asked the question, but she already knows the answer as well as I do.

Her father gives it all the same.

"What you want stopped mattering the day you dropped a positive pregnancy test on our kitchen counter." His mouth is a firm line. Even my mother doesn't dare argue. "We'll go back to South Carolina and pack your things. Henry, you better start shopping for houses."

"They'll stay here," Mom says. She studies Kimberly, sympathy softening her features. "If I'm gonna watch the baby, it makes the most sense. Then y'all can put away your money for a nicer house when you're out of school." She rises from the table like that's the end of discussion. I guess, for her, it is. "Now, does anyone want some tea?"

August 23rd, 1997

Pastor Timothy glares down at me from the pulpit, a self-satisfied smile twisting his lips. I shift my feet, Dad's oxfords dragging on the green carpet at the foot of the stairs. My mom is seated in the front pew, face swollen from the unrelenting tears that have been spilling out of her all morning. The room is sweltering in the late summer heat, like the pastor couldn't even be bothered to turn the AC on for us. That's how beneath him this wedding is.

"I hope this sets you straight, boy. I hope you step up and

make a good husband of yourself. A good father. Time to start setting a good example. You can't be thinking about just yourself anymore. Not with a wife and a baby on the way." His voice is low, meant only for me to hear. "Your daddy would be so disappointed in your actions these past few months. Now's your chance to make it right."

I don't give him the satisfaction of meeting his dark stare. Instead I try to catch Lucy's attention. She's sitting at the piano with her fingers poised over the keys, talking to Waylon in hushed tones. His arms are crossed over a plaid button-down. His dark hair is slicked back. An ironed pair of khaki slacks complete the look. He certainly plays the part of the pastor's pet well, which I'm sure is how he managed to get that engagement ring on Lucy's finger. The sight of it when we walked into the church nearly brought me to my knees.

Why? I want to ask her. *Why him?* The girl who played a masterpiece at my side, who slipped me notes and snuck out of her house and held me as I collapsed under the weight of my grief… How could she agree to marry Waylon? Anyone else I could've accepted. But not him. The territorial way he stands guard over her. His treatment of any girl he could get his hands on when he was in school. The cool, calculated mask he wears when he's tailing the pastor, mimicking his every move.

None of it settles well in my stomach. Blame it on jealousy, I don't care. I know he's not good enough for her, because I'm not either, and he's a hell of a lot worse than me.

"Eyes on your bride, son. She's coming your way."

The music has started. A choppy wedding march fills the cavernous sanctuary. My brows furrow. I know for a fact Lucy can play better than this. Does it hurt her to be here? Does she feel the ache in her hands, the sickness in her stomach, the way that I do? My head swims, the room spinning, as I tear my gaze from her face, which is half-shrouded by the piano's cover. I find

Kimberly already halfway up the aisle, accompanied by both of her parents. Resignation tugs the corners of her mouth down. Our eyes meet, and a shiver runs the length of my spine.

We're about to promise a forever to each other that neither of us had a say in. One day I will grow to love her, I'm sure. A lifetime together will do that at least. But will my heart ever be so enraptured with her that her presence feels like a warm fire burns beneath the surface of my skin? Will the mere thought of her ever pull music from my fingertips? Enough to fill an entire church with its sound.

My hands flex. The scent of vanilla candles burning on the pulpit fills my nose, clogging my throat. Or maybe it's the tears that I suddenly can't choke back. They fall freely, and as I turn to search for my handkerchief, it's then that I finally catch Lucy's gaze. Her chest heaves. Her arms tremble with every note. And her eyes, the blue-gray of a summer sky, are filled with tears.

"Who gives this woman to be married?" Pastor Timothy's voice reverberates in his throat, thick with the weight of his own self-importance.

"I do." Greg unravels Kimberly's arm from his and cradles her hand reverently as he places it in mine. For the first time I see the dam of control break in his eyes. He's scared, possibly devastated, to be giving his daughter away. It's there in the twist of his quivering lips. In the pool of unshed tears gathered over his hazel eyes, the same shade as Kimberly's. "You take good care of her, son."

I nod. "Yes, sir."

The pastor launches a monologue on the sanctity of marriage. On the ways it binds two souls together so that they become one life in the eyes of God. It reminds me of my parents. When Dad left, it broke my heart in two. But Mom? She buried half of her soul that day. I study Kimberly. The tight pinch of her lips, so similar to her mother's. Her wide, determined gaze. The simple lace gown she chose hangs like a sheath over her body. The swell of her stomach is beginning to show, and I find myself smiling despite the fear that quickens my gut.

I can't yet imagine Kimberly as the other half of my soul, but already I feel that way for our child. And that is more than enough.

"Do you, Kimberly Anderson, take this man, Henry Ridgefield, to be your lawfully wedded husband? To have and to hold from this day forward, for better, for worse, for richer, for poorer, in sickness and in health, to love and to cherish, for as long as you both shall live?"

Kimberly's lips part, but it's not her words I hear. It's Lucy's soft inhale, audible now that the music has faded out, that captures my attention. I glance her way, noting the subtle shake of her head at the same time Waylon does. His stare locks on me and hardens in a warning.

"Henry?" Kimberly whispers.

My gaze jolts to hers. I've missed her answering the pastor, I realize. Missed that it's my turn to speak, based on everyone's expectant gazes, in the time I've spent watching Lucy.

A single tear falls from the corner of Kimberly's eye. "Could you at least try to pretend like I'm the one you wish was standing here right now?"

All warmth drains from my face, replaced by a fresh wave of shame. "I am." I wince. "No, that's not what I mean. I'm sorry, I —" I close my eyes and draw a deep breath, gathering myself. When I open them again, everyone in the room is waiting for me to answer a different question than the one she levied. A more important one, in my opinion. Because wishes mean nothing at the end of the day. They're the stuff of fairy tales. Of fictional worlds where fathers don't die young and soulmates always end up together.

But vows? Those matter. They make up the foundation of a life. First my parents', and now ours.

I hold her gaze and try to convey the weight of my words as best I can. "I do."

Her eyes drift closed at my words. She stands there, unmoving, as Pastor Timothy declares us married before God and everyone in this room. She's still motionless as I take her in my arms and kiss her for the first time since that night.

When her eyes finally flutter open, a wall has come up behind them. One made of steel, same as her rigid spine. I'm afraid I'll spend my whole life searching for a way around it.

Chapter Twenty-One

Delilah

"Since when do we have places this cute in Fly Hollow?"

Alicia turns to look over her shoulder at the room. The News Room was once someone's house, now turned into a cozy cafe. It has the original creaking floorboards and framed news clippings from the local paper on the faded olive walls. In what used to be the kitchen, a lanky teenager took our order and grumbled our total to us, which Alicia insisted on paying. I couldn't talk her down, so I bought two biscuits with chocolate gravy while she collected our coffees, to make up for taking two weeks to answer her invitation.

Two weeks spent mulling over what Truett had said, both on the road home from the school as well as at his house. Two weeks spent wondering if I could forget how it felt to be so close to him again, to have his lips brush mine, this time knowing full well it wasn't for practice.

If what he said was true—if he's always wanted me—why wait until now to admit it?

I can't make heads nor tails of it. But he was right about one thing: I'm not immune to mistakes. Nearly allowing myself to kiss him, to ruin the fragile arrangement we have for my dad by giving in to a temptation with no chance of a future? I'm proving the apple doesn't fall far from the tree. And if I want to believe I can be better, then I have to believe Alicia can, too.

Her gaze slips from the closest news story, meeting mine with an amused spark. "A few years back the local government allotted grant money for any business plans that would improve the town and bring fresh blood to Fly Hollow. Since then we've cycled through a couple cupcake shops, one Italian restaurant that lasted a single summer—"

"Let me guess, no one wanted food they didn't know how to pronounce?"

"Listen, Delilah, *speziata* just does not roll off the tongue with an accent this strong." Her expression is mock serious as she takes on an affected drawl. "They'd honestly do better if they stuck with a classic. I'm thinking McDonald's, KFC, et cetera."

I divert my laughter into my cheeks, puffing them out. "Have they tried a Dollar General? That'd drum up some interest. I think this might be the last small town in America that doesn't have one."

"Not yet." She sags in her seat, suddenly listless, and swipes a hand dramatically over her forehead. "But a girl can dream."

I snort, then hiccup, choking on the sip of coffee I'd been in the middle of taking. "Dream a little bigger, Alicia."

She grabs a napkin from a nearby table and passes it to me. "But anyway, through all those failed businesses, this one is the only to have thrived so far."

I finish wiping the coffee spittle from my chin. "With good reason." I spear a bite of biscuit with my fork. "Their food is delicious."

Her gaze drifts up the walls, settling on a framed clipping featuring a photo of a man and his son in black-and-white, tilling a small garden. The headline reads, *"Local family starts vegetable garden for the needy."*

She smiles. "I think it's because it feels like home."

She's right. And not just because it *is* one. It's all the things I loved about this town, once upon a time. Even the surly cashier knew Alicia by name and cracked a smile when she asked him about joining concert band in the fall. There's a group of white-haired women gathered in the corner, holding a gossip counsel they've disguised as a book club. Each story on the wall celebrates an achievement, like the ground breaking for a park near the town square, or the year Renee Holt turned one hundred and five. The big and small wins that make up a life.

I know my mom always found it stifling. Since leaving, I've tried to convince myself I do, too. But Truett was right. A fact I'm afraid to look too closely at, lest it apply to other things.

"So how've you been? How's your dad?"

"He's all right." I tuck a strand of hair behind my ear and bite the corner of my lip. "His meds keep him calm, and he's altogether pretty alert most of the time. Nights are hard. Talking is getting harder for him now. It takes him a while to find words once he forgets them. The doctor recommended a speech therapist, so he starts there on Monday."

Her normally serene face crumples with pity. "I'm so sorry, Delilah. I hate that you guys are having to go through that."

Her words settle over me like a balm to a wound I didn't know I had. So often I think of this as something my dad is going through that I'm simply bearing witness to. But she's right. *I'm going through it, too.* Losing your parent is never easy, I imagine, but how cruel of the universe to make me do it day by day, hour by hour for however many years Dad has left. Wouldn't it be better to lose him all at once, rather than waking to find pieces of him have disappeared in the night, never to return again?

"It's been really hard," I whisper, my voice fracturing. I suck in a deep breath. My lungs ache with the pressure of holding it.

"He'll be fine all day, and then it's like a switch turns, and he panics. Or retreats into himself. I'm not sure which is worse."

"But you have help?"

I nod. "His caretaker, Roberta, comes during the week. And Truett—" I cut myself off, pressing my lips together. My eyes burn. Even with me avoiding him, he hasn't wavered. He checks in on Dad a few times a week. Brought the mower by on Monday. He even texted me instructions for starting it and cutting the engine off so I wouldn't have to ask for help. He's giving me space when he could so easily force his way in. He showed his hand, then left it up to me whether I want to play.

Alicia tilts her head. "And your mom?"

I flinch, and she clicks her tongue.

"I suppose I could've guessed as much." Her hand, smooth and scented with vanilla lotion that wafts up to my nose, settles over mine. "I'm glad you're not alone in this. And I'm here if you ever need anything."

My responding smile is wafer-thin. "Sorry it took so long for me to get back to you on making plans."

"I didn't really think you'd meet up with me, if I'm being honest." Alicia takes a sip of her latte. Milk foam pools on her upper lip, and she releases my hand to swipe it away with a napkin. "You didn't seem too keen when I initially asked."

The sound of conversation ebbing and flowing, of coffee grinders buzzing, fills the silence between us for a beat. I suck in an aromatic breath and let it out slowly through barely parted lips. The truth is, Truett was right about people changing. About letting people grow, letting them become someone we might not have believed they could be. And since I'm too terrified to apply that logic to him, I picked the next logical person to call.

Alicia doesn't look at me with any expectation written in her wide brown gaze. She laid it all bare that day in her new class-room, and now she's giving me the option to do the same. I get the sense I could brush the question off with a nonanswer, and she'd let it go. But that wouldn't gain me any friends, and Truett hit too close to the truth on that for me to bear. I've isolated myself for too long, and for what?

"To be honest, I didn't plan to at first." I move a piece of biscuit through a pool of chocolate gravy, back and forth, forming a divide. "I want you to know I'm not angry at you. Not anymore. What you did hurt me a lot back then, but you were a kid. We all were."

Her throat tenses as she swallows. Her eyes are glassy, cheeks hollow. "I'm so sorry I left you alone to deal with that mess. When Truett said you'd left town, well… I couldn't help but think it was my fault."

"You weren't the one bullying me."

"I didn't stop it, either." A tear puddles on the apple of her cheek. I recognize the sheen of regret in her eyes. I'm sure mine look very much the same.

I drop the fork and reach for her hand. "We've all made mistakes. The important thing is that we learn from them."

"God, you sound like Truett." Her laugh is part sigh. A relieved smile softens her mouth. Today her lipstick is a vibrant pink that reminds me of the azaleas growing wild along the roads. It suits her.

I think of their easy conversation that day at the school. "Do you two hang out a lot?"

She shakes her head. "No. We see each other around town as much as anyone, but we're not nearly as tight as the two of you were. There was this one time, though, when I was home on break from college. I ran into him at the Crow Bar and we got to talking about life. About you."

I imagine the two of them in the local dive, discussing me over a couple of beers. My cheeks warm. "What about me?"

What few sharp edges she has go soft. I feel her gaze tracing my features, and I wonder what it is she's looking for. Her cheek twitches, the prelude to a smile, and that's the only hint I get.

"We both had a lot of regrets about how we handled things, that's all." She sucks in a breath, sits up straight, and rearranges her face into her normal brand of sunshine. "But you two seemed to work things out, yeah?"

The bell over the door jingles, signifying the pseudo-book club has concluded their discussion. I watch them leave, hoping beyond hope that Alicia no longer possesses the uncanny ability to read me like a letter. "Sure."

"Oh, come on." She nudges my shin with the toe of her sandal beneath the table. "Explain that look."

I sigh. *Of course.* "Glad to see you haven't changed a bit."

"I've changed a ton," she says, puffing up her chest. "But you're still terrible at hiding your emotions. What's wrong? Haven't told him you're in love with him yet?"

"I'm not in love with him," I grumble. My biscuit is stodgy and cold at this point, but I take a bite anyway to have something to do.

"I know I'm not a doctor, but my husband is. I'll bet I could get him to prescribe you something for that denial." She swirls a finger in my direction.

I roll my eyes, and she chuckles.

"In all seriousness, Delilah, can I give you a piece of unsolicited advice?"

"It wouldn't be unsolicited if I said yes."

Her grin is wicked. "Exactly."

I ball my napkin up and toss it at her. She dodges, and the employee cleaning up the book club table scowls at us.

"Sorry!" I scurry over to collect my garbage and bring it back to the table. Alicia is trembling with laughter by the time I return. "Go on, before I get us kicked out of the nicest restaurant in town."

"Uh-uh. The *only* restaurant in town."

I point my fork at her. "How could you forget the Grille?"

"Does the Grille count if it's technically outside of city limits?" She shrugs. "I'm just saying."

I roll my eyes but smile. "Touché."

Her smile softens. She trains her gaze on me, watching for my reaction to her words. "Anyway, I think you should be honest with yourself, and be honest with Truett. I imagine your parents, and mine too, would've spared a lot of people so much pain if they'd done that."

A stone sinks in my chest, weighing me down. I part my lips to say something, anything, but nothing comes out.

She leans forward, places a hand on mine, and offers one of those half smile, half frown expressions that says, *I know it sucks, but I'm here with you,* in a way that fits right into the hollow of my heart.

"Thank you," I manage to force out.

She pats my hand. "What are friends for?"

I've grown so accustomed to getting my mother's voicemail that it takes me a few seconds to realize she's answered when I call her on my way home from the cafe.

"Hello? Delilah, can you hear me?" She scoffs. "Godforsaken town with its shitty cell service."

"I can hear you," I interject. Early afternoon sunlight filters through the canopy of oaks overhead as I drive down the main road through town, creating a kaleidoscope on my dash. I retrieve my sunglasses from the center console and slide them into place. "Sorry, I didn't think you'd answer."

"And why not?" Her tone is tight. Poised for an argument I

wasn't prepared to have. Hell, I wasn't even prepared for a *conversation.*

"I don't know, Mom. You just haven't lately, I guess." I don't want to go home with her on the phone. Not when Dad's awake to hear every reply. I flick my blinker, then take a turn down a winding dirt road that leads to another access point for the river that flows through Truett's farm. Groves of dense forest line either side, broken up every so often by double-wide trailers painted varying shades of washed-out beige.

"You haven't either," she retorts.

Because you call in the middle of the night, I want to say, but I grind my teeth over the unspoken answer. Mom has always been a night owl. Sometimes she'd climb the stairs to my floor at two in the morning, tiptoe into my bedroom, and shake me awake just to talk about the movie she finished, like I wasn't dead asleep moments ago.

So often it felt more like we were two college students sharing a too-big apartment rather than a mother and a daughter. I wonder if she was trying to recreate an experience she never really got to have. I know she was a freshman in college when she got pregnant with me and moved to Alabama to marry my dad. How much did she miss because of me? How much did she give up?

Sympathy stretches my impatience out like taffy, working it into something more malleable. More forgiving.

A wooden bridge appears in a break in the trees ahead. I slow, pulling into a small dirt parking lot. There are only a few other cars right now, but come Saturday, the road leading here will be lined with cars overflowing the lot. It's a popular spot to swim on sweltering summer days. I crack my window, and the sound of children splashing in the river filters in.

"I'm sorry, Mom. I've just had a lot on my mind."

I hear a door close on her side, followed by a wrapper being split open. The image of her raiding our pantry for a pack of

Veggie Straws fills my mind, the familiarity of it tugging at my heart.

"What's been going on?" she asks around a mouthful of her favorite snack. I smile at her predictability. Sometimes I wonder if I know her better than she knows herself.

That thought triggers something in me. A reminder of Truett's words, and the truth he hinted at but wouldn't explain. On impulse I decide to ask Mom, hoping someone in my life can shed a little light on things. "I've been spending time with Truett—"

"Lucy's son? I didn't think you wanted anything to do with him after—"

"Yes." I close my eyes, pinching the bridge of my nose. "I mean, no. I didn't. He was helping out with Dad before I came back." I'm toeing the edge of honesty, staring down from this precarious ledge. For reasons I don't look too closely at, I want to keep parts of him to myself. Who he's grown up to be. The moment we shared in the kitchen. But there are things he hinted at, things I need to understand, that push me over the edge. "He said some things about the affair, and I just feel like there's so much I don't understand. I was wondering if you could help."

She laughs. It's a harsh, painful sound. My hand flutters to my throat like I can soothe her ache.

"What's there to understand? Your dad cheated. That bitch was always prowling around, and she finally got what she wanted. They didn't even have the decency to do it in private, for Christ's sake." Her voice grows louder, more heated with every word. She sucks in a shaky breath and adds, "I know you're not supposed to speak ill of the dead, but God help me if that isn't karma."

A tear snakes beneath the rim of my sunglasses. Falls down my cheek. I shake my head, knowing she can see me about as well as she can understand how much it hurts for her to talk about someone I loved that way. Someone I lost, too. Which is to say, not at all.

"Was that night the first time that something happened between him and Lucy?"

"Why? What have you heard?"

"Nothing." I sigh heavily, but it relieves none of the weight in my chest. "It just doesn't make any sense. Why would Dad cheat out of the blue? I know you two didn't always get along—"

"We got along fine."

I bite my cheek, allowing the searing pain to clear the fog of annoyance. Denial is a stage of grief, I suppose. Is it possible that she's still grieving her relationship with Dad after all this time? Before, I would've said it's unlikely. But maybe my absence has brought it all back into focus. "Right. But was something going on that you guys didn't tell me? Were you two fighting?"

"Why can't you believe that your father did something bad without accusing me of causing it, huh? You've always worshipped him, but he's not perfect either, Delilah."

"I'm not accusing you of anything, Mom." I force my tone to remain level, my version of crouching low to approach a cornered animal. "I'm simply trying to understand."

She mutters unintelligibly—something unholy, I'm sure— then bites out, "What lies is he filling your head with?"

"None, Mom. It's not like Dad and I are taking a deep dive into our family trauma given his condition."

She pauses. In the silence, the sound of families enjoying the beautiful day rushes in. I envy them with such intensity that it knocks the breath out of me. I want to stagger from this car, from this conversation, and sink into the cool river below. Build sand-castles and throw Frisbees and just enjoy life for once. I can't remember the last time I did.

I picture a different part of the river and a shirtless, blond-headed man with water spilling over the contours of his abdomen. A shiver unspools down my spine.

When Mom speaks again, all her guards are up. "So why the third degree then?"

I let loose a captive breath. It stretches my cheeks, and I feel the pull of sticky skin where my tears have dried. "I just asked if there was more to the story, that's all. Hardly a third degree."

"Seems to me like the more time you spend there, the more you allow yourself to be manipulated into believing your dad was the victim in all this, when I was the one humiliated in front of the whole town."

I'm so tired. Tired of being torn between the two of them, never able to decide for myself how I feel or what I want to believe. My bones ache from the weight of her expectations. Her need for absolute loyalty, when Dad has never once tried to convince me of his innocence. If anything, in that first year when he still called, his words were laced with guilt. Shame. When Mom sent him my letter, that must've confirmed every deeply held fear he had. That he was unforgivable. And for a long time, I was sure he was. But now?

"I'm not being manipulated. No one is trying to sway me to one side or the other, Mom." *Except you.* "Me being here to help care for my sick father is not some jab at you." My next inhale stings my lungs. Fuels my fire. "Maybe I'm just finally out from under your umbrella of control and you hate that because then you can't influence my perception of you *or* Dad. Like you have the past nine years, trying to convince me that *he* was the villain." She gasps, but I push on. "And maybe no one was really the villain in the first place. Or everyone was, at least a little bit. Hard to say when you refuse to even discuss things with me. It was my life, too, you know."

Her choppy sobs fill the speaker. "I gave up *everything* for you, Delilah. I don't understand how you could be so cruel to me, saying things like that."

Just as quickly as anger filled me, it dissipates, leaving me rotten and empty. My chest caves in from the weight of the guilt. "I'm sorry, okay?" I open my eyes. Even with sunglasses, the light is blinding. "I'm under a lot of stress, and I'm just trying to make sense of everything. I didn't mean to take it out on you."

Her cries die on a whimper. A self-soothing hum meant to ease the ache. It's her signature epilogue. The way she's ended her crying fits for my entire life. "Delilah, I just don't think being there is the best thing for you." Another hum. This time low, contemplative. "Maybe it's time you come home."

I exhale, deflating entirely. My shoulders sag. The seat cushions embrace me as I sink in.

I don't know how to tell her that when I hear that word, I don't picture the sprawling house the two of us shared. There's no grand staircase or arched doorways or vaulted ceilings. *Home* whispers through my ears, and I see live oaks blown by a summer breeze. The heady scent of spring blooms mixed with the earthy aroma of hay and cattle. I'm on a front porch, with Dad's black Converse kicked off by the door and an old, rusted chain squeaking in tune with the lazy sway of the porch swing it supports.

Despite all the pain, all the uncertainty, when she says *come home,* I look around at the dark river, and the tall pines, and the bright blue sky, and I think to myself, *I'm already here.*

I picture Dad playing guitar in his window seat. I feel worn hardwood beneath my bare feet. I see him scanning the kitchen cabinets for cat food he'll never find. That ache in my chest turns to agony. My home is changing, and I am too, right alongside it. That's not my mother's fault. But that doesn't mean she's spared from the repercussions.

Rather than try to explain it all, I just sigh and say, "He needs me here, Mom."

"And I don't?"

My head meets the headrest with a muffled thud. "Why does it have to be a competition?"

I didn't mean to say it aloud, and by the hiss of breath coming from her end, I should've bitten my tongue.

When she finally speaks, her voice is dripping with indignation. "It's not, but I certainly know where I'd fall if it was. I've got to go, Delilah."

"Mom—" I start to say, but the call is already cut off. "*Fuck.*"

I tear my gaze from the river, the trees, the sky. The steering wheel is warm beneath my palms as I back out of my spot, shift into drive, and head toward home.

Chapter Twenty-Two

Delilah

"PLEASE REMIND me never to store spaghetti sauce in a white container again," I grumble. The soiled Tupperware is the first thing I see when I open the dishwasher. A deep red stain stares up at me defiantly from the base of the bowl. "Or if I do, only let me store it in *this* container, since it's already ruined."

When I get no response, I peer into the living room to find Dad has drifted off to sleep, mouth gaping, with a dark spot of drool forming on the Ridgefield Family throw pillow he's propped on. I laugh softly, padding across the room to gather the quilt from the back of the couch and spread it over him. Without thinking, I press a kiss to his forehead.

"Night, Dad," I whisper.

He stirs, the wrinkles around his eyes deepening for a moment, before his face relaxes back into restful bliss.

The low hum of conversation coming from the television accompanies Dad's muffled snores as the only sounds in the house. The sun sits low in the west field, casting a warm glow over Truett's land and spilling onto the hardwood floors through the window. There's still an hour or so till it sets completely, but already there are hints of pink and purple streaking the sky. It's always been my favorite part of summer, that the days seem so endless. So full of promise.

My phone buzzes on the countertop, dragging my attention away from the fields. A text from Mom pops up beneath a notification that I've missed a call from her. I squint, not entirely believing my eyes. Normally her silent treatments last a lot longer than two days. One time, after I chose a business degree instead of attending the flight attendant program for Delta Airlines that she suggested, she made it a whole three weeks. It would've been impressive if it wasn't so depressing.

MOM

Call me ASAP. I'm at the hospital.

Panic lances through me. My heart seizes. I glance over my shoulder at Dad, reassuring myself he's actually asleep, then step out onto the porch, careful to avoid the tattletale floorboard by the door.

Before the first ring has finished, Mom answers, breathless, "Oh, thank God."

"What's going on?" I grip the wooden railing to hold myself steady. Breaths come in thin, rapid puffs. "Are you okay?"

"I fell." Her voice warbles. "I'm waiting on the X-rays now, but the doctor said it looks like I broke it."

"Broke what?" My mind goes straight to her hips. Though I know she's only in her forties, it just goes hand in hand. Parents falling equals hips breaking. Next stop, motorized chair lift on the stairs.

"My ankle!" she wails. "I don't know why I ever let Debbie talk me into that damn hike. I have not been athletic my entire life. Why on earth would I start now?"

"Your... *ankle?*"

"Yes, Delilah. My ankle. I fell down a slick spot and twisted it something awful, and now it's swollen to the size of a grapefruit. I swear. I'll text you a picture."

"You don't have to—" I start, but my phone is already buzzing. Sure enough, her ankle is a gnarly shade of purple and a few sizes too big. But it's an *ankle.* My pulse stalls. Heat fills my cheeks. I pull in a deep breath and blow it out. "Mom, I was worried something terrible happened to you."

For a beat too long, the only sound is a distant monitor beeping and the low hum of chatter in what I assume is the emergency department.

Then, "Do you remember when you broke your wrist?"

I bite my lip, letting a sigh flow through the gap. "Yes."

"And how did it feel, huh? I seem to remember you were in a terrible amount of pain."

I wince, pressing the pad of my thumb to my throbbing temple. "I get what you're saying, but typically when someone says to call them ASAP because they're at the hospital, there's been a heart attack or a car accident or…"

"Or a dementia diagnosis?" Her tone is clipped. Knowing. We've circled right back to our conversation two days ago, and we're no closer to common ground. "How come when it concerns Henry, it's an emergency, but my pain isn't good enough for you to bother with?"

"I didn't say that at all."

She scoffs. "For your information, they're talking about surgery options. This type of break could put me in a boot for over a month."

I flop onto the porch swing. The chain groans under my weight. I want to echo the sound, but I bite the inside of my cheek hard, tamping down the temptation. "I'm so sorry, Mom. I hate that this happened to you."

A low male voice calls her name distantly, and then the sound of a hand muffling the speaker scrapes my ears. I empty my lungs. I try so hard to push the guilt out with it, but it simmers in my stomach, unwilling to be expelled.

She releases the speaker, and the sound of her world comes rushing in. "How soon can you be here?"

My racing thoughts falter, then freeze in place. "What do you mean?"

"I'll need your help post-surgery."

"So you *are* having surgery?"

She goes on like I haven't spoken. "If I buy you a flight, can you be here Monday morning? You can use my car while you're here so you don't have to drive all that way. Unless you'd like to drive. This could be a good time to transition care for your dad to something more permanent…"

"Mom, what are you talking about?" I lurch forward, elbows stabbing into my knees, and bury my head in my hands. "There's no transitioning of care. *I'm* the permanent care. And I can't just up and leave. When is your surgery? How long will you need me?"

"You *up and left* for him."

Swallowing takes effort. My throat is dry and sticky, my hands trembling. It's too much to think about. Too many directions I'm being stretched in. I feel paper-thin. So easily torn. But she's my mother, and she's right. I came when Dad needed me. I'm all she has to depend on. How can I offer her anything less?

"I have to work a few things out before I can say for sure, but I'll try, Mom. I'd need to arrange for someone to stay here with Dad, I think. I have to ask Roberta what her opinion is. Some nights are fine, but I don't even know how long I'd be gone, and—"

"You know, when your nana couldn't be alone overnight, that's when we started looking for a facility."

"*He's not going to a facility.*" The words are finely ground by my teeth. I sigh heavily. She doesn't need vehemence right now.

She's hurting. What she *needs* is my help. "I'll figure it out. Just send me the info on your surgery and I'll let you know when I have an answer."

I hear another voice, this one familiar. Debbie must be there with her. Relief courses through me that she's not alone at the hospital, at least. But Debbie has her own family, with two kids still at home. She can't stay with Mom and take care of her after surgery. That's my job. And I don't wish it wasn't, I just wish it came at a different time. Or that I could tear myself in two and take care of them both.

It's one of the few times I've wished for a sibling.

"I'll send you flight options. I've got to go; they need my pharmacy information. I love you, baby. I know you'll do what's right."

She ends the call, but her words linger. They're intentionally heavy-laden, a weapon she's always known how to wield. It weighs on me, compressing me like a closed fist until I'm standing, gasping for air. I want to be free of it all for just one fucking second. To remember what it was like when the only burdens I carried were my own.

Before I can second-guess myself, I pull up Truett's contact and send him a message, my thumbs hitting the screen rapid fire. To my surprise, he answers immediately.

ME

If I say I'm sorry, will you allow me access to the river?

TRUETT

Sorry for what?

I pause, weighing my thoughts. I dole out what feels like enough, without laying it on so thick it's unbelievable. I *am* sorry. Sorry that I took things further than I should've.

ME

Sorry for making a mistake.

He must pause too, because his next message takes forever to arrive, and I bite off half my fingernails while waiting.

TRUETT

That spot is as much yours as it is mine, Temptress. You don't need my permission or forgiveness.

ME

...but can I have it anyway?

TRUETT

Sure, you little rule follower. You have my permission.

ME

And your forgiveness?

TRUETT

That, too.

Three dots appear and then fade. Appear and then fade. I stare, completely rapt, wishing I could pull the thoughts from him like a loose thread. Like I could unravel all the tension between us so easily.

His message appears, and my cheeks flush.

TRUETT

Want company?

The image of him, water droplets pooling in the valleys of his abdomen, pops into my mind. I wet my lips, sucking in a sharp breath. I'm not sure if it's hope or anxiety causing the tremors in my hands when I type out my reply.

ME

Will you keep your underwear on?

TRUETT

You'll have to wait and see. ;)

Nervous laughter rattles my chest. I press the phone to my stomach and breathe deep, trying to calm myself. Energy crackles through me anyway. I'm tired. I'm upset. I'm turned on. And underneath it all, I'm still unsure of him. It's a maddening combination. How do I face him, knowing what almost happened between us last? More importantly, how do I face him if he's *naked?*

You could be naked, too, the more salacious part of my brain suggests.

I shake my head. The thoughts are still there, clamoring around, but I force myself to ignore them. To open the door and check on my father. To write him a note letting him know where I'll be and place it on the side table next to the couch. And when I finally feel at least partially in control, I fire off a reply, letting Truett know I'll meet him there.

TRUETT

Need a ride?

ME

No, I'll take the exercise. I need the time to think.

TRUETT

About...?

ME

Mom called.

I'm already to his property line by the time I send the last text. I tuck the phone into my back pocket and lift my head, filling my lungs with hot evening air that's as thick as syrup. I will it to clear my mind—and my body—of so many unwanted feelings. It's got about twenty minutes to do its job.

When I arrive in the clearing, sweat pools in all my crevices, leaving me sticky. It doesn't help that Tru's shirt is already off. He's laid out in the shade of the willow tree, using his wadded-up T-shirt as a pillow. His straw cowboy hat covers his face. The sun is fading fast, casting an orange glow through the meadow. It glistens on his exposed chest, slick with sweat and though pale compared to his tanned arms, still golden from days where he works the fields just like this.

Shirtless.

His breath is slow and even. I envy that—the ability to fall asleep so quickly and on just about any surface this earth has to offer. I also envy the light. Spools of gold settle on ridges of muscle where they've slipped through gaps in the willow's branches. A precocious flash of orange illuminates the path of the V-shaped muscles carving his lower abdomen, then disappearing beneath the waistband of his Wranglers. I want to trace them with my tongue. Taste the sweat there. Savor that delicious orange light.

"You're drooling."

My jaw slackens. "You're awake?"

He sits up, propping himself on two hands braced behind him. It pulls his biceps taut. His hat falls to the side, and I'm left with Truett. Bare and unfiltered. His golden hair falls over his forehead. There's a smudge of dirt on his freckled nose. A smirk perched on his lips.

You're beautiful, I almost blurt out. I bite my tongue.

"How was the walk?"

I struggle to remember *how* to walk, but I do manage. I put one wobbly foot in front of the other, closing the distance between us. "Helpful in some ways."

"And in others?" One eyebrow pulls up, wrinkling his sun-kissed forehead. He reaches into the cooler beside him and retrieves a beer, which he opens, then offers to me.

"Thanks." I take a long pull of the ice-cold liquid, letting it soothe the heat rising in me. Or hoping it does. "Turns out, no matter how long you think about problems, they still exist when you're done."

He offers a sympathetic frown as he rises to his feet, dusting his hands on his thighs once he's up. "Yeah, ain't that a bitch." He grabs a beer for himself. The cap flies off, lost forever in the tall grass beyond the willow's reach. "Do you want to talk about it? Or does that fall under the same sad truth, that it still exists even after we've dissected it to the bone?"

I weigh my options. Even if that is the sad truth of it all, I realize I don't want to be alone in my thoughts anymore. "Mom called."

He nods. "You mentioned that."

"She broke her ankle, and it apparently needs surgery."

The bottle stills at his lips. Drops slightly. "I'm sorry to hear that. Is she going to be okay?"

"I guess so, but she wants me to fly home to help with her recovery."

"When's the surgery?"

I scrub a hand over my elbow and shift my weight. "Not sure. I don't think it was scheduled yet. But she mentioned something about Monday."

His gray eyes settle on me, tracing the lines of my face. I hear his voice in my head calling me *remarkable,* and heat flares in my cheeks. I can reason away the kiss we shared beneath this tree all those years ago. He wanted to practice before his date with Molly Evans. I wanted to know if his lips were as soft as I'd always dreamed. Friends help friends. But do friends call their friends remarkable? Do they look at them like they are?

"Do you want to go?"

Heat flares in my cheeks. I'd drifted somewhere far off course, and it's a rude awakening to return. Part of me doesn't want to. I take another pull of the beer while holding his gaze, then lick the remnants from my lips. Energy hums beneath the surface of my skin when I catch him looking. When he licks his, too.

"I don't know," I answer honestly. "But I don't want to think about it anymore. Got enough of that on the walk over."

The corners of his eyes crinkle. "You know what can help with that?"

I chug the remaining beer, refusing to answer his question. Mostly because I know what I'm hoping he'll say, and I don't want that hope to color the sound of my voice.

"That's right, *skinny-dipping.*"

I set the bottle by my foot and then grab another. I remove the cap while looking Tru in the eye. "I'll skinny-dip on one condition."

A smile takes over his face, revealing sharp canine teeth in a flash of white against his bronzed skin. "I knew I'd win you over eventually."

"Aren't you going to ask what my condition is?"

His hand is already at his fly. "What's your condition?"

"Underwear stays on." I toss back the beer, my throat working to get it down. When it, too, is empty, I discard it at my feet and kick off my shoes.

His gaze darkens along with the setting sun. "What if I'm not wearing any?"

"Truett!" I throw a sock at him, which he dodges easily.

"What?" His hands fly up, the picture of innocence. "You texted while I was out in the field, and I came right here. Not a lot of time to go back for boxers."

"Why weren't you wearing any in the first place?"

He shrugs, returns his hands to his fly, and pops the button free. "It's laundry day."

"All right, new condition." I twirl my finger, gesturing for him to turn around. "No peeking."

He does as instructed. I swallow hard. His jeans are tight against the sinful curve of his ass, the long planes of his muscular thighs. The boots come off, followed by his socks. He loops his fingers in his waistband and tugs it down just enough that I can see his tan line when he stops, glancing over his shoulder. "That rule goes both ways, missy."

I spin before he can see the look of pure lust on my face.

I make quick work of my clothes, not allowing myself time for second-guessing. A cool evening breeze rushes in to kiss my skin, pebbling my nipples as my bra drops to the ground. I'm left with my thumbs hooked in my underwear, eyeballing the distance from here to the river's edge. "Hey, Tru?"

"Yeah?"

"How are we gonna get to the river without seeing each other?"

He thinks for a second. A heartbeat, really. And then I hear footsteps thudding against the earth followed by a whoop of joy and turn just in time to catch a glimpse of his bare ass before he disappears beneath the dark surface with a splash.

I scramble to rip off my underwear and follow behind him, hoping I can make it in the time he takes to resurface. My heart is in my throat, pumping so hard my pulse echoes in my ears. I make a running leap. My lungs seize around my last breath. Cool water rushes up to meet me, swallowing me whole.

I come up gasping, giggling, spraying water. "Oh my God, it's *cold!*"

"Excellent form. Ten out of ten."

My mouth forms a perfect O. I throw water in his direction, which he dodges. "You looked!"

"You wish," he chides, winking.

That wink *does* something to me. Or maybe it's the sensation of water flowing over my bare skin—every inch of it—that has me heating from the inside out. I dunk myself, smoothing a hand through my hair. I don't know what's gotten into me. There's no version of me I could picture doing this. Not the careful, responsible daughter who picked up her life to move back here and care for her father. The same one who is now torn over whether to do the same for her mom. Certainly not the shy high school girl who was in love with the man standing naked in the water a mere ten feet away.

But I'm here. Living my life. Doing something just because I want to.

When I resurface, Truett's not looking. His head is tilted back, capturing the last purple rays of light on the column of his throat. The sky is already filling with stars, tiny pinpricks of light that flood the darkness in the east sky. I wonder if he's looking at them. If he's searching for his mother.

I swirl my fingertips over the glassy surface of the water, disturbing the reflection of that twilight sky. I'm in the deepest part of the river, where the water reaches my collarbones. Tru has remained in the shallow end, looking like a statue in this pose. I'd almost believe he was if it weren't for the rise and fall of his chest in time with his breathing.

"Tru?"

His eyes drift closed. Does he grimace? Or is it a trick of the light? "Yeah?"

"How did you forgive your mom?"

Our gazes meet. Twin wrinkles appear between his eyes, which are wrought with an intensity that pierces my chest. "For the affair?"

I shake my head. How do I explain what I mean? I'm not concerned with the result, but the trigger. Not the side effect or even the medicine that caused it, but the disease it was meant to cure. Like the way my parents were never truly happy. Or the way his dad treated his mom.

"For marrying your dad in the first place."

His blink is slow. Measured. His voice the same. "I lost her. Once she was gone, all that stuff—the anger at how he treated her, the resentment that she stayed. Even the fact that her choices cost me you." His throat works over some unseen knot, and I trace the movement with my gaze, unable to look away even for a second. "It seemed so insignificant in the face of losing her."

And now I'm losing my dad. Is that what makes it easier to forgive the part he played in all this? Or is it because I feel a kinship to him, floating weightless in the river as I fully admit to myself the feelings I've held captive for this particular Parker for my whole life. The ones that never really left. Perhaps a weakness for them is genetic. A trait I inherited from my father.

"I'm sorry for avoiding you," I whisper. "And for almost kissing you."

He takes a step closer. The water moves around his hips reverently, like it's an honor to touch him. My heart cries that it would be.

"Are you?"

"Am I what?"

"Sorry." He says it flatly, like I should know this.

I blink. "I just said I was."

"But why? Why be sorry, when we're two adults who clearly have feelings for each other. What's there to be sorry for?"

I suck in a breath and hold it till it burns my lungs. Setting it free does nothing to shake the nerves out of me. "You don't have feelings for me, Truett. You're just lonely and I'm around and we're stuck in this emotionally heightened situation together with my dad. But don't worry. It'll pass."

He presses his lips together. "Do you know why I call you Temptress?"

The change in subject tilts me off axis. I adjust my footing, hoping it'll land me on solid ground. "Because your grandfather being a pastor gave you a complex about Bible stories?"

"No. Because I have always been tempted by you. Even when I knew I shouldn't be. When you were my best friend. The child of the man my mom cheated with." His chin dips, and his voice becomes a low baritone. "Even when you hated me. I tried to stay away, to protect you—"

"To protect me? How?"

"I didn't want to make things worse for you, start even more horrible rumors. After we kissed… Delilah, I have always wanted you with every ounce of my heart, of my body. But kissing you made it unbearable to keep pretending you were only a friend. And then, because of our parents, a friend was all you could be. But even all this time that has passed changed nothing for me. You're still so impossible to resist."

He takes another step closer, and I cannot move. I'm so close to falling off the edge of the only universe I've ever known. The one where I want Truett more than oxygen and he's seen me as nothing more than a friend.

"You can't say things like that to me, Tru."

"And why not?"

My voice registers just above a whisper, so soft I'm certain the chorus of insects filling the night air will drown me out. "Because I might believe them."

He's right in front of me now. So close that if I looked down, I'd see everything. So close that I can't look anywhere but at his face.

"Do you want to know the truth?"

"Yes," I breathe. More than anything.

His hand cradles my jaw. The soft pad of his thumb brushes my bottom lip. I'm still as a statue, afraid to fracture this moment by taking too deep a breath, by opening my mouth wider to invite him inside.

"I want you to believe them. I want to embed myself in your heart, become as vital to you as breathing. I'm tired of pretending like I haven't thought about you every day since you left. To pretend I haven't imagined you exactly like this." His gaze rakes over my face, and his chin dips closer, closing the distance between us till I can feel my breasts brush against his ribs and we both inhale sharply. Something like a growl resonates deep in his chest. "Delilah, I dream of what it would be like to taste you."

"You've kissed me before."

The corner of his mouth twitches. "I'm not talking about kissing you."

I shake my head. "Truett, I—"

"I gave you your space." He swallows thickly, pain flashing in his gaze. "But I needed to let you know how I feel. How I've always felt. No more wondering. No more hiding. I said it was a mistake because I knew it felt that way to you, but Delilah? The only mistake I made was not kissing you anyway, Ollie be damned." He gives me the world's saddest smile. "There. Now you know everything. The ball is in your court."

Everything. Everything except how to let go of the hurt that still feels so near to me. Everything except how to be enough for everyone who depends on me, let alone for him.

"I'm getting cold," I whisper. A shiver runs through me for emphasis. Coarse chest hair scrapes my nipples, stealing the breath from my lungs. I want nothing more than to rise up on my tiptoes and press my lips to his. To see if he's as passionate a lover as his words lead me to believe. But I can't. Not with so much uncertainty left between us. So much fear.

Shutters close on his eyes. He steps back, and I feel his absence like a knife through my sternum. My lungs burn; my ribs crack. On instinct I reach for his hand. Capture it between mine. He studies me, brow furrowed, as I place his calloused palm over my pounding heart.

"I don't know how to do this." My voice is shredded. Stripped down to bare bones. His thumb moves absently over my skin like he can soothe the ache this way. And perhaps he can. "But I'm trying. There are things I don't know how to let go of. How to forget."

He smiles, and it's the saddest expression I've ever seen in my life. Upturned mouth, downturned eyes. Parentheticals that could break your heart. That do.

"I can be patient."

Tears finally spill from my eyes. He doesn't make a move to wipe them away. He simply lets them exist. Lets *me* exist. And for that I'm grateful.

"Let's get you home, okay?"

I nod. "I need to call my mom."

His expression turns to stone, or a close cousin of it. He glances above me to the tree line. "Whatever you decide to do, I support you. If you need me to stay with Henry, just say the word. You need a ride to the airport, I'm your guy." His firm gaze returns to mine. "You need me to tell her to fuck off, I'm also your guy."

A sharp chuckle cuts from my lungs. "Got it."

He leans forward and presses his lips to my forehead. I'm surrounded by the scent of fresh water and the wide-open sky and *him.* I suddenly wonder how I ever breathed another type of air.

"Come on, Temptress."

This time I don't correct him.

Chapter Twenty-Three

Henry

August 30th, 2003

"It's time, Henry."

A glance in the rearview mirror tells me Delilah has tuned us out. She's gazing out the window while swaying back and forth in her booster seat. Phil Collins's croons fill the air. The girl's got good taste. The smile that stretches my lips is lackluster, but it's all I can manage. I've been spread so thin for so long I have nothing left to offer in the way of joy. It's why I know Kimberly's right, even if I don't want her to be.

"You've done more for her than most kids would, but it's time for us to live our own lives." Kimberly doesn't lower her voice, even with our daughter in the car. She never has. *You coddle her too much,* she says. *It's good for her to hear what real emotions sound like, what real problems are. She'll be more prepared when she grows up.*

Agree to disagree, I always retort. We're a lot like a broken record these days.

Delilah hears that, too, and though she's only five, she picks up on the tension between us. I see so much of myself in her, and so does Kimberly. Our daughter is sensitive, and she doesn't like conflict. She makes herself smaller to leave room for everything —and everyone—who dares to be bigger than her. I worry one day this world will swallow her whole.

"What if I'm not ready?" My voice trembles. I don't want it to, but it does. Even with the episodes getting more frequent, even with my mom's care needs growing beyond what we can handle, the idea of leaving her in a facility somewhere feels impossibly cruel. After everything we've been through together, after she took Kimberly in and helped us care for Delilah while Kimberly finished her degree… These last two years of turmoil feel like a drop in the bucket of what I owe her.

The symptoms started off easy to ignore. She'd forget where she left something or how to properly load the laundry. No problem, I could put in a load after my shift at the factory. Kimberly could fold when she got home from class. Mom started to skip showering for days, then lie about it when we asked. She'd get angry. Belligerent. Still, we reasoned that she was just getting older. Quirky. A bit stubborn.

But then we got a call that Mom had shown up at the fire department with Delilah in tow, saying she'd found her in the woods and did they know this child? I drove straight over from work. Delilah was crying, begging for her nana, and my mother didn't know who she was. Didn't remember that I'd even had a child.

Delilah went to daycare. Kimberly started work. But every night when we came home, it became more and more clear that Mom needed round-the-clock care. After a year, I switched to nights to be home with her during the day, and Kimberly cut her hours to be there when I couldn't be. Now even that doesn't seem to be enough.

"What if *I'm* ready?" Kimberly bites out. Delilah notices, because she always does. I watch her gaze flit to her mother and widen. Kimberly continues, unaware or uncaring or both. "I know you love your mom; I do. But I can't do this anymore. I can't worry which version I'm going to get of her each day, or that she's going to run off the moment I turn my back. I deserve more than that. Your daughter deserves more than that."

"I love Nana," Delilah whimpers. She brushes her hair—the same muted brown tone as mine—back from her face with a flat palm. "She's gonna be okay, right?"

I stop at a red light and turn to glance over my shoulder at her, offering my most reassuring smile. "Nana's gonna be fine, sweet pea. She just hurt her ankle on her walk today, so they're keeping her at the hospital till she's all better."

Delilah's expression tells me she doesn't believe me, but she keeps her lips pressed tight.

"She has to have surgery because she walked off into the woods in the middle of the night and broke her ankle. She's not gonna be fine, Henry. A facility is what she needs, with a whole team of people. I'm one person. I can't do it all." Kimberly's lips are pursed, just like her mother's were the day we sat across that table. I want to reach for her, to smooth them out, but the light turns green and she jerks her chin forward. "Go."

"I'm with you, you know."

"What do you mean?"

I capture the hand on her lap and squeeze. "You're not just one person. We're in it together."

"I wish that were enough for me, Henry, but it's not." She sighs, her shoulders sagging. Not with relief. With finality. "It's not up for debate anymore. She goes, or I do."

My spine stiffens and my throat dries. I glance in the rearview mirror. Delilah's already looking at me, lashes damp with quiet tears. She hates when we argue, and we do it too much.

"Okay," I whisper. "I'll start looking on Monday."

"Today." Kimberly slips her hand from beneath mine and

crosses her arms over her chest. She stares straight ahead and doesn't say another word for the rest of the drive home.

Before I've even placed the car in park, she's unbuckling and opening the door. She rounds the hood and heads for the front steps without sparing a glance in mine or Delilah's direction.

I watch her go, wishing I felt more than abject terror at the idea of her leaving me. Not heartbreak. Not sadness. Just fear—that she'd take Delilah with her to spite me. That I'd never see my daughter again.

Delilah is staring out the window again, this time in the direction of Abel Johnson's farm. He passed last year, leaving the grass overgrown and the house abandoned. Delilah likes to watch it the way I always have. It's a beautiful, peaceful place. Something we sorely lack in this house at the moment.

As much as I'll feel like a failure of a son, if we keep going like this, I'll be a failure as a dad. And I can't fail my little girl.

A line forms between her pale brows. "Who's at the farm?"

I follow her gaze. "Looks like someone's finally moving in."

There's a trailer stacked high with furniture parked in front of Abel's old house. I squint, a ripple of shock hitting me square in the chest when I realize it's attached to Pastor Timothy's white Ford. I snort, but there's no humor in it. It amazes me that all this town sees when they look at him is the pastor who helps a church member move on the weekend, never mind the man who stood across from me as I planned my father's funeral and threatened me to stay away from his daughter.

My eyes scrape like sandpaper when I blink. You'd think it wouldn't hurt so bad anymore.

"Can we go say hi?"

I clear my throat. "Um, they're probably really busy right now. Maybe another time, sweet pea."

She kicks the back of my seat. "Please, Daddy!"

Refusal dies on my lips when I catch a glimpse of long blonde hair disappearing behind the truck. *Not possible.*

"Look, they have a kid!"

Sure enough, a child races out of the house, trailing after the woman. They reappear at the back of the trailer, where she bends over to listen to something the little boy says. He takes off running for the edge of the nearest hill, where he lays down and starts to roll down the slope.

"I wanna go play, Daddy. Please!"

My heart hesitates to beat. From this distance it's so hard to make out their individual features, but I swear my body knows it's her even from here. Senses her. My stomach twists in on itself, but the words bubble up anyway, as if by their own volition.

"Sure, sweet pea. Let me just tell your mom."

She squeals with delight and gets to work on releasing her seat belt. I rise from the car on shaky legs and help her from her booster seat. We hold hands as we walk toward the house, her skipping to keep up with my strides. I study the crown of her hair, the narrow bridge of her nose. It's all I can see from this angle, but it's enough.

She's my whole world. The only thing that matters. And she deserves to play, to have fun like a normal kid. Especially after the morning we've had. If that means facing Lucy Barlow —*Parker,* I correct myself, wincing—for the first time in years, then so be it.

"Hey, Kim, it looks like there are new neighbors moving in. Delilah wants to say hi." I shout it into the house through the open front door. "You wanna come?"

"They have a kid like me!" Delilah adds.

There's no response. "Wait a sec," I tell Delilah, and then I make my way to our bedroom and glance inside. Nothing. I retrace my steps, this time going toward the hall where the bathroom is. Light slips under the door, so I knock. "Babe, did you hear me? Delilah wants to go say hello to the new neighbors."

"Go, then. I'm fucking exhausted. I'm gonna take a bath and then a nap while we have some peace and quiet in this house."

I flatten my palm against the door and nod, though she can't see me. "Got it. Give us a shout if you need anything."

There's an answering grumble that sounds a lot like, "*Like hell I will.*"

I drop my arm and return to Delilah, who's practically vibrating with excitement. I smile, mussing her hair when she's within reach. I think a lot about life when I look at my daughter. Not the life I once dreamed I'd have, like Kimberly sometimes tends to do when she drinks too much and waxes poetic about what could've been. Instead I think about the life I want *Delilah* to have. This one we've been living lately is not it.

I'll do better, I promise her silently. Out loud I say, "Ready, Freddy?"

"My name's not Freddy!"

"Is it not?" I mock surprise. "I could've sworn that's what I wrote on the birth certificate."

She giggles. "Can we go?"

"Yeah, we can go," I say, laughing. Then I take her hand and we head for the farm.

The minute Lucy glances over her shoulder at us, all certainty that I'm man enough for this seeps out of my body. I've very purposely avoided stepping foot in that church since the day of the wedding, and between work and Mom's doctor appointments, I don't spend a lot of time out and about where I run the risk of bumping into people. I've managed to go five years without seeing Lucy for more than a split second at the grocery store or in passing at the post office. Seeing her now has my heart dropping all the way to the dirt beneath my shoes.

"Henry?" Her gray eyes widen. Her hand pulses at her side. For a split second I think she might reach for me. Cup my face in her palm. I think it because I want it to be true, not because it's possible. Then her gaze drops to Delilah, and her smile falters. Briefly, but I see it. Then it goes so wide it resembles the late summer sun beating down overhead. "And who might this be?"

Delilah squares her shoulders, beaming up at Lucy with a toothy grin. "I'm Delilah! Do you have kids?"

Lucy laughs. "Wow, you don't beat around the bush. Yes, I have a son. He's playing on the hill if you'd like to join him. His name's Truett."

Delilah nods. "Thank you. Nice to meet you!"

"It's wonderful to meet you, too." Lucy pinches her shoulder playfully, then sends her on her way.

I watch her go, my throat suddenly thick with all these words I shouldn't say. *Couldn't* say.

Kimberly and I may have our problems, but that life I want Delilah to have? It involves two parents who love her. Who stay. I won't do anything to jeopardize that.

"She's a cutie," Lucy says, breaking the quiet that's settled between us. "How old is she now?"

"Five."

"Truett, too."

I glance back at her and try to ignore the way motherhood has softened her features, her curves. I'd heard they had a kid. It's one thing to avoid crossing paths, but avoiding news of her altogether? Impossible in a town like this.

Still, I hadn't realized his age. How close it was to Delilah's. "Really?"

A blush floods her high cheekbones. "Yep. We got married

that fall after you and Kimberly, and he was born nine months later. To the day, almost."

A half smile tugs at my suddenly chapped lips. "I wasn't questioning your virtue, Lucy. I just didn't realize y'all had a baby so soon after us."

"I know, I just…" She bites her full bottom lip, tilting her head as she gazes up at me, then shakes her head. "Never mind. How are you? How's Kimberly?"

"I'm good; she's good." I glance at the ground, nudging a clump of dirt with my toe. Lying to Lucy doesn't feel right. It sits on me like an itchy sweater. And why should I? She's the one person I've always been able to tell the truth to. "Things have been hard lately. Mom has been having some health issues, and it's getting to the point where it's a bit too much for us to handle at home."

Fingertips brush my forearm, drawing my attention upward. Her touch drops to my hand, where she squeezes once, tightly, then lets me go. "I'm really sorry. Anything we can do to help? As your new neighbors?"

"Did I hear someone say neighbors?"

My skin crawls as Waylon's voice registers. He rounds the back end of the trailer, and Lucy takes a measured step back, putting distance between us. His arm settles on her narrow shoulders, locking in tightly with a squeeze.

"Hi, Waylon." I nod at him and offer my hand. "Welcome to the neighborhood."

He clasps my hand and shakes it, jerking his chin in the direction of my house. "That you and the missus down there?"

"Yes, sir. And our little girl." I point toward the two kids who are gearing up for another log roll down the hill. "Delilah."

When I look back, Waylon's shaking his head. "Well, let's hope she's nicer to Truett than her namesake was to Samson."

Lucy squeezes her eyes shut. When they reopen, there's an

unspoken apology there. I wish she'd say it out loud. But I don't get the vibe that Waylon is the type to take kindly to criticism, and I'm not trying to make her life harder than it needs to be.

"I'm sure any boy of yours can take it," I say, voice flat.

His gaze hardens, while his smile remains perfectly lazy. "So what are you doing now, Henry?"

"Something with music, I hope," Lucy adds. It's meant to be a peace offering, but it lands more like a physical blow.

I shake my head. "Nope, I'm at the factory still. Had to put that dream to rest in light of the circumstances."

Said circumstances come barreling toward us, dirt smudging her cheeks and eyes bright with laughter. Truett follows closely behind, giggling like a madman. He has his mother's gray eyes and blond hair, slightly darker but still golden. His dad is there in the cut of his features but not in his laugh. It's all music. All Lucy.

He grins up at his parents, mischief clear in his gaze. "Can Delilah stay for dinner?"

"Not tonight, bud. We're still getting unpacked, and I've gotta get Grandpa's truck back to him by this evening." Waylon drops his arm from Lucy's shoulders, and I swear I hear a sigh of relief. He sweeps that arm out toward the expanse of land between our houses and adds, "We're starting a farm. I'm gonna raise Angus on this land. Get it back to its former glory."

I follow the motion with my gaze, tracing the fields I've memorized at this point after all the years I've spent staring at them out my kitchen window. "They look pretty glorious to me."

"What about tomorrow?" Truett presses, not swayed by his dad's tangent.

"Another time," Lucy replies, reaching out to tousle her son's hair. "I'm sure we'll be seeing lots of Delilah now that we live next door."

Delilah grins ear to ear, her gaze cutting from Truett to Lucy. "We can ride the school bus together and everything!"

"I don't ride the school bus," Truett says. "Mama drives me."

"I'm a teacher now, so he rides with me to work," Lucy explains.

"I told her she didn't have to work, but she insisted." Waylon rolls his eyes, leaning in toward me like we're conspiring on the conversation. "Once the farm's up and running, I'm sure she'll change her mind. I'll get her barefoot and pregnant again in no time."

"How do you do that?" Delilah asks, nose wrinkling.

"I'll explain later," I reply, bracing a hand on her shoulder while shooting daggers at Waylon.

"I worked really hard to get my degree while raising that wild son of yours. Not giving it up anytime soon," Lucy chides, pride sparking in her words. I feel it too, unfurling in my chest. I'm glad she stands up for herself, even in this small way. "You should consider teaching, Henry. Music teachers with talent like yours are hard to come by around here."

I can see Waylon's neck reddening, his gaze sharp, so I quickly speak up before he can cut her down. "Is that what you do? Teach music?"

"No," she says, laughing, "English. Though I do piano lessons at the church a couple nights a week if you're ever interested, Delilah. I'm sure your dad's already taught you everything he knows, but I have a few tricks up my sleeve, too."

"I have a keyboard!" Delilah says. "Well, it's Dad's. But he lets me play it sometimes."

"All the time." I haven't played it in ages. Haven't had time to. I squeeze her shoulder and smile. "She's a natural."

"I bet," Lucy says. Her eyes are lost in memory even as she's looking at my daughter. I wonder if she's seeing what could've been.

I know I am.

"Well, we've gotta get going on the rest of this." Waylon slaps a nearby dresser strapped to the trailer. "See y'all around?"

"Right. Yep. We'll let y'all get back to it." I capture Delilah's hand in mine and take a step toward home. "See ya around."

"Good luck with your mom," Lucy says. Her gaze is laced with sympathy, hands folded at her hips. "We're here now, if you ever need anything."

"Thanks, Lucy." I smile. It's the closest to the real thing I've done in months. I just hope it's convincing.

Waylon grabs a chair and starts heading toward the door. "Grab that other one, would ya, Luce?"

She frowns but says, "Yep. Coming." Then, glancing down at Truett, "Why don't you go get cleaned up, love?"

"Bye, Delilah!" He waves, a spot of dirt marring his palm, then follows after his dad.

"Think about what I said, Henry. You've got time to follow your dream." She shrugs. "We're still young, even if it doesn't feel like it."

Her hair dusts her shoulder as she hoists that chair up, turns back toward the house, and leaves my daughter and me standing together, holding hands. Leaves me feeling at once ancient, because so much time has passed since I last let myself consider the possibility of music, and at the same time impossibly young. I've spent five minutes with the woman, and already I feel like I've turned back time. Become the seventeen-year-old I was when I loved her.

I try to recall the exact moment when I stopped. It feels fuzzy. Just out of reach.

"They were so nice," Delilah sighs as we make the long trek home. "I think he's gonna be my new best friend."

I smile. "I'll bet he is."

Kimberly is bent at the waist, peering into the refrigerator when we return. A fuzzy bathrobe hides most of her shape, but I still find myself pausing to admire her. For all our problems, my heart still stands still when she straightens, glancing down at our little girl who's come up to hug her thigh.

"I made a friend, Mama!"

Kimberly smooths a hand over the crown of Delilah's head. "Isn't that nice? Wish I could make one." Her eyes move to meet mine, sharp as barbs. "Just don't seem to have the time these days."

"You could be friends with his mom!" Delilah says. "What was her name, Daddy?"

"Lucy." It comes out gargled, half choked on. I clear my throat. "Lucy and Waylon Parker bought the farm. They've got a boy about Delilah's age."

Kimberly stills. Her face is smooth, unreadable. "Of course they did."

I shrug like, *What can you do?*

Kimberly shakes her head and turns away.

Chapter Twenty-Four

Delilah

I CAME to school because I didn't want to face the hell that is being home with my parents right now. Between Mom spending every second berating my father to me, and Dad holing up in his office, I feel like a soldier conscripted to war. One where I don't agree with either side fighting.

But school brings with it a different type of suffering. The kind I didn't anticipate.

My shoes squeak against the polished linoleum. All around me, life ebbs and flows. Lockers slam and fluorescent bulbs buzz. Voices rise and fall over each other. It's a normal Monday morning, for all of about two seconds.

A beefy arm locks around my shoulders. I glance up. Brody Chamberlain—the resident loudmouth jock I've known and detested since kindergarten—smiles down at me with a wicked grin. "Hey, Ridgefield, heard your dad and Mrs. Parker were making their own kind of music after the band concert Friday night."

A few of his teammates form a huddle behind us. They erupt with laughter like this is the most original joke ever told. I shrug his arm off, scowling as best I can. "Leave me alone, Brody."

His eyes flare. "So it is true?*"*

Any student within earshot falls silent. A good twenty pairs of eyes settle on me, making my skin crawl. My ears and throat heat. Bile hits the back of my tongue, and I turn, earning a collective "Ooooohhh" as I slip into the girls' bathroom.

I slap open a stall door and kneel on the disgusting tile. As my meager breakfast of a boiled egg and some stale Cheerios splashes into the bowl, I contemplate whether the small squares that make up the floor were always brown or if our custodian is just that bad at mopping. Knowing Mr. Pugh, probably the latter.

I wipe my mouth with a wad of single-ply toilet paper, then flush it down the toilet alongside the contents of my stomach. My backpack thuds when it hits the floor. I lock the stall door, collapse onto the toilet, and rest my head in clammy palms. I don't understand this new version of reality. My dad and Lucy? Of all people, why her? Why did it have to be Truett's mom?

I unzip the front pocket on my backpack and retrieve my phone. No new messages. I click on Truett's name, smiling despite myself at his contact photo. It's a shot I took last summer right before he did a backflip off the riverbank. I called his name and he turned, bright smile flashing, the sun glinting off beads of water on his tan skin. I captured him like that, carefree and bright and looking at me with warm amusement in his eyes. It's how I always saw him when I closed my eyes. That is, until Friday.

Friday, when we were lounging against the trunk of the willow tree and he told me about his upcoming date with Molly. He admitted he was nervous. That he'd never really kissed anyone beyond a peck during spin the bottle. Even that revelation sent jealousy spearing through my gut. But then he turned to me with a sheepish grin and said, "Will you practice with me?"

Now, when I close my eyes to block out the slew of unanswered messages I've sent him since Friday night, that's the version of him I see. Gray-blue eyes glimmering with hope. Lips pocked with scars where he chews them too much. Nose splattered with freckles. He's leaning close, a breath away, and I can smell the sunshine on his skin and the scent of his parents' laundry detergent. Gain Apple Mango Tango. I begged Mom to get it after I smelled it on Truett the first time. Lucy even offered us a coupon. But Mom refused. She said it was too fruity.

I'm about to type out another message, thinking this might be the one to finally garner a response, when the door to the restroom opens. The noise from the hallway rushes in, then just as quickly disappears with the closing of the door. I hear bags slap against the counter. Through the crack in the stall door, I make out flashes of two girls standing at the sinks.

Emily and Katelyn pass a lip gloss between them. Their brunette waves are swept into messy buns, with small tendrils falling to frame their faces. Emily's brown eyes go wide as she glances at Katelyn in the mirror. "Did you hear what happened with Mr. Ridgefield and Mrs. Parker?"

Katelyn shifts out of my line of sight. "No, what?"

"Jessica Mathias caught them having sex in the band room on Friday night after the concert."

"Oh. My. God."

"Right?" Emily smirks. "I heard they were doing it on the piano!"

"Ew! They're going to burn that, right?" Katelyn audibly shudders. "That's so gross."

"I mean, Mr. Ridgefield is pretty hot."

"Yeah, but at school? That's disgusting."

They both giggle. I clamp my hand over my mouth to hold back the sob that wants to creep out of me. It's bad enough hearing the CliffsNotes from my parents. The unabridged version is humiliating.

Katelyn recovers first, asking, "Did Delilah show up to school today?"

"Yeah, Jessica said she saw her with Brody this morning." Emily snorts. "Maybe she's gonna take after her dad and become a skank herself."

"Oh, come on. You know she's been in love with Truett since grade school."

"Oh my God, you're right! How fucked up is that! Now they're practically related."

Katelyn shifts into view, rolling her eyes. "That's not how genetics work, but all right." She loops her purse back onto her shoulder and collects her books.

"But, like, imagine if Mr. Ridgefield and Mrs. Parker get married. Then Truett will be Delilah's brother.*"*

They both make mock vomiting sounds. It's almost enough to send me back to the floor, if I had anything in my stomach left to lose.

"Do you think they will?" Katelyn asks.

The door opens, and any response is lost in the crowd as the bell rings, signaling one minute to class.

One minute to English class. Which Lucy Parker teaches.

Surely she called in a sub, right? Dad did. And in a town this small, God knows what'll happen in a few days when word gets around to the other teachers. The principal. Hell, the fucking superintendent's daughter is a freshman this year. Is Dad even going to have a job when all this is over?

I loop my backpack over my shoulder and exit the stall. I try to focus on the hot water rushing over my hands instead of my spiraling thoughts, but it doesn't work. All I can think about is what Emily said. Are my parents going to get a divorce? If they do, is Dad going to marry Lucy?

Once my hands are dry, I fire off another message to Truett.

ME

I need to talk to you. Right now.

Either he's truly ignoring all my messages, or he's turned off read receipts for the first time in the history of our friendship. They show delivered, sure, but he's not opening them. I growl in frustration, my hands balling into fists. I never understood in movies when people punched holes in walls, but suddenly I'm tempted to slam my fist against this splotchy mirror and watch it shatter. My next breath is more hiccup than inhale. My eyes are red, face ghostly white. I choke on a sob, and that's the last straw. Tears pour down my cheeks. Snot pools in the valley of my cupid's bow. I draw in breath after ragged breath, scraping my throat with the effort of it.

The final bell rings, signaling I'm late to class. My hands are trembling when I retrieve my phone from the counter. I send another message, this time to Alicia, letting her know which bathroom I'm in and to come quickly. I can't do this alone. I don't know how to do this all alone.

ALICIA

Can't, I'm in class.

ALICIA

I'm sorry about what happened with your
parents.

ALICIA

My mom doesn't really want me talking to you
right now. I'll get in trouble if she even sees
these messages. Sorry, Delilah. I wish I could
help.

ME

To me? Why? I didn't do anything wrong!

My normally blue message bubble comes up green. Like she's turned her phone off. Or blocked me.

I turn the water on cold and gather a handful, splashing it against my face. It dribbles down the curve of my neck, dampening the front of my shirt. I'm no better for it. My face is still mottled. My breaths still come in short gasps. Now I'm panicking and wet. Perfect.

The hallway is empty save for Mr. Pugh pushing his wide dust broom down one side of the corridor. I move in the opposite direction. Away from the janitor, away from Lucy's classroom. I turn down the science wing and find the classroom at the end of the hall, my hand landing on its cool metallic doorknob before I think better of it and loosen my grip.

I glance in the window, a tall, narrow pane with black latticework disturbing the view. Even so, I find the desk I'm looking for. Truett is slumped in his seat, a camel-colored Carhartt hoodie covering his messy hair. Mr. Graves must know what's happened, because he hasn't forced Truett to put his hood down, and Mr. Graves never tolerates hoods or hats in class.

I'm considering barging in, no matter how crazy it would look, when Truett glances up. Our eyes meet. He doesn't look the least bit surprised, as though he could sense I was here before he even looked. The way I have always been able to feel him entering my orbit.

My eyes widen, and I do my best to look as desperate as I feel. After years spent masking my emotions around him, trying to cover the fact that I've loved him for as long as I can remember, it's difficult to let the mask slip. But I force it down because I need him. I need my best friend. The only person in the world who understands how I feel right now.

His jaw tenses. He sucks in his bottom lip and bites down, rolling it beneath his teeth. I glance from him to Mr. Graves's desk and back. The man is teaching chemistry with too much enthusiasm for eight o'clock in the morning. Everyone else is pretending to listen while fighting sleep. But not Truett. He studies me like I'm a problem on the board. Something to be solved—or at least endured, depending on your feelings about chemistry.

Please, *I mouth.*

He winces like he's been struck. Those gray eyes harden. I'm watching him retreat right before my eyes, and he's not even moving. Until he does, and I wish he hadn't. Because with the subtle shake of his head, he breaks my heart in two.

I don't bother going to class. One bonus of Dad's overwhelming guilt is that he let me drive his car since he didn't come to school today. I leave campus without a word. Instead of going home, I park at the river access point where Alicia and I go sometimes to swim in the summer. I give Truett one last chance. I text him my location and tell him I'll wait for him. And I do. I wait for hours, till my stomach is hollow and the sun dips low in the sky. Till Mom has filled my phone with missed calls and texts complaining about being left alone in the house with Dad, and Dad has texted to make sure I'm okay, telling me to take all the time I need.

But not a single message from Tru. That day, or any of the days that follow. Not when Emily and Katelyn corner me in the hall the next day for details. Not when my dad resigns from his position. Not when an anonymous note appears in my locker, telling me all the disgusting things the person is going to do to me in the band room if they can catch me alone and force me in there.

So I agree when Kyle shows me an ounce of niceness by inviting me to the bonfire. It's the first I've received since news of the affair broke out. And when even that turns out to be a lie, Truett doesn't say a word. But this time, neither do I.

When the movers come, I climb into the car with Mom and let myself be driven away. I don't look back. Not for nine years.

"Penny for your thoughts?"

I glance over at Truett. He's traded his cowboy hat for a faded ball cap and his normal T-shirt for a loose-fitting flannel button-down. His eyes pick up the blue in it. And even though they're sad, they're beautiful.

I try to shake the residual memory. To think of anything else, but my brow furrows. "Why don't you use that apple-scented laundry detergent anymore?"

His dimple pops as he fights to suppress a smile. "You remember what detergent I used to use?"

I snort half-heartedly. "Technically Lucy used to use it. I doubt you were doing your own laundry back then, Mama's boy."

"You're right." He shakes his head. "This mama's boy stopped using it because he prefers easy-peasy Tide pods. No measuring involved."

I roll my eyes. "There are literally lines marked in the lid to tell you the measurements."

"You're just mad because you miss the Apple Mumbo Jumbo."

"Apple Mango Tango."

"Apple Mambo Number Five?" He quirks a brow.

"You're ridiculous, you know that?"

This time he doesn't fight the smile. It spreads over his face like dawn breaking. I force myself to turn away, to face the scenic view of palm trees mixed with tall pines that line the road leading to Pensacola's airport. If I don't look at him, it'll be easier to remember why everything he said Saturday at the river shouldn't matter.

I've been slipping in and out of the memory of those miserable days following the affair since early this morning, when we left Fly Hollow to head to the airport. Mom's surgery is tomorrow, and I'm going to stay for a week while she recovers. She's hoping it turns into more, no matter how many times I assure her it's not. And true to his word, Truett showed up bright and early in his truck to shuttle me here. He and Roberta are going to trade off staying with Dad while I'm gone. The fact that I was able to pay her overtime with my quarterly bonus fills me with pride, and I focus on letting that emotion take priority. On pushing those lingering feelings of confusion over Truett even deeper into the recesses of my mind.

The drop-off lane is surprisingly empty for a Monday morning. Truett parks alongside the curb, but neither of us makes a move to get out.

He draws in a deep breath, and I force myself to look at him, praying my mask holds.

"Call me if you need anything, okay?"

I smirk. "You gonna hop on a flight to help me give Mom a bath?"

He sucks in his cheeks, then releases his lips with a pop. "Maybe just moral support then?"

"Got it."

I gather my purse and reach for the handle. The midmorning heat rushes in when I open the door. It's not so bad here, with the bay nearby to move the air around a bit. But it's still Florida, and every breath feels like I'm inhaling a bucket of water.

Truett strides around the front of the truck and places a hand on my arm, stopping me from opening the back door to retrieve my bag. "I got it," he says.

I step back, and he easily hoists my overstuffed suitcase onto the curb.

"Thanks, Tru. For this and the ride."

His lips start to form a smile, but they turn down at the corners. He studies the glistening pavement, one thumb hooked into his belt loop, and sighs. "I'd hoped we'd spend at least a portion of the drive talking about what happened at the river."

My lungs squeeze like they've taken on some of that water I'm breathing. "You didn't bring it up."

His gaze narrows on me. "Neither did you."

I gesture lamely toward the airport entrance, hoping it offers some form of explanation. But we both know I'm avoiding things. It's my MO, and he's finally copping on.

He sighs heavily, his gaze cutting past me and then back to my face. He studies me like he doesn't know what to do with me, which makes two of us.

"Just take care of yourself. I'll be here when you come back. We can talk then."

Tears sting my eyes. I blink them away, shaking my head at their presence. He's so patient with me, and that patience feels a lot like a gift I don't deserve right about now. "Be careful driving home."

He nods solemnly. When our gazes meet, that sadness from before is amplified. "Bye, Temptress."

"Bye, Tru."

Neither of us moves. We stand on the sidewalk, a foot apart, suspended in uncertainty.

It's okay to want things just for yourself.

I hear those words, spilling from Truett's lips over and over again, as I rise up on my tiptoes and press a kiss to his warm cheek.

Then I turn away, saving myself from his reaction. From the consequences of wanting what I shouldn't.

The hard plastic armrest digs into my side. I shift again, still unable to find a comfortable position to read in. The terminal waiting area is nearly full now, and a burly man takes up the armrest on my left while a toddler juts her feet beneath the one on my right. I have to sit at an angle to avoid her light-up sneakers, not that her mom has noticed. Or cared.

After an hour delay, they finally announce that we're going to begin boarding. I pull out my phone to text Mom and let her know, and it starts to vibrate in my hand. Roberta's name lights up the screen.

"Hello?"

"Delilah," her voice is thin, punctuating my name in a way she never has, "please don't panic."

I immediately panic. "What's wrong?"

"Your dad has wandered from the house."

"He *what?*" My brow knits together. I lean forward on my knees as though it'll make her words clearer. "Like he's on a walk?"

"He took your car keys from the junk drawer while I was in the bathroom. He left his cell phone behind." She blows out a breath. "We haven't found him yet, but the fire department has been called and they're out looking. I'm here in case he comes home or someone calls."

"He's *missing?*"

The burly man's gaze cuts to me. There's no sympathy in them, only annoyance that I've shouted loudly enough to penetrate his AirPods.

"Yes, but we will find him, Delilah. I just wanted to let you know right away. Truett said your flight was delayed?"

I'm already on my feet, gathering my carry-on and my purse. "Yeah, it was. I'm leaving the terminal. We hadn't boarded yet. Is he there with you? He should be back by now."

My heart pounds as I race toward the terminal exit. Passersby give me a wide berth. And who could blame them? I'm running in the wrong direction, away from all the planes. And I'm crying, I realize. Tears pool at my chin and drip onto my white peasant blouse. My leggings are slipping. My carry-on bag has a wheel that's dragging. And I have no clue how I'm going to retrieve my luggage or get home for that matter; all I know is that I have to go. I have to find my dad.

My dad is missing.

The terror slams into my chest, blowing the sob right out of me. It almost drowns out the sound of Roberta's reply. Almost.

"He's still there."

"He's here?" I repeat, unsure if I heard correctly.

"He was waiting until you took off safely."

I burst through the glass doors, and he's here all right, tires squealing as he pulls right alongside the curb and leaps from the driver's side.

"We're coming, Roberta." I say it like the wind has been knocked out of me. And then it has, because Truett sweeps me into his arms and crushes me against his chest.

"I'll call with any news," she says. Her voice sounds so far away. I feel like I'm in a tunnel. All I see is Truett's face right in front of me. Everything else is black.

Somewhere in the corner of my mind, a bitter part of me wants to tell my mom, *This is an actual emergency.*

I open my mouth to speak, but nothing comes out. Truett sees it. Sees everything about me. He scoops the bag from my grasp and tosses it into the back seat of the truck, and then he offers me his hand to guide me up. By the time I remember to reach for my seat belt, he's already there, buckling me in.

"I don't know how to get my luggage," I murmur.

"I'll call the airline once your dad is safe. Get it shipped to the house." He closes the door and rushes to the other side. Before I know it, we're out of the airport and racing past rows of tall palm trees toward the interstate. Toward my dad.

"He's missing." The words are on the other side of that tunnel. So far away. It's still only me and Truett and the dark path between us. "Dad is missing."

"We're going to find him."

"Why the fuck did I leave my keys where he could get them?" I'm gasping, but the oxygen isn't helping. The world feels even farther away, my panic looming closer. "What if he's hurt? He could've crashed again."

"Delilah, listen to me." Truett's hand retrieves mine from my lap. Our fingers weave together, and he squeezes once. Twice. Three times. I squeeze back. It's weak but it's there, and his relief is an exhale that fills the car with the scent of Big Red gum. "We are going to find him. Henry is going to be fine. He probably went to the store or the post office. Maybe even the school. We'll find him."

I bite my lip. Tears blur my vision. The interstate is a swath of gray before us. "How could I be so stupid?"

"You aren't stupid," he says through gritted teeth. Like he doesn't believe it either. And who could blame him?

I gasp, ripping my hand from his as I clamor for my phone in the mess of my belongings Truett tossed in the back.

"What are you doing?"

"I have to call my mom."

He nods. In my periphery I notice his chin wobble, and it breaks something in me. He's scared, too. He's disappointed in me, too.

She doesn't answer, and after three calls, I decide the next best thing is to let Debbie know what's going on so hopefully she can get ahold of Mom if I'm busy looking for Dad.

Where on earth would he go?

"Hello?"

"Debbie, hi, it's Delilah." I sit up like that'll help anything, and Truett lifts an eyebrow. I put her on speakerphone, mostly so I don't have to relay all of this to Truett when it's over. "I can't get ahold of Mom. Can you let her know I had to miss my flight? Dad is…" I can't bring myself to say it to her. It feels too imminent, too real. "Something happened and I have to go back home and help. I won't make it in time for the surgery."

"Delilah, baby, what surgery? What's going on?"

"For Mom's ankle."

Debbie snorts. "For her *sprained* ankle? That woman is so dramatic. She's my best friend, so I can say that. But good Lord."

Truett's hand finds mine again, and this time I'm certain it's meant to be an anchor. Because I'm cut off, adrift, and it's the only thing that keeps me from being carried away.

"What do you mean, *sprained* ankle?"

"Has she not called you since we got the X-ray results? They couldn't find a break, thank God. Just a bad sprain. She'll be all right so long as she keeps it wrapped and elevated for a bit." Debbie tuts like it's just another day in the life of knowing Kimberly Ridgefield. And I suppose it is. "Now what's going on with your daddy?"

"I have to go, Debbie." All the life goes out of me. All the fight. I sag against the seat and draw a reluctant breath. "Just tell Mom I'm not coming, would you?"

"I'll tell her," she drawls. "Hope everything works out with Henry!"

I end the call. My phone slips from my grasp, clattering into the floorboard. I make no move to pick it up.

"Delilah—" Tru starts.

"Just drive." I close my eyes. The tunnel has only gotten longer and darker. I can't even see his face anymore. If it weren't for his firm grip on my hand, I'd be lost entirely. "I want to find my dad."

Chapter Twenty-Five

Delilah

Dirt spits into the air, thrown by Truett's spinning tires. I spill from the truck before he's even put it in park. There's a bright red fire engine parked on our street, an ambulance idling behind it. The front door to the house is ajar. Roberta stands at the threshold, and for the first time since I met her, she looks disheveled. Uncertain. Her mouth is flat, her silver-streaked hair tied back in a low ponytail. When our gazes meet, her lips form a gentle smile, but it wavers at the edges, and my heart falters right along with it.

"Delilah!" She opens her arms for me, and I fall into the hollow she's created. The door catches us, holding us upright. "Everything's going to be okay. I promise. We're going to find him."

She smooths a hand through my hair, and I shiver, drawing back. She's blurry now. I can't make out the fine edge of her pointed nose. The soft lines that caress her face. I blink, but it does nothing to combat the flood of tears.

"Where all have you looked?" Truett asks.

I turn in her arms to find him stomping up the front porch steps. His truck is parked haphazardly behind the ambulance. The driver's side door still hangs open. He's looking at a fireman, who

I now realize is standing behind Roberta, observing our exchange with a piteous glance. It fills me with irrational rage. What good is his pity if he's not doing something? Why is he *here* when he should be out *there* where my dad is?

"Chief Davidson." The man, slightly older than my dad with a clean-shaven face and brown eyes, reaches out to capture Tru's hand in a firm shake. "Police are en route from Foley to help. I've got the rest of my guys out in their personal vehicles searching town." His gaze, the same shade as the dry earth at the end of winter, locks with mine. "The ambulance is here as a precaution."

Tru releases Chief Davidson's hand and places his palm gingerly against the base of my spine. It's another point of contact, alongside Roberta's arm wrapped around my shoulders, to anchor me in this world when I feel so untethered. I want to melt into it, but instead I simply meet his gaze and nod, hoping he understands how much gratitude exists in that gesture.

"Have you searched the woods around here?" Tru asks.

Davidson glances from Truett to Roberta and back, a deep rivet forming between his salt-and-pepper brows. "Well, no, sir. We haven't. Since the vehicle is missing, we can assume—"

"We can't assume anything," Truett bites out. His hand flexes against my spine. "What about the farm? Did anyone check my land?"

Davidson grimaces and Roberta's mouth pops open in surprise. She narrows her eyes at the man and bites out, "Daniel, you know better than this." She releases me, stepping back into the kitchen to retrieve her keys from her purse. "I'll go. Delilah, you stay here in case your dad comes back. It's going to stress him out having all these people in his space, so try to keep him calm and—"

"I'm not waiting here doing nothing." I glance up at Truett for reassurance, and his eyes glimmer with something I cannot name.

Pride, maybe? I grip the front of his button-down firmly. "You're going, right? I'm coming with you."

His dimple pops as his lips form a knowing smile. His gaze seems to whisper, *There she is.*

Not pride, then. Recognition. Like for once I'm exactly who he remembers me being.

"Wait here, Roberta. We're going to search the farm." He laces our fingers together. "We'll call with any news."

I ignore the buzzing refrigerator, the rumbling engines, the timid remorse in Davidson's stare. I focus on Roberta. On her steady hand brushing my shoulder as she whispers, "Be careful."

I nod. "Thank you."

"Here, son." Chief Davidson tosses a radio to Truett, which he catches in his empty hand. "In case you don't have a signal. Let us know your location, and we'll send the bus if needed. I'll search the woods out front just in case."

Tru jerks his chin in acknowledgment, and then we're off, racing back toward the truck the same way we came. Our pounding footsteps and my galloping heartbeat pulse in perfect sync. It's the only sound I can hear, even when I'm no longer running. Even when the truck roars to life and we're barreling toward Truett's property line. There's still that steady thrumming to drown out all the fear and anger and hurt. A drumbeat to focus on. A song to lose myself in.

"What if we don't find him before he gets confused? Or hurt?"

"We'll find him." Tru places his hand on the console, palm up, and I take it. His gaze finds the rearview mirror, and he shakes his head. "I can't believe Davidson didn't think to search around the house."

"I mean, he's right. Why take the car if he's not going far?"

Truett arches an eyebrow. "The same reason we're driving right now. The farm is huge."

We launch over a pothole, and I leave my seat for a second too long. When I slam back down, the breath rushes out of me. "On behalf of your suspension, *ouch.*"

He smirks, but his eyes are tight at the corners. "Keep making jokes, Temptress. It's much better than watching you suffer silently for the entire drive home and being unable to fix it."

My lips flatline. He's right. I haven't spoken much since I got off the phone with Debbie. I'd have powered off my phone if I weren't hoping for Dad to call. As it stands, Mom has already left six voicemails and a slew of texts I refuse to read. The minute we find Dad, I may sink my phone in the river. If we don't find him…well, maybe I'll go in with it.

We're climbing a winding road that branches out of the valley behind his house. Fencing lines either side of the dirt path. Besides a few stragglers dotting the hill, this part of the pasture is mostly empty of cattle. We're far from the feeders, and grass is sparser on the hillside. Instead, dense clusters of hawthorn bushes interspersed with towering oaks keep the ground mostly bare beyond the graveyard of their fallen leaves.

Graveyard. Oh God.

"Tru, are we driving toward the cemetery?"

His lips flatten and he swallows. It's answer enough.

We crest the hill and veer left. The trees part to reveal my car parked in front of a waist-high wrought-iron fence. It's intention-ally secluded, cradling its visitors in a cocoon of privacy. There's no way Roberta or the firefighters or even Tru's farmhands could've seen my white sedan tucked away up here. I know that logically. But as my gaze lands on Dad's slumped shoulders where he sits on a stone bench in the center of the small cemetery, I can't help but feel a wave of anger roll through me. It settles in the pit of my stomach, simmering.

All that panic and he was here the whole time.

Truett blows out a breath just as I draw one in, filling my

lungs to bursting. I climb from the truck on wobbling legs and stagger forward. The little iron gate is propped open. Moss should grow here in this shaded spot, but the fencing and gravestones are immaculately clean. There are only a few plots. Tru's maternal grandmother, who passed away when we were in middle school, is buried to my right. I'd forgotten this place, her funeral, but the memory of it comes flooding back. Sitting with Tru in the pasture while the sermon was delivered, holding his hand while he cried.

The man who owned this land before Truett's family had lost a son when the boy was only six in a farming accident. His headstone is massive, taking up the entire back left corner of the small cemetery. Abel Junior has a garden in front of his stone, and though the flowers are done blooming for the year, their leaves are a vibrant, healthy green. A smaller stone beside it honors his parents. There's a hummingbird feeder hung from a garden hook over Abel Sr. and Marie Johnson's grave, filled to the brim with sugar water.

They're cared for. All of them. With a tenderness that strikes me square in the chest.

I glance over my shoulder to find Truett. He's standing at the entrance with his hands tucked into his jeans. His gaze isn't trained on me or even my father, but on the stone in the center of the private cemetery.

Lucy Parker's headstone is almost as beautiful as she was. It has live edges that glimmer where sunlight filters through the canopy overhead. There's a stone slab over her body with the words from an old hymn engraved. Beneath the two dates that bracket her life, a simple *"I'll love you forever"* is carved into the face, which is embellished with roses along the borders.

"Dad?" Leaves crunch underfoot, announcing my approach. He doesn't look up. Doesn't react. I steel myself, prepared for whatever version of him I might get, as I round the bench and sit by his side. I rest my hand on his knee. "Are you okay?"

His gaze is transfixed on the headstone. A tear slips from his blue eyes, scaling his stubble-pricked skin. Shaving has been hard for him lately. Soon he'll have a full beard, because I'm too scared to take a razor to his skin.

He inhales sharply, his bottom lip quivering. "I miss her."

He's here with me. His words are slow, but they're his.

"I know you do."

I study his profile, so similar to my own. Our noses have the same soft arch. Our eyelashes are both straight as a board but long. So long they brush his cheeks when his eyes drift closed and he lets out a low whimper.

"Mom always forgot Dad was gone, toward the end." He turns to face me, eyes clear as a bright summer sky. "Sometimes I think she chose to because it hurt a lot less."

I tilt my head. That simmering anger in my gut stills as a dart punctures it, letting out the air. "Do you choose what you forget?"

A tear snags on the wrinkles at the edge of his eye. "I don't wanna forget anything."

My heart sinks low in my chest, heavy as an anvil. Or an anchor.

"You know, I loved your mom."

I force myself to swallow. To breathe through the grief. "Yeah, Dad. I know."

"But Lucy was so special."

My forehead falls against his shoulder. We both suck in air that is at once painfully thin and so, so thick. "She was."

A sound rattles his throat, caught somewhere between a hum and a groan. His hand smooths my hair. His mouth parts, then closes. I sit up, studying his face. He rolls his lips together, searching for words that don't come easily anymore.

He shakes his head, as if giving up on what he wanted to say and settling for what he can. His voice is filled with yearning when he whispers, "Lucy could hear the music."

Then his fingers begin to drum against his lap, a phantom melody only he and Lucy can hear.

I try to find Truett's eyes. To plead for rescue from this heartbreak. But he's walked away from the cemetery and now stands in the first patch of sunshine beyond reach of the trees. The radio is raised to his mouth. His gaze is pointed toward home, where I imagine Roberta sagging with relief at the news that Dad is safe. That he is fine. Something we would've known hours ago if the fire chief knew what the hell he was doing.

Something that never would've happened if I hadn't left the keys out in the first place. *Or gone off to rescue a mother who didn't need saving,* my mind whispers.

Anger returns, this time mixed with a heavy dose of shame. It burns so hot that it feels like it's going to erupt into a boil. I cycle through the emotions: relief, overwhelm, nausea, disbelief. No matter what, I keep coming back to anger. It trembles in my limbs. My face is scorched with it. I force myself to breathe deeply, evenly, but I'm losing my grip on even that. I want to scream into these silent woods. I want to shake my mother for being so selfish. I want to drown in the ocean of my responsibilities, if only to be relieved from them for a moment.

Footsteps approach behind us. Dad rises from the bench and turns, but I can't. The best I can manage is a glance backward.

"Delilah?" Truett says.

I barely see him through the haze. My vision is seared white and so hot. I press my eyes closed, desperate to escape this feeling that claws at my throat. I never lose control like this. *Never.* And I'm not about to start now.

"Henry, we were really worried about you. Chief Davidson with the local fire department is driving Roberta up here, and she's gonna take you home in Delilah's car. They might wanna check you over when you get there."

"I didn't go far," Dad mutters, confused.

"I know that." Truett looms over me now. He's so close I swallow a breath of his sunshine scent like water, desperate to wash away this burning anger. This residual fear. "You just forgot to let Roberta know where you were headed."

Dad sighs. "Did I?"

Truett claps his shoulder. "Yeah, you did. It's okay. Happens to the best of us."

I chance a peek and find my dad staring at Truett incredulously. Like he knows he's being placated. It's the same look I get when I remind him to eat something other than vanilla bean ice cream for lunch.

Tires crunch over fallen leaves, announcing their arrival. I push off of the stone bench, its grainy surface biting my palms, and sway for a moment before catching my balance. Dad is halfway to the exit by the time I circle the bench and follow in his footsteps.

A hand clamps down on my hip, stilling me midstep. "No, you don't." Tru uses his grip to turn me toward him. "Roberta's got your dad. You and I are gonna stay here for a sec."

My eyes flare. That flame in my chest burns brighter, hotter. More indignant. "No, we aren't. I'm going home with my dad."

"Delilah." His voice is low. "Just stay here. Please."

I don't know why I listen. Probably because my legs no longer feel connected to my body, or because the canopy overhead is spinning. Not because I want to. Certainly not because I have to.

I'm losing my grip, and it's agony. I want to be the one escorting my dad to Roberta's side. Closing the door behind them. Watching them till they're driving safely toward home. But instead I'm standing here, tempted to vomit or scream until my lungs give out. I want to run, but my legs won't comply.

"Delilah, talk to me. What's going through your mind right now?"

He's here. Right in front of me. I try to lock on to Tru's gray eyes, or the smattering of freckles on the strong bridge of his nose. But it's all out of reach. All lost on the other side of too many emotions I don't want to feel. My face heats. "Nothing, I—"

"You're mad. I can see it in your face. It's okay; just talk to me. You'll feel better if you talk about it."

"I'm not mad." I shake my head. My hands curl into fists. "Just…"

"Just what? Just upset? Just disappointed? No, Delilah, I don't buy that. You are mad. And you have every right to be. You don't get any awards for having superhuman patience. Let it out. Be mad. I've got you."

My gaze finally finds him. I stumble back, desperate for space. For air. For logic and reason and the safety of having things under control, but it won't come. It slips through my fingertips, slicing my palms as it goes. I'm trembling from head to toe. Suddenly everything I've forced down comes rushing up. The fear for my dad. The horror at my mother. The abandonment from Tru. The fucking *anger*.

"Okay. I'm mad, Truett. I'm fucking pissed. Is that what you want to hear?" I throw my hands up. "What good does it do? It doesn't fix anything to be angry."

He's still in the wake of my admission. His face is calm. Carefully blank. "What are you mad about?"

"Are you insane?" I scream. Birds startle and take off, abandoning the branches overhead in a flurry of wingbeats and rustling leaves. "What do you *think* I'm mad about?"

"Oh, I'm fairly certain I know what you're angry over. But you've got to face it, Delilah. You've got to give it a name. It's the only way you'll ever be free of it."

He steps closer. We're near the gate now, so I stagger through it, putting more and more space between me and Truett. Between me and Lucy's headstone. Between me and all the brokenness in my life that I'm helpless to fix.

"Let it out. Scream some more. But don't keep forcing it out of sight, thinking you can avoid it." He follows me through the gate, grabs my shoulders, and holds me steady. "You cannot outrun it. So go on. *Tell me who you're mad at.*"

It bursts like a dam in my chest. All that heartbreak, all that hurt. It roars to life inside me, swirling and stoking the anger higher and higher, until it's a fever pitch scalding my lungs. My throat. Ripping its way out of me just to get some semblance of relief.

"I'm angry at my mom!"

"Why?"

I want to say, "*Why not?*" but instead I say, "Because she lied. She lied about her surgery to make me feel bad so I'd come home." My chest caves in. I gasp for breath, refilling it just enough to press on. "I'm mad that she has fucking season passes for guilt-tripping me into doing what she wants, like it's somehow my fault that she got knocked up too young or that my dad cheated or that he's sick and I have to take care of him."

"Good." His gaze is hard on mine. He nods as his thumbs pulse against my shoulders. "What else?"

"I'm mad that neither of them could get their shit together for my sake and just be fucking happy together." My voice tapers off. Falls into the pit my admission carved out of my heart. "I'm mad that my dad is dying, so I can't even be mad at him anymore."

His eyes flutter closed, and he presses his lips together. He nods again. When his eyes open, they're unguarded and lethal in their honesty. So filled with anguish but edged in pride. "What else?"

I shake my head, biting down hard on my lip. "Isn't that enough?"

"It's more than anyone should have to endure." He swallows

hard, the column of his throat working over the same knot twisting mine. "But it's not everything. Come on, Delilah. I'm a big boy. I can take it. I won't break."

"But I might," I whisper.

He shakes his head softly. "You won't."

Tears well in my eyes and I try to look away, to let them fall where he won't see, but one of his hands releases my shoulder and cups my jaw instead. The pad of his thumb strokes my skin gently, and I come all the way undone.

"I'm mad that you were my best friend in the whole world, and you left me when I needed you most." I breathe in the scent of him. The scent of home. My stomach twists. "I'm so fucking mad at you for that. I don't understand how you could be the kind of person who did that to me, but also one who would wait in an airport parking lot for hours for my flight to take off. I'm mad that I don't know which version of you is real. The one who walks away or the one who stays."

He doesn't flinch. He holds my gaze and continues tracing my skin with his thumb. "Can't I be both? A stupid kid who made a mistake, but also the man he grew into, who would do anything to make it up to you? To take care of you?"

"You said it yourself that you thought you were taking care of me back then, too," I whisper. "But you didn't even give me a say. I would've chosen you anyway, rumors be damned."

"I know that now." He leans forward and presses his lips to my forehead. "I shouldn't have taken that choice away from you. You're right, and I'm sorry."

You're right, and I'm sorry. Such simple words. Such powerful ones. How many times would it have made all the difference for Mom to admit that to me? Rather than to double down on her lies just to be the one who wins in the end. How much would it have meant if Dad had replied to my letter all those years ago, with nothing more than that sentence?

It would've meant the world. It would've meant nine years that we'll never get back.

I tilt my head back, capturing Truett's gaze with my own. His thumb moves to my bottom lip, tugging it from the trap of my firm bite. Leaves rustle all around us, cocooning us in a world of our own. Away from the responsibilities and the fear. Away from the past and all the burdens it left us with.

"You can push me away. You can lash out. You can feel whatever you need to feel." He tips my chin up, brushes his lips featherlight against mine. "But I'm never going to walk away. I'm never going to stop taking care of you. I will prove to you every day that I am this man. That I will not abandon you again."

I surge upward, capturing the word *again* with my mouth. It tastes bittersweet like regret, but that quickly gives way to the cinnamon spice of his breath. To the warm slip of his tongue between my parted lips. I wrap my arms around his neck and pull him close to me. Our mouths move in a dance perfected by time apart, making this moment of reunion so much sweeter. He's not shy anymore, and I'm not nervous. I've screamed the anger out, and with it every ounce of reservation. And he's here, just like he said he'd be. I'm not alone anymore.

My teeth graze his bottom lip, scraping the ridges left by his constant worrying bites. He groans softly. Warm breath washes over my mouth, down my neck. Goose bumps ripple my skin. My breasts heave with each gasp, brushing the plane of his muscular chest. I've wanted him for so long—a feeling that I've always kept at arm's length. To embrace it is overwhelming and heavy. It's saccharine in its sweetness, exquisite in its pain.

His fingers weave into the hair at the base of my skull and tug softly, pulling me away from the kiss like if I get too close, he won't be able to stop. Still, I reach for him. The locks of my hair straining against my scalp only stoke the flame higher. I need him here, like this. Around me and moving inside me. Yearning pulses between my thighs and I squeeze hard, but the ache remains.

His eyes are heavy with lust, a gray so dark it could be charcoal. "I need to get you home before I lose all ability to let you go."

I blink through the haze. He's right, though I've never wanted him to be wrong more than I do at this moment.

He smiles like he's read that thought as it comes to me. "Don't worry, we've got time. Now that I've got you, I'm not letting you go that easily. But your dad needs you more right now."

Letting me go, like he's so sure that he already has me. Have I ever been so sure of anything in my life?

I'm sure of this: the panic rising rapidly in my chest. The idea of being alone in the aftermath, left to wonder if any of it was even real—it strips me bare. Leaves me shivering.

"Will you stay with me tonight?" My voice breaks on the request. "Not like, *with* me, but you know…"

His eyebrow lifts. My fingers itch to smooth the soft ripple of his forehead wrinkles. Now that I've touched him, stopping seems impossible. By the way his hands flex against my scalp, I know he feels the same.

"Yeah." His hand finds mine and squeezes. "I know. Let's go home, Delilah."

And we do. Together.

Chapter Twenty-Six

Henry

December 13th, 2003

"WHY DO you even want to go back to school? I thought music was just some hobby you finally grew out of. It's not a career, Henry." Kimberly passes another ornament to Delilah, who places it too close to the other baubles on the tree for her mother's liking. Kimberly sighs, reaches past her, and moves it to a better location. "We finally have a bit of free time now that your mom is out of the house. Do you really want to fill that with classes and homework?"

I focus on the knotted string of lights in my hands, realizing it looks a lot like how I feel. All tangled up inside. If only I could find the right loop to pull to make it all unravel in my hands. "Music has always been more than a hobby to me, and you know that."

"But you make so much more at the factory than you would teaching."

Delilah's eyebrows lift. "If you're a teacher, does that mean I don't have to ride the school bus anymore? Like Truett?"

"Yes," I say at the same time her mother says, "No."

Our gazes meet but part just as quickly. I add, "We'll talk about it when the time comes."

"*If* the time comes," Kimberly corrects.

Delilah's shoulders droop, and the corners of her mouth follow. She reminds me so acutely of my mother when she makes that face that a fist clenches around my heart and squeezes. I know Mom has more hands-on care now than we were able to provide at home, but I wish I could've had this one final Christmas with her. I would've slowed down, taken more of it in.

When Dad died, I often wished I'd known ahead of time what was coming so I could say the things I wanted to, do the things I should've. Yet even though I've watched my mother deteriorate for years, I still didn't make the most of it. I don't know if you ever can.

There will always be one more memory, one more word. What little time we get together will never be enough.

"You're finally in your career. Delilah's in school." I shrug, probably looking as lost as I feel. Our cat, Skittles—a tiny, calico sweetheart—rubs herself against my calf, and I reach down to stroke her back absent-mindedly. "I want to do this one thing that will make me happy. Surely you can understand that."

Kimberly's gaze goes flat. No longer sun-warmed fields but the dull brownish-green of fall grass. "Are you not happy now, Henry? Is this life we've built not enough for you?"

"That's not what I'm saying. I—" My gaze drops to my hands. Once calloused from guitar strings, now rough from manual labor. This life is not bad. But there is so little of the version of me I used to be in it. I tried so hard to make space for Kimberly to have that. To go to school, finish her degree. Have her career. Is it so bad to want a little of that for myself, too? I shake my head. "I want to make music. And I want to give music to other people. To kids." I smile sadly at my palms. Curl my fists closed. "That's all."

"I can learn music!" Delilah interjects, glancing quickly between her mother and me. "We can play together. Miss Lucy said she'd teach me. You wouldn't have to hear it if I was at her house, Mama!"

"No," Kimberly says, a tight-lipped grimace stretching her mouth taut. "No lessons. You can do what you want, Henry, but Delilah isn't getting dragged into that bullshit." She passes another ornament to our daughter, holding her gaze when their fingertips brush. "You're gonna make a good life for yourself, Delilah. A big life. Piano lessons with Lucy Parker aren't going to do that for you."

"Kim—"

"What?" There's a dare in her eyes. An invitation to disagree, but only if I have proof that she's wrong. And I don't. Not really, anyway.

Delilah places the shimmering red globe on a low branch, and it slips, shattering on the hardwood floor. She jolts back, startled, and brings little hands to her wide-open mouth. Skittles darts beneath the couch.

Kimberly groans. "I knew I should've just done this myself."

"You all right, sweet pea?" I sweep an arm around Delilah's waist and pull her close. Her sniffles vibrate in my ear, and I squeeze tighter. "It's okay. Accidents happen."

"Sure do," Kimberly mutters, dodging my glare as she stares at the mess on the floor.

March 4th, 2006

The days are so long when you're in them. But now, looking back, they seem unbearably short. I would take a million more long, back-breaking days over a single one like this.

The church cemetery is overflowing. Patrons from the diner, ladies Mom used to brunch with, even the nurses from her care facility show up. I asked the director at the funeral home to lead the ceremony, but Pastor Timothy still insisted on attending. He stands at the back of the crowd, head leaned close to hear something Waylon whispers. Lucy looks on, offering me a soft smile and polite wave when I catch her gaze on my cursory scan of the crowd.

Delilah sits on the lowest branch of the big live oak near the entrance to the cemetery. Truett is perched beside her. She hasn't said much since we told her Nana passed. Not to me, anyway. As the choir begins to sing a slow rendition of "I'll Fly Away," Truett slings an arm over Delilah's narrow shoulders. She sucks in a breath so big I can see it from here, and I hold the same one. I'm glad she has him. Some small part of me wishes I could climb up in a tree and observe this from afar, too. Maybe it'd hurt less that way.

As it stands, I get to be the one to stand up here and listen as everyone tells me how much they'll miss my mother, like it's anything compared to how I feel.

"So sorry for your loss," Odette Love says, reaching for Kimberly's hand, then mine. "Your mama was a good woman."

"The best," I try to say, but my throat swallows up the words. Odette smiles in understanding, like she speaks the language of grief.

"She kept us laughing till the very end," one of Mom's nurses at the memory care facility says. She places a hand on my forearm, a breathy laugh stretching her pink lips into a smile. "She was so determined not to be bathed by us that she'd hide in her bathroom and wash herself with a rag in the sink! Said she was a dignified woman, and she could take care of herself." The nurse —Lana? Lena?—shakes her head. "She was a strong woman. You ought to be proud."

I don't remember how to make this kind of small talk. How to laugh at these well-meaning jokes when inside I'm falling apart. All I want to say is that the real Loretta Ridgefield was dignified and proper, but she also loved to dance in the living room with my dad and garden with no gloves just to feel the earth between her fingers. She was so much more than the confused, scared woman her disease reduced her to, and they can't even see it. They don't even know.

"Thanks so much for coming," Kimberly offers on my behalf. The nurse smiles, dips her chin in a nod, and leaves.

"I want to go home," I whisper.

Kimberly plasters a smile on her face and takes my hand, but her eyes fire a warning shot in my direction. "You're not leaving me here with all these people."

I sigh. Of course I'm not. But that doesn't mean I don't dream of doing it every second until the line finally dwindles to our closest family. *Kimberly's* closest family.

I have none left, I realize. My grandparents are gone. My parents are gone. It's just me, Kimberly, and our little girl. The family I created.

"You might want to tell that daughter of yours to wear hose the next time she climbs a tree in a dress," Nancy, Kimberly's mom, chides. "Reminds me of Helen at that age. Such a tomboy."

"She's just having fun," I say.

"Delilah!" Kimberly yells. "Get down from there, please."

Our daughter and Truett exchange a glance. He nods, then launches off the tree branch and lands with a thud in the dirt below. I start toward Delilah, but his arms go up and she leaps. The idea, I assume, was that he'd catch her, but they both tumble to the ground in a heap of flailing limbs instead.

Giggles ring out, and it's sweeter than any music the choir sang. So at odds with our surroundings. So joyous. I stop in my tracks and listen. Let it calm some aching part of me.

"She's moving to Italy for the summer, you know," Nancy says.

Kimberly's head whips around, meeting her mother's gaze in a flash. "Who?"

"Your sister." Her father smiles and shakes his head. "She called last week with the news."

"What for?" Kimberly asks.

"Oh, some boy she met told her about an art program. It's three months long. She'll basically be in a commune, from what she says." Nancy loops an arm through her daughter's and starts toward the tree, where Lucy is dusting dirt from Truett's little suit and Delilah's baby-blue dress. *You don't dress kids in black,* Mom always said. So I didn't.

"You know how she is. Helen's always off on some new adventure," Greg muses.

"Of course she is." Heat floods Kimberly's cheeks. I reach for her hand, but she dodges it. The air around us compresses, like it's holding its breath for what comes next. "She's gallivanting around the world with zero responsibility while I'm stuck here in the middle of nowhere working as a glorified assistant rather than an actual accountant. My life consists of shuttling an eight-year-old to birthday parties and making small talk about the latest fad diet with the other boring moms who also have no life." She throws her hand, cutting the air.

Greg's gaze meets mine briefly, brow raised, then slips back to his daughter's profile. "You could always move."

"No, we can't. You think my husband is ever going to let us leave this town?" She says it like her *husband* isn't walking right beside her.

"Kimberly," Nancy whisper-shouts. She may agree with her daughter on some level, but she hates a scene. And with the heads of a few stragglers turning our way, that's exactly what this is becoming.

I can't bring myself to care. I'm so numb, all the way to my core. This has been the worst day of the worst week of the shittiest year of my life, between balancing school and Mom's declining health and Kimberly's digs. If she wants to be angry about her sister living the life she wanted, so be it. My body aches with exhaustion and residual grief. I want nothing more than to get my daughter and go home.

I double my step, putting distance between us at the same time I'm closing in on Delilah. She turns to me and smiles. "Daddy!"

I sweep her up into my arms and hold her for the first time in ages. Her legs are getting long and she's heavy enough that my back will ache in the morning, but I need this. Need her.

The one thing I did right in this life.

Waylon and the pastor are locked in conversation with the funeral director up ahead, and he glances up, measuring the distance between me and his wife. *About four feet,* I want to tell him. *But don't worry, I can smell your piss from here.*

"You okay, Henry?" Lucy says, voice as cautious as her eyes. Her delicate fingers are clasping Truett's shoulders, holding him in front of her.

"Yeah," I reply gruffly. My breath disturbs Delilah's hair, sending it off on its own wind. "Just hate funerals."

She nods. Her gaze is wide and knowing, a shimmering slate backdrop for all the words I can see brimming in her mind. But she keeps her mouth shut. After all, Kimberly and her parents are mere steps away.

"They're more fun from a tree," Delilah says sweetly. Her hands are folded together at the nape of my neck. She leans back to get a good look at me, holding tightly to her anchor point. "You think Nana minds?"

My vision glosses over. "No, sweet pea. I don't think she minds one bit."

"Sorry about your mama," Truett drawls. Tears well in his

eyes as his gaze slips from mine to Lucy's. "I don't ever wanna lose mine."

"No one does," Kimberly interjects. "Thanks for being here today, Lucy. Truett." She doesn't look at them as she says it, only me. "Let's go home, Henry?" Her voice lifts like it's a question, but her eyes say it's not.

"Right." I swallow past the lump that's been living in my throat for the past week, ever since we got the call that Mom was gone. I press my lips together. I want so badly to crumble beneath the weight of it all. But I don't. I can't. So I wet my lips and nod, turning away from Lucy and her son to follow my wife out of the cemetery, where I'll leave both my parents behind. It's the finality of it that weighs like a stone in my gut. I pat Delilah's back. "Let's go, sweet pea."

"Bye, Tru!" Delilah calls over my shoulder.

"Bye, Delilah!" a small voice replies, already muted by the space I've put between us.

August 3rd, 2009

I thought the reality of it all would hit the moment I started student teaching. Or when I walked across the stage, diploma in hand, to start this phase of my life. Maybe even when I sat for the state teaching exam.

But it's not until this moment, when I step into the classroom that will be my own, a box of recorders in hand, that it really starts to sink in.

I did it. I'm here.

I wish my parents could see this.

If Dad were alive, he'd pat me on the back and ask where he gets to put an Alabama football poster. Mom would roll her eyes, then lean in and kiss my temple, leaving behind a smudge of red lipstick. I didn't get to have many of those moments with them. Dad was gone too soon, and though Mom was so proud of me becoming a father, it's not the same as this. Being Delilah's dad is the thing I'm most proud of in the world, but becoming a music teacher? Going back to school when it would've been so much easier to keep trudging forward in the life I fell into? I wonder if this is how it felt for Kimberly.

It's the first thing I've done for myself in so long, and I want to revel in it. Soak it all in.

"Knock, knock."

I turn too fast and nearly drop the recorders as I do.

Lucy's standing in the doorway, arms intertwined in front of her body. She's in jean shorts that brush the tops of her knees and a pink T-shirt with a logo I recognize as the camp the church takes the youth group to every summer. Her golden hair is swept up in a claw clip, with a few strands falling softly around her face. She tucks one back, an amused smile playing on her lips. "Sorry, did I interrupt something?"

My mouth snaps shut. I shake my head. "No. Just thought I was the only one here other than the custodian… What was his name?"

"Woodrow Pugh. The other teachers call him Woody." Her nose wrinkles, and she snorts a laugh. "The kids call him Pee-Yew."

"Wow, kids are assholes."

She unfolds her hands to point at me. "Watch your language, sir. There could be children listening."

I make a show of glancing over both my shoulders, then level her with a flat look. "Nope, no kids. Summer is still in full swing for them."

Lucy sighs, her shoulders sagging. "Yep, for a couple more weeks anyway. I think Tru and Delilah have been down at the river every day this summer. I'm surprised they haven't shriveled up from being waterlogged."

"Don't you miss that? Summer as a kid." I walk over to the piano and set the box of recorders down beside it. "No responsibility, just playing outside and getting a tan."

"I was usually taking care of a little sibling or two," she says, laughing. I hear her footsteps on the tightly woven carpet as she follows me. "Or cleaning the church."

"Yuck." I glance over my shoulder. "I mean, no offense to your siblings."

"But offense to the church?" she deadpans.

"Well…"

She manages to hold the expression long enough to make me uneasy before bursting into laughter. "I'm just picking on you. And besides, my siblings would probably agree with you."

I take a seat at the piano bench and peer up at her. "What are they all up to now?"

"Cyndal moved out to California. Something about becoming a scriptwriter. I'm lucky to hear from her on holidays and birthdays. Always a text, never a call. Colton swore off God and everybody after he graduated and hasn't talked to any of us in years."

"Wow, I'm really sorry."

Her gaze flutters to the carpet between us, lashes brushing her cheekbones. "Can't say I blame them. Dad is nothing if not overbearing."

My eyebrows lift. She glances up.

"What?" she asks, a little wrinkle forming between her brows.

"Nothing," I say, shrugging. "I've just never heard you be critical of your dad before. Or anyone, for that matter."

"Oh, I can be critical. I just keep most of it in my head."

"What a wild place that must be to live." I smile, my gaze traveling over her face.

The creamy skin on her neck flushes crimson. Her gaze flits past me to the piano I'm sitting at, and the corner of her mouth twitches. "I'm really proud of you for doing this, you know. You have a real gift. The world deserves to witness that."

Nerves unravel in my stomach. "I don't know if I'd call Fly Hollow the world."

It's her turn to shrug. "It's our world."

I click my tongue. "Right you are."

"Whether that's a sad thing or not is still up for debate."

I groan, tipping my head back. "Now you sound like Kimberly."

Lucy doesn't reply. When I lift my head to face her again, her expression is guarded.

"Sorry, I didn't mean that the way it came out." I run a hand through my hair, then drop it onto my thigh. "Do you feel like your life here is sad?"

Her gray eyes are storm clouds, building toward an inevitable downpour. She blinks, clearing the clouds, but the memory of them is there. The smell of rain. "Not sad, really. How could it be when I have Truett?"

"I say the same thing about Delilah."

She smiles. "Delilah is one exceptional girl."

"I'd be inclined to agree."

"You know, last week she helped me bake ten dozen cookies for the church fundraiser. I didn't even ask her to; she saw me making the dough and told Tru they needed to help." Her gaze sparkles in the dull classroom light, her hands moving as she talks. "She's good for him."

I think of the way Truett brings Delilah out of her shell. Helps her live in the world I always worried would be too tough for her. "He's good for her, too."

Lucy closes the distance between us, walks around the opposite side of the bench, and sits facing the keys. It's a simple spinet piano, but it'll do for now.

"Sometimes I get so caught up in thinking about how life would have turned out, if only one little thing had gone differently. If I'd married someone else." Her gaze nearly meets mine, then darts away at the last second. "If I'd gone away to school. But then I wouldn't have Truett. And a life without him is a life I never want to see."

I'm toeing a line here. Lucy and I have been friendly over the years. We've had to be, with kids as close as ours. But I've always kept it surface level. Refused to stray too far. Looking at her, with that forlorn expression painting her face melancholy, I know exactly what question I want to ask. I also know it's not my place.

"He's a lot like my dad."

"Truett?" My brow furrows. I've never thought of the kid as anything like the pastor. He's kind and confident, a little wild but so good-hearted. Nothing like the man I know his grandfather to be.

"Not Truett. Waylon." Her gaze finally meets mine. "That's what you were going to ask. If I was happy with him, or some iteration of it."

"Iteration. Good use of your SAT vocab, English teacher."

She rolls her eyes, but when they return to mine, they're a little bit brighter. "Are you happy? With Kimberly?"

I blink. "I can't remember the last time someone asked me that."

"Well, I'm asking you now. Are you?"

There's always an undercurrent when Lucy's this close. A spark that flows beneath my skin, jolting me awake. I feel it now, pulsing. It's the kind of thing you could get addicted to, even when you know you shouldn't.

"I'm happy now"—I sweep my arms out toward the barren classroom—"with this."

She presses her lips together and nods. Settles her fingers over the keys. "Okay."

Before I can reply, she starts to play. At first I assume it's an original, but then a familiar swell reverberates through my chest and I remember a different piano, in a room with green carpet and vaulted ceilings. I remember a girl with a purity ring and a yellow sundress, and the song we played together.

I pivot on the bench and join in, rusty at first and then in perfect sync. There are so many words we'll never be able to say to each other. A lifetime of conversations missed. But in this way, we can be honest with each other. With ourselves.

We are happy. And we are sad. We want more from this life, and yet we'd never change it. All these things can be true at once. We're not bad people for it. We're just people. Just Lucy and Henry. A breath apart, but also a lifetime.

Chapter Twenty-Seven

Delilah

AWARENESS FLOODS me with the scent of freshly brewed coffee and something so masculine it makes my stomach clench. Rain splatters against nearby windows. There's an ache running the length of my cheekbone, up to the shell of my ear. I try to pull away from whatever firm, flat surface I've knocked out on, but that surface has arms that tighten when I put the tiniest bit of effort into moving.

"Back to sleep," Truett groans, his voice thick. "Too early."

This time when I yank backward, he lets me go. I prop my palms on the hard plane of his chest, arching my back to create space between us. I orient myself, blinking the blur of sleep away to find my father sitting at the table sipping his coffee. He glances up at me and smiles like it's normal that I'm sprawled over Truett Parker on our living room couch, a spot of my drool seeping through the front of his shirt. Like yesterday never happened.

For a moment I wonder if it did. But if it hadn't... How else would Truett be beneath me now?

The front door creaks open. Roberta doesn't knock anymore. Lately her absence is felt more strongly than her presence. That's how integrated she is in our family. How necessary. I don't know how I'd make it through the long days without her. How I'd have survived yesterday and calming Dad down in the aftermath, if I didn't have Roberta.

If I could go back in time and talk with the version of me who thought she could do this alone, I'd laugh in her face. *Gently.*

Roberta kicks off her rain boots on the porch and steps inside. When her gaze lands on the two of us, an easy smile spreads over her face. "Well, don't you guys look cozy."

Heat floods my cheeks, and I scramble the rest of the way upward and over, till I'm sitting at the other end of the couch next to Truett's feet. He grunts when my knee narrowly misses his groin and cracks one eye open. "Careful there; I need those."

I shoot him a glare. How did I end up asleep in Truett's arms? The last thing I remember was dragging my blanket out here at half past midnight, telling him I couldn't sleep for fear that Dad would slip away in the night unnoticed. Truett had tucked his legs in, making room for me at the opposite end of the couch, where I planned to sit vigil the entire night.

He's staring at me now through the narrow slit of his eyes. He wipes a hand over his tense jaw, and it slackens, his mouth parting into a lazy grin. "Morning, Temptress."

I elbow the soft underside of his foot and he yelps. "How'd I end up down there, huh?"

"Apparently you're not the only one who's irresistible."

"Funny," I deadpan.

Roberta empties the remainder of the coffee my dad prepared into a cup and passes it to me as I approach, righting my oversize tee where it had slipped off my shoulder. I hear Truett stretch and groan behind me. The pop of his joints fills the room with the sound of firecrackers. "Are you seriously taking the last of the coffee?" he says.

"Relax, I'm making a fresh batch," Roberta calls over her

shoulder. "I gave her that one because Henry let a few too many grounds slip through."

Truett laughs. Dad glances up sharply. "I did not!" He peers into his cup, grimacing.

I pour a bit of creamer into my coffee and wrinkle my nose. "You did."

I feel the heat of Tru before I see him. He steps up behind me and peers over my shoulder at the coffee grounds floating in my mug. One of his hands locks on my hip like it's the most natural thing in the world to touch me like this, to wake up beside me. And in some ways it is. He fits into my mix-and-match family better than I do most days. I peer down at his hand splayed over the hem of my cotton shorts and remind myself not to imagine his fingers slipping beneath that hem, dusting sensitive skin as he blazes a path to—

"…speech therapy today. Delilah, are you working?"

"Hm?" I pivot and Truett's hand slips. I miss it so acutely I can hardly take my next breath, let alone answer Roberta's question.

Truett coughs to cover a breathy chuckle. When I glance up, I find mirth dancing in his gray eyes.

Roberta glances between the two of us and smirks. "I said, Henry and I are going to speech therapy today, then to a doctor's appointment. Are you working?"

She and Truett are watching me for an answer. Dad continues to stare at his mug with a frown.

"Er, no." I step out of Truett's orbit, hoping a little space will clear my mind. Coffee splatters the sides of the sink as I dump it and rinse the mug. "I haven't told Cameron yet the surgery's off. Haven't exactly had the time." *Or the energy.* How do I explain what my mom did to my boss? Or to anyone, for that matter. I can't even explain it to myself.

"Who's having surgery?" Dad asks, finally glancing away from his coffee cup.

"Mom was. But she's not anymore."

He nods, rolling his lips. "Mom."

"Kimberly," I explain.

His gaze flits over my face, like the answer to his problem can be found there. "Do I know Kimberly?"

"Yeah, she was you—" I start.

Roberta cradles my elbow as she steps close, and my voice peters out. I'll never get used to it. How he can be with me one moment and lost the very next. I lean into Roberta, drawing strength from her calm, and blow out a breath. Let the explanation die on my tongue.

Truett busies himself with gathering his wallet from the counter, his flannel overshirt from the back of the couch. But I can tell by the way his head is tipped, his shoulders taut, that he's listening as intently as we are to see where my dad goes from here.

"Are you Kimberly?" Dad says. He's squinting at me. "What surgery are you having?

Roberta squeezes my side. "No surgery anymore, Henry. She's all better."

He fills his cheeks with air, shaking his head. "I'm glad. I had surgery once. It fucking sucked."

Truett covers his mouth with his hand. I laugh despite myself, some of the anxiety rattling loose in my chest.

"Jim did it. He's not even a surgeon!"

Roberta hands me a fresh cup of coffee, then passes another to Truett. I pour creamer in, relieved to find no grounds come floating up from the depths. "What was Jim, if not a surgeon?"

"A damn insurance salesman." Dad's eyes are wide and so, so far away. "But get this, he's not actually an insurance salesman.

He just thought he was. He was actually being filmed secretly for this TV show."

Metal clambers against granite as I drop my stirring spoon on the counter. "You sure his name wasn't Truman?"

He snaps his fingers and points at me. "You're absolutely right. Truman. What a strange guy."

I fill my mind with the memory of my dad's happy chatter the night we sat and watched *The Truman Show* till the sun rose and flooded the room with soft morning light. It takes the sting out of this moment, if only for a second.

"Strange indeed." I swallow past the knot in my throat. "Are you going to be okay going with Roberta today? I can take you, if you'd like."

"I can drive my truck," he says, glancing out the window. His brow furrows. "Where's my truck?"

I've never known my dad to have a truck. I'm still stumbling over that question when Roberta shrugs and, without missing a beat, says, "In the shop. But I'm happy to take you, if that's okay?" She shakes a few pills from his organizer into her palm and retrieves a yogurt from the fridge. "I've also got some meds for you. You weren't feeling too great last night, and these should help."

His blue eyes lighten as they land on Roberta. "You're Lucy's friend."

She nods, a sad smile playing on her lips. "I am."

"Okay," Dad says, accepting her outstretched offering.

Truett and I let out a held breath simultaneously. I try to catch Tru's gaze, but blond lashes shield his gray irises from view. He dusts an unseen particle off his jeans and clears his throat. The sound is so rough. So full of unspoken pain.

It's the simplest moments that rip your heart into pieces. This is one of those.

I sigh, trying to push the ache out on my exhale. My phone

vibrates on the counter. I don't even react. It's probably another message from my mom, and I'm not in the fucking mood. Don't know if I ever will be. "Okay. Well, if you two are going, I guess I'll need the mower, Tru. I can come get it or—hey!"

Truett reaches for my phone and flips it over, gaze scanning the screen. The corner of his mouth curves upward. "Relax, it's Alicia." He tosses it to me. "I'll mow. You go make nice with the locals. You deserve a day off. A *real* one."

"You *are* the locals, and I've made nice with you," I retort, ignoring the way his words make my heart stutter and skip. A day off. When was the last time I had a real one of those?

"Yeah, you have." His expression turns downright scandalous, and I force my gaze down to my phone to avoid meeting his.

ALICIA

Going to the News Room with Tess Monroe—
you remember her? Couple years older than us.
She just got back into town and I'm done
stripping the classroom so we thought we'd let
loose with some mimosas.

ALICIA

Anyway, that was a weird way to phrase it, but
I'm inviting you. I can pick you up in an hour, if
you're not busy?

I glance at Roberta, still too warm in the cheeks to face Truett, and lift an eyebrow. "She wants to go to brunch, but I can totally say no—"

"Go, Delilah. Have fun." She smiles softly, an expression meant only for me. "Live your life. That's why I'm here."

My teeth clamp down on the inside of my cheek. "Are you sure?"

"Yes, ma'am. And I'd commit to it before that one changes his mind and makes you mow." She points over my shoulder with the teaspoon she was using to dump sugar into her coffee.

Tru swallows the sip of coffee he'd taken and smacks his lips. "Now that you mention it, it is really fun to watch her spin in circles when she forgets how to steer."

"That has *never* happened."

"I thought those were crop circles," Roberta tuts, ignoring me.

"All right, I'm going." I fire off a reply to Alicia before I can second-guess myself. "But first I've got some laundry to fold. Need a shirt, Dad?"

He shifts in his seat. When our eyes meet, there's gratitude there, replacing the fear of uncertainty. "That'd be great."

"Good deal. And Truett." I point at him, and he splays a hand over his heart in mock surprise. I narrow my gaze. "Try to do a better crop circle, I dare you."

Amusement glimmers in his eyes. "Challenge accepted."

Tess has already commandeered a table for us when Alicia and I arrive at the News Room. Of all the mismatched furniture in the place, the one she's chosen is by far my favorite. Chrome edging, white tabletop, with bright turquoise chairs to complete the vintage feel. Tess suits her seat perfectly, like she dressed knowing it'd be waiting. Cat-eye sunglasses hold back her shoulder-length blonde hair, and she's paired a gingham-print babydoll blouse with flared jeans to complete the outfit. Her face is small, delicate in a way I've never been. She glances up as we approach, green eyes flashing with recognition when they land on me.

"Delilah! You came. What a nice surprise." She stands, encircling Alicia in a tight embrace. Then it's my turn, and though I've barely spoken two words to her in my life, she offers me a hug that's equally as familiar. "I ordered a flight of mimosas to share; then we can pick a flavor we like and order our own. Sound good?"

"Sounds great." Alicia smiles brightly. We slip into the chairs opposite Tess, who lifts the paper napkin she left on the table and sits, spreading it over her lap.

What little I know about Tess has me studying her, checking her confident exterior for cracks. She lost both parents in a car accident when she was a junior and we were freshmen. That was in the spring, and we didn't see her again until fall. Her grandparents had taken her in so she wouldn't have to change schools. When she returned, she seemed unchanged. She maintained her spot on the cheerleading squad, and when I passed her in the halls, she was smiling and laughing. I didn't understand how a grief like that could leave someone so unmarked. Now, as I stare down the possibility of losing my own parent, I wonder if pretending everything was normal was the only way for her to make it through.

The same surly teenager who took our order last time we came saunters up to our table and places a water glass in front of each of us, though his gaze lingers on Tess the entire time. "Do you know what you want to eat?"

Alicia and I exchange a glance. Tess answers for us with a cheery, "Not quite!"

He nods and scuttles away. I watch him retreat to the counter, which I can just see through the widened doorway behind me. A line of waiting customers turn to glance at our table, their expressions as confused as I feel.

"How did you get him to bring your order to your table?" Alicia asks.

Tess shrugs. "He offered."

My brow furrows. "I didn't think this was that kind of restaurant."

"It isn't, unless you're Tess, apparently." Alicia snorts. She pops a straw from its wrapper and drops it into her appointed water glass, which is already sweaty with condensation from the balmy summer morning. "How was Colorado? Do anything fun?"

"Mostly spent time with my uncle, Gary." Tess's eyes widen. "Still weird to call him that."

"Tess recently found out she has an uncle she's never heard of," Alicia explains. Her gaze flits back to Tess. "How'd you find him again?"

Tess shrugs. "One of those DNA testing kits. Apparently my grandpa knocked someone up in college and she never bothered to share the news. Gary didn't even know the man who raised him wasn't his dad."

"That's wild," I say.

"Right? What's crazy is, it felt like I'd known him forever." Her gaze softens, the corners of her mouth drooping. "He reminds me so much of my mom."

"Did he have a wife? Kids? Do you have a bunch of cousins, too?" Alicia asks.

"No, his wife had already passed, and they didn't have any kids." Something in Tess's expression shifts. "Lots of friends who he treats like his children though."

Alicia smirks. "Including the guy who was determined to woo you?"

"Yes. That guy was a menace." Tess waves her hand dismissively. "Gotta give him credit for persistence, I guess."

I snort. "He sounds like Truett."

Tess's gaze shifts to me. "Is that your boyfriend?"

The sip I'd taken catches in my throat, and I cough. "God, no."

"Truett Parker. His family had that cattle farm off Sowell Mill Road," Alicia supplies.

The waiter returns, buying me time to clean myself up. The mimosas are a myriad of colors ranging from classic orange to an unnaturally vibrant blue. He places them on the table, narrowly avoiding taking out my water glass.

"Ready yet?" he asks, eyes on Tess.

"Sure." She sighs, passes him a paper menu she must've lifted from the checkout counter, and orders with a charming smile that sends him swooning.

Now I see how we got tableside service.

Alicia and I panic-order from memory, which certainly gives her a leg up, since I've only been here once before. The cashier-turned-waiter scrawls it all down on the back of his hand, then disappears to calm the masses waiting at the counter.

"I remember Truett, I think, now that you mention it. Blond hair, dimple, painfully attractive?" Tess giggles, unaware that she's brought this entire restaurant to a standstill with her beauty.

Now *that's* what I call remarkable.

Jealousy sparks in my chest, unwarranted and irrational. I take a sip of the bright blue mimosa—artificially sweet but delicious— to bury that feeling.

Alicia shoulder-bumps me. A smirk stretches her vibrant pink lips. "How are things going with him?"

"Ooooooh." Tess braces her elbows on the table and perches her chin on folded hands. "Gimme the scoop. Is he as dreamy out of those jeans as he is in them?"

"I thought you didn't know him," I quip, stalling. Heat creeps up my neck and shoots down my spine. I shift in my seat, but there's nowhere for that feeling to go. It settles within me, a permanent fixture these days.

Tess laughs. It's bright and breathy as a summer breeze. I wish I could be like that, all carefree and unaffected. No one meeting her would ever suspect her past is so marred. Meanwhile I carry mine around on my shoulders, a heavy coat even on a sweltering day like this one. People probably note it immediately as out of place. Note *me* as out of place. And I reinforce it by isolating myself further.

"I'm terrible with names," Tess explains. "But I always remember a nice ass in Wranglers."

I scan her features, each one more perfect than the next. She's all things feminine and yet simultaneously so confident that she commands the room, even from this corner table. I couldn't compete with a woman like that on my best day, and after yesterday's events, I am certainly not at my best.

"Relax." Tess reaches across the table and smooths her forefinger over the skin between my eyebrows. "I can practically hear those gears in your head working overtime. I'm not interested, just an admirer of fine art. Promise."

"And besides," Alicia adds, returning what smells strongly like a lavender mimosa to its slot on the board with a grimace, "Truett has only ever had eyes for you, Delilah."

Tess claps excitedly, wriggling in her seat. "Oh, I love that! Soulmates!"

"I wouldn't go that far," I caution. "We're—" What are we, exactly? More than friends but less than a couple, certainly. We have so much history. But how much future is possible when mine is so unclear? So dependent on my dad's illness. And when Dad is gone? What happens when it's time for me to go home?

Where even *is* home for me anymore, if not in Fly Hollow in that little clapboard house with my father?

"…feeling things out?" Alicia offers. "Did something happen with you two?"

I start to shake my head but pause, grimacing. "We kissed."

"*What?*" Alicia shouts a little too loudly, while Tess wriggles her fingers together maniacally. The few diners sharing this room with us turn to glare, already irritated with us since we got special service. "Sorry!" Alicia whisper-shouts, shrinking into her shoulders a bit. Her gaze returns to mine and widens. "When did this happen?"

"Yesterday. My dad had wandered off and emotions were running really high, so I don't know how sincere it could possibly be."

It's a lie, one I sense the moment it passes over my lips. When I close my eyes, I can still see Truett standing in front of me, telling me he's never going to walk away. The sincerity in his tone, the heat in his gaze… He may not have truly meant never, but he certainly meant for a long while. For as long as I'm here. *Right?*

Alicia's brow furrows. "What happened with your dad?"

Tess's face has gone blank. All the light that seemed to warm her golden skin a second ago is gone, and she's pale by comparison.

I recognize her grief. I see it in the mirror all the time.

It helps a little bit, to know she's not immune. Not perfect. It makes it feel like I don't have to be either.

"He decided to go for a drive and didn't tell anyone. Took my keys and drove off while his caretaker was in the bathroom. I was in Pensacola, about to fly home for a surgery my mom lied about having, and had to race back to help find him." I blow out a long, slow breath. "Just a really bad day all around."

Tess offers an empathetic smile. Her green eyes are glistening with tears.

Alicia sighs. "Are moms meant to fuck us up? Is that their sole purpose in life?"

"My mom was great," Tess whispers. Her bottom lip quivers, and she bites down on it with shiny white teeth. "Not to brag or anything, but she really was."

Alicia reaches across the table and smooths a hand down Tess's forearm. "That's not bragging. That's how it should be."

Tess sucks in a breath through her nose and leans back in her chair, tucking her hair behind her ear with a ring-laden hand. "What's wrong with your dad, if you don't mind me asking?"

"He has dementia," I explain. "He hasn't really expressed a desire to go anywhere by himself since I've been back, so I never worried about him taking the keys. It was stupid of me."

"Not stupid," they correct simultaneously.

Our food arrives. The kid drops mine and Alicia's plates unceremoniously but offers Tess a nervous smile when placing her avocado toast on the table. She barely glances up as she thanks him. He scurries away, but not before I note the sheen of sweat coating his brow.

"You just broke that boy's heart," I say, cutting a bite out of my pancakes. They're nowhere near as good as mine, but I groan as they melt in my mouth all the same.

Tess glances up, eyes wide. "What'd I do?"

"She doesn't know the effect she has on people," Alicia explains, waving her fork. "Don't change the subject. What are you going to do?"

I nod, remembering the plan we discussed in the quiet of my dark living room while I tried to drift back to sleep. "Keep my keys hidden at all times. I'm thinking about getting a doorbell camera or something installed, too. Just so I feel better."

Alicia swallows a bite of bacon and chases it with a sip of the normal mimosa. "How long is this sustainable?"

My nose wrinkles. "What do you mean?"

"I mean, you're twenty-six. How long are you going to be able to live like this? Putting your life on hold to be a 24-7 care-taker?" Alicia asks.

Tess studies me, her eyes kind, and offers a sad smile. Alicia goes on eating like she hasn't just asked the million-dollar question.

I consider telling her I'm not putting my life on hold at all, but the thought immediately rings as untrue. Aren't I doing exactly that? Making sure someone's watching Dad when I can't. Worrying about him at night. Dealing with his outbursts like they don't chip away at who I am a little at a time. It's exhausting, and for a moment I let myself feel it so deeply my bones ache, before shoving it back into the box where I keep those kinds of feelings.

I shrug, hoping it comes off as lighthearted. "My parents put their life on hold to have me. It's the least I can do."

"Do you really think he'd want that for you?" Tess asks.

My fork clatters on the glass plate as I drop it. My heart stills, bracing for the pain that line of questioning brings.

Tess sets her fork down too, with more grace than I did. "As someone who lost her parents, I spend a lot of time thinking about what they'd want for me. What kind of life, what kinds of choices." Her gaze is distant, glossy. "Especially lately. Consider that, and be really honest with yourself. Would your dad want the same life for you that he had? Would he want you to make the same choices?"

"I—" I start, but she holds up a hand.

"No need to tell me," Tess interjects. "Just think about it, okay? Promise?"

"I promise," I say, working to breathe around the knot my throat has become. "I'll think about it."

"Good." Tess punctuates the word with a smile, her confidence shifting back into place. "Now, which mimosa do you ladies hate the most, and why is it the lavender one?"

Chapter Twenty-Eight

Delilah

TRUETT

Delilah Jean Ridgefield, we're going on a date
tonight.

ME

Who are you to middle name me, my mother?

TRUETT

Not your mother. But you can call me Daddy if
that's something you're into?

ME

That is especially gross when I'm sitting right
next to my ACTUAL father.

TRUETT

...so that's a no on Daddy. *crosses off list*

ME

What else is on the list?

TRUETT

You'll see ;) Pick you up at 6. Already paid
Roberta to stay late!

I FEEL like I'm seventeen again.

Nerves bubble in my chest. Clog up my throat. I'm hyper-analyzing myself in the mirror, checking for flaws in makeup that took me too long to make this little a difference. I scan my hazel eyes and mousy hair, trying to understand what it is Truett claims is there. But I don't. And right now I'd much rather strip the too-tight jeans and slim-fitting crop top I'm wearing off and meet him outside in cutoffs and a loose tee.

I'm highly considering it when Dad raps twice on my cracked-open door and pushes inside. He finds me at my vanity and smiles. "You look beautiful, sweet pea."

Those nerves unfurl, leaving something glimmering and soft in their wake.

"Thank you." I tilt my head, scanning him. He looks good. Vibrant. He had a music lesson earlier, and that always makes him feel better. I hate the idea of missing even a few hours with him when he's like this, so fully himself. It's getting rarer and rarer lately. Especially since the graveyard incident. "You sure you're okay hanging with Roberta tonight?"

"Absolutely! You need to go out and have some fun. Hanging with your old man all the time isn't good for you." He glances around the room. When he notices the pile of discarded clothes in the corner, he chuckles. "Is that the 'no' pile?"

"Ugh, yes." I purse my lips, eyeing the black cowl-neck tank on top of the stack that my crop top just barely edged out. "Should I have picked that black one instead?"

Dad shakes his head, still smiling at the pile of clothes. "You look perfect. And he'll have me to contend with if he says otherwise."

The idea of my sweet, loving father being someone to contend with is laughable. Especially when he loves Truett arguably more than he loves me. Even so, my chest grows impossibly tight. "I love you, Dad. You know that, right?"

His gaze flicks to mine, blue eyes now glossy. The blades of my ceiling fan dance in their reflection. "I know. And I have no clue what I did in this life to deserve it."

Tears pool along my lash line. I blink them back, clearing my view of him. It feels like we're really seeing each other for the first time in weeks. Perhaps in years. I don't want to let the moment go. Lately I see so much of him in me. And the more Mom shows her true colors, the closer I look at my feelings for Truett… It's getting hard to feel justified in blaming my dad for everything that's happened in our family. At least entirely.

And I want his forgiveness, I realize, for ever blaming him in the first place. But I don't know how to ask for it in light of everything. So I ask for what I can.

"Just don't forget it, okay?" I whisper the words, afraid they'll upset him. But it feels impossible not to say them. I'm not sure who it is I'm pleading with, if it's him or the universe itself. All I know is that this disease is so cruel. It's taking something so precious from me. From my dad. I just want him to have this one thing. The knowledge that he is loved.

Maybe it'll outlast the knowledge that I left. That I stayed away for so long.

"Never." He chokes on the word. We both know it isn't up to him. But I am my father's daughter, and I'll pretend for as long as he will.

The growl of an engine shatters the fragile moment. I tap my phone, noting the time. "He's early."

"He's excited." Dad smirks. "As he should be. He's been waiting since the two of you were kids."

"Did everyone know that except for me?"

He shrugs. "Pretty much."

I rise, grab my purse off the bed, and perch on my tiptoes to place a kiss on Dad's stubbled cheek. It strikes me that we never got this experience. I wasn't dating in high school—I was too caught up on Truett to see anyone else—and then I moved away. We're doing things over, all of us, and I'm filled with gratitude that I get this chance before it's too late.

"Love you. Don't wait up."

"Make good choices." He winks, but the way he clears his throat cuts through the playfulness. He's as sentimental as I am, and I know this moment means something to him.

"Always do."

"That you do." He chuckles as he steps to the side and sweeps his arm out, offering me the right of way. "Definitely didn't get that from me."

What did I get? I wonder. Besides a propensity for people-pleasing and an unhealthy obsession with a Parker.

That's when it hits me: I'm going on a date with Truett Parker. *How in a million years?*

"Have fun tonight! And tell that boy to be a gentleman!" Dad calls.

"Or not to be," Roberta adds in a low voice. She's standing at the kitchen counter, separating Dad's medications into his weekly pill holder. The doctor upped his dosage, and while it seems to be helping, I can't stop myself from grieving this little progression. A step closer to the end.

Roberta flattens her lips, but there's a smile written in her twinkling brown gaze.

"Heard that," Dad retorts.

Roberta nudges him with her elbow when he joins her at the counter. "I don't know what you're talking about."

He gives her a flat look, and she laughs.

"You two behave," I call over my shoulder. I slip on my dirt-smudged Keds as the door shuts behind me. I have nicer shoes since Mom sent my package, but it feels meaningful to wear the ones he got me. It feels right.

Tru's parked behind my car, leaning against the door of his truck. I pause at the top step, admiring him. The late afternoon sun glistens on his disheveled hair. It's brushing his ears and neck, long overdue for a cut. My fingertips itch to comb through it. To lace there as he settles between my legs, those gray eyes glinting with desire…

"Normally I'd never tell a woman this, but you might want to hurry up."

I startle. My skin sizzles under his scrutiny. The way he's looking at me, it's like he knows exactly where my mind was headed. Impossible. And yet I flush scarlet. "Excuse me?"

He braces one hand on the hood of his truck. Veins pop along his corded forearm, and I have to force myself not to trace their path with my gaze.

"Believe me, I could stand here and look at you all night. But unfortunately one of the cows has other plans."

"What do you mean?" I jog down the steps, aware of his gaze on my exposed midriff as I go.

"We've got a calf stuck." He meets me halfway, loops an arm around my middle, and pulls me flush against him. "Our date has been derailed by childbirth."

"I'm pretty sure my mother said something similar to my father about twenty-six years ago."

His nose brushes mine. He's so close I wish he'd close the distance and kiss me, but he doesn't. He just holds me, gaze locked on mine, and breathes a laugh over my lips. "Funny, Temptress." He gives my butt a firm pat. "It's an emergency. Calf is coming backward."

My eyes widen. The heat in my core subsides. "Why are we still standing here, then?"

"Jason's with her. Doc's on the way." He tilts his head. "And I wanted to soak up this moment with you."

I playfully slap his chest, but a blush highlights my cheeks. "Let's go, lover boy. There's a calf that needs pulling."

A wry grin stretches his lips, and his dimple pops. "That's my girl."

I've only attended one other calving in my life, and I was too young at the time for Truett's dad to let me get close. That calf was too big, his mama a petite heifer. He was gone before Waylon and his farmhands could get him free.

I cried. So did Tru, until his dad told him to stop.

I see it now, in the determined set of Truett's shoulders and the hard glint in his eyes. He's not letting this one go without a fight.

"Just be sure to give the mama some space, all right? She's in a lot of pain and a bit unpredictable." Truett squeezes my hand, offering me a tight smile. He's all business now, that flirtatious man from before forgotten.

I think I like this version even more.

We veer to the right of the barn in the valley behind the main house, where a black pickup truck is already parked. The barn is a simple structure, with pens parsed out inside using more of that steel fencing they used to construct the WeightWatchers field. I chuff at the memory, but my laughter is cut short. Truett bounds ahead toward the farthest pen in the barn, where I can see the tall redheaded farmhand working with a cow. Truett strips off his shirt as he goes. The muscles in his broad back coil and unspool with the swing of his arms, and I watch, mesmerized.

"Watch where you step or I'll be buying you another pair of shoes!" he shouts.

I glance down just in time to dodge a sizable patty and groan.

His laughter wanes quickly, replaced with the tight purse of his lips. The steel pen clangs loudly beneath his shifting weight as he hoists himself over the barrier and lands with a solid thud in the bed of hay on the other side. He sidles up to Jason, who's working to tie chains around the dew claws dangling from the cow. Turns out, Truett taking his shirt off had nothing to do with vanity. Jason's baby-blue T-shirt is covered in a mixture of fluids that will be impossible to remove. That shirt is going in the trash before the night is through.

I've hooked one leg over the pen when another voice calls from behind me, "Oh yeah, that calf's backward all right."

The shiver running down my spine nearly knocks me off-balance, but I manage to right myself on the steel fencing. I glance back, eyeing the short, wiry gentleman with a shock of white hair and a mustache so thick that a younger version of me once wondered how he breathes through it.

"Delilah Ridgefield, is that you?" He sets a bucket down at the barrier of the fence and peers up at me through narrowed eyes.

"Yes, sir," I say, though it's barely above a whisper.

"I'll bet you don't even remember me. I'm Doctor—"

"Van de Berg," I say. "I remember you."

His hooded eyes widen in surprise. He's right to think I wouldn't. After all, the last time I saw him, I was about thirteen years old. My cat, Skittles, had developed kidney failure. Dr. Van de Berg sat with me and explained everything as he put her to sleep, his faint Dutch accent making the words sound more like a fairy tale than a tragedy. It was one of the worst days of my life up to that point, and he softened that blow as best he could. Even my dad, who loved that cat arguably more than I did, sobbed in the tiny back room of the local vet's office. It's the kind of day you don't forget.

Which is why I was so shocked that Dad did, that first day when I arrived back into town.

He nods, his lips disappearing in what I assume is a smile beneath that bushy mustache. "Right, well, we'll catch up after. Got a job to do."

I salute him and he chuckles, unbothered by the apprehension pulling the air taut around us.

"Have we tried pulling with the chains yet?" He directs the question to Jason and Truett, who stand bracketing either side of the cow's hind end.

"Nope, just got them secure," Jason offers.

"Good. Don't pull till I check her out inside. A torn uterus equals a dead cow." Dr. Van de Berg unbuttons his short-sleeve Happy Tails Veterinary Clinic shirt and slips out of it, tossing it on a clear patch of ground. He climbs the fence with surprising grace for his age—I offer him a hand, which he huffs at—and drops down on the other side near my dangling legs. "Is this her first?"

"Nope," the other two reply in unison.

"Okay." The vet slips a hand in around the dangling calf hooves, closing his eyes as he feels for…well, for what, I don't know. Placement maybe? "Let's try with the chains, and say a prayer that this little one behaves."

I haven't prayed in a long time. Not since I was a little girl, trying it on for size and realizing it wasn't my thing. But I say one now, sending up a plea to anyone who will listen to let this little baby make it. I meet Truett's tense gaze, and he nods. We both need this bit of positivity in our life, this proof that the universe can sometimes be kind, too.

"You two pull while I guide the calf. All right?"

"Got it," Truett says. He passes one chain to Jason and takes the other for himself. "Tell us when."

"When," Dr. Van de Berg commands.

The two men lean back, pulling with all their might. Jason's freckled arms flex, and Truett's back ripples with the effort. Sweat beads on Truett's forehead, dampening his dirty blond hair till it's nearly brown. I can't look at Jason or the vet, or the poor cow who bellows as they pull. The puckered line where the steel fence was welded bites into my palm. I grip it harder, my hands be damned. My entire body coils tightly. They pull, pause for Dr. Van de Berg to readjust, then pull again. Over and over with very little progress.

"Can I help?"

Truett opens his mouth to answer, but it's Dr. Van de Berg who speaks first. "There's a calf puller in the back of my SUV. Big metal thing that braces on the cow's hind end. Would you grab it, please?"

"I can grab it," Tru says, releasing the chains.

"No, it's fine." I hold up a hand. "I've got this."

The corners of his eyes soften and he nods. "Watch for patties."

I kick off my shoes, letting them fall beside the vet's discarded shirt, and Truett lets out a guffaw that cuts the tension thoroughly.

While I'd never admit to Truett that I was nervous, relief courses through me when I throw open the Forerunner's back hatch and identify the only thing that could possibly be called a calf puller. It's heavy and awkwardly shaped, but I'm determined to be helpful. I hoist the thing up and race back into the barn without even pausing to close the hatch.

"Here." I pass it through a gap in the fencing to Dr. Van de Berg. I have what I'm choosing to believe is mud in between my toes and bits of hay stabbing me in the soft soles of my feet, but I scrape it off on the rough edge of the steel panel and start climbing, this time until I'm all the way over and standing a few feet back from the action.

Dr. Van de Berg braces the crescent-shaped bracket against

the cow's hindquarters, below the dangling hooves. Truett attaches the chains to the center point of what I'm realizing is basically a jack, and locks eyes with the vet.

"Go slow," Dr. Van de Berg cautions.

"Got it, Doc." Truett grabs the cranking mechanism and begins the arduous process of pulling the calf inch by inch, now with a bit of the effort taken out of it for him.

"You're doing great, girl." Jason pats the cow's dark hide. She throws her head back and bellows, letting him know just how great she thinks she's doing right about now, and he flinches. "I know. We're trying."

"Finally, making some headway!" Dr. Van de Berg smiles, his teeth flashing beneath that mustache. "Let's get this little one's rump out and things should go smoothly from there."

What was once hooves becomes knobby knees and, eventually, hindquarters. Truett quickly unhooks the jack, and the vet tosses it to the side. On instinct I surge forward and take the other chain. Tru glances down at me, surprise widening his features. Then he smiles. "Come on, Delilah. Show me what you're made of and *pull*."

We each put our whole bodies into it. The chain is slick from blood and other fluids, but I notch my hands between the loops and pull with everything I've got. Jason disappears over the fence, and then it's just the three of us, with Dr. Van de Berg coaching us through. We give it one last yank, leaning all the way back, and the calf slips out with a wet squelching sound. I lose my footing and fall, hitting the ground at the same time as the glistening black calf.

Truett drops the chain, concern lacing his features as he turns and reaches for me, scooping me off the ground. He braces me against the steel fence and smiles. "You did great."

"Is the calf alive?" I ask, biting a lip and glancing past him to the unmoving pile of limbs and midnight-colored fur on the ground.

"Get some water!" Dr. Van de Berg says.

"Already ahead of you." Jason holds a bucket up over the fence, and Truett grabs it from him.

I turn just as Truett dumps the bucket of water on the newborn's head. It lurches upward, head swinging, and sputters through its first breath.

"Congratulations, it's a boy!" Dr. Van de Berg reaches out to smack Truett's shoulder, but Tru dodges it.

"Not with that hand, you don't. I know where it's been." Truett laughs, and the older man joins in. The anxiety that filled the room is gone, replaced instead by a contagious joy. Jason and I let out breathy chuckles that turn into full-on belly laughs, and I swipe at a tear that spills down my cheek with the back of my hand.

"Well, she's clearing the afterbirth on her own. I'd say you're all good from here." Dr. Van de Berg's gaze cuts from Truett's to mine and softens. "What a pleasant surprise to see you, Delilah. I trust your parents are well?"

I press my lips tight and try to nod, but it comes out as more of a tremor. Dr. Van de Berg's shoulders droop, and he sighs heavily. "I'd heard your dad resigned from the music school. Guess I'd hoped he won the lottery or something and got to retire early, unlike the rest of us." He smiles, and it's full of kindness. Enough to steal my breath. "Tell him I wish him well, okay?"

I tilt my head and do my best to smile in return. "Will do, Doc."

The corners of his eyes crinkle and he nods. His gaze cuts over my shoulder to the redheaded farmhand behind me. "Jason, help me carry that calf puller to the car? I'm an old man, after all."

"An old man who could out-pull any of us, I'm sure," Jason quips, his tone playful. "Yeah, I'll get it, Doc."

They gather his supplies and head for the exit. The calf glances up at me with big brown eyes, his thick lashes blinking slowly. He's precious—and alive. My heart tumbles over itself at the sight of him.

"What are you gonna name him?"

Tru glances from me to the calf. "Don't typically name the bull calves, for obvious reasons."

My stomach plummets. I know how farms work. I know what happens to the steers in the feeder lot. But I look down at this baby who worked so hard to be born, and my heart can't take it. "Can we make an exception for him? Please."

I bite down on my bottom lip. I'm covered in hay and questionable liquids, and my arms are still trembling from more exertion than I've put in, in months. But all I care about is this little calf, staring up at me with his precious, dopey eyes. Not this one, I reason. This one is special.

Tru braces his hands on his hips and sighs, his shoulders caving in on the exhale. "What are we naming him?"

My eyebrows hit my hairline. "You mean it?"

He laughs, his whole body trembling with it. He's dirtier than I am, but he's never looked so attractive. "Yes, I mean it. So what's the name?"

"Well, I need time to think about it." I purse my lips. The mama cow turns in her stall and nuzzles her baby, cleaning his forehead with a swipe of her long tongue. "I've gotta make sure it's perfect."

"Understandable." His eyes are alight as they dance over me. My skin heats, and I'm suddenly aware that every effort I put into how I look has gone out the window. I shift my weight, and Truett tracks the movement, a smile quirking the side of his mouth. "In the meantime, wanna head up to the house and get cleaned up? Not that afterbirth doesn't look amazing on you, because it does."

It snaps the nerves, the agonizing, the floundering all in half. I let out a laugh so loud it startles the cow, and she glares, letting me know I've overstayed my welcome.

"Yeah. Yes." I shake my head, hoping to loosen some of the anxiety leaving me dizzy. "I would like that."

He tucks his chin and offers a hand to assist me over the fence. "After you, then."

I take his hand, and he lifts me up. "Such a gentleman."

His reply is almost lost in the thud of my bare feet on the other side of the railing, but I swear I hear it. Sense it, down to the marrow of my bones.

"I'm certainly trying to be."

Chapter Twenty-Nine

Delilah

It's the quickest shower of my life, mostly because I'm pushing every thought of Truett naked in this very spot out of my head. I refrain from inhaling the scent of his body wash. His two-in-one shampoo and conditioner. All the intimate details that make him *him*. I don't slip my fingers between my legs and let myself imagine the water pooling in the valley of his spine, running over the perfect globes of his ass, and down the thickly muscled planes of his thighs…

"Delilah?"

I spin the water dial off so quickly I'm shocked it doesn't come away in my hand. "Yeah?"

"I'm leaving a shirt and some sweatpants on my bed for you. I'll toss your clothes in with mine, try to save them while there's still time."

The scrape of rough terry cloth over my face brings me back down to earth. I scrub the threadbare towel down my throat, across my shoulders, and wring out my hair, then wrap it around my torso. "Okay. I'll be out in a sec."

"Can you pass your clothes to me?"

I glance at the puddle of discarded clothing on the bathroom floor and grimace. *Right.* I separate out my bra and panties, because there's no way in hell, and crack the door. "Here."

His gaze catches on my face, and I swear his eyes darken. Realistically, I must look like a drowned rat. But the way his throat is working? The way his breathing picks up? I feel more beautiful in this moment than I did an hour ago, sitting in front of my vanity with a full face of makeup.

My lips twitch, threatening to spread into a grin. "You gonna take them or what?"

"You know"—he swipes the bundle of clothes from my hand —"you're entirely too tempting in that outfit."

My brow lifts. "It's a towel."

"You heard me," he says, and then he retreats without another word.

I finger comb my hair as best I can and don my underwear and bra. The sweatpants he laid out for me are way too big, so I roll them a few times over my hips and hope they'll stay. There's a faded Fly Hollow Rodeo T-shirt that does fit, mostly because it's left over from his brief stint with the association back in middle school. It's not polite to pry, but I find my gaze flitting around the room, noting the framed photographs of his mother on his dark wooden dresser. There's one of us, too, with bony arms slung around equally knobby shoulders. A shit-eating grin on Truett's face and one of pure adoration on mine, glancing up at my father behind the camera.

It was the day they let me jump off the riverbank all by myself for the first time. Even when Mom was certain I'd drown, Dad said, *"Let her try."* Try I did, and the minute I hit the water, I started kicking, determined to prove I was strong enough to move myself out of the current. When I made it to Dad's arms, Lucy and Truett erupted in applause. Dad looked down at me like a negative diagnosis from an oncologist.

A miracle when you were preparing for the opposite.

I tear my eyes away, full now in a way they weren't before, and scan the rest of the room. There are a few discarded socks littering the floor, a raggedy cardboard box in the corner labeled *Misc. Cords* in Tru's messy scrawl. His bed is made, which surprises me. I wonder if his pillows smell like him, but force myself not to check.

I pad out of the master bedroom, past the hall bath, which is still coated in steam from Truett's shower, and find him standing over the stove, shimmying a frying pan. Shirtless, of course.

He's turned slightly away, so I can only see the contours of his side profile. My gaze falls down his frame like rain, catching on all the ridges and gathering in the valleys. On his rib cage, the outlined bouquet of flowers flexes and pulls with each movement.

He glances up, jaw tightening when he catches sight of me in his clothes.

I panic, aware that he's caught me staring, and blurt out the first thing that comes to mind. "Why do you still have a T-shirt from the eighth grade?"

He blinks a few times, resurfacing from whatever rabbit hole he'd fallen down in his thoughts.

"What?" I do a spin. "I think I pull off my *dumb cowboy* cosplay quite well."

When he laughs, I breathe a sigh of relief. The smile opens his face up. He's the Truett I know intimately. The happy-go-lucky boy who would laugh at any joke, no matter how shit it was.

I relax. That simmering awareness just beneath my skin eases. This version of him I can handle. It's the one who was looking like he'd happily devour me that I don't know how to navigate.

He shakes his head, clicking his tongue. "What am I gonna do with you?"

I climb onto a barstool and balance my chin on steepled fingers. "Preferably feed me." The scent of butter and whatever else is in that pan has my mouth watering, more than what the sight of him was already doing.

He turns to look at me, one eyebrow crumpling his tanned forehead. His low-swung sweats perch on the precipice of his hips, leaving the broad expanse of his chest exposed all the way to the valley beneath his navel. He looks relaxed, amused, and far too attractive for my heart to withstand.

Perhaps kissing him was a terrible mistake, because now it's all I seem to think about doing.

"Grilled cheese sound good?"

"Sounds delicious," I say, groaning.

He holds up the spatula, wagging it at me. "Don't make that noise."

I don't know what's gotten into me. Maybe it's the fact that I was just in his shower or the intimacy of this moment as a whole, but I find my spine straightening under the heat of his gaze. "And why not?"

A muscle in his jaw ticks. "You know, I had my hopes that I'd eventually get to see you moaning in my clothes, but didn't think it'd happen this quickly. Keep it up and I won't make it through dinner."

My mouth pops open. I knew I was toeing the line, but he just jumped a few miles past it.

"What?" His head tilts, eyes wide. "I told you I'd do everything I could to prove I mean it when I say I want you. And part of that is being honest with how badly I do."

I swallow thickly. "I think the grilled cheese is burning."

He reluctantly drags his gaze from mine, already moving the pan off the heat. The burner dies with a rattling click. There's another sandwich to the side already plated. He passes me that one and sets the slightly burnt one on a paper plate in front of the barstool to my right, where he sits a second later.

Suddenly the hunger has evaporated. What's left in my

stomach is a different kind of need, one that makes it difficult to focus on anything but the thrumming pulse in Truett's clean-shaven neck and the thick ridge pressed against the front of his joggers. I want to reach for him. To close the distance between us and really let myself savor this feeling.

From the corner of my eye, I watch him take a bite, and for a second nostalgia swells so thick in my throat I'm not sure I could breathe if I wanted to. I picture every decision that led us here. Every version of us we had to grow through, to become who each other needs in this moment.

I picture the boy who kissed me in a meadow, then broke my heart, neither of us realizing he'd one day be the man who mended it, too.

"Did you know you were my first kiss?"

He wipes his mouth off with a napkin and turns to look at me, brows furrowed. "Really?"

"Yeah." I scrape a fingernail over the golden crust of the sand-wich. "I guess I'd been holding out. Not that anyone from school was exactly beating down my door for the chance, but still."

There's a pause. When he finally speaks, his voice makes the same scratchy sound as the bread. "Why's that?"

"I was pretty awkward back then. Shy. Boobs didn't come in till senior year—"

"Not that." He drops the sandwich and turns completely in his chair. I glance up as he grabs the edge of my barstool and spins me to face him. Our knees bracket just like they did that day when Ollie interrupted us.

No risk of that now. The farmhands have all gone home. It's only us here, and as that knowledge washes over me, it leaves a trail of goose bumps behind.

His eyes roam my face, pausing at the swell of my bottom lip, then lifting to meet my gaze. "I hate when you talk about yourself like that, you know. And I wasn't asking about that part because I know it isn't true. You weren't awkward at all." He pauses, daring me to object. When I don't, he nods, satisfied. "I meant, why were you holding out?"

Heat begins the slow crawl up my throat. I swallow thickly. Remind myself to breathe. "I think we both know why."

His mouth twitches. It lands somewhere between a smile and a frown. "Pretend I don't. I've been confessing a lot of feelings lately, and you've been confessing none."

"That's not true!"

The look he gives me is incredulous, and I still. I've always assumed the way I felt for Truett was glaringly obvious, especially after our first kiss. Surely I wasn't that good at hiding my crush.

Was I?

Fortune favors the bold, and I could use a bit of good fortune. So I decide to tell the truth, no matter how vulnerable it makes me feel. "I was so in love with you back then." I shrug like it's nothing, when really it's everything. "I didn't notice anyone else."

He doesn't miss a beat. Doesn't even flinch. "What about now?"

I shake my head gently. "What do you mean?"

"What do you feel about me now?" His gaze is intense, searching my face for feelings I'm not yet ready to name. Not when the ground we stand on is still so unsteady.

"Tru, this is our first date," is what I manage to say.

"You're right." He clears his throat, playing off a wince. But I see it. Ache for it. "So let's do what everyone else does on first dates."

My lips flatten over the smile that threatens to form. Nervous laughter bubbles in my chest. A welcome kind of tightness, after the nerves from my confession. "Is now the right time to tell you I'm not that kind of girl?"

"Not that." He waves a hand dismissively, then winks. "Though I wouldn't be opposed."

I chuckle, lowering my gaze to his exposed abs. "Actually, neither would I."

He wasn't expecting that. A cough erupts from his lungs as he chokes on a bite of grilled cheese. I take advantage of the moment and finally tuck into my sandwich while he marinates on my words. For a beat, the only sound in the room is the hum of the refrigerator and my soft chewing. Oh, and the gears audibly turning in Truett's head.

"What *did* you mean, then?" I say once I've swallowed.

He pushes his plate aside and rests an elbow on the counter. His undivided attention falls on me, sending a shiver down my spine.

"We could ask each other questions. Get to know the things we thought were already known just because we've been friends our entire lives."

I narrow my gaze on him. "Okay, you first. Who was *your* first kiss?"

He smiles. "Also you."

My jaw slackens. "No way. You said you had kissed girls during spin the bottle."

"I lied."

My stomach flips over. I circle a small hole in the hem of the shirt he gave me with the pad of my thumb, trying to process that information. "Wow, no wonder you wanted practice for your date."

"Also lied about that." He pushes a hand through his hair, this time having the decency to at least look sheepish. "And I'm sorry, for what it's worth. I didn't know how to bridge that gap between being your friend and being more."

I try to blink away my confusion, but it's stubborn. "What else did you lie about?"

"That's it." He places a hand gently over mine and squeezes, his callouses scraping my skin. "I promise. My turn?"

"Yeah," I answer thickly. "Your turn."

"Who did you lose your virginity to?"

My eyes widen. "Oh my God, you did not just ask that! No one asks that on a first date!"

He shrugs. "I do."

"And now I understand why you're still single." I shake my head at him, but he's not letting up. He stares, unblinking, until I finally relent. "Someone from college. Not anyone you would know. Why?"

His gaze is open, and so deep I'm afraid I might drown in it.

"I always thought it'd be me."

It hits me like a blow to the chest, knocking the air from my lungs. "Honestly?" I croak, my gaze trained on his hand where it rests over mine. "I did, too."

He absorbs that with an equal amount of shock. He studies me like I'm brand-new, and I feel like I might be. We thought we knew everything about each other, but it turns out, we didn't know the half of it.

"We can pretend it's the first time." He smooths his thumb over my knuckles, then flips my hand and begins tracing the latticework of veins beneath my skin. "None of the people who came before matter, not to me. Not compared to you."

A wave of desire flows through me, settling deep in my core. I bite down on the inside of my cheek. The pain pulls me back from the brink, if only slightly. Enough to rasp, "No more pretending, Tru. Pretending's what got us here in the first place." I grimace. "Unless you lost yours to Jessica Mathias, in which case I can never forgive you."

His hand releases mine to clamp down on my thigh, and he throws his head back, laughing so loud my ears hurt in the best way. "No," he manages between quick breaths. "Definitely not the girl who caught our parents hooking up."

I bite the inside of my cheek, mulling over how to say this without sounding utterly pathetic. Turns out there's no cool way to ask for reassurance, but I forge ahead anyway. "So you've thought of me then? Like… well, like that?"

The laughter dissipates, leaving us in a quiet cocoon of awareness. I sense his proximity to me like a bloodhound. His nostrils flare when I tuck my hair behind my ear. There's so much to focus on that I can't focus on any of it. Only that there is him, and there is me, and the distance between us is too far. And yet not far enough.

The hand that was resting on my thigh slides to my hip. He watches its path like he can't really believe it's his hand on my body. "Delilah, the amount of times I've thought of you naked in my bed is downright sinful. And yet I've never been able to feel the least bit ashamed of it."

My skin heats; my stomach flips. I lick my lips to buy a little time, because I'm not sure I still have the ability to speak. Instead of words, a scoff escapes me. My absolute shock manifested.

His gaze pops up to mine in a flash. "Why is that so hard to believe?"

I glance at my hands where they rest in my lap, itching to touch him but so, so afraid to shatter the fragility of this moment. I shake my head. A half-laugh, half-cry kind of thing scratches my throat. "If I tell you, you're going to say you don't like it when I talk about myself like that. *Again.*"

"And I'd be right. Again." His free hand pinches my chin, pulling my gaze back to his. When they meet, his brow furrows. "I hate that you think so little of my favorite person in the whole world. You're a remarkable little thing, Delilah, and you can't even see it."

My pulse roars to life in my ears. The fire is everywhere,

smoldering beneath my skin. I brace myself internally, everything cinched up tight. Swallow the weight of my insecurities and whisper, "Why don't you show me, then?"

His gaze heats. The hand at my chin drops to frame my other hip, and then both slip under the waistband of my sweats. "And how would you like me to do that?" The rough pads of his thumbs scrape the crest of my hip bones while his fingers press into the soft flesh of my ass. "Tell me what you want, and I'll give it to you on a silver platter."

My spine straightens, allowing that heat to rise within me uninhibited, all the way to my head, which spins, dizzy with the headiness of it. Breathless, and without much thought for once in my life, I say, "You."

A groan rips from his throat. It's guttural. Almost threatening. Those fingers press harder into my ass, and I surge forward, bracing my hands on the warm skin of his chest. A light dusting of chest hair scrapes my palms, and then it's my turn to groan.

"I want you to say it again."

My gaze meets his from beneath my lashes. I swallow hard and say it louder this time. Confident in a way I've always wished I could be, asking for what I want. "You, Truett. I want you."

"Is that so?" I nod, and he cocks his head to the side, suddenly predatorial. "Well, you have me. I'm all yours. Have been since we were two kids who didn't know any better. And I've had a lot of time to put together a laundry list of things I dream of doing to you." He slips the waistband lower. Cool air brushes over my skin. Goose bumps prickle my flesh. I gasp when his fingertips trace their arrival down the globes of my ass until he runs into the barstool I'm seated on and practically growls. He's staring at his hands where they bracket my hips as he whispers, "It's not about me, though. I want to know what *you* would like. What would make you happy?"

Images of every fantasy, every daydream I've ever had of him flit through my mind. My pulse moves south until my clit throbs between my thighs. I wet my lips. Truett's gaze tracks that swipe of my tongue. I swear his pupils blow from that alone, turning his irises every beautiful shade of midnight.

I've never been good at asking for what I want. Truett's right. I prefer the shadows, the sidelines. The supporting role. But in the spotlight of his undivided attention? His obvious desire? For once I feel like I can put a voice to all those wants. All those fantasies.

With him, I feel safe saying, "I want your head between my legs."

He doesn't turn away. Doesn't laugh at the need painting my voice. Instead his jaw ticks and his lips quirk in a wicked smile. He pushes off his chair and kneels before me, hooks those hands in my waistband and tugs at the swell of my ass. I lift up enough to let him pull them and my underwear down, down, down until they're caught at my ankles and he frees each leg, one by one. When at last I'm sitting on this barstool wearing nothing but his old rodeo T-shirt, his rough hands grip my knees and force them apart.

His teeth scrape over his bottom lip as he gazes up at me. "Delilah, you temptress. Come here and let me taste you." Then he grabs the legs of the barstool and jerks me closer till he's exactly where I asked him to be. Hands moving to grip my thighs, head between my legs, tongue spreading me open for him to devour.

His mouth encircles my clit, and he sucks, pulling at the most sensitive part of me while I reach for anything that will keep me seated. I end up with my hands laced in his damp hair, gripping it like reins as he laps at my core. I cry out, something like, "Don't stop," but also, "Please," and even a breathless, *Fuck me, that feels so goddamn good.*"

One of his hands remains in a vise grip on my thigh, which I'm certain will leave a mark that I'll beg the universe to let me keep forever. The other releases me and slips below his chin. Then I feel his fingers press into me, hooking to stroke every nerve ending until I'm panting, my stomach clenching, certain this will be over before it's even begun.

"Wait," I breathe. "I want you inside me when I come, Tru."

He stops flicking my clit with his tongue and instead swipes one long lick over it before pausing to look up at me, fingers still moving inside me. "Oh you'll do that, too. But you're going to come on my fingers first, like the good girl you are."

My thighs are trembling, chest tight. It's a miracle I'm able to force out, "But I can't do that."

One eyebrow rises. "Do what?" He slips a third finger into me, and I cry out. With him touching me this way, I can't even catch my breath to answer him. Luckily he doesn't make me. He clicks his tongue, cool confidence painting his features, and nips my clit. "You think you can't come more than once, Temptress?"

I shake my head. I'm so close to the edge, if he so much as breathes on me, I'm a goner.

"Well, you're going to, baby. I promise that." His gaze is hard, not an ounce of doubt in those gray depths. "Forget what happened before. You're mine now. And I *always* take care of what's mine."

Then he shows me just what being his really means.

His tongue and fingers move in tandem, regaining the rhythm that had been stoking the flame in my abdomen higher and higher until I'm certain I'd come careening off this chair if it weren't for his grip on me. I buck against him. Cry out nonsense. Every nerve in my body erupts into a fireworks show, sparking and sizzling through wave after wave of delicious pleasure. My thighs are locked tight around Truett's head, but when I finally remember to look down, I'd swear the man looks like he's in heaven.

"Beautiful," he whispers, pressing a kiss against my inner thigh as his fingers slip from inside me. "Remarkable." He says it like he dares me to disagree. Another kiss, this time punctuated with a bite, just above my knee. Then he slips his fingers into his mouth and his cheeks hollow out. "Delicious."

"Amazing." That one's me. And when he looks up, the sentiment is echoed back to me in his eyes.

He stands and steps into me, wrapping my legs around him as he leans down to kiss me. I taste myself and blush crimson. Then I taste him, and that ache returns with a vengeance.

His hands brace beneath me and he lifts like I'm light as air, and for a moment I am. Breathless, completely undone. He carries me down the hall, only breaking our kiss to throw me onto that made bed of his, messing it up completely.

"You look so damn good in my bed." He stands back, admiring me, then hooks his thumbs in his sweats and drops them to the floor.

His cock swings free, thick with desire and glistening at the tip. My mouth waters. He's bigger than I imagined, and so perfect like this I could paint him. And I try to, using my gaze as the brush. I trace every curve, every hard plane. Explore the way light lives and breathes on his body.

"What are you thinking, Delilah?"

My gaze is heavy, lips languid. "That I'm tempted to ask you never to wear clothes around me again."

He laughs. "Might get weird around town."

I shrug. "Worth it."

"Such a smart mouth." He fists his cock and pumps once, twice. "It'd look even better wrapped around my cock, don't you think?"

My skin is a thousand degrees, I'm sure of it. I lose the ability to speak. Instead I nod and rise to my knees, grab the hem of my shirt, and pull it over my head. He continues stroking himself as I undo the clasp of my bra and let it fall away, leaving me as bare before him as he is before me.

On even ground. He took care of me, and now I'll take care of him. How it should be. How it always should've been for me.

"Do you want me to get down on my knees, or do you wanna fuck my throat while I lie in your bed?"

I see that question rock through him, from his shoulders squaring to the way he rolls his neck and swallows to the movement on the column of his throat. Every motion is tight, arduous. Like he's trying to keep control of himself and losing.

And I want him to lose it all. To be reckless with me. Unhinged.

Finally he points to the edge of the bed right in front of him. "Lie on your back, and hang your head over the side. I want to play with you while you choke on my cock."

"Yes, sir."

He groans, and it fills me with power. Such an unfamiliar sensation, knowing that I could bring this man to his knees with my words. With my touch. Now that I've had it, I never want to let it go.

I crawl to him slowly, drawing out the moment. His jaw is tight, and so is his grip at the base of his cock when he squeezes there in an attempt to pace himself.

I settle onto my back and tip my head over the edge, bringing his muscular thighs and rigid length into view. Then I open my mouth wide.

He nudges the head against my parted lips. Teasing. I stick my tongue out and lap at the drop of cum on the tip, and he groans. Two can play at that game.

"Spread your legs, Temptress."

I do as he says, opening myself to him. He drags the smooth head of his cock against my tongue with one hand as he spits in the other, then runs those damp fingers through my core. He circles my clit slowly. Pushes into my mouth at the same pace. There's so much of him, and I want it all. I'm tired of waiting. I reach up and grab his ass, so perfect and muscular and taut, and pull him into me. He bottoms out at the back of my throat, and I gag, opening up to him.

This time it's he who says, "*Fuck me.*"

I moan, letting him know that's exactly what I want him to do, and he gets the message.

His thrusts are slow, controlled, but his breathing is ragged. I release his ass and cup my breasts. I pinch my nipples and roll them. Pleasure makes my pussy slick, and I feel his fingers slip through it, burying in me and stroking me until I'm nothing but a shrine to this moment, to my desire for the man standing over me. He's everything I've ever wanted, and now he's filling me, touching me, surrounding me. My nerves coil tight, and I open my mouth wider, hoping he'll lose himself to the pleasure of me the way I am to him.

And lose himself he does. He fucks my throat frantically, abandoning the control he'd so carefully honed. "Delilah, you feel so fucking good. Your body... Fuck. It's incredible. *You're* incredible." He shudders. He buries himself in my throat and holds, quivering against me for a moment before withdrawing. Not just from my mouth but from me entirely, stepping back and combing a hand through his hair. He's shaking his head as I flip over, a question in my eyes. He whistles. "Didn't want to finish there, when I haven't even felt you around me yet. But fuck, I wanted to make you swallow every drop."

"I would've." I move to lounge on my back with my head on the pillows, legs drawn up so I'm on display for him. I draw a finger through my lips and spread that wetness over my clit. "I still can."

"Come here," he growls and kneels on the bed, hooks my knees, and drags me to him. He settles over me and locks his mouth with mine, our tongues moving against one another. Our chests heave, breaths intermingle. He's so close and yet not close enough.

I mewl against his lips, bucking my hips toward him. "I want you."

"The feeling's mutual." He nips my bottom lip, and then he's gone, rocking back on his heels and reaching into the top drawer of the side table, where he pulls out a foil packet. He rips it open and drops the condom onto my stomach. "Put it on me."

Heat flares in his gaze as I roll the condom over the length of him, then stroke his dick in my closed fist once, twice, before lining him up with my core. I'm nervous and turned on and so fucking ready. I swallow, gaze trained on the place where our bodies meet, and watch as he stretches out over me and rocks forward, entering me.

Truett. I'm having sex with *Truett*.

My chest swells with desire, with emotions I don't dare name. Inch by torturous inch, he fills me, until he's buried to the hilt and I'm whole for the first time in my life.

I gaze up at him, eyes wide and marveling. "It's never felt like this," I whisper.

His fingertips glance over my jaw, brush my swollen mouth. "That's because you're mine, Delilah. Always have been. Always will be. There's nobody else. Not for you and me."

My throat constricts. And then, before I can find a single word that will do my feelings justice, he retreats and slams home, emptying my thoughts with a single thrust.

My vision blurs. My back arches, reaching for him in every way that it can. I cry out as wave after wave of pain and pleasure course through me, threatening to drag me under. His hands lock around my wrists and pin them by my head. It almost hurts it's so tight. Yet I want it tighter.

"That's my girl." Thrust after thrust, my thighs spread wider for him, beckoning him in. He revels in it, taking everything I offer and more. "You're so fucking strong, Delilah. You can take it."

"Yes!" I slip one hand from his grasp, reaching blindly for him. His arms, his sides, anything I can touch. I want it all. Every inch of him. *Mine.* "That feels so good."

The only light in the room spills in from the hall, but with it, I can see everything that matters. The sweat beading on his forehead. The contours of muscle that tell the story of his body. His cock thrusting into me over and over, marking me as his. Claiming me.

"Flip over." He slips away from me and grabs my hips, guiding me into position. He gathers my hair in his fist and pulls, arching my back with the movement. "Just like that."

When he enters me again, my entire body reacts. I feel him so deeply I forget how to breathe. How to speak. I forget everything except him and the sensation of his body moving within mine, building that fire in my core till it burns so hot I'm certain I'll combust.

"Do you want to feel really good, baby?"

"Yes!" *I already do.*

"Mm, I knew you'd be so good. So willing." His hand cups my ass and he spits. I feel it land between my spread cheeks. His thumb strokes through it and then presses into my ass.

Oh. *Oh.*

I arch into the sensation, so wholly new. So fucking hot.

"Look at you," he moans. His thrusts strike my core, and as he plays with my ass with one hand, he uses the other to reach around and stroke my clit. "*You're mine.*"

At that, I *do* combust.

I buck wildly against him, feeling him everywhere. He's staked his claim on every inch of my body and I unravel for him, screaming his name over and over. He loses his pace. His thrusts are harsh. Erratic. Then he plunges into me and lets out the most guttural sound of pleasure as he collapses over me, utterly spent.

I'll be chasing this feeling forever. I already know it. One time isn't enough.

He slips from me, and I'm so empty I ache with it. I want to weep. Now that I've had him, I never want to be without him. It's a dangerous feeling. Yet I can't escape it. It's everywhere. He dropped a match in the middle of a forest, and now that fire is marking everything in its path.

I go limp against the mattress. After he discards the condom, he joins me, completing me like the answer to a question I've been asking my entire life.

I don't know how long we lay there, the only sound our mutual breathing, before he buries his face in my neck and whispers my name against my skin. When Truett says it, it doesn't feel like a sin, the way his grandfather's stories once suggested it was. It feels like a prayer for every good and holy thing. For once, suspended in this moment with him, I almost believe I could be that for him.

I tuck that thought away in my heart. Maybe there it'll be safe from reality, which always has a way of ruining the things I love most.

I turn over in his arms, taking him in, in all his disheveled glory. His hair is wild from my fingers, eyes heavy with the remnants of desire. He smiles at me. "What are you thinking about?"

Gingerly I trace the outline of his ribs, drawing a shiver from his skin. "What are these?"

He lifts his arm to get a better look. "Carnations."

The inked skin dips beneath my touch. I note each frayed petal. The ribbon that binds the stems together. "What is it for?"

His gaze finds mine, and it's suddenly so heavy, so raw that

I'm tempted to look away. "I got it because it reminds me what's most important in life."

My throat dries up. The way he's looking at me. Waiting. His muscles drawn tight with anticipation… *No. No way.* "Tru, you didn't."

His seriousness breaks into a smirk. A dare if I've ever seen one. "Didn't what?"

I almost back down, but I know what I saw in his gaze. What I felt. "You did not get a tattoo for me."

He lifts a brow. "I never said it was."

A blush blooms on my cheekbones. How stupid. How *embarrassing* of me to assume. I flop onto my back and cover my face with my hands, wishing this damned mattress would swallow me whole already.

Strong arms envelop me. Draw me in close. When I peek between my fingers, Truett's smiling down at me. He plucks one hand from my face and then the other, trapping them at my sides with a firm grasp. "I never said it wasn't either."

"But—"

My objection dies on his lips. His mouth covers mine, teasing and tasting my embarrassment. My confusion. My hope.

He retreats slightly, only enough that breath can pass between our mouths. I still feel the brush of his lips as he speaks, like his words are my own. "Like I said, the tattoo is a reminder of the most important things in my life, of which you happen to be one."

He buries his face in my neck, planting kisses like he plans to stick around and watch them bloom. I tilt my head back, giving him better access. Enough space for a garden of carnations to grow, if he wanted. Because Truett Parker got a tattoo for *me,* and I've never felt more remarkable.

The ceiling is painted with strokes of light. I glance at it, trying to find reason in the shapes. Make a world where there can never be one. "Are you really going to keep the calf?"

"Yes." He says it like there was never another choice. "Of course I am."

I smile at nothing. "Can we call him Beau Vine?"

With anyone else, that would shatter the moment. But Truett melts into the laughter just as he melts into me, body slung over mine in the midst of his rumpled blankets. We're slick with sweat and so breathless our laughter is more rasp than music, but we're happy.

At least, I know I am.

"We can call him anything you want, as long as I can make love to you again."

I nod a little too eagerly. "Deal."

When his lips find mine, I forget about our parents and all the unknowns that still surround them. I forget about first kisses and losing virginities and all the things I thought would matter so much when I was seventeen. I even forget about the fear of what's to come, if only for a moment. As his mouth slants over mine and his tongue slips between my lips, it all falls away and there's only this. It's my first time feeling a want like that—the kind that makes you feel like you'll combust if it isn't satiated.

It's the best kind of first. One that promises a *next*.

Chapter Thirty

Henry

September 5th, 2013

THE ASPHALT GLIMMERS in the late afternoon sunlight, causing me to squint against oncoming traffic. I rap my fingers on the peeling leather steering wheel, half because it's hot and resting my hands for too long leaves them scalded; half because Delilah's anxiety is making the air too thin to breathe.

"I could fry an egg on the nervous tension in here." I lick my finger and hold it up in the air. "I mean, it really is palpable."

Delilah's brow furrows. "That makes zero sense."

"Neither does you being nervous. You're going to kick ass tonight."

"You're obligated to say that because you're my father." Her shoulders sag, and her eyes search my profile like my expression might tell a different story than my words. "What if I don't kick ass, Dad? What if I suck?"

I click my tongue and offer her a shrug. "We'll sell you to a convent."

That earns a throaty groan. At least her leg has stopped bouncing.

The classic rock station that plays in the background succumbs to static. We both wince. I reach forward, spinning the dial to mute it. "I'm serious, sweet pea. You've got this. And I'll be there to cheer you on the whole time, in case you forget how amazing you are."

She smiles softly, letting her head fall against the seat. She's petite for her age, still growing into her lean limbs and delicate frame. But there's a spark in her eyes that never existed in mine, something I'm not even sure she knows she has yet. I'm grateful for its presence. For the hope it gives me that she'll be a fighter in this life rather than a mere observer.

"Why isn't Mom coming?"

Her words cut through me. My throat grows as dry as the brittle grass turning brown along the shoulder of the road. Whoever called it Alabama the Beautiful didn't stick around to see everything die off at the end of summer, long before fall sweeps in to paint the world in a palette of oranges and reds. Still, I love it.

Still, I don't know how to answer my daughter.

I roll my bottom lip between my teeth, nibbling on the truth. Or what I suppose it is. I know what Kimberly said. The noise of a crowd in the gymnasium drives her crazy. Nothing, not even her daughter's first volleyball game, is worth that suffering in her opinion. But a part of me suspects that it's something else. She's never really cared for the ancillary parts of parenting. The parent-teacher conferences, the field days, the award ceremonies. The doctor's appointments and driver's permit tests. And while I love that it's time I get to share with Delilah, I know it'd mean the world to her if her mother showed up for once.

It'd mean the world to me, too.

For years I assumed that what we lacked in a relationship before our marriage could be built during it. And damn it if I haven't tried. It seems like the more I reach, the more she retreats. I feel so helpless to fix it, both for myself and our daughter.

I sigh, swiping a hand over my face. There's a tractor holding up traffic at the one intersection in town, and I take advantage of it to turn and look at Delilah. She's growing so fast, becoming an adult before my very eyes. It's still my job to protect her, though. I want to hold on to her innocence a little bit longer, even if she doesn't.

"She gets those migraines, you know. The noise in the gym can be a bit too much for her."

Delilah's lips flatline, and her stare hardens. "I'm not stupid, Dad."

I arch a brow. "I never said you were."

"But you're acting like I am." She crosses her arms with a huff. "Why can't you just say that Mom doesn't want to spend time with you?"

"With me?" I splay a hand over my heart. My calloused thumb finds the opening of my button-down and scrapes against my skin. I grimace, telling myself it's because of the sensation rather than Delilah's words. "I don't know what you're talking about."

"Well, the alternative is that she doesn't want to spend time with me"—she pauses, lifting an eyebrow—"and that would suck. So I'm hoping it's you."

I'm momentarily stunned and a little bit out of my depth. Sure, Kimberly and I don't always get along. What couple does? But I'd hoped we were doing a bit better at keeping that under wraps. I don't know why I assumed—or at least hoped—our daughter was blind to the tension. Now I feel stripped bare and wholly unprepared, like an unqualified survivalist on that show *Naked and Afraid.*

And I *am* afraid. Afraid that Delilah will base her self-worth on her mom's and my issues. Afraid I'll fail her in this way, among so many others.

We finally roll through the intersection, silence unraveling around us like spilled thread.

"She likes to spend time with you." I pause, choosing my words carefully, then add, "And with me. She just…prefers to do it in ways that she enjoys."

"And sports isn't one of them?"

I shake my head. "Sports isn't one of them."

She quirks a brow. "Or music?"

I wince. The sun-bleached red brick of the school appears on my right, and I flick the blinker on while clearing my throat. "Or music."

Thoughts I've kept buried for so long come bubbling up, filling my head with pressure. I tell myself that's why Kimberly never wanted Delilah to take lessons. Why she'd fill the house with angry sighs whenever our daughter would play around on my keyboard while I strummed the guitar. Maybe she really didn't see how it could be a career for Delilah, or maybe she just doesn't like music as a hobby. Deep down, though, I suspect the real reason is that I love it, and therefore our daughter can't.

Is this really love? I wonder. Worrying the person you're with resents all your passions, solely because they're yours?

I shake my head, but the thought won't come loose.

I grab a spot near the front of the recently repainted lot. All the spaces are outlined in a blinding shade of white. I turn away from it, blinking back the moisture in my eyes caused by the glare. Delilah's watching me, gaze guarded. She doesn't say a word when I wipe my eyes.

"You're gonna do great today. And I'll film it all so your mom can watch it later. With the volume down, of course." I wink. The move is rusty. Forced.

She smiles, but it doesn't quite reach her eyes. That same

nervous energy from before crackles through the air, bringing my pulse up a couple notches.

It's the weirdest part about having a kid. The part that took me the longest to get used to. When they hurt, you feel like you're bleeding out. When they're happy, you're on top of the world. Right now Delilah is anxious. That makes me terrified.

I rest a hand on her jittery knee and squeeze. "What can I do to help, Delilah?"

She peeks up at me, tears welling in her eyes. "I'm just glad you're here. That's all." She turns to glance out the window, swiping a hand over her cheek where she thinks I can't see. She's a lot like me in that way. "Don't call me Delilah, okay? No matter how old I get, I'm 'sweet pea' to you. Promise?"

A fist closes around my heart and squeezes. Still I manage to force the words out. "You've got yourself a deal."

She nods. "Cool." There's a chill in the air when she opens her door, letting herself out into the September evening. Fall begins here, in the cool evening hours as the sun dips low. By late October it'll encroach on the heat of day, making the air bearable once more.

"I'll see you inside?"

I nod. "Wouldn't miss it."

She smiles. A real one this time, with shiny teeth and that lopsided tug on her lips that I love. Then she's gone, jogging toward a group of her teammates who are making their way into the largest building on the school campus where the locker rooms and gym are housed. I huff a laugh, mostly to release some of the tightness in my chest, and run a hand through my hair.

So often I feel completely out of my depth with her. Like I'm screwing everything up. But at least she knows she can count on me to show up. To cheer her on no matter what.

I pull myself from the car, simultaneously weighed down and completely hollowed out. I'm wondering how that can be when my footsteps on the pavement are interrupted by a lilting voice drifting up from behind.

"How's our girl feeling?"

I turn my head and find Lucy jogging up the sidewalk to meet me, Truett hot on her heels. There's a bouquet of flowers in his hand, bursting with color. He ducks his head when he catches me noticing them, a blush rising on his cheeks.

"Nervous," I say, eyeing the flowers. "But I'm sure those will make her feel better."

"Oh, I just…" Truett glances up at me quickly. Shrugs. "You know."

I chuckle. "Eloquently put." His normally bronzed face turns an even deeper shade of scarlet. I clap his shoulder, catching his gaze when it rises. "She'll love them."

He smiles, braces flashing. It's gone as quickly as it came, replaced with an expression of practiced disinterest. He may think he's stealthy, but I see the way he looks at my daughter lately. I can't say I'm the least bit surprised. Delilah, however, seems absolutely clueless.

Lucy sighs. "Oh, to be fifteen again."

My gaze finds hers, a smile quirking my lips, but it quickly falls flat. "What happened to your eye?"

Delicate fingers flutter to the purple bruise at her temple. She untucks her blonde hair from her ear, but it does nothing to hide the gash splitting the bruise in two.

"Newest calf was a bit squirrelly." She shrugs, breaking eye contact with me in favor of the chipped polish on her fingernail. "Caught me with a hoof. It'll heal in no time."

Truett's jaw ticks, but he doesn't say a word. Something in his slumped shoulders, his guarded gray eyes, sets me on edge. I force myself to swallow, then nudge Lucy's elbow with mine.

"Are you sure—"

"How's Delilah doing with her serve?" she interjects. Her

hands fill the pockets of her cardigan, and she strides forward, not waiting for Truett and me to follow. "I know she was nervous about getting it over the net."

"She does fine in practice; she's just afraid she'll fuck it up in front of a crowd," Tru mumbles. His mother glances back at him with a warning in her eyes, and he manages to look sheepish. "Sorry, *screw* it up."

Lucy snorts, our momentary tension forgotten. "Watch it, kiddo."

"I'm, like, fifteen, Mom. Not a kid anymore."

Now it's my turn to snort, loosening some of the uneasiness in my chest. I hook an arm around his shoulder, keeping his pace as we trail behind Lucy. "Your mom and I thought that, too, back when we were fifteen."

Lucy's steps lose their cadence, slipping into something haphazard and wandering. We catch up to her easily, and when I step into her orbit, her gaze finds mine. This time her eyes are painted with a sheen of tears that she quickly blinks away. I can't help but stare at the bruise even as her gaze begs me not to.

"Maybe you'll be better at it than we were," she whispers, then clears her throat. Shakes her head.

"Better at what?" Tru asks.

A ghost of a smile passes over her lips. I wonder if I really saw it or merely wished it were there.

"Being fifteen." She juts her chin toward the flowers. "And in love."

The noise he makes is pure teen horror. "I'm not *in love* with Delilah. Gross." He holds the flowers out to his mother. "You give her these. It was your idea anyway."

Her hands haven't fully closed around the stems before he's off, jogging toward the gym doors so he can enter on his own, with no association to the discarded bouquet.

"Do you remember those days?" Lucy muses, gaze following her son.

I hum an answer. My steps falter, then stop. She does the same, turning to me with a question tugging at her eyebrows. "Everything okay?"

I bite the inside of my cheek, only releasing it when I'm sure I can be calm. "Was it really a calf, Lucy?"

She goes completely still. It reminds me of squirrels in the middle of the road. They see your car barreling toward them, danger so clearly imminent, and yet they freeze. Unable to fight. Or run. To do anything to protect themselves.

Lucy's not like that, right? She'd fight. She'd run.

She'd ask for help.

I'm telling myself that even as she starts shaking her head, chin wobbling with the effort to press her lips together around all the things she will not say.

"Just a calf." Her head tilts. "I got in the way. My fault."

I reach for her on instinct. "Luc—"

She lifts the flowers to block my outstretched hand. "Gotta get these to Delilah. See you inside?"

She walks away, carrying her secrets with her. It takes everything in me to follow her into that gym instead of driving right back to the farm where Waylon no doubt sits in his big La-Z-Boy, sipping a beer, not an ounce of guilt in his mind over the bruise on Lucy's face that I can't help but believe he caused.

Not only does Delilah's serve make it over the net, but her team wins their very first game. Joy splits her face into a burst of pearly teeth like twin rows of stars. Truett races to the gym floor and sweeps her into his arms. For a split second her delight becomes my euphoria, and then Lucy and I look away to give our kids a moment.

On the surface, I'm the picture of normalcy. In the back of my mind, I'm reeling. Considering the possibilities.

Maybe I'm mistaken. Maybe it *was* a calf. Delilah witnessed a birth one time. She said it was a hectic affair. I have no doubt someone could get a black eye, or worse, in the middle of so much chaos.

But Truett's body language when Lucy mentioned the injury? Her own stillness when she dodged the question? I can't shake it. Can't get out of my own head long enough to even try.

Delilah joins her teammates for ice cream after the game to celebrate their victory. I ride home in silence, never bothering to search for a better station with less static. I can't even bear to roll down the window and let the night flood in and drown out my thoughts. Once I'm free of the cluster of traffic near the school, it's just me and the occasional truck passing in the oncoming lane. There are no streetlamps in Fly Hollow, so the world passes by in darkness save for the few fireflies who haven't given up on summer quite yet.

When I get home, Kimberly is curled up on the couch beneath a pile of tufted blankets, sipping wine and chatting on the phone. My foot hits the same old floorboard she's always begging me to fix, and she glances up sharply. I don't know what she sees on my face, but she mutters, "I've gotta go, Mom," and hangs up the phone. "How was the game?"

I can't find it in me to so much as grunt in response. Instead I pluck at the buttons of my shirt, exposing my chest and then my abdomen and finally letting it fall from my shoulders on the way to the bathroom. I open the door, flick on the light, and toss the shirt into the corner.

"Excuse me?" Kimberly calls out. "I asked you a question. What's wrong with you?"

I hear but can't see her wineglass land on the side table, then her soft footsteps pad across the hardwood until she's standing outside the bathroom door. She doesn't so much as glance downward when I drop my jeans and underwear to the ground.

Her arms cross over her chest. "You storm in here like something bit you and don't even say hello?"

The water squeals through the old pipes. When it finally rushes from the faucet, I pull the knob to enable the shower. Kimberly stands in the doorway, looking unimpressed.

I sigh, my shoulders sagging. My thoughts are all over the place. None of them make any sense. And somehow, despite her being the one person I should, no part of me wants to confide in Kimberly.

"Did Delilah lose?" She shrugs, looking unsurprised. "I told you, she—"

"She did great. Their team won." I peel the curtain back and step into the flow of water. When the curtain is closed, cutting me off from Kimberly, I relax for the first time since I saw Lucy's face. The bruise.

"Then what's the problem?"

I push my hand through my hair, dampening it to the roots. My scalp screams when I pull, but the pain is a distraction. A welcome diversion from the truths I'm trying so desperately to believe are fabrications.

Waylon might have hurt Lucy. Kimberly probably can't stand me. I'm deeply unhappy in my marriage.

Only one of these things can be said aloud. So I say it, just to let some of the pressure out of my chest.

"I think Waylon hit Lucy."

Silence. Then the door shuts, and for a moment I think she's walked away. The faint whisper of clothing falling to the floor restarts my heart, though, and then the curtain is pulled back, revealing a naked Kimberly.

She steps into the shower and pushes me backward, clearing a space for herself beneath the warm spray of water. I stand there, shivering from the cold or anger one, as she tips her head back to dampen her hair.

It's been a long time since Kimberly and I showered together. I let my gaze rove the soft swells and sweeping valleys of her body. She's beautiful. Always has been. There is no lack of want in my body for her, as evidenced by my swelling dick. It's her that never wants to be intimate. Either because she's tired from work or too full or simply not interested. I can't remember the last time we slept together, and for a moment it's all I can think about.

"What makes you think he hit her?" She doesn't open her eyes as she speaks. The column of her throat works when she swallows stray droplets that fell into her parted lips. I look away, willing myself to focus, even as that dormant need surges to the forefront of my mind.

"She has a bruise on her face, right beside her eye." I brush my fingertips over Kimberly's temple, right where Lucy's skin was mottled and swollen. "She said it was from a calf, but I just don't know. Everything about her body language was off."

Kimberly's eyes flash open, and she finally lifts her head, letting our gazes meet. "Why were you even with her?"

My brow furrows. "That's what you're concerned about? From that whole statement, the one thing you wanna ask me about is why I was with our friend to see the *giant bruise on her face.*" I wipe my face with a damp palm, trying to maintain my calm. "She brought Truett to the game to support our daughter, for Christ's sake."

She snakes her arms around my waist, pulling me close. Her breasts press into my rib cage. My dick is tucked against her soft stomach. I swallow hard and look away from her heated gaze.

Her finger plucks the cord of my exposed collarbone. "She's not our friend. Her son is Delilah's friend. *She* is our neighbor."

She shrugs, and it shifts her breasts over my skin. I fight against the warring voices in my brain. One that wants so badly to take what his wife is offering, the other who knows she's only doing so out of misplaced jealousy. Or something worse, like an actual disdain for Lucy's well-being. "Since when are you so attuned to Lucy Parker's body language that you would know if she's lying? If she said it was a calf, it was a calf."

Jealousy it is, then.

"I just have this feeling." I shake my head. "I can't explain it."

"How come you never have these kinds of feelings about me?"

Now I'm frustrated *and* confused. "What are you talking about?"

She steps into me, and I move backward. We repeat this until my back is flush against the cold porcelain tile, and her body is aligned with mine. "You're never this concerned about me. Never give a shit that I'm upset or I'm unhappy or I'm stuck in this miserably redundant life, but you're all up in arms over Lucy Parker's imagined abusive husband." Her hips retreat from mine, and her hand closes around my dick, squeezing one long stroke as she locks eyes with me. "If you care so much, why don't you fuck her then?"

The fight leaves me. I slump against the tile, muscles screaming at the cold seeping into them, and shake my head. Her eyes are dark and turbulent, like the river after a heavy rain. I thread one hand into her hair and hold her there, gentle in every way that her touch is not.

"Miserably redundant life, huh? Is that all we are to you?"

She doesn't flinch. Doesn't react. The fire goes on burning beneath her skin even as it dies out in mine. I go limp in her closed fist, and she drops me like I've insulted her.

I press on, finding my voice for once after so many years of letting her speak to me like this. I can't stand it. Can't stand the idea that on the other side of the pasture, Lucy is taking the same treatment from Waylon. Telling herself that because she chose him, she deserves what she gets.

It's what I've been telling myself for too long.

"You say these things to me like there will be no consequences, Kimberly. You tear me down. You tear our *daughter* down." I place my hands lightly on her shoulders and push her back, giving myself space to breathe. "How long am I supposed to take that until I break? How long do you expect me to pay penance to you for what happened when we were kids? For upending *both* of our lives, mind you. You're not the only one who had to give up everything. Who lost something. But we gained our daughter, and while that has always been worth it to me, you've made it more than clear that it's not to you."

Her eyes widen and her jaw clenches. "How dare you—"

"Do you think she doesn't notice?" I keep my gaze level with hers, even when she tries to look anywhere but at me. "How do you think she felt tonight, when she looked up and her mom wasn't there to see her finally serve the ball over the net? When her team won and she saw all their moms cheering them on, but hers was nowhere to be seen? All because you couldn't stand a little *noise.*"

Her lips part and then close. The vein in her forehead pulses. Her cheeks are hollow, jaw working, as she decides which bullet to fire my way.

I'm surprised, I'll admit, when it comes out as a whisper.

"If it wasn't for Delilah, do you honestly think we'd be married?" Her eyes dart between mine as she sucks in a tight breath and squares her shoulders. "Do you think in a million years we'd have chosen one another if we hadn't been forced to do so?"

I blink. My stomach knots itself, sending acid stinging up my throat. She doesn't waver even as I do. Doesn't back down when all I want to do is cower from a truth so obvious, so heartbreaking that I've never allowed myself to think it, let alone say it aloud.

"I didn't think so." She cuts off the water, not bothering to ask if I'm done. She is, and that's all that matters. She rips open the curtain, snatches her towel from the rack, and covers her body quickly like this is a locker room and I'm a stranger rather than her husband. When she turns to look at me, a droplet of water spills over her cheek. I could almost convince myself it was a tear if I couldn't see its track all the way from her hairline glistening in the dull bathroom light.

"Delilah is the reason we're together. And I'll stay with you as long as she's here. But when she's not? When she goes off to college to start her life?" She jams a finger into her breastbone, right where her heart should be. "I get to start mine, too. Do you understand?"

I expect the heartbreak, and it does come. Fear and sickness turn over in my gut. Anxiety, too. An overwhelming sense of failure. It all crests over me like waves, crashing and building and crashing again.

What I don't expect is the buoy of relief, floating on the surface when the tide slows. It's out in the distance, too far to swim to right now, but I see it. I cling to the knowledge that it's there.

My nod is a jittery, broken thing. "I understand completely."

Surprisingly, the words are clear, even when nothing else is.

Chapter Thirty-One

Delilah

WORKING from my dad's office was meant to be an improvement. More desk space for my extra monitor. A large picture window allowing buttery sunlight to filter in and brighten my days. Yet lately I find myself zoning out from the task at hand, letting my gaze wander the spines on the far wall of bookshelves or study the way the light glistens on the brass surface of some of his instruments. They're beginning to gather dust, aside from the guitar and keyboard, which he still uses often enough. It's the sight of that thin layer dulling their glow that squeezes my heart.

I want to be a good employee. And I do try my best. But some days real life gets to be so overwhelming that the idea of logging into a meeting and dragging a group of strangers through a tutorial they'll forget the details of in mere hours gets to be a bit much. It all feels so meaningless. Why waste my breath on some corporate bullshit when what I really want to say is: *My father is suffering from dementia, and even the good days aren't easy because I spend them dreading the bad days to come.*

Or, *My mother might actually be a horrible person, and yet I love her, so what does that make me?*

And finally, *The last man in the world I should want is the only one I do. And I'm still grappling with the fact that he wants me, too.*

But I can't say any of that. Instead I have to repeat, "Click the X in the *right* corner. No, your other right," ad nauseam until my voice cracks from overuse.

Emails are stacking up in my work inbox, but I find myself staring at my phone where it rests on the smooth, dark oak of Dad's desk instead. There's an automated message from the office for Dad's speech therapist, letting me know she's sick and needs to reschedule. A text from Truett asking what Dad and I would like for lunch from the Grille. And finally, the latest in a long thread of unread messages from my mother.

Why should I read them when I know what they'll say? Line after line telling me I have no right to be upset. That it wasn't even that big of a deal. That she wouldn't have had to lie if I loved her as much as I love Dad, so really it's my fault that it all happened in the first place.

Months ago I might have believed her. Those words would have torn me up inside until I lay at her feet, eviscerated by guilt and begging for forgiveness. Now all I feel is the exhaustion filling my head. Seeping into my bones.

At what point do you stop hoping your parents will change and finally start to accept them for who they are? People who are equally as damaged as you, and doubly as set in their ways.

At what point are you justified in saying that their love isn't worth having if you must cut yourself open and bleed in order to keep it?

I lock my phone and push back from the desk. My joints crackle as I rise and stretch my arms toward the ceiling with a groan. I yank open the bottom drawer of Dad's filing cabinet, where he used to house cleaning materials for the instruments. Spare bottles of valve oil rattle in protest as I search the contents. I retrieve a microfiber cloth from a stack at the back and a half-empty can of cleaner, then use it to dampen the cloth in my hand.

It doesn't take long to wipe down Dad's trumpet and return it to its case, which is worn at the edges and rusted at the clasp. I dust off the other leather cases and his music stand for good measure, then drop the cleaner back into its drawer. When I turn toward the door, prepared to discard the rag in the laundry room down the hall, my gaze catches on the box of items Alicia gathered from his office at the school. He still hasn't gone through them, or at least, hasn't bothered to put them away.

Guilt spears me. *I should've offered to do it for him.* I press my thumbs against my temples. The lemon scent of cleaner lingers on my skin, burning my nose and making my eyes water. I blink, trying to clear it. Sometimes it's so hard to remember that the person I once needed help from now needs it from me. Even in these small, seemingly insignificant ways. It tangles the map I'd drawn from my parents to me, and leaves us with something far less direct. With no beginning and no end. Just a never-ending loop of give-and-take until, one by one, we disappear altogether.

There are a few trophies in the box, no bigger than the palm of my hand, for superlatives given out by his fellow teachers at the end-of-year staff parties that Dad always volunteered to DJ. I flip one over. On the base they've engraved the words *Most Likely to Bail You Out of Jail*. Laughter bubbles in my throat, effervescent. Another reads *Band Teacher of the Year*. It's Dad's favorite. I remember it being displayed proudly on his desk, the first thing you'd see when you walked into his office. Never mind that he was the only band teacher in the school. The sentiment still meant the world to him.

How badly he must have felt about what he'd done, to have left it behind.

Looking back, it's so easy to see how he was a different person at school than at home. Completely in his element.

Outgoing and playful in all the best ways. Other students used to tell me how much they wished he was their dad, and my chest would swell with pride. But at home? He made himself so small. We both did. We cut our edges into the exact pattern of Mom's roughest ones, just to make it all fit a little better. Keep the peace a little longer.

I blow out a long, weary sigh. I take the trophies to his bookshelf and add them to the few already there. Maybe it'll make him smile to see them again. It doesn't begin to make up for all the years he spent compartmentalizing those parts of himself, but it's something.

In the bottom of the box are binders of music sheets with my dad's signature scrawl coating the pages. I turn them over, smiling at each enthusiastic reminder to pause a little longer, draw a note out beyond the cliff of its stanza.

Savor it, he'd always tell me. *Hold the music on your tongue and really let yourself taste it.*

I set those binders in one of the drawers of his filing cabinet. When I glance back at the box, amid a few framed photos and loose cards from students through the years, I notice a cluster of papers wrapped in a rubber band. Some are torn at the edges, others folded into squares. Dark pen marks bleed through the thinner sheets. I can just make out my dad's handwriting on the top one.

I grab the stack and take it over to the desk. The age-weakened rubber band snaps when I go to remove it. The top paper is thin and soft to the touch. When I unfold it, a back-and-forth exchange fills the page, starting with my dad's chicken scratch and followed by a loopy cursive that feels two degrees shy of familiar, like I've seen something close before but not quite the real thing.

To my co-composer,

So, what did you think? I'm on the edge of my seat waiting to hear how much you loved the man, the myth, the legend. PHIL COLLINS!!!

-Mozart (this will never not be weird to write)

To the next Mozart (just accept it),

Ok. You were right. I listened to the CD you made and Phil Collins is totally incredible. Against All Odds was my favorite, as you predicted. Are you psychic?

Love, your co-composer

To my co-composer,

If I were, I'd have seen that pop quiz coming in English. So much for going out this weekend with the guys. I'll be grounded once Dad sees that grade.

-Mozart

To the next Mozart,

Let me know if you ever need a tutor. I'm more than just a pretty face, despite what my father seems to think.

Love, your co-composer

. . .

Beneath that note, my dad's handwriting starts and then stops a few times. A dark line has been scratched through all the random letter combinations that never made it into words. What remains is a simple thank you to Co-Composer, followed by a scribbled smiley face.

A knock on the door shatters the silence cocooning me, and I jump, sucking in a breath through my teeth. "Yeah?"

The door cracks open, and Truett peers inside. As soon as I see him, that tightness in my chest melts away.

"I brought lunch." He grins. "You didn't answer, so I got you a shrimp sandwich. Hope that's okay?"

"You didn't have to get me anything."

My stomach growls in disagreement. I clamp a hand over it. He steps into the room, chuckling, and slides an arm around my waist. His nose dips into the space where my neck slopes into my shoulder, and he inhales deeply.

"I didn't have to. I wanted to." His lips brush against my skin, which breaks out in goose bumps. "Whatcha looking at?"

I hold out the note for him to read. It only takes seconds before he's letting out a breathy laugh, something like nostalgia softening his features.

"What?" I ask.

"That's my mom's handwriting."

I glance at the page again. That nagging sense of familiarity suddenly clicks into place, and I see it so clearly, our parents as they must've been twenty-something years ago, scrawling notes to each other on torn notebook paper.

He reaches for the stack and removes another page, filled with more of the same. "Where did you get these?"

I point to the box on the ground. "It was in the stuff from the school."

"Were they passing notes at work?"

"No." I shake my head, glancing back at the note in my hand. "He talks about his dad being mad about his grades. They were kids."

Truett laughs, a warm smile illuminating his face. "That's cute."

"Cute? I didn't even know they knew each other back then."

His smile falters. Gray eyes widen, opening up so I can see them clearly. "You still haven't talked to your dad, have you?"

"No, I—" I catch my bottom lip with my teeth and roll it. "I guess I've been scared."

"Scared of what?"

I shrug, letting my hand fall to my side, note still clasped tight. "Scared I'll upset him. Or myself." My gaze roves his face, taking in the sun-darkened freckles on his nose and the split in his lip where he bit it too hard. What's new, and what's always been there. Though it all feels familiar just the same. "For years I told myself it was this one-time ordeal. But what if it's worse? What if everything I believe about my life is a lie?"

"You believed me wanting you was a lie." He smirks, but it's soft at the edges. "Look how much better the truth turned out to be."

My responding laugh is harsh. Fragmented.

He catches my chin between his thumb and forefinger, holding my gaze. It's unnerving to be seen like this. Up close and personal, and completely out of control. When you're the one taking care of things, you get the benefit of standing back. Holding it all at arm's length. Letting someone in, letting them take a bit of that burden from you… It also means letting them close enough to see you clearly. Trusting them not to run when they do.

His gaze dances from eye to eye. He clicks his tongue like what he finds there breaks his heart.

"I'm not gonna pretend that I know everything that happened between them, but I do know this." He leans forward and brushes his lips over mine, soft as a whisper. "There's a lot to be learned from it. A lot we could do differently, to spare ourselves the heartache our parents endured. It's not a bad past, Delilah. Just a past. We've all got 'em."

I rise up on the tide of him pulling away, stealing one more painfully gentle kiss before he's standing upright, out of reach.

"Now, there's a shrimp sandwich out there with your name on it, but if we linger here any longer, your dad might eat it and his both. He's in a feisty mood today."

I raise an eyebrow. "Feisty?"

"Yeah, but don't worry. We're gonna channel that energy into something productive."

The intensity of our conversation slowly leaks from my bones, and I relax into him, my worry momentarily forgotten. "Oh yeah? What's that?"

He reaches into the back pocket of his jeans. There's a shuffling noise of something being removed, and then he holds up a brand-new deck of cards, still in their packaging. "We're gonna play Rummy."

I purse my lips, not wanting to burst his bubble.

"What?"

"It's just, what if Dad doesn't remember the rules?"

Truett's sigh bleeds into a laugh. He slips an arm around my shoulders and guides me toward the hall. "Not to worry. I have it on good authority he's been whooping Roberta's ass at this game on the regular since she started. They used to play a lot when Mom was sick, and your father held a grudge because Roberta took him to the cleaner's every. Time."

My dad? Hold a grudge? "This I've gotta see."

"Oh, Henry!" Truett singsongs.

Dad glances up as we step into the kitchen, his hand poised

over a takeaway box from the Grille. Another sits empty to the right. He flushes, drops his hands, and glances away like a child caught in the act of shoplifting.

Truett lifts a brow. "Were you about to eat Delilah's sandwich?"

"N-no." Dad shakes his head, still staring at the ceiling. "Yours."

I snort. Truett's jaw drops. Dad pauses for a moment to reconsider, then reaches forward to pop open the container, steals a fry, and walks away.

"Feisty indeed," I mumble.

"You were warned!" Truett quips. He grabs one of the containers and follows Dad to the table. "This one's yours, Delilah." He sets it down across from Dad, then points at him. "I'm watching you."

I pour two glasses of water, take them to the table, then fix a third while Truett shuffles the deck. He's placed his meal in the center of the table, and he and my dad take turns plucking fries from it. They squabble over an extra crispy one, but ultimately Truett lets him have it. I laugh as I set the final glass in front of my seat and slide in beside my dad.

"Do you…" Dad rolls his lips. The word is on the tip of his tongue. Satisfaction glints in his eyes when he seizes it. "Play. Do you play, sweet pea?"

"I have once or twice, years ago." I study the hand I've been dealt, then the card on the discard pile. "You'll go easy on me, right?"

Tru snorts but doesn't look up from his cards. "Not a chance."

Dad chuckles, then offers me a shrug. "It's Rummy."

I scowl at the two of them in turn. "What does that mean?"

"All's fair in love and Rummy," Truett says.

I roll my eyes. "No one says that."

"Your dad says that."

I glance at my father, and he nods. "I think I do say that."

"Good to know." I elect to draw a card from the stack and add it to my hand. The two men watch me. Dad is outright staring, and Truett is gazing over the top of his cards. When I gather a four-card run of spades and flatten it on the table, Tru's mouth pops open.

"Your turn, Dad."

"Ridiculous," Truett scoffs. "We've been bamboozled!"

Dad shakes his head but keeps his eyes on me the whole time. "Well, fuck."

I giggle nervously, then swallow hard. "Beginner's luck."

"Nah." He nudges me with his elbow. "Talent. So talented."

"We'll see about that," Tru says. His lips curve upward, and he cocks a brow at me in a clear challenge.

Dad draws a card and, just like me, gathers four cards together to place on the table. A six in every suit.

Truett's gaze widens. "What are the freaking odds?"

"Pretty good if you have a shit dealer," I say, shrugging.

Dad loses it. He holds his cards to his chest as he succumbs to wave after wave of laughter till there's no sound left. Just the shaking of his shoulders.

Meanwhile, Truett's shaking his head at me with mischief glinting in his eyes. "You'll pay for that later."

"Later?" I do my best to sound coy. Which will only work if Tru can't see the tremble in my hand when I reach for my water. The blush creeping up my neck as I take a sip.

For a moment I swear I can feel his lips on my skin. His hands roaming my curves. I'm lying in his bed, legs spread wide for him, feeling him everywhere and yet endlessly craving more.

Tru winks like he knows exactly what I'm thinking. The swell of his cheek hollows out his dimple. He is equal parts man and mischief. Every inch of him rugged and rough-hewn, yet boyish in the most charming way.

"I'm taking you dancing." He turns to Dad. "If that's all right with you, Henry?"

"Sure." Dad waves a hand. "I'm all good."

I shift in my seat. "Are you sure…?"

Dad leans into me and smiles. It'd be reassuring if it weren't tinged with such sadness. "Feel right as rain. Those…um…new meds. They help." He swipes a hand over his lower abdomen and winces. "Just give me a hell of a stomachache."

"Probably all those extra fries you ate," Truett says.

Dad makes a *pfft* sound and waves a hand at Truett. "Take your turn, boy."

Truett snickers. Dad joins him. Some of that tension releases from my shoulders.

Truett draws, then discards. "Roberta will be here too, Delilah. I already asked her." His gaze meets mine, full of warmth and knowing. "I owe you a date. One that doesn't involve childbirth."

"I said that to my wife once." Dad shakes his head at his cards. "I lied."

I'm laughing so hard tears pool in my eyes. I point at Dad, but my eyes are on Tru. "See where I get it from?"

Tru shakes his head, but his shoulders are rattling with laughter. "Can't take you two anywhere."

"Except dancing," I clarify.

He meets my gaze once more, expression serious as sin. "Except dancing."

I draw another card, and this time it's not luck that brings me my third ace. I have to believe it's karma. That after so much bad, I'm finally getting some good.

I lay down my cards.

Chapter Thirty-Two

Delilah

FELIX CROW OPENED the aptly named Crow Bar in 2007, when I was barely old enough to register the disgruntled rumblings it started among my neighbors. Mostly the church ladies, in line at Sunshine Grocery on Sunday afternoons getting a bucket of fried chicken to bring home from the deli. Dad would scoff and smile down at me, whispering, *"Their husbands would all be first in line to patronize the bar if their wives would allow it. Instead they settle for lukewarm beer they keep hidden in their garages, and ibuprofen to dull the headache from all the complaining."*

I didn't really know what that joke meant back then, but as I walk into the dimly lit bar with an industrial-style exposed ceiling and neon beer signs lining the walls, I find myself laughing at it with a renewed sense of perspective. Small-town people with their small-town secrets, so afraid that if word gets out that they, too, have vices, they'll never be forgiven.

Felix glances up from behind the bar. He's in his late fifties, with tattoos lining each arm that have faded into a mess of gray ink, and a beard in a matching shade. His bald head is polished, belly stretching the limits of an AC/DC shirt. When he sees us, he smiles, and it softens all those hard edges at once.

Tru laces our fingers together, tugging me through the small crowd of people already gathered this early on a Friday night. "What do you like to drink?" he calls over his shoulder.

"Oh, I shouldn't—"

A body slams into me. When I turn, alarmed, I'm met with Alicia's wide gaze. "Surprise!"

"Alicia!" My gaze cuts from her to Truett and back again. "What are you doing here?"

"Your *boyfriend* invited me." She pinches my shoulders, then moves her hands to cup my face. Her brows nearly hit her hairline. "And it sounds like I swooped in just in time. I know you weren't about to say you shouldn't drink. We're cutting loose tonight!" Her gaze rolls to meet Truett's. "Right, Parker?"

Tru releases my hand to slide his arm around my waist. His fingers thread through my waistband, and he pulls me into him. The movement is natural, like it's the millionth time rather than the first.

He offers Alicia a cheeky grin. "Exactly."

"Perfect." Another face-splitting smile from Alicia. "Oh! This is my husband, Destin, by the way." She steps to the side and gestures to the booth a few feet behind her where a man sits, watching her with bright-eyed admiration. He's got dark hair, shaved to the skin at the sides and left slightly longer on the top. What looks like an old scar splits his right cheek down the middle. He startles when he notices us staring, and a closed-lip smile stretches his lips as he waves. That scar disappears; pain erased by joy.

"He thinks he's not dancing tonight." Alicia turns back to us and winks. "But he's wrong."

Tru leans in and kisses my temple. "You don't have to drink if you don't want to. But if you want to, I've got you." His lips brush my skin with every whispered word, sending a shiver down my spine.

As he pulls away, I glance up and smile. When was the last time anyone had my back instead of the other way around? Too damn long ago.

"I'll take a margarita on the rocks, if you don't mind."

Pride flashes like lightning in the storm cloud of his eyes. "Don't mind at all." He points at Alicia. "You or Destin want anything?"

"I'll second Delilah." She glances back at Destin, who's nursing a beer in his fist. "You want another, babe?"

"I'm good, thank you." His voice is deep and smooth. Decisive. He doesn't offer more, and Alicia doesn't wait for it. He seems quiet, which is good, because Alicia has always been anything but.

"Two margaritas coming right up." Truett's hand slips from my waist. I didn't realize how much I loved his warmth until I lost it. I catch myself pouting. *Pouting.* Like I'm a toddler rather than a grown woman. Pathetic.

"You've got it *bad,*" Alicia taunts, poking me in the side. Her smile falls to a thoughtful shrug. "I'm glad things are going well. Tess will be proud."

"Where's she at tonight?"

Alicia tosses an arm around my shoulder and starts guiding me toward the booth where Destin sits. "Working. I think this time it's as an instructor at a fitness class? I never can keep up. The woman has a million odd jobs. She can't stand still to save her life."

Trying to keep her mind busy, I'm sure. I don't know Tess very well, but I feel a kindredness with her that I can't explain. Not quite that we are the same, but that we will be someday, whether I like it or not.

"Destin, this is Delilah. Delilah, my husband." She says the word *husband* like it's a lollipop she's licking. When her gaze falls on him, I cease to exist for a heartbeat or two.

I slip into the booth opposite the two of them. "Hi, Destin." I offer my hand over the table, and he takes it. "I've heard a lot about you. Alicia says you're a doctor?"

"Yes." He casts a sideways glance at her. "Well, I'm still in residency. But yes."

"More of a doctor than I'll ever be," Tru interjects. He passes a margarita to Alicia and sets one down in front of me, then plucks a beer bottle from his back pocket. "Though I *have* delivered a baby."

"Really?" Destin asks, brows raised.

"A calf," I clarify.

Tru shrugs. "Cow baby."

"Hey, if it looks like birth and smells like birth"—Destin wrinkles his nose—"it counts."

"Hear, hear." Truett offers his beer, and Destin clinks his against it.

"Disgusting," Alicia says.

Truett laughs and Destin joins in with a breathy chuckle. It's lost to the thrum of music coming from the jukebox in the corner of the room. There's a pool table beside it, illuminated by a single swaying overhead lamp. Two women that look to be a few years younger than us pass a vape back and forth while making commentary on the pool game of the men they're with. The dance floor is a humble ten-by-twenty-foot expanse of hardwood on the other side of the bar, where a single couple shimmies slowly despite the quick tune bouncing through the speakers.

"How's your dad doing?" Alicia asks.

Their gazes all find me in turn, until despite the noise filling the space, my head goes quiet.

"Okay." I find myself glancing at Destin, searching his face for any sign that Alicia has given him the rundown. I don't want to rehash my father's condition. Not here. Not on a happy night.

Destin's gaze is kind. Undemanding. It reminds me of Roberta and the way she always seems to know without ever having to ask. The corner of his mouth lifts. "I'm glad you're getting out. Living your life. I did an elective rotation in geriatrics and saw time and time again that the caregivers were neglecting themselves because they thought it was selfish to do otherwise. But it's not. The best thing you can do for your family member is take care of yourself." He blinks, then glances at Truett. Back at me. "Sorry, you asked for none of that. Please ignore me."

"No, it's okay. Really." I'm grateful for the loud music. Hopeful that it hides that my voice is breaking. I take a long pull from my margarita and lick the salt from my lips. "I think I needed to hear that."

Alicia strokes a hand down Destin's bicep and smiles when he turns to look at her. "Destin doesn't usually out-talk me, but if there's one thing he'll lose his voice over, it's his patients."

Her husband ducks his head, bowing to the compliment.

"How'd you decide to be a doctor?" Tru asks.

Destin runs a finger over his scar absent-mindedly. "I was attacked by a dog as a kid. The doctor who did the reconstructive surgery on my face made a really scary situation a lot less intense." His hand drops to the table, and Alicia lays hers over it. "I guess I liked the idea of being able to do that for someone, too."

"So will you go for plastic surgery then?" I ask.

He nods, and Alicia chuckles. "Yeah, once he's practicing, I'm gonna make him give me implants."

Destin chokes on a sip of beer. His cheeks flush red. "Jesus, babe."

I raise a brow. "Can we get a two-for-one deal on that? Or is it four-for-two."

Alicia throws her head back, laughing. When she finally sucks in a lungful of air and blows it out with a high note, she offers me her glass, and I clink mine to hers. We both finish off our margaritas and slam down our glasses.

The arm Truett had been resting on the back of the booth falls to my shoulder and tugs me into him. His lips find my ear, and his tongue slips out to tease the shell of it. "Don't you dare, Temptress. Your tits are perfect the way they are."

His comment courses through my veins. Hot and pulsing. It settles between my thighs, leaving me squirming beneath the table.

"We'll go get another round," Alicia offers, a coy smile playing on her lips as she glances from me to Truett.

"Thank you," I say. It comes out breathier than I'd like, which only makes her smile harder.

As soon as they're out of earshot, I smack Truett on the thigh.

"Ouch!" He removes his arm from my shoulders so he can rub the sore spot. "What was that for?"

"You can't say stuff like that to me in public!"

An impish grin sweeps over his face. "Or what?"

I glance past him to verify our friends are still well out of earshot. When my gaze lands on Alicia, she makes an obscene hand gesture that Destin pretends not to notice. I giggle and bring my gaze back to Truett. "Or you'll have me all turned on in public with no way of getting off."

His eyes catch flame. I feel his hand move to my thigh, heated against my bare skin. It snakes higher, higher, until his fingertips are kissing the hem of my jean skirt. "Are you saying you're turned on right now?"

I don't honor that with a response.

One brow shoots up. His hand dips beneath my skirt now, and my clit throbs at the proximity. "You know I could easily tell…"

I should stop him. Smart, responsible me would do just that.

But I'm not her tonight. I'm the me who knows what Truett looks like on top of me, inside me. I'm the me with a margarita already lightening her limbs, softening her vision. I part my legs ever so slightly, an invitation that Truett senses the moment it's given.

The tips of his fingers brush my pussy through the thin fabric of my panties. I nearly arch off the booth but force myself to remain still. Any second, Alicia and Destin will return, and we'll be caught red-handed. I should stop this before it goes too far.

But there's a part of me that wants just a little bit more.

He tugs my underwear to the side and slips a finger through my wet center. "So wet for me already. It's almost like you enjoy me talking about how much I love your tits. So perky, with pretty pink nipples that I love to play with almost as much as your pussy."

I gasp. He leans into me, nestling his face in the crook of my neck where he bites me lightly, then sucks. His finger slips inside me then, curling to stroke the place that drives me crazy.

Then, just as quickly, he retreats. He sucks the remnants of me off his fingers, a smirk playing on his lips. Lips that find mine and open, pleading with mine to open too. I do. And his tongue moves against mine, tangling and unraveling again and again, till I'm convinced I'm going to have to beg him to take me home and fuck me *right now.*

I pull away, and the world is hazy. All except Truett, who exists as he always has for me: in Technicolor. "Tru—"

"I brought shots!" Alicia's holding two up over her head. "Well, for Delilah and me at least. Beer for the gentlemen per Destin's request."

I blush scarlet. Alicia and I have just gotten close again, but she said it herself. She's always been able to read me like an open book. One look at me and she'll know I'm guilty as sin.

She places one shot in front of me. It's clear, likely vodka since there's no lime. My stomach burns at the sight of it, but when our eyes meet and she gives me a knowing wink, I decide even the worst shot in the world is better than facing her right now.

"Cheers!" She holds hers out. Destin passes a beer to Truett, and they both join in as well. "To good health. Old friends. And forever loves."

"Cheers," Destin echoes.

I swear Truett nudges me as he chimes in.

Finally I echo them all and down the shot before I can hang too much hope on a simple toast.

"Okay, now I promised you dancing"—Tru slides out of the booth and reaches back for me—"so dancing is what you shall get."

I giggle. I'm doing a lot of that tonight, despite not being a particularly giggly person. Before I know it, my hand is in his and I'm floating across the room to the little dance floor. "It's Your Love" by Tim McGraw spills from the jukebox, whether on purpose or by sheer dumb luck. I grin up at Truett, who sweeps one arm around my waist and uses the other to take my hand in his, and shake my head. "How did you know it'd be a slow song?"

"I have my ways," he says, then glances over my shoulder. I follow his gaze and find Alicia has managed to get Destin out here after all. When she catches us looking, she shimmies her shoulders and offers a thumbs-up.

"I love her," I say, sighing. The room is spinning, probably because we are too. But it feels good. Light and carefree in a way I haven't been in years. Or ever.

"I'm glad you have her." Tru steps away from me and guides me under his arm, capturing me as I spin away from him and lowering me into a dip.

"Truett Cole Parker, since when did you learn how to dance so well?"

He looks at me, eyebrows raised.

I raise mine too. "What? You're the only one who can whip out middle names?"

He snorts. We're moving in tune with each other as though we've done this a thousand times. He retreats; I follow. He pushes in; I let him guide me away. When our gazes meet again, he says, "Yes, I can dance."

"Some other talent you picked up while I've been gone?"

Something sad flashes in his gaze, but it's gone before I can hyper-analyze it. It's replaced by a simmering heat so visceral I'm right back in that booth in a second, his fingers inside me, thinking I'll make a fool of myself by coming from his touch alone.

"I've got so many talents I've been saving for you, Delilah."

The music fades out, leaving us locked in this breathless embrace, his hard length pressing against my stomach and a responding warmth spreading through my limbs.

In the brief silence before another song loads, I hear an alert come through on my phone. I'm about to ignore it when another follows suit. Truett's brow furrows. "You might wanna get that."

"Already on it." I pluck my phone from the back pocket of my jean skirt and glance at the screen. "It's Roberta."

Alicia and Destin step into our orbit as Truett asks, "Is everything okay with Henry?"

"Is your dad all right?" Alicia adds.

I squint at the screen, trying to make it make sense in my alcohol-induced haze.

Roberta: I hate to interrupt, but your dad isn't doing well. Very agitated and confused.

Roberta: It may be best if y'all come home.

"He's not having a good night." I glance up at Tru. "I've gotta get home."

"But he was fine earlier?" Tru holds my shoulders as he peers down at my phone. "I wonder what's got him upset."

I try to think through all the events of the day. His mood. Possible triggers. My brain is lagging, running on a terrible signal. "I-I don't know. I thought he was doing okay." I glance up at Alicia. At Destin, who's holding her close and studying me with a sympathetic gaze. "I shouldn't have come out. I'm sorry, guys."

"Don't be. It's not your fault," Destin offers.

Alicia reaches for me, but I'm already moving, albeit clumsily, toward the door. I hear their voices but don't really listen. Hear the voice on the jukebox but not the words. Truett's footsteps thunder behind me, one after the other, and then he's ahead of me, opening the door to let me out into the night.

The moon is a sliver, leaving the world blanketed in darkness. Gravel crunches underfoot. We reach the truck in mutual silence, and Truett opens my door. Offers a hand to guide me in. I sit, staring blankly ahead, as he strides around front and climbs inside. The engine rumbles to life, settling my fears inside me like a lullaby.

"It's gonna be okay," Truett offers.

I bite at my lip. "You don't know that."

For Roberta to ask, it has to be bad. We both know that, deep down. I feel myself bracing before we've even left the parking lot.

Silence. We roam dark streets. His headlights strobe the overhang of branches and occasional twinkling yellow gaze in the brush. The metal fence lines and dust-coated mailboxes. Mile after mile, minute after minute. So much of it is monotonous. Enough to get lost if you don't know your way.

"You know it's not your fault. This didn't happen because you took time for yourself."

To that, I have no response. Because I don't know. How could anyone say with confidence it isn't my fault, that my absence isn't what upset him? Maybe I could've noticed, redirected, prevented. If only I'd stayed home, I could have protected him from this.

When we arrive at the house, I hear my dad shouting the minute I open the truck door. The house is old; the walls are thin. It's a shocking sound, one I never heard before his diagnosis. I take the front steps in twos and I'm at the door, pushing inside in the time it takes Truett to call out my name.

"I don't wanna go!" Dad shouts. "I don't know you!"

He's wearing an old Alabama football jersey and slacks, with house slippers and his robe on top. He glances up as I enter the room and holds up a hand. In it, he's white knuckling his wallet. "You can have it. Take it. Just don't hurt the baby!" He throws the wallet and runs down the hall.

I briefly meet Roberta's gaze before following after him. He slams open my bedroom door and gasps. "The baby! She's gone!"

"What baby, Dad?"

He turns to me, shock and confusion and horror all warping his features into someone I barely recognize. "I'm not your dad. I'm hers." He points to the wall, where a photo of me as an infant is hung in a gilded frame. "Where is she?"

"I'm right here, Daddy." Tears spring forth. I can't stop them any more than I can stop his confusion. Any more than I can make him remember. "It's me. Delilah. I'm your daughter."

Roberta's hands cup my shoulders. I start, spinning around to find her holding up a phone.

"We need to get him to the hospital. Usually with a sudden shift like this there's something medical going on. If nothing else, they can give him something to calm him down."

I open my mouth, then close it. Truett appears just over her shoulder. I can't look at him as I say, "I can't drive him. I've had too much to drink."

Shame twists my stomach, and I'm certain I'm going to be sick. The only virus I can blame this time is my own selfishness.

"Stop it! You all need to leave!" Dad yells from behind me. "I'll call the police."

"Henry, it's okay. We're here to help. We wanna find your baby, too," Roberta says sweetly. "We're going to call the authorities and they'll help."

"You will?" Dad asks, disbelief breaking his voice.

"You will?" I whisper, glancing at the phone in her hand.

"Yes. In his state, it's not wise for any of us to drive him. We'd get in a wreck," Roberta says to me, her voice low. She grabs my hand and pulls me backward. Turning to Dad, she says, "We're going to call them now. This is Truett." She pats his arm when he's within reach. "He's gonna stay with you while we call." She peers up at Truett and smiles, though there's tension tightening her gaze. "We're gonna step into the kitchen. I'll be right back."

I bring myself to look at Truett, and I wish I hadn't. There are tears spilling from his eyes, which are trained on my dad. He nods. "I'll stay with you, Henry."

"Do I know you?" Dad asks, squinting.

"You do," Truett says, stepping closer. "We're friends."

Dad nods, slowly at first and then so fast I'm afraid he'll have whiplash. "They took my daughter. I can't find her anywhere."

"We'll find her," Truett says. He glances back at me as I'm pulled around the corner, his last words echoing in my ears. "I'm sure she's around here somewhere."

"Hi, yes, I need an ambulance at 211 Sowell Mill Road." Roberta glances up at me to confirm, and I nod. "I'm an in-home care provider for a gentleman with dementia. I believe he's having an episode of delirium and needs medical attention."

I listen to her rattle off the details. To Truett on the other side of the wall calmly helping my dad search for a baby he'll never find. I cry, cry, cry for that baby, because all she wants, all she *needs* in the whole world is her father. And with every moment like this, he slips further away.

How unfair. How unnecessarily cruel.

Chapter Thirty-Three

Henry

March 20th, 2015

It takes a little over a year for me to make it through all five stages of grief.

The denial lasted longer than I expected. I wasted months believing Kimberly would change her mind. Come around. That we could be happy together, the way I always wanted us to be. I couldn't believe the curious, affectionate girl I met that night on my school's gymnasium steps was the same woman now telling me our marriage was worth nothing to her, and she'd be discarding it like expired milk as soon as she possibly could.

After she declined couples' counseling for the third time in as many months, I moved on to anger. Anger that spread my patience so thin I became a version of myself that I hardly recognized. Students complained I was getting my period. Kimberly nearly took my head off for snapping when she made one of her signature biting remarks. Even Delilah, who remained level-headed as I usually was, asked me if something was wrong after I overdid it when she came home with a less-than-stellar exam grade. That shook me loose from my distemper. I couldn't let my suffering become hers, too.

Bargaining was brief. Not much to bargain for when you've already given up so much, and none of it good enough.

I thought I knew what depression felt like. I remembered the months following my father's death, and then my mother's, in which it felt like all the light had been drained from my world. But there was pain in that darkness. Agony in its truest sense. When depression finally arrived, it cast a cloak of numbness over my heart and mind. Left me desolate. Bereft. If grief is feeling everything all at once—anguish over the loss, longing for their return, even joy at the memories you once shared—then depression is the complete lack thereof. There is no pain, no hope, and certainly no happiness. I suddenly understood why people contemplate self-harm, if only to feel something. Anything, rather than nothing at all.

Acceptance arrived out of the blue one day, without much fanfare or even a signaling shift in the air. It was a parcel placed inside my mailbox, one that was lost somewhere along the journey but found its way to me after a few missteps and wrong deliveries. A little rough for wear, and long overdue, but here all the same. The day I woke up and realized that life was handing me a second chance and I better not fuck it up, I shook off the dark cloud that'd plagued me for far too long and finally started looking forward to the future and all the possibilities it could hold.

Which is why I'm sitting at the bench of my classroom piano, bathed in only the dim light coming from my office, dreaming about those possibilities.

Delilah will be off to college in a year. And then what? Kimberly leaves. I'll be left with a house I inherited, in the town I was born into, with only my former childhood love and a few coworkers for friends. It feels like a recipe challenge on a cooking show. How do you take these ingredients and make a meal worth eating? How do I take these pieces and make a life I could love?

My hands fall roughly on the keys, filling the room with a note so jarring I flinch.

"Yikes, you've really gone downhill in recent years."

The bench groans as I pivot, glancing over my shoulder to find Lucy leaning against the cinder-block wall just inside the doorway, a teasing grin playing on her lips. My thoughts go blissfully blank in her presence. And thank God, because I'm so tired of thinking myself in circles.

"I'm kidding, of course. We both know you're the next Mozart." She accompanies her wink with a giggle, so girlish that for a moment I see her as she once was, with fewer curves, no fine lines framing her face, but the same bright sparkle in her gaze.

I sigh heavily, hoping it'll loosen my suddenly aching chest. "I forgot about that."

"I did, too, actually." She produces a small stack of papers from behind her back, all bound together with a rubber band. "Found these the other day when I was cleaning out a closet. I was coming by to drop them off on your desk when I heard the world's worst piano solo."

I laugh, but it's pinched at the edges. My gaze is trained on that small stack, my breath a little sharper as I take it in. "Is that what I think it is?"

"Yep, all our notes." She waves the stack in the air by her head. "Well, the ones where the conversation ended with me, anyway. Obviously."

I shake my head, my jaw slack with surprise. "I can't believe you kept those all these years."

"Technically I didn't know they were still around until I evicted the dust bunnies from our spare bedroom closet, but yes. I kept them." She shrugs, her narrow shoulders shifting beneath the loose silk of her pale green blouse. "They meant the world to teenage me."

A knot forms in my throat. I wring my hands in my lap, because if I don't, I'll be tempted to get up from this bench and cross the few feet that separate us. To wrap my arms around her and not let go. I'm starved for affection and far too emotionally raw to allow myself to step into her orbit, even for a second.

She jams a thumb over her shoulder toward the hall. "I caught the tail end of the concert. The kids did great."

"Thanks," is all I manage to squeeze out. My lungs are tight, compressed by my pounding heart. It's the millionth time I've been near her, so why does it suddenly feel so nerve-racking? I stand and smooth the wrinkles from my slacks to hide the tremble in my hands. "What's got you here so late?"

"We've been reading *Great Gatsby* for the past few weeks, and I promised the kids that if they had an average of eighty percent or more on their comprehension test, I'd throw a party for them, 1920's style." She bounces on her toes, smiling widely. "They took it today and nailed it! Nearly eighty-seven percent as the average score. So I stayed late to decorate my classroom. If I never see another art deco print, it'll be too soon."

My responding chuckle shakes a bit of the tension out of me. "It's been a while since I read Gatsby, but if I'm understanding correctly, you turned your classroom into a speakeasy? For teenagers?"

"Not quite." Laughter floods her cheeks with color. She fans herself with our bundled letters, sucking in deep breaths until it's reduced to residual giggles. "We'll be leaning more into the Prohibition side of the roaring twenties, if you know what I mean."

I suck in air through my teeth, grimacing as I shake my head. "Oh, well, in that case I'm going to have to skip that party."

"As if you were invited!" She pushes off the wall and takes a step in my direction. Her hair is swept into a low ponytail that swings over her shoulder, revealing delicate gold hoops hanging from her ears. Her fingertips brush one lobe like she's caught me looking. I meet her gaze, and I swear a shudder runs through her, but it's gone before I can convince myself it was more than a trick of the light.

She closes the distance between us, holds out the stack of notes we once passed each other, and arches a brow. "And besides, since when do you drink?"

I pluck them from her grasp and turn them over in my hands. Ink bleeds through time-worn paper, a testament to the history between us. The reason she knows I don't drink in the first place. Save for the night of prom, and that was enough to turn me off it forever.

"You caught me," I say, raising my hands in a show of innocence. "Drinking has never been my vice, thankfully."

"I'm not sure I believe you have *any*. You're too in control."

I toss the stack of notes on top of the piano, hoping the sound will drown out my pathetic, "Oh, you have no idea."

It doesn't, of course. When I glance back at her, Lucy's brow is furrowed. Her gray eyes flicker, catching on something in my expression that makes her say, "Name one," so softly I have to lean close to make it out.

You, I almost utter. But what good would that do? She's still married to Waylon. I'm still with Kimberly, if only in name. Our opportunity long passed us by. I know this deep down, no matter how much I wish it wasn't so.

In the silence following her command, she winces as her words echo back to her. She tucks a stray hair behind her ear and casts her eyes to the ground. "Sorry, I didn't mean…I wasn't trying to insinuate—"

"You didn't." I reach for her hand without a thought. We both stare at this point where we connect, her lips parted in a drawn breath and my lungs bow-string tight. I drop her as though I've been burned. "I'm sorry. I— You didn't insinuate anything. I'm a little slow on the draw, that's all. I promise I don't mean to be. I've been all over the place lately."

I rub my palm against my thigh, trying desperately to forget the feel of her skin. Lucy's right. Control is my strong suit. So why am I struggling to maintain it?

A wrinkle forms between her eyebrows. "If something's going on, you know you can talk to me about it, right?"

"Like you talked to me about what happened with your black eye?"

Her lips flatten. I've broken the unspoken rule, and we both know it. I expect to see vitriol in her gaze, perhaps even disgust that I'd bring this up after she made it clear it wasn't a topic up for discussion. And I'd deserve it. I don't know what's gotten into me, that I'd be so abrupt. I open my mouth to apologize, but she speaks before I can.

"You were right," she whispers. There's a quiet grief lacing her expression. An understanding. "About Waylon. He's not usually like that. Things got a bit heated, and it went too far that time. He felt really bad about it."

I scrape a hand over my mouth. "You could've told me, Lucy."

Her watery smile could break a thousand hearts. "I know. But like I said, it was a one-off. There was no need to worry you over something so stupid."

Rage blinds me momentarily. No amount of time, distance, or regret from his sorry ass could lessen it. My mind races with all the things I want to say, wondering if any are words she needs to hear. I nearly grind my molars to stumps trying to hold back every curse, threat, and promise that comes to mind. Finally I force out, "One time is a time too many, Lucy."

From the way she swallows, tilts her chin up, and meets my

gaze with unwavering resolve, I'd guess she knows that already. But I don't regret saying it, just in case.

"I couldn't have any more babies after Truett." Her lips quiver, but she does not look away. Doesn't close her eyes even as tears fill them. "We tried for years, but nothing happened. Secondary infertility, they called it. But Waylon just called it my fault.

"I always wanted a house full of babies. It was the only good part of my life growing up. Having a brother and sister to lean on when times were hard, to laugh with when they were good." She snorts softly, crinkling her nose. "Maybe it was a blessing in disguise. Maybe they'd have ended up exactly like my siblings and me. After all, Waylon is so much like Daddy. I worry sometimes that Truett's so sick of it that he'll leave when he turns eighteen and never come back. And the worst part is, I wouldn't blame him."

This time I don't stop at grabbing her hand. I use it to pull her into me; then I wrap my arms around her shoulders and squeeze tight. The scent of honeysuckle floods my senses. I nuzzle into her hair, drinking it in. She exhales against the curve of my neck. Goose bumps break out along my flesh. I feel every inch of her molding to me, and it's perfect in ways that Kimberly and I never were.

"That boy will never abandon you. He loves his mama too much." I stroke a hand down her spine. Her blouse is so thin I can feel the heat coming off her, and I allow it to thaw the anger filling me till it's nothing but its molten core.

"I'm gonna leave him." Her words are a whispered confession. One that sets my heart to a gallop in my chest.

I pull back enough to see her eyes. To measure the truth there. "What?"

She blinks rapidly like she's surprised at her own confession. "I've been saving up my money. Once I have enough, once I know I can afford to do this and put Tru through college if he wants to go, I'm leaving." She bites her bottom lip. "You can't say anything. Truett doesn't know. Waylon would lose his mind—"

All that control I'm famous for disappears in a flash. For a moment there is no Kimberly or Waylon. The years that separate us from the kids who wrote those notes on the piano cease to exist. There is only me and my strong, brave Lucy. Only her lips and my desire to taste them.

Only a second chance, and my determination to take it.

My mouth slants over hers, fusing us together. A whimper spills from her lips. She arches into me, her breasts pressing softly into my ribs. Electricity courses through my body, grounding itself in every place Lucy and I touch. I search for more. Need it like I need the very breath in my lungs. My tongue strokes hers. Her teeth drag my lips. It's bold in all the ways our first kiss wasn't. Perfect in all the ways that it was.

I find the hem of her shirt and slip beneath it. Her spine, the soft flesh of her sides—I trace it all like a road on an atlas. My fingertips brush the space I vowed years ago to kiss, to rewrite the harshness of her father's touch, and I outline a heart against her skin. It's a mark on the map that my lips can later follow, if only I can get this shirt off...

"Mr. Ridgefield?"

The moment fractures. One second she's everywhere. Everything. The next, we're five feet apart, staring down one of my students in the doorway.

"Jessica," I say, my voice a fault line at risk of breaking. "Did you need something?"

Jessica has a thick head of dark brown curls and tawny skin that makes her green eyes pop in contrast. A spitting image of her mother, Angie, who met me once at a school event and asked me out on the spot, despite my very present wedding band. I politely declined. Next thing I knew, Angie was signing her daughter up for band, and herself up to chaperon every competition. Never mind that Jessica absolutely despises playing clarinet. And, subsequently, my class.

So when a smile curves the corner of her mouth, dread spills through me, freezing my organs in place. Jessica pops her lips, rocking back on her heels briefly, and lets her gaze drift slowly from me to Lucy, who I swear is about to faint on the spot.

"You know what?" Jessica says, shrugging. "I forgot what I needed. Oh well. Sorry for interrupting." Then she pivots on her heel and bolts down the hall, back toward the front of the building where the auditorium is.

"Fuck," Lucy groans. "Fuck, fuck, fuck."

My hand is at my throat. I don't know how it ended up there. I'm out of my body, somewhere above, looking down on this moment in absolute horror. I've risked not only my job but Lucy's, too. And what about our kids? There's no chance Truett and Delilah's friendship comes out of this unscathed.

I turn to Lucy. Her chest is heaving. Panic widens her gaze. *I* did that. My recklessness did that. It took our first chance from us all those years ago, and now I've swept our second right from under our feet.

Damage control. I have to do damage control. I might've signed myself up for a one-way ticket to hell, but there's no way I'm taking Lucy down with me.

I just hope I can make Delilah understand.

Chapter Thirty-Four

Delilah

IT TAKES a lot of coaxing and a healthy dose of sedation, but eventually Dad falls into a restless sleep in his hospital bed. His eyelids flutter with movement. Every once in a while, he moans or mumbles something unintelligible. *It's an improvement,* I tell myself, ignoring the tubes and the monitors and the thin, scratchy hospital sheets. At least he's not afraid anymore.

I fold myself into the recliner in the corner. A kind nurse fixed it up with a plastic pillow and a thin sheet to match Dad's. It's no Four Seasons, but it's comfortable enough. I won't be sleeping anyway, not after the night we've had.

They found a urinary tract infection but are waiting on blood tests to be sure it hasn't spread to Dad's kidneys. I fired off a text letting Roberta and Truett know what was happening, and that we'd be staying overnight at a minimum. Roberta responded saying that it wasn't unusual for dementia patients to get them and to be extra confused as a result. Truett responded with a phone call.

A call I declined the second it appeared. Much as I hate myself for it, I know it's for the best. Tonight showed us one thing for certain: I cannot let myself get swept up in Truett's orbit, because it'll be my dad who suffers if I do.

My head flops against the pillow. Its flimsy plastic cover squeaks in my ear. I swap it for my hand, propping my chin on my palm as I study my father. To be so young, he suddenly looks ancient. A complete stranger with his scraggly beard and graying hair that hangs limply against his sweat-slicked forehead. I want to brush his hair back and thread a dollop of hair cream through it, revealing the tousled starving-artist look he had before I left. My fingers itch to take a straight razor to that beard, like I might shave it off and find the father I once knew hiding beneath, patiently waiting for his chance to say, *Gotcha!*

A tear rolls down my cheek, dripping from my chin onto the fake leather armrest my elbow is indenting.

This wasn't supposed to be how it went. I was supposed to come here and find answers that could finally mend my heart. It wasn't supposed to be broken further. I certainly wasn't meant to break someone else's in the process.

As if on cue, my phone lights up on the mobile bedside table. Truett's name hits me like a bullet aimed by a talented marksman. I blink rapidly, but it only spreads the tears across my vision with added vigor. By the time the phone goes dark, I'm underwater.

Time ticks by, each second punctuated by the clock on the wall by the door. Eventually my shoulders sag and I loose the breath I'd been holding. I grab the foam water cup the nurse left on the table and stand, my sheet pooling at my feet. My phone lights up again, this time with a text. I unlock it with shaky hands, but my heart is still. Braced for the blow it knows is coming.

TRUETT

I hope you're getting some much needed rest.
I'll be by in the morning to check on you both.
Do you need anything from home?

My teeth scrape over my bottom lip. I debate backing out of the message and powering down my phone when another comes through on the first's heels.

TRUETT

You know you have your read receipts on, right?

"Shit."

Dad stirs, rolling toward the sound of my voice with a grimace and a moan that plucks right at my heart. I hold still until he settles once more, and then take the phone and the water cup into the hall, closing the door behind me with a soft click.

ME

Sorry, it's been hectic. We can't have visitors, unfortunately, but thanks for offering.

TRUETT

I understand. I can drop them off but not stay, if you'd like. Bring some warm food for you?

ME

I'll be fine. Don't worry about it.

I find the nurse's station mostly abandoned save for a woman in her midforties with long braids gathered in a knot at the nape of her neck and a stern expression aimed at the computer in front of her. When I set the cup on the counter, she glances up, that tightness melting into a gentle smile.

"Everything all right, sugar?"

"Yes, ma'am." I offer my best smile in return, but it feels pained. I can only imagine how it looks. "I was wondering if I could refill my dad's water cup?"

"Absolutely. It's right this way." She stands and navigates around the U-shaped desk to meet me where it opens into the hall. There's another opening a few feet later, which she guides me into. It's a hallway connected to their station from a center juncture, with a sink, some cabinets, and a water and ice machine. She pops the cup under the ice maker with one hand while retrieving a second cup from a nearby drawer. To my raised brow, she says, "We can't have you getting dehydrated in this dry hospital air, now can we?"

I smile, more genuinely this time. "Thank you."

"No problem." She hands me both cups. "I'm Judith. You call if you or your dad needs anything, okay?"

"Yes, ma'am," I say. Then, when she glares, "Er, Judith."

"There you go." She shuffles toward that juncture and turns. By the time I walk back by the counter, she's tucked back into her chair, gaze locked on the computer once more. Our moment falls by the wayside, a drop in the bucket of her day.

When my phone vibrates again, I slip both cups carefully into the crooks of my fingers on one hand and retrieve it from my pocket. He's calling again. I watch it, forcing myself to bear witness to my undoing until his contact disappears.

Only to be replaced by a voicemail.

I laugh, but there's no humor in it. It is not lost on me that this all started with a voicemail. And here we are, ending it all with one, too.

I can't be what Truett needs. Hell, I can't be what Dad needs. So what's the point in any of this? In dragging someone along toward my own unhappy ending?

From my spot outside Dad's door, I can barely see the corner of the nurses' station. I anchor myself to it. A point in the distance. A reminder that what I've done is not the end of the world; it's only the end of us.

I press play and drag the phone to my ear.

"Delilah, I know you're awake. Hell, you're probably staring at the phone as this call comes through and biting that pretty little lip of yours while you wait for me to give up and stop calling. News flash, Temptress. I'm never giving up."

I tip my forehead into the textured wallpaper and press the foam cups against my heart. Something like ice for a fresh bruise. Only this isn't a bruise, it's a fucking massacre.

"You're running, and I get it. You're scared and feeling like you let your dad down tonight. I know because I've been there. But here's the thing, Delilah. You can turn tail and run all you want, but I'm not the same scared boy you left behind nine years ago. The one who sat back and let you go without a fight. I'm all grown up. I'm the man who will come for you. Who will find you and bring you home as many times as I have to until you finally realize I'm not giving up on you."

Sobs rack my body. Through the blur of my tears, I catch Judith peeking around the corner. Whatever she reads on my face keeps her from coming closer. I'm left alone in the hospital corridor, but I've never felt less lonely. Truett's words offer comfort I haven't earned—which is honestly the kind I struggle to accept the most—but he knows that. Knows *me.* And he offered it anyway.

I'm trying to see the blessing in that, but it's so damn hard. Nothing feels clear anymore. Nothing feels guaranteed.

I lock my phone and slip it back into my pocket, then use my free hand to wipe my face clean. I take a moment to tuck this all away so I can go in there and be strong for my dad, even when I don't feel it.

Even when I'm too afraid to let Truett be strong for me.

"I should've known." I push the orange chunks around my fruit cup, searching for any remaining pineapple I might've missed. "How did I not see he was sick?"

Roberta sits with her chin resting on interlocked fingers, watching me thoughtfully. I'm glad she's here, even if I feel guilty for inviting her. I told Truett we couldn't have visitors, but really I just couldn't handle him. Couldn't trust myself to stay focused with him around.

A twinge of pain turns my stomach. I drop my fork.

Roberta's gaze tracks the movement. Her eyebrows pull together. "Do you remember that night you and your dad got the stomach flu?"

"Yeah. He was a little confused, but nothing like this."

She shakes her head. "That's not what I mean." Her chest rises and falls around a deep breath. She's measuring her words carefully, which is how I know to lean in and listen closely. She nods when I do, like she's acknowledging that I'm ready. "Think about that night. Before you went to bed, how did you feel?"

I try to think back without dwelling too much on the endless vomiting or the man who pulled my hair up when I was too weak to do it myself. I purse my lips and shrug. "I guess I felt normal. Nothing crazy or out of the ordinary."

"Exactly." She thumbs her nose and shrugs. "Sometimes illnesses are like that. The symptoms were so minor, if they existed at all, that your dad didn't really have the awareness to call it out. But then it got so bad it disoriented him. It happens a lot. You had no way of knowing."

I think of the stomachache he complained about during our card game and wince.

Roberta misses nothing. Her gaze flickers over my face, and her lips turn down at the corners in a rare frown. "Do you wanna talk about what's really bothering you?"

A different version of me would say, *Absolutely not.* She'd clamp her lips shut and insist on taking care of everyone else in order to keep the spotlight off herself, even if it meant leaving her bruised and battered heart unmended. But I'm exhausted, ashamed, and more than a little desperate for comfort. And maybe Truett's on to something, whether I like to admit it or not. Perhaps it'd be nice for someone to find me for a change. To see me, in all my brokenness, and tell me I'm not too far gone to be saved.

I may not be ready for Truett, but Roberta feels like a safe place to start.

"I couldn't even drive my own father to the hospital because I'd been drinking." I stare at the fruit cup. The cheap plastic table. The cuticle sticking straight up on my thumb. Anywhere but at her. "So fucking irresponsible. I'm supposed to take care of him."

Her hand covers mine. Rings glint on every finger, a mix of silver and gold. They catch the fluorescent light as she rubs my knuckles softly. "You're twenty-six years old, Delilah. You're allowed to make mistakes. To be the child in the relationship. This disease takes so much. It doesn't have to take your whole life, too. Your dad wouldn't want that. He doesn't. He's told me as much, not just now but long ago when we watched Truett walk through the very same ordeal with his mama.

"You two are such good, kind children. You love your parents a whole awful lot. Anyone can see it. But Delilah…" She tilts her head to capture my gaze and offers a smile that's meant to be reassuring. "You've gotta love yourself too every once in a while, you know?"

No, I don't know. And I'm not sure how to tell her that. To make her see all the obligations, the sense of fealty that weighs on me so heavily. That in all the gaps between who I am and who I should be, I find myself lacking. Unlovable.

That it feels impossible to trust Truett to feel something for me that I can't even feel for myself.

I clear my throat. "I should go check on him. They said he could be discharged soon." I rise, gathering my trash in my hand. "Thanks for coming by, and for bringing the car."

"Always. I was happy to help." Roberta stands and reaches for my forearm, pulling my gaze to hers. "You two are family to me, Delilah. And I meant what I said that first day. I'll be here through it all. I promise."

It's too early in the morning for mercy. And I'm not quite sure I deserve it, anyway.

I duck my head, studying the scuffed tile at my feet. "Thanks, Roberta."

She pulls me into one of her million-dollar hugs. I'm two seconds from collapsing and begging her to stay, to make all these decisions for me. To take this immovable burden from my shoulders, if only for a second so I can breathe without the weight of it compressing my lungs.

Before the words can tumble out, though, I extricate myself from her arms. Take two steps back. Breathe in, then out. I allow myself one more glimpse at the compassion in her face. File it away for a time in the future when I can look at it and believe I'm worthy. It's not everything, or even a lot, but it's as much hope as I'll allow myself here in this sterile place where the reality of my father's condition looms so much closer than it ever does at home.

"See you later."

Her lips stretch into a feeble smile, but her gaze is strong. Determined. "Call me when you're home."

I wave a hand by way of response. She's still watching me with that same intensity when I turn the corner toward the elevator and disappear from view.

Chapter Thirty-Five

Delilah

ANTISEPTIC STILL BURNS my nose as our house comes into view. It stings with each lungful of air, reminding me where we spent the last forty-eight hours. Even though we've left the hospital, the hospital hasn't left us.

"Can we go see Lucy? Just for a few minutes?"

I white knuckle the steering wheel over a new pothole the latest summer rain must've carved from the road. I brace myself, my tired, weary brain snapping to attention, as I say, "I don't know if that's the best idea, Dad. Lucy is…"

Busy? On a road trip? I want to lie, to spare us this conversation, but my mind won't compute a solid answer.

"Damn it, I know she's dead. I'm not stupid."

I blink back tears and wonder absently if it'll ever get easier to convince myself he doesn't mean these things. That it's not really him.

I doubt it.

"I never said you were."

He meets my worried gaze, his own clearer than it's been in days. Whatever he finds there dissolves the irritation in his voice.

His face crumples, regret evident in every fold. "I'm sorry. I-I know she's gone. I just wanna talk to her."

I sigh. At the mouth of our driveway, I put the car in park and pull out my phone. Truett followed up his voicemail with a few more texts. Not pressuring or pushing, but merely offering to help when he noticed we stayed at the hospital longer than one day. It doesn't matter that I don't respond. He keeps showing up for me. Coming for me. Waiting for me to be ready to be found.

It's his consistency, his care, that'll be my undoing, when I finally have time alone to come undone.

As much as I know that cutting things off with Tru is the best thing for everyone involved, it takes every ounce of my strength to ignore the voice that tells me to call Tru right this second and admit I need him to get me through this. To hold me and tell me it'll all work out. That I'll make it, because I have to.

But Dad deserves to have one hundred percent of my attention. And Truett deserves better than whatever shell of me is left over when this is done.

I fire off a text, and hope beyond hope that me ignoring the rest doesn't hurt him as badly as it hurts me.

ME

Finally out of the hospital. Dad wants to visit Lucy. Is that okay?

TRUETT

He's welcome any time.

TRUETT

I made soup.

TRUETT

I can come by later, once you two are settled?

I lock the phone and put the car back into drive, but not before a silent tear slips from my lashes.

The cemetery is cocooned in an otherworldly quiet. Not *silence,* per se. The birds still call to one another. The breeze ruffles the leaves here, too. But it's muted. Delicate. Like nature knows to hold its breath for the souls laid to rest in what was once an empty hilltop meadow. I hold my breath too, as Dad makes his way through the opening in the iron fence. He settles easily into the bench at the foot of Lucy's plot, like he's slipping into an old pair of shoes. Familiar and formed perfectly to fit him.

I take the open seat beside him. Cold seeps from the stone bench through my jeans and into my skin. During her visit, Roberta brought a change of clothes and some toiletries for me to freshen up. A godsend, when I was in the middle of my own personal hell.

Fresh flowers are lying at the base of her stone. Beautiful white carnations, like the ones forever memorialized on his ribs. I think of Truett coming here all alone to sit with his mom, and my throat constricts. One day it'll be me visiting my father. The thought swallows me whole, till it's all I can see when I look around.

"Thank you, sweet pea." Dad hums a breath, his gaze locked on Lucy's stone. I let mine drift closed, afraid I'll see his name if I allow myself to look again. His shoulder brushes mine, and he sighs. "It's good to see her."

He's calm. The antibiotics helped, though the doctors said his confusion might come and go more frequently as he fully recovers. Still, he's here now. I can't think of another time to ask. "How did you two meet?"

"We went to church together."

My eyes fly open. "You? Church?"

"It was for Nana, mostly. I was in it for the fifteen minutes I got every day after service to play at the baby grand." He smiles, gaze lost to memory. Sometimes he exists better there than he does in the present, it seems. Like this moment is blurry, but thirty years ago remains in hyper-focus. "Lucy sang in the choir. We didn't talk for a real long time. Then, one day, she sat down with me and we played some beautiful music together."

"Did you two date?"

"Oh no, her dad wasn't having that. I don't know exactly what his bone to pick with me was. Maybe he could see right through my paper-thin faith, or he saw the hard-on I had for his daughter—"

"Dad!" I shout before catching myself. I know being a bit too honest is par for the course with dementia, but there are some things you never want to hear your father say aloud. Still, he looks guilty. Embarrassed. So I pat his knee and say, "I'm sorry. Go on."

It takes a minute for him to find his footing again, to draw the words back from where they disappeared to, but when he does, his face softens around the memory like a candle set alight. "We couldn't date. But we were friends. Good friends."

"You wrote notes to each other, right?"

His eyebrows leap to his hairline. "How'd you know about those?"

"I found them in the box of your things from school. They're in your desk if you'd like to read them."

"Well, thank you for that." He rolls his lips, tears pricking his eyes. "I'd forgotten about those notes. Lucy brought them back to me after finding them in a closet she was cleaning out. I couldn't believe she held on to them for all those years."

My heartbeat slows and my breath catches. "You must've meant a lot to her."

He nods. "She meant a lot to me, too."

I don't want to upset him. Not after everything that's happened the last couple days. But there's a question itching just beneath my skin, begging to be let out, and I have to know. Before it's too late. "Did you two… was there…"

He blinks at me, confused.

I draw a breath and try again. "The affair. How long had it been going on?"

"It was just that one kiss. I—" His lips shutter closed. "I shouldn't say j—*ugh*." He rubs at his mouth, his beard crinkling against his touch. "I shouldn't say 'just.' One kiss is enough. I cheated. It was wrong."

My heartbeat slows to a crawl. I shake my head, more at myself than at him. "All this time I thought Jessica caught you sleeping together."

He barks a laugh. "I wish!" Silence swallows his laughter, and a grimace steals the joy from his face. "Sorry. No. We never slept together."

He said that to me once, on his knees in the kitchen as he pleaded his case. But a part of me never believed him. Not with the rumors—and Mom's accusations—filling my head with another story. Not until now, when he has no reason to lie.

I press my fingers against my temples, trying to make sense of it all. "But there were feelings before? Right?"

"For who?"

"For Lucy."

He opens his mouth, a little sound of realization escaping, and nods. "Yeah." The word is wistful. Breathy. "I've loved her my entire life. Or at least for every second she was a part of it."

Now my head is really starting to hurt. "But you married Mom?"

His brow furrows. "Kimberly?"

"Yes."

"She was pregnant." He mulls it over. "With you, as a matter of fact."

A squirrel shoots across the cemetery, startling us both. My mind is at once spinning and holding incredibly still, trying to keep up while attempting not to move too fast and miss it all in the process.

I lay a hand over Dad's. His skin is bruised where they gave him an IV, so my squeeze is gentle. "Were you ever happy?"

His lips curl upward, crinkling the corners of his eyes. "I was happy being your dad."

"But not with Mom?"

His head drops. "Kimberly is a…difficult person."

I snort. I don't mean to, but it slips out. A flock of starlings evacuate the oak branches overhead, calling out their distaste. Dad chuckles, too, though there's something broken in it. In us.

When the laughter subsides, it leaves behind a raw ache in my chest. I push my palm hard against my breastbone, but the pain remains just out of reach.

"Were you and Lucy together after Mom and I left?"

He shakes his head. His bottom lip warbles.

"Why not? There was nothing standing in your way. Waylon was gone. We were gone. Why not go after Lucy, if you had truly loved her your whole life?"

"The only person I love more than Lucy"—he glances up at me—"is you."

I blink. "I don't understand."

He opens his mouth to speak, and the words stall. This time I'm not sure if it's because of the dementia or because some things simply cannot be explained, no matter how hard we try.

Like why neither of us stood up for ourselves when it came to Mom, or how we both ended up in love with a Parker. Across time and circumstance, I find myself walking the same path he did, right down to supporting him through the very disease that took his mom from him in the end.

There are no words for a pain like this. Him, looking at his past while I'm staring into my future. The two looking so painfully similar.

"I wanted you to come home, sweet pea. There had to be room for you to come home." He turns to Lucy's stone, and tears slip from the corners of his eyes. "Lucy… She understood."

For me. Even when I had been so cruel as to cut him out of my life.

"I'm so sorry, Dad." I lay my head on his shoulder. A trembling hand crosses over his chest to stroke my cheek. I suck in a breath and hold it, trying to capture it and this moment in the very same grasp. "I would've understood. I—"

How do I explain to him that I think I know exactly how he felt for Lucy, because it's the same love I've held for her son for my whole life? It's the torch I've carried, one I didn't even know my father passed on to me before today. One I never would've had if he'd gone after what he truly wanted.

One that still isn't mine to keep, given the circumstances we're in.

His hand drops to my knee. He pats it gently, like I'm a child again, being comforted even when I intended to do the comforting.

"It's okay. It's done." He squeezes my knee. "You two are better than us in every way, and now you have each other. That's all we could ask."

But it's not okay, I want to say. How do I go on, knowing my father gave up everything for me? Not only his life, but his one chance with the woman he loved. For the first time I see so clearly what Truett meant about my father sacrificing himself at the altar of everyone around him. At the altar of my happiness. The same way Truett accused me of doing for everyone else.

Like father, like daughter. No matter how much you might wish it wasn't so.

Dad sighs, and I swear the weight of the world comes out on that breath.

"I'm ready," he says.

"Okay." I swallow past the lump in my throat and rise, dusting imagined dirt from my legs. "We can head back to the house. I'll order some pizza and we can watch a movie. Maybe *The Truman Show*?"

He smiles, but it doesn't reach his eyes. There's a resignation to his sloped shoulders. His solemn gaze. He's looking right at Lucy's stone when he says, "No. I'm ready to go to a home."

The air stalls in my lungs. "What?"

"It's time." His breathing is rapid, and for a moment I'm worried I'm losing him, but his gaze is alert. Intense with passion rather than delirium. "I don't want this for you. I never wanted this."

"I'm happy to do it, Dad. I don't mind at all."

He chuckles under his breath, like this is exactly what he expected me to say. "I'm ready, sweet pea." He turns to me and meets my gaze. "I want to go now, while I'm still me. Some of the time."

"All the time," I correct. "You're you, even when you're confused."

He sighs. "I'm so tired."

"Let's go back, then. You can take a nap. I'll order food." I offer my hand to help him rise. "It'll be okay. You'll see."

He doesn't let my gaze drop. He grabs hold of my hand and repeats softly, "I'm ready."

And perhaps he is. But I don't know if I ever will be.

Chapter Thirty-Six

Henry

March 20th, 2015

WHEN I ARRIVE HOME, light is spilling onto the front yard, painting the grass a dull yellow. I shut off the car, but I remain seated long enough to second-guess my resolve. Long enough to see Lucy's headlights as she passes. To worry for her, before guilt steals that from me, too.

I force myself to get out. I put one foot in front of the other, but I don't hear a single step. My ears are crowded with the rush of blood evacuating my face. My shoes are on one second, and then they're off. I don't register discarding them in the pile by the door. The door creaks as I push inside. Shudders closed behind me. I follow the sound of reality television into the living room, half-blind thanks to a blur of white-hot shame clouding my vision.

I find Kimberly there, curled up in the corner of the sofa with a throw blanket draped haphazardly over her knees. A half-empty glass of white wine glistens on the side table. I pause for a moment, but no sound comes from the back of the house. Delilah's not home yet. There's still time.

I swallow hard. "I need to talk to you."

Kimberly doesn't look up from her show. "About what?"

"Could you look at me please?"

She huffs a breath but tears her eyes away for a heartbeat. It's long enough. Whatever she sees on my face grabs her attention. "What's wrong now?"

My airways are closing. My stomach is inside out. I try to speak, but the words won't come. Only tears. Sticky, hot tears that I wipe away as quickly as they fall, but there's always more to replace them. I give up eventually. They soak my face, my throat, the collar of my shirt. I'm sodden by the time I manage to yank each mangled word from my lips.

"I kissed someone else."

Her face is perfectly blank for a moment. It shatters when she rolls her eyes. "Good for you, Henry. I couldn't care less."

"W-what?"

She groans as she reaches for the remote and pauses her show, then untangles herself from her blanket to rise from the couch. She takes her time straightening the navy-blue cotton shorts and matching top she has on. When she faces me once more, her expression is one of cool indifference. "If you think jealousy is the way you're going to get me to stay, you're sorely mistaken. We've been over this. I'll stay through next school year, but when Delilah moves out, I will too."

My mouth opens. Closes. The tears slow to a constant drip. "I'm not trying to make you jealous, Kimberly. I'm trying to tell you I fucked up. Trying to have an adult conversation about it."

Her gaze flickers over my face. Scans the length of my entire body. She takes a step closer. Curls her nose as though she smells Lucy's perfume coming off me in waves. When our eyes meet again, hers are wide. "Who? Who did you fucking kiss?"

I know. I know it shouldn't matter. Not after everything she's said, everything that's happened over the last year. Over the last seventeen years. But seeing her anger, knowing I deserve it for once, rips my heart out and shreds it in one fell swoop.

I cast my eyes downward, unable to watch the wound open when I whisper, "Lucy."

"*WHAT?*" She steps forward, plants her hands on my shoulders, and shoves. "You better not be fucking serious. Lucy? Of all the people in the world you could screw, you picked her? I knew it. I damn well knew from the day we got married and you couldn't keep your fucking eyes off her." She pushes me again. Steps back to look at the whole of me in absolute disgust. "How could you?"

I throw my hands up. "You said you were leaving."

"I haven't fucking left yet! Damn it, Henry, you had one more year. One. More. Year. You couldn't keep it in your pants till then? You don't think you owe me that much?"

"I didn't…we didn't… It was a *kiss,* Kimberly. I swear." My brow furrows. "I'm telling you because I know I fucked up, and I'm sorry I disrespected you. But we've been over for a very long time. You made that incredibly clear."

"We're still married, Henry!" She swipes a candle off the end table and throws it my way. I dodge it, barely, but hear it shatter on the hardwood behind me. "You expect me to believe you didn't fuck her? You're a fucking cheat! I gave up *everything* for you, and this is how you repay me?"

This time it's her wineglass, the contents of which soak my feet upon landing. The smell of alcohol burns my nose. My foot stings. I glance down to see a small shard of glass sticking upright in my skin, right behind my big toe. A drop of blood leaks from it like a rusted tear slipping over my skin.

Good, I think. *I deserve this.* Because she's right. We are still married. I made a promise to her, and I broke it. All I can do now is try to minimize the damage.

"I know, Kimberly. I'm sorry. I'm so fucking sorry." I flatten my palm against my heart, mostly to reassure myself that it's still there. "Whatever you need from me, you've got it. I'll quit my job. I won't be near her. For as long as you stay, I'll be loyal to you and to this marriage. But we've got to figure out a solution that doesn't hurt—"

"Mom? Dad?"

The words die on my lips. Kimberly is frozen with her hand around a picture frame. In it, she and I are smiling. Delilah is standing between us, large Mickey ears on her head. It's the only family vacation we ever took. One of the happiest memories we share.

A snarl twists Kimberly's face. She holds up the frame, gaze fixed over my shoulder. "Delilah, if you learn one thing from me, let it be this." She slams the frame on the floor. The sound is like a clap of thunder in the small house, startling everyone but its maker. "Don't waste a minute of your life on any man."

I glance over my shoulder. My daughter, the light of my life. My kindred spirit. She looks stricken. Her narrow face is pale, eyes wide. Her light brown hair flows wild and unruly from her crown. A sprig of grass sticks out from behind her ear. But what eviscerates me is her gaze, which flicks from her mother to me, unsure of who to trust.

Her whole life, I've tried to be the constant. The steady hand through the storms of her mother's moods. The person she can depend on, no matter what. How could I have let her down so monumentally, that I've now taken that away from her? I'm the rug stripped from beneath her feet, and I'm watching her free-fall before my very eyes.

"I'm so sorry, Delilah," I say.

"What's going on?" she asks, brow scrunched tightly.

"Tell her, Henry. Tell her what you did."

Another crash. Delilah and I both turn toward the sound. This time it's a wedding photo on the ground. Delilah stumbles forward, and I put out a hand. "Careful. There's too much glass, sweet pea."

"Oh, don't pretend to be this perfect caretaker now that she's here." Kimberly points at me, but her eyes are on our daughter. "Not gonna tell her? Fine. I will. He fucked your friend's mom, that's what he did. He cheated. He's a goddamn cheater. He ruined everything."

"Dad?" Delilah's voice is so small, so childlike that for a moment I'm transported back in time to when she was little and afraid of the dark. I'd tuck her into bed, but inevitably about ten minutes later, she'd tiptoe down the hall and find me watching TV on the couch, her soft voice dragging me from whatever show to go do the whole closet-check routine over again.

This time she's looking at the monster. A fact that strikes shame down my spine, grounding itself at my feet.

"I kissed her. I kissed Lucy. And I shouldn't have. I'm so sorry." I drop to my knees, hearing but not feeling the glass crunching beneath my weight. "Please, Delilah. Please forgive me. I love her. I'm so sorry."

"You LOVE her? Is that what you fucking said?" Our bedroom door swings open, slamming into the wall behind it. A second later my duffel bag comes flying through the doorway, landing with a dull thud at my side. Clothes are thrown in an array of colors, so fast that I can barely make them out. Kimberly follows soon after, her face mottled red with anger. "Get out. *Get. Out.* I can't look at you right now."

"But, Delilah…"

"You should go, Dad," Delilah says softly. Her gaze is guarded, one hand braced on the kitchen counter for support. She catches my eye and shakes her head. "It's better if you go."

Better for whom? I want to ask. But it's not my place. I gave up that right when I let myself be so damn selfish for a split second. A split second that shattered my world, and hers right along with it.

"Okay," I say, my voice a raw croak. "I'll go."

"And if you go see that whore, so help me God—"

"Mom," Delilah interjects, her voice weary.

"What?" Kimberly snaps.

"Lucy's my—"

"Your what, Delilah? If you think she's anything more to you than some woman who used you to get close to your dad, you're as stupid as your father."

"Don't talk to her like that," I say, rising from my knees. "This has nothing to do with her."

Kimberly's lips pinch together. She holds my stare for so long I consider the possibility that we'll stay like this till we're old and gray, neither giving an inch, while the world goes on spinning around us.

"Out," she commands. Then she pivots on her heel, marches into our bedroom, and slams the door.

I turn to Delilah. "I'm so sorry. I can explain."

Her gaze drops to the floor. She starts toward me, and for a moment hope rises in my chest, but it quickly crashes when she walks around me to the laundry door, which she opens. She retrieves a broom and dustpan, shuts the door, then gets to work cleaning up the shattered candle.

"Please go. It'll make it harder on everyone if you stay." Her voice drops off, but I still hear it when she mutters, "Especially me."

My heart plummets, but I do as she asks. I gather my clothes, not bothering to look at what Kimberly tossed my way. I shrug the bag onto my shoulder. Cast one more glance around the bedraggled remnants of our once peaceful home, now splintered apart irrevocably.

"At least let me help you," I say, reaching for the broom handle.

She jerks it away. There's a fire starting in her eyes, the sparks of betrayal, when she glances up at me. "Dad." It's a warning. A boundary.

So I heed it. I back carefully over the glass shards toward the door, never taking my eyes off her. When I reach it, I grab the handle but keep my gaze trained on Delilah. "I love you. I'll come back in the morning. I won't leave you, I promise."

"Good night," she mumbles, but she doesn't look up. I'm being dismissed.

I shut the door behind me, cocooning myself in the quiet night. It's too cold out still for birds to sing, for crickets to chirp. As I pluck the glass from my skin and slip into my shoes, that fresh cut stinging, I spare a glance for the farmhouse on the hill. All its windows are aglow, floating in the darkness. I think of what it is Lucy is facing, and I pray she's safe.

Then I load myself into the car and pull away, unsure of where it is I'm heading, only that I have to keep going.

Chapter Thirty-Seven

Delilah

WARM WOOD PRESSES against my skin, no doubt imprinting the looping pattern of its grain on the backs of my thighs. My laptop hums quietly on my lap. A gust of equally hot wind rips through, giving the swing I'm sitting on an invisible push. The swing Dad installed for Mom as a gift, a place for her to lounge on summer days like this one, with a perspiring glass of sweet tea in hand. Yet another thing that wasn't enough to make her happy.

Sometimes I wonder if I was the first, or if her disdain started long before I came to be.

My gaze rakes over the ebbing fields of Truett's farm, settling on a lone figure bent over a downed fence post in the closest pasture. The one the females and their calves graze in, lazily scarfing down endless supplies of green grass this time of year. I squint. I can just make out a straw cowboy hat, sitting low on the figure's head. Hope leaps in my chest. Even from this distance, it'd be a relief to see Truett. The unscrewing of a pressure valve, letting off a bit of steam.

The figure removes the hat, and my heart sinks to the bottom of my stomach, heavy as a stone. Dark hair is disturbed by gloved hands. Ollie. Truett's farmhand replaces the hat and gets back to work.

I shouldn't care, but my shoulders sag with disappointment. It's a telltale sign that while I might know in my head that a relationship between us is the last thing I'm capable of right now, my heart sank its claws into a different narrative—one it's not tempted to let go of quite yet.

I'm so lost in this round robin of thoughts that I miss the sound of tires crunching over discarded acorns. Don't look up until footsteps thud against the weather-worn wood of the front steps and draw my attention away from the field.

"Hey, stranger," Alicia says. A bouquet of brightly colored mums interspersed with greenery and bursts of baby's breath sits clenched in her fist. She holds the bouquet up, a light pink blush settling high on her round cheeks. "Brought these for you." Her other hand moves from behind her back, producing at least five Caramellos trying to spill from her grasp. "And these are for your dad. Please tell me he still loves these things, because there are about ten more in the car."

I swallow the rising tide of nerves and second-guessing and force a smile on my face that I pray is more convincing than I feel. "Did you clean out Sunshine?"

She nods, expression morose. "I did. But it was the price that had to be paid for the great Henry Ridgefield. Citizens of Fly Hollow will understand."

I snort softly, and a relieved smile blooms on her face. No lipstick today. It makes her seem younger, more like the Alicia I knew at seventeen. And twelve. And five.

A dark red indent cuts through my palm when I lift it from the keypad and gesture to the space opposite me on the bench. My back rests against one of the arm rails, but I tug up my legs to free a seat on the other side. "Care to join me?"

"Sure!" She balances the bouquet carefully on the handrail

wrapping the porch and piles the candy bars beside it. When she sits on the swing, it rocks beneath us, then finally settles. "What are we doing? Admiring your cowboy from afar?"

"That one isn't mine." *None of them are,* I almost add. Even if my broken heart disagrees.

"Oh?" She flattens a hand over her eyes and squints, blocking out sun that's already been shielded by the roof. "Where's yours then?"

Now would be a good time to correct her, but that damn heart of mine has clamped its hand over my lips.

My gaze skirts the field once more, taking stock, but Truett is nowhere in sight. "Not sure."

She hums her understanding. When her gaze flits to my laptop, a wrinkle appears between her brows. "Are you working?"

"Not exactly." I scowl at my computer screen. "I'm researching memory care facilities in the area."

I found the list in a folder Truett had left in Dad's office, along with the burial plans and other forms he'd taken care of before I ever arrived in town. The temptation to call him, to ask for his help, was so strong I had to power down my phone to keep from acting on it.

Alicia's eyes widen briefly, but she catches herself. Relaxes the surprise as quickly as it arrived. "What changed your mind?"

"It hasn't changed. Not really." I release the breath scalding my lungs and pinch the bridge of my nose. It stings with imminent tears that I fight to hold back. I'm so sick of crying. I've been doing it all week, and it's gotten me nowhere except knee-deep in a migraine that even the strongest pain reliever won't touch. When my eyes peel back open, Alicia is a little blurry. I blink, bringing her empathetic frown into focus. "I don't know what to do, honestly. Dad says he's ready to go, but I feel like I'm failing as his daughter if I put him there."

She stretches one leg out alongside mine, our skin sticking

together in the damp summer air. It's a comfort though, to have her so close. To sit like we did what seems like a million years ago and talk about our problems as though they can actually be solved.

"What does Truett think of all this?"

I roll my bottom lip between my teeth. I should've known I couldn't skirt past this with Alicia. If anyone's gonna find out the dirt I'm hiding, it's her. I sigh, letting the fight go out of me along with the air. "I haven't really spoken to him since everything went down."

"And why not?"

"With everything going on, I just can't…" I wave a hand in the air by my head and widen my eyes, searching for an explanation in the forest across the street. When one doesn't magically appear, I drop my hand, defeated. "I can't pursue him *and* take care of my dad. I'm not capable of doing both. Not well, anyway. I certainly proved that last week, which is probably why Dad is suddenly hell-bent on going into care sooner rather than later."

The words singe my throat. It's a truth I've been too afraid to utter aloud, even in the quiet of my bedroom long after Dad has drifted off to sleep, yet I've served it up to her on a silver platter. *Here, judge my shitty performance as a daughter.* Like I'm not hard enough on myself as it is.

It's not judgment I find swimming in her brown eyes when I glance up. Understanding wells in her gaze. It hugs the downward curve of her lips. Everywhere I look on her face, there grace is, just waiting to be found.

"Have you ever considered that it's not that you aren't capable of this, but rather that you're capable of so much more? That your dad sees it, and wants it for you? A life he was never willing to take for himself but has the chance to offer you instead."

I drop my gaze to the laptop. To my hands, trembling against the keys. "Even if I wanted to, I don't think I could afford it. Truett helps pay for Roberta as it stands."

"I don't suppose you'd want to ask him for help with a facility…?"

I shake my head before the words have finished falling from her lips. "No."

She shrugs. "What other options do you have?"

"Sell the house, I guess. That was the plan they had before I came home, at least." I glance up at the wooden beams above my head. The same ones I've sat beneath since I was a little girl, and my dad before me. It's not that I want to live here forever. I just never imagined losing my childhood home like this, with no time to prepare for that particular goodbye. Tears prick at my eyes. My laugh is a wild animal, equipped with claws that rake my throat. "I thought about calling my mom to ask about the money my grandparents left for my wedding one day, but then I remembered my mom would rather die than help my dad in any way."

It's not like I need the money for its intended purpose. The only wedding I've ever been able to imagine for myself involves Truett and I eloping in one of his fields, wildflowers tucked in my hair and my father's arm looped through mine. And I'll never have that. So why hoard money away that could be better used to help me now?

Compassion creases Alicia's features. "I could sit with you while you call her, if that would help."

My lips flatten. I imagine Alicia overhearing the kinds of things my mother says to me on a normal phone call, let alone when I ask her for money to help her ex-husband get the care he needs. Shame climbs the column of my throat and lodges itself there, immovable against the pull of me swallowing.

Because that's the thing, isn't it? No mother should ever speak to their child in a way that they'd be ashamed for others to over-hear. In a way that completely rewrites the voice in their child's head for the worse. I can't remember when my inner monologue became colored by my mother's chastisements. All I know is when I suspect I'm failing at something, it's her voice that confirms my worst fears. Hurls them back at me with a few extra concerns added on for good measure.

I know she's wrong for being that way, and yet I can't help but want to protect her—and myself—by hiding these ugly truths away.

"There's no point," I whisper. "It's not like she'll listen."

Alicia's frown deepens.

I quirk a brow. "What?"

She leans forward and rests her hand on my knee. "Maybe that's because no one ever made her." She catches my gaze, daring me to disagree. When I don't—*can't*—she nods and reclines back against the armrest. "Listen, as someone whose mother will also walk all over her if not put in her place, I get it. But you're not a child anymore, Delilah. You get to decide how people treat you. Talk to you. You may think it's some kind of failure to let others help you, but there's power in that, too—in who you choose to lean on when times get hard. And times are really fucking hard right now.

"If your mom won't be someone you can depend on, then fuck her. I know that's harsh, but I mean it. You deserve better than the bullshit hand you've been dealt, and I'm sorry it took me so long to say so. Sorry that I ever played a part in making you feel like you're less than, or lacking, or that you only have your mother so you have to put up with that kind of treatment lest you be left alone." Her voice grows hoarse. She forces herself to pause and swallow, but the pain remains like a heartbeat in her gaze. Steady. Life-giving.

"But you're not alone. Not now. You have me. Your dad. What's the caretaker's name—Roberta? You have her." She tips her head toward that farmhouse on the hilltop, one eyebrow raised. "Truett, if you'll let him."

Tears spill down my cheeks. More and more, they are becoming the language for a type of pain that English simply doesn't cover. I realize that's probably why my father loves music so much, even now. It's a language that conveys what spoken words cannot. Grief that pours out from his fingertips, while mine leaks from my eyes.

"You're right. I know you are." I shrug flimsily, my shoulders suddenly too heavy to lift. I'm weighed down by so many decisions that I wish weren't mine to make, by burdens I don't know how to let go of. My gaze meets Alicia's through the watery mess of my tears, and I tell her the honest truth. "But I don't know how to be anybody else."

"Not someone else. You." She smiles. "Just less of an island. More of a peninsula, maybe, to start with?"

I crinkle my nose. "Was that a geography joke? I thought you were a music teacher."

"What can I say? I'm a woman of many talents." Her laughter reminds me of the wind chimes that once hung from the rafters on Tru's front porch, their music summoned by the slightest breeze. She lets it fade, the wind gone still, as her gaze levels mine. Her legs sweep to the floor as she sits up, reaches over, and slips my laptop from my grasp. "Call your mom, Delilah. Get whatever answers you need. Then we can decide how to proceed. No matter what she says."

We can decide. It shouldn't mean so much, that little pronoun, but in this moment it might be the most beautiful word I've heard in my entire life. My chest deflates even as fear pebbles my skin with goose bumps. When all you've had is yourself for so long, it's scary to risk depending on someone else. But it's scarier to face everything alone.

So I reach for Alicia. Hold her hand as the phone rings

through to my mother, who answers the call with a heavy sigh and a distracted, "Delilah, I'm a bit busy right now."

I swallow back the bile coating the back of my tongue. My hands tremble, but Alicia doesn't let go of the one she's holding. She squeezes it tighter.

"I need to talk to you." I draw in a shaky breath, forcing the fist clasping my lungs to loosen its grip. "It's important."

"You've been ignoring me for weeks, and I'm supposed to drop everything because you've decided you're ready to talk? That's very selfish, you know that?"

I bite down so hard I'm afraid I'll shatter my molars. I have to force each muscle to relax, one by one, until finally I can speak again. "I… Well, Dad, he's… He's ready to go into care, Mom. He wants to."

"Well, that's great news!" The immediate cheer in her voice grates on my ears. "So you're coming home?"

I haven't even gotten there yet. What happens to me in all this? Where do I end up?

"One step at a time," Alicia murmurs as though she can hear my thoughts.

"Is someone with you?" Mom asks. I picture that thin little wrinkle appearing between her eyebrows. Something so familiar that for a minute I can't breathe around the wound missing it opens.

"No." I shake my head, though I know she can't see me. "Mom, I'm not calling because I'm coming home. I'm calling because I need help."

"Help?" Her tongue curls around the word in disgust. "What do you mean, you aren't coming home?"

"I didn't say that; I just—" Heat rises up my throat. Fills my cheeks. I feel ill with a fever all of a sudden, like my entire body is revolting against this conversation. I want to give in. To say never mind and tell Alicia I'll figure something else out. Anything else but this.

But then I think of my dad, sitting beside me on the bench at Lucy's grave. His wide, somber gaze as he told me he was ready.

And I decide if he can be, then so will I.

"You know the money Grandma and Grandpa set aside for my wedding?"

"What?" She pauses. I've tilted her off axis, and it takes her a second to recenter. "Is this some kind of joke? Who the fuck are you marrying? Lucy's kid? Delilah, so help me God—"

"I'm not marrying anybody, Mom. That's exactly the problem." I lock eyes with Alicia. Hers brim with courage I don't feel. Tears that I very much do. "I'm not getting married any time soon, but Dad needs to go into care, and I could really use the money to help him."

"Sell the damn house."

I blink. Alicia doesn't.

"I can't, Mom."

A chair scrapes against some faraway floor. She's pacing now, which is how I know I've really pissed her off.

"And why the hell not?" Mom bites.

Something cuts loose inside me, and suddenly everything I'd been holding so tightly comes unraveled in my hands. *"Why not? How about because it's my father's? Or because I still want to be nearby in case he needs me. I can't dump him at a home and then abandon him."*

"Sure you can. He did the same thing with us, dumped us for Lucy like—"

"All he did was kiss her!" I push off the swing and brace my hands on the railing, gaze trained on the spray of flowers. Alicia's brows hit her hairline. "Jesus Christ, Mom, all this time you made it out like they had some wildly sordid affair, but they just fucking kissed. And I know that's wrong—I do. But you watched me

suffer for years, and all you ever did was double down, heaping coals on top of his head. You wanted me to hate him as much as you did, so you wouldn't be alone. You told me he didn't love me or miss me. But he did, Mom! He *does.* He loves me and I love him. He's my father. And what happened between the two of you never should've been my business in the first place."

Silence deadens the line. I don't think she's breathing, but neither am I. We're in a standoff that spans hundreds of miles and all the years I've spent burying my feelings inside to keep the peace. *Her* peace, while my own heart was torn to shreds.

"That money was meant for you. For your wedding. Your future. You're not gonna shack up with some dumb hick in a plain church with no one around to care." Hurt beads on the surface of her words. It spills through the line, and I'm drenched in it. "I will not let you throw your life away for that man. Not like I did."

I close my eyes. Squeeze them so tight stars burst in the darkness. "That man is my father. And I'm sorry that your life didn't go the way you planned, but that's not my fault. I don't care about some theoretical wedding that I may or may not one day have. What I do care about is taking care of my dad, the same as I'd care for you if the situations were reversed."

I bite hard at my bottom lip, drawing blood. It's sharp and metallic on my tongue, and so bittersweet. All of this is so damned bittersweet. Realizing how much I didn't understand, how much my father loves me, just as I'm running out of time. Finding Truett again, falling for him all over again…but not having the courage to let him in.

Finally standing up to my mother, while knowing it may very well mean I lose her, too.

I'm here now. Might as well go for broke.

"Mom, I love you. I do. But if you want to have any kind of relationship with me when this is all over, then you need to think really carefully about what you decide."

"Are you threatening me?" she bites out.

I turn toward Alicia. She's watching me carefully, a fight lighting her eyes that reminds me I'm not alone. It's weird how anger gets such a negative rap. It can be such a source of power, of drive. And having someone be angry *for* you? That can change your life.

"Not a threat, Mom. The truth. My grandparents left that money for me. And if I want to use it to help my dad, then that's my choice. But if you decide not to cosign on that? Well, you can keep it. Because whatever wedding I have one day, you won't be invited to it."

"Delilah—"

"Let me know, Mom," I interject; then I hang up the phone.

Alicia and I stare at each other, holding our breath, for so long that I choke on my next inhale. My lungs burn. My chest is tight. And my eyes are raw with tears that fell silently, without stopping, for the entire call.

But I did it. So why don't I feel proud of myself?

"It's not like in the movies," Alicia finally says, her voice heavy with compassion.

I don't have the energy to lift a brow. I feel like I've run a marathon, despite only making it a few steps across the porch. "What do you mean?"

"You know, where the hero wins the fight and rides off into the sunset, beating his chest in triumph." The corners of her mouth dip as she rises, crosses the distance between us, and grabs hold of my elbows. "That only happens for Superman. Or men in general, I think, because life isn't fair." She snorts at her own joke, but her gaze is hard. "No one ever tells you that standing up for yourself involves killing off the version of you that allowed that treatment to go on all this time. It feels like shit because it's murder, Delilah. A vigilante killing, but a killing all the same."

My gaze flicks between her somber eyes. I suck in a breath;

then I'm reaching for her. Pulling her in tight. She smells like jasmine and my childhood, all wrapped into one.

"I can't believe you called me a murderer," I murmur into her hair.

She pulls back enough to look me in the eye. "But, like, the good kind?"

I snort. Grief scrapes the surface of my heart, and I don't just let it. I beckon it deeper. Because at least the pain means I wasn't complacent. Stagnant. No longer a rock that the river runs through but the river itself, carving its own path forward. "Thank you for being here."

"I'm about a decade late"—she taps my nose and smiles—"but I owed you one."

"Better late than never," I say, glancing over her head at Truett's farm.

Chapter Thirty-Eight

Delilah

"ARE YOU READY?"

I shift my footing. Loose bits of rock scrape underfoot, fragments fallen from tires onto the faded cement of the parking lot. It grates my ears, almost as much as my voice when I say, "I'm trying to be."

The edges of Dad's eyes soften. "Take your time."

Time. It unspools like sand through the threads of my fingers, spilling onto the ground beneath me. I made the mistake once of thinking I had a whole beachfront full of it, only to realize now that all along it was an illusion. The scene of a beautiful vacation, encased in the finite boundaries of a snow globe.

I shook it the day I came home. And here we are, looking at what was stirred up.

The grounds of Edgewood Assisted Living are immaculately landscaped. Square-edged bushes surround the red brick building, and large magnolia trees tower at each corner. Carefully pruned wisteria vines weave through gardening arches that line a walking path off to my right. The building itself is stately and classical, with large columns standing guard on the front porch and windows lining the facade, allowing light to pour in at every angle.

It's an enormous complex, with the assisted living building up front and a dedicated memory care facility on the back. Dad would start in assisted living and stay for as long as he can handle some independence. The memory care facility is for when the disease outpaces therapy and meds and *time,* which I pray we have more of than we think.

Mom called me late last night, long after I'd tucked myself into bed and tried to sleep. I don't know how long I tossed and turned, going over every word I wished I'd said differently. Analyzing each held breath, every sniped comment. When my phone lit up, I was sure she was calling to let me have it for being so disrespectful. And I was prepared to agree with her.

"You're right," she whispered through the receiver, something I've never heard her say before. Words I wasn't even sure she was capable of uttering.

I had to stop myself from saying, *I am?* Instead I repeated the mantra that had been living in my head all day. *It's a murder, but a necessary one.* Then I mentally thanked Alicia for the morbid pick-me-up, almost missing Mom's words in the process.

"He said all they did was kiss. I know that. But I couldn't believe it, Delilah. He had been so pissed that I said I was leaving him, but he had the nerve to do that? *With* her?"

"You were going to leave him?"

"Once you graduated. That was the deal I made." She sighed, and I could hear the tears on her breath. *"I was miserable there, Delilah. Wasting away. I had to get out."*

In the dark I reached for my heart. Fumbling through tangled blankets and the rodeo T-shirt I never gave back to Truett, I finally found my own skin. Pressed against my chest, my palm vibrated in tune with my pulse. Lifted on the tide of every breath. Up and then down. Inhale the truth, exhale the lie.

"I'm going to give you the money. You're all I have left. I can't lose you." Her tone curdled, making otherwise sweet words rancid. *"But I'm doing it for you. Not for him."*

Good enough, I thought. Then, and now. As I look up at the ornate building, with all its drama and flair, those words trumpet in my brain. Our shoes aren't littering the front porch, but it's good enough. There's no crooked floorboard to greet you, but it's good enough.

It's not at home with me, but it's good enough.

I reach for Dad's hand and squeeze. "Ready."

A gentle smile crinkles the softest parts of his face. "Okay."

The foyer is lined with black-and-white tiles that remind me of an old manor house from the British drama television Dad and I have taken to watching when he can't fall asleep. His newest meds are supposed to help with that, but they either haven't kicked in yet or he's immune. Our shoes scuff and squeak as we make our way to the front desk. A young lady with tightly coiled hair and skin as dark as umber glances up at us and offers a bright smile from behind the desk.

"You two here for the tour?"

Her voice has a soft twang to it, the kind that embraces you from the inside out. I find myself leaning in close, elbows braced on the smooth wooden countertop, while Dad glances around with his mouth popped open.

"Yes, ma'am. We're the Ridgefields."

The corner of Dad's mouth twitches. A smile that matches my own. We're the Ridgefield family. The two of us. And no matter what Mom has tried to make me believe, there's nothing sad about that.

"Perfect. My name is Kesha. I'm one of the care coordinators here, and I'll be showing you around today." She steps out from behind the counter and offers her hand to me and my father in turn. "It's so nice to meet you both."

The way she smiles, the soft grip in her hand. It reminds me so much of Roberta. I text her to tell her so, and my heart warms when she responds that she's proud of me for doing what's right even when it's hard.

I still don't know about right, but it makes me feel like everything might at the very least be okay.

We tour the memory care facility first. I imagine it's so we don't end on such a sad note. It's clean, well-appointed, and the staff seem nice, but it's still depressing. I'm glad it's brief.

We take the wisteria-lined path back to the main building, and there we see a small movie theater, salon, and a room they've decorated to look like a soda shop. You can tell the intended resident is a lot older than my father by the choice of decor and movies on the roster, which only adds to the unfairness of it all. But Dad takes it all in stride, even asking for a photo with a cutout of a woman sporting big breasts and a tray of milkshakes in hand that they keep propped behind the counter of the soda shop. I snap the shot with tears in my eyes.

The residents' rooms are more like apartments, with small kitchenettes that host mini fridges and countertops but nothing that can catch fire, and a lounge area that leads into the bedroom and bath. Dad sprawls on the couch and props his feet up. "I could get used to this," he says, grinning.

Kesha laughs good-naturedly. I bury my hands in my jean pockets and force a chuckle.

"We'll check out the dining room last. Lunch will be served soon, so you can meet a few of the residents while you're there!" Kesha tosses this over her shoulder as we stride down the hall, past framed images of beaches and faded florals and one of a dog and a cat snuggling close. It reminds me of the doctor's office, and I can't help but grimace.

The place is nice for what it is. I understand that. But I can't possibly imagine driving off and leaving my dad here alone. That is, until we step into the dining room.

The chairs and tables where they serve food are offset from the main room in an atrium, with light pouring in from all sides. An older woman and gentleman sit at a white-clothed table, chatting animatedly. There's a family in the farthest table. They have a little boy, about six years old, who plays checkers with the resident they must be visiting. The kid skips his checker an absurd number of times, then collects everything in its path. His laughter is maniacal. The man who plays opposite him grabs a white napkin from the table and waves it in the air in defeat, which only makes the little boy laugh harder.

My gaze skirts past all of it, taking in the joy and normalcy and life that thrums in the atrium, before settling on a sleek baby grand piano standing sentinel in the main room.

Dad notices it at the same time as me. His lips audibly pop as they part, his jaw slackened. I try to meet his gaze, but he turns to Kesha, who's watching his reaction with a raised brow.

"Can I...?" His words drop off, though I don't know if he's forgotten or is simply too thrilled to bother saying *play.*

"Go right ahead, Mr. Ridgefield."

"Henry," he corrects in a soft voice. Then he meets my gaze. "Will you...?"

So he has forgotten. Sometimes certain words slip through the cracks in his mind, and it can take days for him to find them again. If he ever does.

"You want me to play with you?" My voice wavers, tripping over the emotions left behind from our tour. "I haven't since I was a kid."

"That's okay." He offers me his hand. "I can teach you."

The bench creaks beneath our weight. My hands tremble, awareness of how many eyes are turning toward us making me regret agreeing. But excitement sparkles in Dad's gaze, holds his head up. He dusts his fingers over the keys with reverence, then meets my nervous stare with a wink meant to ease.

"I don't remember much," I admit.

"Don't worry. I'm a good teacher."

He starts slow, with a nursery rhyme that makes the elderly couple nearest us giggle and clap. I mimic his movements, letting those long-forgotten memories float to the surface. There was a time when I thought I could've been as talented as him. I'd tinker with his keyboard while he tuned his guitar. I even tried to take lessons with Lucy, an excuse to spend more time with her. But Mom never liked the whole music thing, and I wanted to make her happy, so I quit. Now, as my fingers drum along the keys, I wonder why I never cared about my own happiness.

Dad slips into a classic from Phil Collins. "Against All Odds." The only full song I ever learned to play on the piano, simply because it was Dad's favorite. I smile, remembering Lucy's note. Of course it was his favorite. All along, it's because it was hers.

Slowly the resentment I've held for the torch he carried for her gives way to understanding. To sorrow, that it ever had to be that way at all.

When Dad plays, he turns into something else. Himself, but so much more. He *is* the song. It's the air flowing in and out of his lungs. The blood coursing through his veins. For this moment we're suspended in time. There's no dementia here. No pain. And I could weep for it, that sweet reprieve, as I lose myself in it as well.

We play the song all the way through. Dad carries most of the harmony, while I keep us on track with the melody. Kesha's jaw drops somewhere around the second verse and stays that way till the very end. When the very last note breathes its last, the few people gathered around erupt in applause. He turns to me, flushed and wide-eyed, and smiles. "I like it here."

"Yeah?" I murmur. I inhale, but my lungs won't fill up. My hand is still trembling as I bring it to my chest and push, willing the ache away.

His brows gather close. "What's wrong?"

"I just—" Tears rush to the surface. Embarrassment knots my stomach. I can't believe I'm doing this here, in front of everyone. Kesha must see the look on my face, because she's suddenly very interested in the floor. I force my gaze to meet my father's, but all I want is to crawl in a hole. "I'm so sorry. For blaming what happened on you. For not understanding that you and Lucy…" My throat fills, and I swallow, trying to clear a path to breathe. "You loved her, Dad, and I'm sorry I couldn't see that. Didn't want to see that. I shouldn't have punished you for it. I was so cruel. I didn't even try to understand."

His hand settles over mine, where it has fallen into my lap. "You were just a kid."

"Yeah, but that letter—"

"That letter," he interjects, "made me so proud."

My breath catches. "W-what?"

"All I ever wanted was for you to be able to stand up for yourself. To say what you wanted, rather than what you thought we wanted to hear. I was proud of you for writing that letter." His gaze catches on mine and he grimaces. "I should've reached out to you sooner, but I wanted to honor your wishes."

Tears puddle in the corners of my mouth, dampening my words. "I was so selfish, Daddy."

He uses his free hand to swipe some of those tears away. The other remains on mine, squeezing every time a sob rattles my throat.

"Being selfish isn't as awful as people say. There are bad ways to be selfish, sure. Not being careful and getting someone into a situation they shouldn't be in. Marrying them so no one thinks you've done the wrong thing, even when you know your heart lies with someone else. Giving in to desires that will hurt everyone you love." His eyes go wide, unseeing, like he's in another time, rather than here with me. "But there are good ways, too. Like going after your dream job or living someplace just because you love it. Taking the one you love for yourself. Believing you deserve it. Because you do, sweet pea. I made the wrong decisions in my life, but I'm glad you were selfish. I hope you'll continue to be selfish in the very best ways."

The words are slow, stilted. I can hear the effort he puts into each one, and then into stringing them together to form a coherent sentence. It's a gift I'll never be able to thank him enough for, that he managed to give them to me.

By the time he falls quiet, I can't see him through the tears. I collapse into him, my arms tight around his neck, and let myself cry in my father's arms. Perhaps for the very last time.

"The cost of forgetting you," he whispers into my hair, "is that I'll never be able to make it right. To show you how very sorry I am for the way I let you down."

"I know, Daddy. I know."

He leans back, cradling my sopping-wet cheeks in his trembling hands, and smiles like I'm a miracle in the flesh. "I'd do it differently, you know. If I could. I'd tell you the truth. Set a better example. It's my first time living life, sweet pea, but I wish for your sake it were my second so I had better lessons to teach you."

I nod into his hands, my tears dripping into his palms. His guitar-string calluses are fading. Another piece of him that's slowly passing away. I want to hold on for as long as I can. But I also want him to know I'm capable of letting go.

"You did an amazing job. All the good things I am are because of you."

"No," he says, shaking his head. "They're because of *you*. You're remarkable, Delilah. Don't ever forget it."

I collect his hands in mine and squeeze. My head drops, gaze trained on our gathered hands. "Truett said the same thing."

"He's smart, like his mama was." Dad chuckles, but it's dry and wrought with pain. "Just one more life lesson, then we can do some paperwork and go get ourselves some shrimp sandwiches." He looks at the piano keys, his chin wobbling slightly, as he adds, "If you love him, don't let him pass you by. I promise you'll regret it for the rest of your life."

My face crumples, and his does, too. It takes several long minutes for us to gather our composure and peel ourselves away from the piano. Several more before we can explain to Kesha that despite our display, we do like it here, and we are ready to make that decision.

The whole drive to the Grille, I lose myself in fragile silence. Dad, meanwhile, chatters on about what he'll do if they don't have his shrimp this time, our conversation already forgotten. It's perhaps the only blessing of his disease, that wounds ripped open can so quickly be mended.

Mine remain raw within me, desperate for some kind of resolution. And no matter how many circles my brain travels in, I always come back to the same one, with dirty blond hair and a knowing grin.

Two hours later, when we roll into our driveway, he's waiting on our front porch as if I'd summoned him, my name the only word on his lips.

Chapter Thirty-Nine

Henry

April 14th, 2015

FOOTSTEPS SHUFFLE over the weather-beaten wood of my parents' front porch. Despite owning the house outright since the day my mother died, I still think of it as theirs. A vessel keeping me, like I'm a ship built in a bottle. A thing that looks like it should sail but never actually has.

I glance up as Delilah, who refuses to make eye contact, moves past with the last suitcase from her room. The moving truck isn't even half full. Turns out Kimberly's parents didn't want any of our hand-me-down furniture in their South Carolina estate. So boxes of clothes, some pictures, and Kimberly's exercise equipment are all that made the cut. Everything else will stay, a museum of the family that once resided here, before I blew it all to bits.

Guilt is a half-starved rodent crawling around my insides, gnawing at anything it can get its paws on. Every day that passes takes another piece of me. Soon I'll be nothing but the chewed-up consequences of my own poor decisions, with nothing but the walls to hear my apologies.

I've tried to give them to Delilah. At first she seemed like she wanted to talk. We built a bridge over morning coffee before she left for school each day, when her mom was still fast asleep. That all disintegrated Friday night when Kimberly burst into my office.

"She's coming with me." Kimberly's eyes were bright with malice, her tone laced with it. She knew the weapon she held, and she wielded it perfectly. *"Guess you can't win 'em all, can you, Henry?"*

I sat up in my makeshift bed on the window seat, heart throbbing in my chest. *"What do you mean? Why would she leave? She loves it here."*

"What would you know about how she feels? You only ever think of yourself." She laughed, shoulders lifting slightly. *"Though that'll be perfect, since yourself is all you'll have left."*

I bite down hard on my tongue. Even remembering it has me panicking, my chest tight. I didn't argue with her that night, and haven't since. What do the details matter, after all, when the results are all the same? Semantics aside, I cheated. I ruined not only my life, but Delilah's, too. I deserve everything I've lost. Am continuing to lose.

Delilah turns to me once the truck is loaded. Her hair is braided back from her face, which is mottled with the quiet tears she's shed all morning. I rise to my feet, the bottom step creaking beneath my weight. When she finally lifts her gaze to meet mine, I swear I see an apology hiding behind the accusation.

I'm not sure which breaks my heart more.

I step down onto the dirt. A cloud of dust rises around my black Converse. She doesn't move. Doesn't blink. I chance another step forward. When her eyes flare wide in warning, I stop. Close enough. This has to be close enough.

I haven't hugged her since I left for the concert that night. Now I fear I'll never get to again.

"I love you, sweet pea." I place my hand over my heart, which has been hers since the day she was born. "And I'm so sorry. I'll never be able to make it up to you. I know that."

She whimpers, a tiny sound that escapes her parted lips. She clamps them closed.

"I want you to know that you'll always have a place here. This will always be your home. You can come back whenever you're ready. I—" My voice falters. I've never known how to put my feelings into words. Music? Sure. But this? It's so much harder. How do you teach your seventeen-year-old daughter a lesson you've yet to learn? A moral you're still trying to find in the rubble of your mistake?

"Dad…"

I strain to see her clearly through the blur caused by unshed tears. To memorize every freckle, every quirk. The way she tugs at her braid nervously while she tries to find her words. The arch of her brow when she does.

"You don't have to—" She licks her lips. Glances behind me and grimaces. "Never mind. Bye, Dad."

"I love you," I repeat.

Her gaze is still trained over my shoulder. "You too."

"I'll call."

"Don't bother," Kimberly says from behind me.

Delilah ducks her head and turns. I count each step as though it were her first, right up until she climbs into Kimberly's car and closes the door. Thirty-eight. It takes thirty-eight steps for my daughter to walk out of my life. Selfish. I was so selfish. And now it has cost me the only thing that matters.

"You know, I really should thank you."

I hear Kimberly approach, but don't turn. I won't take my eyes off Delilah till she's gone completely. Even the top of her head through a car window is a lifeline, which I'll hold on to till I lose even that.

Kimberly takes each step slowly. When she finally stands in

front of me, duffel bag on one shoulder and purse on the other, she smirks. "My parents never would've approved if I left you because I wanted my own life. Even at thirty-seven. But cheating? From someone who was never good enough for me anyway?" She shakes her head, gaze scanning the length of me. Whatever she finds, it's lacking. "You guaranteed I'll have their full support."

She reaches across her chest, spreads her purse open, and plucks a manilla folder from it. I take it from her hands and hold it limply at my side. I don't have to open it to know it contains a divorce filing. I don't have to read it to know I won't contest.

She pauses like she's waiting for me to beg. To try and change her mind. When I don't, she narrows her gaze. Crinkles her nose at me in disgust.

"Have a good life, Henry." She shrugs, a biting laugh piercing the air around us. "Or don't. The great thing is, either way, it's not my problem anymore."

When she walks away, I don't bother watching. All those years ago, I didn't see her coming. There's no need to watch her leaving now.

Instead I keep my gaze trained on our daughter. I track their progress over every pothole, past every live oak, till they disappear behind a thicket of holly, too tall for me to see over from here. I continue to watch even as the movers close up the truck and follow Kimberly's Honda Civic down the dirt road. I don't stop even when the sound of the truck's engine fades into the afternoon, or when the afternoon fades into the evening.

I don't know when it gets dark out, only that it does. Only that I'm afraid the light will never come on again. Not for me, anyway.

That's when Lucy arrives. She's wrapped in a quilt, wearing a tight white T-shirt over pajama pants that she's tucked into cowboy boots. Her hair is mussed, her eyes red from crying. She pauses in front of me, head tilted in question, and squeezes the quilt a bit tighter around her shoulders.

"I've been on our front porch for the past hour, and I haven't seen you move a lick. I figured I'd come check if you'd turned to stone."

I suck in a breath, shocked to find my lungs still remember how to hold it. "She's gone."

"Kimberly?"

"Delilah."

Lucy's expression freezes. Slowly, tears begin to stream from her eyes, polishing her irises till they shine. I want to join her, but I don't know how. I want to put this pain down, but I've no idea where to set it.

"I'm so sorry, Henry." She steps closer, a question opening up her gaze. When I don't react, *can't*, she opens her arms and embraces me. Rocks me when I finally start to weep. "She'll come back. I know she will. You've just gotta give her time."

I press my chin into the curve of her neck, trying and failing to regulate my breathing. "How do you know?"

"Do you remember when we were kids and you dreamed of running off to Nashville to make a career as a musician?"

I rise to my full height and glance down at her, one brow raised.

She goes on like she hasn't just thrown me for a loop. "Let's say you did do that. You even made it big. Spent ten, twenty, even thirty years touring with a band. What would you have done at the end of all that? Where would you have gone?"

It's not even a question. "I'd have come home."

"And so will Delilah. She loves it here, even if these last few weeks have made her think otherwise."

My brow furrows. "What do you mean?"

Lucy grabs my hand and nods toward the porch. I follow her, albeit slowly. My joints are stiff from standing in one place for too long. We take our time climbing the steps and settling onto the swing. The wood is cold even through my clothes. A shiver courses through me, and Lucy scoots closer till her body warms mine from proximity alone.

"The kids at school have been…none too kind to her since the news got out. Truett, too, but not nearly on the level of Delilah. He told me last night. I imagine because of this." She gestures toward the driveway.

I stare in that direction, unblinking. "I had no clue."

"Me neither. A bit too distracted by the comments made in the teachers' lounge when I go to microwave my lunch, I suppose." She laughs, but there's an edge to it. Her chin drops, and along with it her gaze. "Maybe I should resign, too. Make things easier for everyone."

"You can't, Lucy." I grab her hand, which brings her gaze back to me. "You worked too hard for this."

"So did you," she whispers.

"But I can work anywhere. I've got an interview at the music school in the city next week."

She squeezes my hand. The corners of her mouth tug downward, and my heart goes right along with them. "I'm grateful for what you did. For leaving, so that I could stay. I never would've asked you to do that, though, Henry. You've got to know that."

"I know." I clear my throat. "But it was the right thing to do. I'm the one who started all this."

Her lips form a flat line and she nods. "Waylon's gone, you know. Even my dad supported him. Told him he deserved a godly woman, and I'd clearly proven I was not one." She snorts softly, shaking her head. "Only time I've ever been grateful for Dad's misogynistic advice."

"How's Truett taking it?"

A smile blooms on her face. "He's relieved. The minute

Waylon walked out that door, I swear a light came back on in Tru's eyes that hasn't been there in years."

"Glad I could help, I guess."

Somewhere in the night, an owl calls. We pause, listening, but a response never comes.

Her gaze searches mine. "I didn't mean to take away from your pain, Henry, I promise. I just—" Her hands flutter aimlessly in the air, grasping for words. "I guess what I was trying to say is, the door is open. We can be together, you and me. *Finally.* Truett loves you and—"

"I can't." The words are out before I even have a second to process them. "I can't, Lucy. I'm sorry."

She blinks rapidly, gaze searching my face in the dim moonlight. "What?" The word is so soft, so malleable I almost want to try and change it. To change all of this and make it better than reality ever is.

But I can't change it. I can only take what is and make the best of it, like I always have. Or have always tried to do, at least.

"If Delilah… If I ever want to have a chance at her forgiveness… for her to come back…" I let my voice trail off. There's no need to say the rest aloud. I think hearing that we can never be together once in a lifetime is more than enough, let alone twice.

"…then you have to leave the door open," Lucy offers. A sacrifice and an acceptance all in one.

I nod. "Exactly."

Lucy Parker is the love of my life. I thought it before, when we were two kids who barely knew each other, but I'm certain of it now. Across time and space, and so many years, she is it for me. I feel it in my bones.

My daughter, though? She is my entire heart outside my body. An organ I can't live without. If she were ever to come back and find that I've moved on with Lucy… That's a break that could never be fixed. A risk I'm not willing to take.

"I'm so sorry." The words are Band-Aids on a gaping wound. Useless to stop the bleeding, but I try anyway. I have to try.

Lucy stands. The cold rushes in, in her absence, drenching me to my bones. She strides forward, blanket wrapped tightly, until she reaches the front step and cranes her neck back, taking in the only clear view of the moon from the porch. She's awash with silver-blue light, so similar to her eyes that it aches. Every gentle angle, every golden strand of hair. She's everything I've ever wanted, and everything I'll never be able to have. Watching her, I could fall to my knees and weep. But it wouldn't change anything.

"I learned a long time ago not to argue with you when you've made up your mind that you're doing what's right for someone else." She glances over at me, half her face cast in shadow. "I just wonder when, if ever, you'll consider if you've done what's right for you."

I open my mouth, but no words come out. She nods, like she expected as much, and steps off the porch. "Good night, Henry."

It's the second time today I've watched a part of my heart walk away. There's so little of it left, it's a wonder it still beats at all.

Lucy doesn't come back the next day. Or the one after that. Or any of the next fifty that follow. I get a job at the music school and start teaching lessons there. I establish some stilted version of a life in the gaping hole of what was, still too afraid to dream of what could be. I'm not necessarily thriving, but I'm surviving. And I call Delilah, because I promised I would.

She doesn't answer, but I leave her voicemails. Maybe she listens to them; maybe she doesn't. Either way, I'll keep showing up for her. Holding her in this small way, until I can squeeze her in my arms again.

And if that day never comes? Well, I try not to think about it much.

I don't know why I know it's coming the day Lucy returns. It's almost as if the air is sharper, the warmth more saturated, the impending evening storm more electric. By the time she steps foot on my porch, I'm already waiting for her at my door.

"I know we can't be together," she says. "But can we at least be friends?"

My smile is wafer thin but so, so genuine. "I'd like that."

I welcome her in. Offer her coffee. We sit in the breakfast nook and watch the rain come down, saying nothing while feeling everything.

The next week, she comes back. And the pattern repeats.

Some days we talk till our voices are raw. Others we sit in companionable silence. We never touch. We don't discuss our feelings for each other. We just *are,* and that's enough. It's more than I ever let myself hope for.

The day Delilah's letter comes, Lucy sits with me in the quiet. Doesn't speak when I dissolve into tears. Nods her head, with pride in her eyes, when I tell her how strong my daughter is. So much stronger than I'll ever be.

Sometimes I make the trek to the farm instead. We sit at the table with Truett and play cards or eat steak tacos or talk about the plans he has to expand the farm. We celebrate birthdays together. Holidays. Time passes, and I don't feel it going, which is a blessing in and of itself. One I forget to be grateful for until it's too late.

The morning of November 7th, 2021, I'm in my office when there's a knock at the door. I barely hear it from the room, since it's the farthest down the hall. It's only when it comes again, louder and rapid as a racing pulse, that I abandon the schedule I was working on for my music lessons through the holidays and make my way to the door, expecting Lucy to be standing there with a new coffee creamer for us to taste, always too sweet but worth trying if it makes her happy.

Instead it's Truett I find, slump-shouldered on my doorstep with his hands in his pockets. He's taller than me, built broad like his father but kind as his mother. His back is to me, and when I open the door, he spins around, stealing my breath with the tears streaming down his face.

"What's wrong?"

"It's Mama," he whimpers.

I haven't heard him whimper since he was eight years old and fell out of a tree he and Delilah were climbing, shattering his collarbone. My lungs squeeze tight. I reach for my throat absently, needing to hold on to something. "What's wrong?" I repeat.

"Cancer," Tru says softly. His gaze lifts to mine, bereft and seeking comfort. "It's bad, Henry. It's so bad."

I open my arms, and he falls into them. He's several inches taller, and broad everywhere I'm narrow, but in that moment he is a little boy collapsing against my chest. And as his words settle into my mind, I come undone, collapsing right along with him.

Chapter Forty

Delilah

THE SKY IS DOING strange things. As if it knows my heart is breaking in two, it's putting on a show meant only for me, to make the moment hurt a little less. Pink, fluffy clouds billow and break around spectacular orange light. The sun is setting, and this is its curtain call. Soon Dad will be home from the band concert, and Truett will be out on his date. A date I didn't even know he had.

Until now.

"I'm probably making a bigger deal out of it than it needs to be," Truett says. He's pacing in the patch of sawgrass, close to the water's edge. It's early yet in the spring, so the grass is still withered and brown. It crunches beneath his steps, breaking up his anxious mumbling. "I mean, Molly told Robin who told Jason who told me. For all I know, it's a prank and when I show up, she won't even be there."

The responding noise sits low in my throat. I gaze up at Truett from my spot resting against the willow tree's trunk. He's beautiful. Always has been, with his mess of brownish-blond waves and eyes that mimic the ocean on a stormy day. He's gangly, sure, but he fills out more each day thanks to long hours spent working the farm with his father. He still doesn't realize it, though. Doesn't see the way girls at school look at him. The way I look at him.

I never had the courage to tell him. And now I'm too late.

"Are you listening, Temptress?"

I curl my nose at the nickname. He only says it because he knows it bothers me. Because I was not, in fact, listening to his rambling, and that name is the only surefire way to grab my attention.

"What did I miss?"

I know all of Tru's faces. The stoic one he puts on when his father is giving out, which involves a taut jaw and guarded eyes. When he's nervous, his cheeks turn ruddy and he carves trenches into his bottom lip with pearlescent teeth. My favorite is when something has him really excited, because his lips spread into a miraculous smile and his dimple makes an appearance, leaving me speechless.

But I don't know this face. The one he makes when he pauses in his path, brow furrowed, and peers down at me with a question in his gaze so soft it's more pleading than inquiry.

His hand pulses at his side. I press mine against my stomach, which has suddenly flipped.

"Would you practice with me?"

My mouth dries out. "Practice? What are you even talking about?"

He closes the distance between us in a few easy strides. Then he's kneeling in front of me, one Wrangler-clad knee brushing the dirt while he rests his sun-tanned forearm on the other. "Kissing. It's been a while, and I don't wanna look like an idiot with Molly."

"Truett, are you sick?" I reach up and press the back of my hand to his forehead. Try to ignore how perfect his skin feels against my own. "Because what you're saying is crazy. Kissing is

like...I don't know, riding a bike. Or wrangling a calf, for you. You don't really forget how."

Not that I would know. But I'm definitely not going to tell him that. Because despite the tingling in my fingertips and the burning sensation in my chest, the nerves and the jealousy, I find myself leaning closer. Parting my lips a touch. I want him to do this, I realize. Even if it's practice for someone else. It might be the only chance I ever get to kiss him, and as a bonus, he doesn't even have to know I want it.

"Please, Delilah." His brows huddle close, and he folds his hands in pleading. "I won't tell anyone. I promise."

There's a shift inside my chest as my heart settles into the chamber of my ribs. I don't want to be a secret to him. I want to be everything.

But looking into his wide gray gaze, taking in the fault line along his full bottom lip, the stubble at his jaw...I know that I'll take what I can get.

Still, I can't look too eager. So I set a boundary and hope his penchant for breaking the rules holds true.

"Fine." I narrow my gaze. "But only one."

He nods. "I can work with that."

"Okay, so..." I hold up my hands by my head and raise a brow. "How do you want to do this?"

"Um, why don't we stand up?"

"Makes sense."

I rise at the same time as him. We dust off our pants—my ass, his knee—in an awkward pulse of silence. When our gazes meet again, his eyes are soft, the gray diluted. They reflect the orange and pink sky back to me; a perfect mirror.

"Now close your eyes."

"Not a chance." If this is the only time I'll ever get to kiss Truett, I want to see him coming.

His hands slap against his thighs. "You can't kiss with your eyes open, Delilah!"

I cross my arms over my chest, ignoring the thrill that courses through me when his gaze drops to my nonexistent cleavage, even if it only lasts a second. "If you're such an expert, then I guess you don't need my help."

"So difficult," he groans.

And he's right, but what he doesn't realize is that I'm only ever difficult with him. Never with my parents, my teachers, or other friends like Alicia. Only Truett.

I give him hell because he can take it. Because he won't think less of me for it.

I shrug. "Those are my terms. Take it or leave it."

He rolls his eyes, capturing a panorama of the sky in one fluid motion. "Whatever. Eyes open, and only once?"

"Eyes open. Only once." My breath is choppy now, my words a kaleidoscope of splintered sounds. It's settling in. Truett Parker is going to kiss me. Me. It's a fever dream come to life.

Except for the part where it's for some other girl. But I can compartmentalize with the best of them.

He steps forward, slipping his hands around my waist. My skin jumps at the sensation, even through the thin fabric of my lightweight sweater. His arms are muscled and firm against all my soft. I melt into them without meaning to.

Our gazes meet, frantic in the fading light. I've never seen him so close. I could count the faint freckles on the bridge of his nose, the one darker beneath the corner of his right eye. Memorize the thousand shades of gold that make up his hair. The purest gray-blue stones that are his irises.

I could, if I had the time.

"Don't be nervous," he whispers. His breath brushes my lips. It's Big Red gum and minty toothpaste, like he knew this was happening all along. "I'll take care of you."

And then he kisses me. Our lips meet, two strangers that somehow know each other already, like they met in another lifetime. It's my very first. And my second. And my third.

My eyes drift closed. Strong, fumbling hands roam my back. I forget my rules. He forgets them, too. We kiss until our lips are bruised and our breath is quick. Until the sun finally disappears and leaves us blanketed in darkness.

The only promise he keeps is his last. He takes care of me. Truett always does.

***

I shut off the car, letting the engine go dead around us. Dad wastes no time releasing his seat belt and opening his door. When he's out, he stretches his arms above his head and groans like it was a long road trip rather than a short drive from the Grille.

I, however, linger in the quiet. The calm before the storm in Truett's eyes. He's sitting on the front porch steps, a faded Alabama baseball cap cradled in his hands. When he glances up, there's pain in his gaze. Anger, too. And who could blame him? The man who was once the boy I kissed beneath the shade of a willow tree, who promised to take care of me, is trying to do so still. And I've done everything in my power to stop him.

As I pull myself from the car, I'm struck by how similar this feels to the day I arrived home. Trepidation quakes in my belly, filling me with a sharp-winged breed of butterflies. But there's determination, too, steeling my spine. I always planned to do the right thing. It just took me until today to finally understand what that truly means. All I can do is hope that I'm not too late.

Dad smiles when he spots Tru, and his arms fly wide. "Truett! Haven't seen you in a minute."

Tru stands, wipes his hands on his jeans, and embraces my

dad when he steps within reach. "Missed you, old man. Whatcha been up to?"

I purposely slow my steps, not wanting to intrude on their moment. Besides, Truett is intentionally avoiding my gaze as I approach, and I'm tempted to forget my plan and instead attempt to melt into the ground beneath me.

"Oh you know, checking out my new digs," Dad says, laughing. He seems so much like himself today. Whether because of the chance to play or the weight off his shoulders, I'm not sure. All I know is if his speech wasn't slow, I'd never know anything was wrong. He rolls his lips, grasping for the next word, and smiles when he finds it. "Did Delilah tell you? I'm blowing this popsicle stand!"

This gets Truett to look at me, and oh, how I wish he wouldn't. There's an accusation in his gaze. Something like fear hides beneath it.

Tru's eyes cut right through me as he asks, "What do you mean?"

I cup my elbow with one hand, the other dangling limp at my side. I study a small dirt stain on Tru's T-shirt, fresh from the looks of it, so I don't have to meet his gaze. "Edgewood Assisted Living. We toured it today."

Dad slips an arm around my shoulders, oblivious to their slump. "They have a baby grand, boy. It's practically Carnegie Hall."

I dare to peek up at Tru through my lashes. His jaw ticks as he grinds his molars together. His hands have found his hips. There's a fresh Band-Aid on his knuckle, with several smaller cuts around it, like he got caught on a bit of fencing. I focus on that rather than the disappointment in his stare. The disbelief.

I'm not sure if it's the fact that I'm putting Dad into care, or the implications behind it, that earn me that look.

"They have a wait-list. So it'll be a little while," I say in case it's the latter.

Truett's nod is curt and quick. "How long is a while?"

I bite the inside of my cheek. Hard. Tears prick my eyes, and I blink them back. "Could be a month. Could be longer."

Truett mumbles a noncommittal hum, though he looks like he's taken a blow to the chest. "Henry, do you mind if Delilah and I chat for a sec?"

"Sure"—Dad wiggles his eyebrows—"you two take all the time you need."

I reach for my father, catching the sleeve of his threadbare plaid button-down. "Are you sure, Dad? It's been a rough day."

The truth is, I *do* need to talk to Truett. But the obligation to check in, to put Dad's needs above my own, is strong. Maybe one day I'll learn to lay them down or to lift myself above, but today is not that day.

He pats my hand gingerly, a knowing smile playing on his wobbling lips. "I'll be all right, sweet pea. Gonna watch some TV for a bit."

"Okay." I let him go, but I find myself checking his gait as he climbs the steps to the front door. Making sure he slips from his shoes where he always does and walks inside without hesitation. No signs that an episode is imminent, but then, there aren't always.

"So that's it, then?"

I tear my gaze from Dad's silhouette through the windows and focus on Tru. His arms are crossed over his broad chest. He's replaced the hat on his head, and its brim rides low, turning his gaze almost black in its shade. This version of him is all hard lines and stony facade. I know it well. I tried to build one like it for myself, only for life to shatter it without a second thought.

"I know you've seen my texts. My calls. The voicemail." His

gaze is hard, daring me to disagree. "I meant what I said, Delilah. I'm not giving up without a fight this time. I'm here on your doorstep to beg you to please talk to me. Let me in." He licks his lips. Draws in a short breath. "So you're what, leaving? Is that what you were avoiding me for? You didn't have the guts to tell me you were done? I think I deserve better than this, Delilah. I really do."

"It's not that. I—" My voice splinters off. I swallow it, adding to the coating of regret lining my throat. Every excuse dies off in my lungs. What good are they? They don't undo the hurt. I know that better than anyone. So instead I reach for Tru's hand. Tug it loose from his folded arms. I hold it like a promise, a prayer, as I take a note from his book and whisper, "You're right, and I'm sorry."

His eyes widen. Perfectly white teeth puncture the plush curve of his bottom lip. He shakes his head slowly, giving my words time to catch up.

"Are you really leaving?"

I open my mouth to answer, but the sound of a cabinet closing steals my attention. My gaze flickers to the house, and my lips flatline.

"Can we go somewhere else to talk?" I nod toward the closest window, at my father who suddenly makes himself very busy with the kitchen sink. "Somewhere a little more private?"

Truett lets out a strained laugh. The color is still leached from his cheeks, but his eyes are lighter. Glossy with unshed tears. "The river?"

I nod. "Perfect."

He releases my hand, sweeping his in front of us toward the four-wheeler I hadn't noticed parked beside the largest live oak. "Lead the way."

I do. But not before calling over my shoulder, "*TURN OFF THE SINK BEFORE YOU FLOOD THE PLACE.*"

I swear Dad's chuckle follows me all the way to the ATV.

Chapter Forty-One

Delilah

WE RIDE IN SILENCE, my hands curled loosely around his waist. The routine is the same: he dismounts, opens the gate. I drive us through. He latches it and climbs back on. When we arrive in the clearing, the sun is beating down on my shoulders, turning them pink. The air is so thick you could swim in it. I'm tempted to strip and run for the dark, cool river, but I force myself to sit in the discomfort. I'm realizing that I have to learn how to get through tough moments like this if I ever want to have anything worthwhile.

So I'm starting here, with Truett and me. Hoping that the outcome really can be different from my father and Lucy if I lay all my cards on the table now.

Truett leads me through the tall switchgrass to the sandy beach that forms the shoreline. We sit side by side, our thighs touching with every shift, fingertips brushing in the sun-warmed sand behind us.

He's quiet. Contemplative. Anxiety churns my stomach as I wait for him to make the first move.

He gathers a handful of sand and slowly lets it spill from

between his fingers. When he finally speaks, his voice is raw. Weary. "So, Edgewood. That's a swanky place."

I focus on that sand rather than my words. Rather than his face, so guarded against what I might say. "I know. It's— well, I never thought I'd be able to afford a place like it. But he deserves nothing less than the best. It'd be a lot harder to let him go if it were anywhere else."

Guilt still weighs on me, pressing on my lungs like a vise. Knowing it's the right thing to do doesn't make it any easier.

As if he knows this, Truett nudges my shoulder with his. When I glance up, his gaze is soft. Full of understanding. "Why didn't you tell me? I would've helped."

"I know you would've." I purse my lips, studying a ripple in the glassy surface of the water. "And this is only a temporary solution. It gets him in, but I still need to figure out the long-term costs. He could live another decade, you know." *A decade.* So long when it comes to costs, yet so short when you're talking about a life. "But my grandparents left a good amount of money for me when they died. They wanted me to use it to have this big fancy wedding. The full-blown Southern affair that they never got to throw for my mother."

Tru scoffs. "You'd hate that."

"Right?" I widen my gaze, feeling vindicated. "I *would* hate that. I'd have done it for them, I guess, if they were still alive. But they aren't. And that money would go to much better use to help me now, with Dad."

"I don't suppose your mom agreed?"

"Not exactly." I swallow, trying to sink the stone weighing on my chest, but it won't budge. So I go on, breathless. "After everything she's done, everything I've learned… I know she was hurt. I can't blame her for that. But she had no right to hurt me in turn, to make it my problem that her life didn't go the way she planned. No right to lie and try to manipulate me into putting her first. I realized that if we were ever going to have hope of repairing our relationship, I needed her to show me that she could put those feelings aside and really listen to me. Trust me to make the right decision.

"I was running at first, Tru. You're right about that. But I realized this was something I needed to do on my own. And before you object, I know that I don't have to do *everything* alone. I get that. You'd be happy to know I let Alicia witness the entire conversation with my mom and only regretted it the tiniest bit." I let my gaze float up, capturing the few clouds blotting out an otherwise clear sky. A billowing array of starlings burst from the trees to dance across my vision, putting on a show. Their distant calls to each other join with the babbling river to create the soundtrack of my revelation. "Dad and I, we're so much the same. More than I ever realized. I think I needed to understand just how much in order to let go. To accept that it's not my place to force him to stay at home. That this is a gift he's giving me. One that no one ever gave him."

A strong, calloused hand finds my bare knee. I'm still wearing the yellow sundress I had on for the tour. It's riding up, exposing the length of my thigh. For a moment my gaze catches there, mesmerized by the sight of his skin against mine.

Tears blur my vision, stealing away that beautiful patchwork. All the places our edges match up. "I shouldn't have cut you out like that. I was panicking. Thinking I'd fucked everything up because I dared to let myself cut loose for one night. I felt like I didn't deserve him *or* you, if I could be so irresponsible."

I blink, and a tear escapes. Soon my cheeks are slick with them. They fall silently, save for a hiccup of air passing over my lips every few seconds when I forget to breathe.

I don't see him lean close, but I feel his breath on my ear. His lips on the hollow beneath as he whispers, "I'm proud of you, you know that?"

I turn to him, brows furrowed. *He can't possibly mean that.* But he does. It's there in his earnest gaze, his parted lips. In the way he releases my knee to stroke my cheek instead.

"How? *Why?*"

"Why not?" He lets out a breathy chuckle. He shakes his head slowly, lips curved into a soft smile. "You are notoriously selfless. To a fault, sometimes? Sure. But I love that about you. Love everything about who you are." He snags his bottom lip and holds. Like he's waiting for me to bolt because he used the word *love,* but it has the opposite effect. I can't run because I'm growing roots. They're sprouting from everywhere we touch, and everywhere we don't. A life blooming in what is and what could be.

When I don't object, he sucks in a breath and pushes on. "Helping your dad do this on his terms was exactly that. Selfless. But doing it the way you needed to? Standing up to your mother in the process?" He peers up at the treetops, where that flock of starlings has settled. His words fade to nothing more than the scrape of flint against steel, igniting a feeling in my heart that's impossible to ignore. "I've said it before, and I'll say it again. You're remarkable, Temptress. Don't ever forget that."

I couldn't, even if I wanted to. It's impressed upon my heart. Eternal.

Love is a lot of things. It's reckless when you want to be careful. Gentle when the world is anything but. It's choosing a life you'd never want for yourself, because you have a little girl on the way with someone you just met. It's kissing your best friend beneath a willow tree in a quiet meadow in the forest. Taking them back there after life got in the way, only to find those feelings never really left.

Love is a cowboy with strong hands and a gentle heart guiding a new calf safely into the world. Holding his mother's hand as she left it. It's that same cowboy finding me when I'm trying so hard to be lost. Showing me the way back home.

Love is this moment, and every other we've shared. The threads that bind our years together. Our entire lives.

It's the gift of the truth, so I say the truest thing I know.

"I love you, Truett. I always have, I think. Since that very first day when we rolled down the hill in front of your house."

He holds his breath for a beat too long. I'm beginning to think I've entirely misjudged the moment when he chuckles quietly. "You managed to dodge the cow patties *that* time."

"Because you didn't have any cows yet! It's hard, okay?" Laughter spills out of me in torrents, a rival to the rain of my tears. I lean into him, nestling my forehead in the curve of his neck. "You ruined me for everybody else."

He angles toward me and threads a hand through my hair, holding me tightly. A heavy sigh rolls over his lips and onto mine, and his gaze settles there. "Is this the part where you rip my heart out by telling me you love me but you can't stay?"

The pain in those words hollows me out. I cover his hand in my hair with my own and shake my head softly. "That's the thing. I'm not leaving."

He pulls away slightly, eyes widening. "You're not?"

"No." I bite my lip. Nerves wring my stomach. He hasn't said he wants this, not really. But I have to trust my instincts when they tell me it's worth it to take this leap. "You were right, you know. About this place. It's where I belong. Where I've always belonged. I'm not my mother, much to her chagrin. I like it here. Love it, in fact." I drop my hand to rest against his chest. His heartbeat pounds against my palm, as fast as my own. I let that give me the strength I need to add, "This is not an obligation to you, by the way. Just because I'm staying doesn't mean—"

"*Fuck an obligation.*" One hand moves from my hair to my waist, the other tossing his baseball cap before finding my other hip and hauling me into his lap in one smooth motion. We're face-to-face, eye to eye. I can feel his desire swell beneath me, pressed against my core. I roll my hips instinctively, and he hisses in response. When his eyes meet mine once more, they're glazed in sweet sadness. The kind that is a prologue to relief. "You are all I've ever wanted, Temptress. You're every dream I've had, every damn hope for my future. Even when I thought you were lost to me, I prayed for you. Swore my soul to whoever would take it if you'd just come back home so I could say I was sorry. Tell you what I'd always known was true but was too scared to say when we were kids. I love you, Delilah. I'm so damn gone for you, it's insane. You will *never* be an obligation to me. You're my whole world."

He doesn't wait for a response. His fingertips dig into my hips as he surges into me, covering my mouth with his. I can taste the sugar of his words on his tongue, the truthfulness in his every breath. We ebb and we flow, as practiced at this dance as the river that flows behind us. We carve notches into each other meant only for us, so that no other will ever fit like this. Like *us*.

Truett and I were made for each other. Written in the stars long before we came to be. We're the best of our parents, and also entirely ourselves. Their unfinished love story and our very own that's just getting started, all rolled into one.

His hands climb the lattice of my spine. If the sun was heating my skin before, his touch is burning me alive. He finds the ties of my straps on my shoulders and tugs them free. His lips replace them, tracing the path from my sloped shoulder to my collarbone to the hollow at the base of my throat. His tongue laps at that hollow, stealing my breath. My thighs tremble against his hips. Pleasure dips low in my stomach. I want him. I've never wanted anything more.

Truett's fingers slip beneath the cups of the dress's corset top and tug it down, freeing my breasts. He captures them in his wide grasp, and I tip my head back, sucking in a breath. I feel his lips press into the swell of my cleavage. His hands dip lower, scooping me into his waiting mouth. His tongue flicks over my nipple, drawing it to its peak; then he closes his lips around me and sucks.

I'm grateful we're tucked away in the woods, because my moan could alert the entire farm.

"Yes, Tru. *Fuck.*"

"Is that a compliment or a command? 'Cause I'll take either."

"Can't it be both?" I sigh. When I glance down, I swear the man smiles against my breast. He tugs at me with his teeth, then releases me to move to the other nipple and repeat the same ministrations.

I'm desperate for more of this. More of *him.* I find the hem of his shirt and tug, forcing us apart for a moment only to come back together stronger, with no barriers between his chest and my peaked nipples.

He cradles my back as he flips us and lays me down in the soft sand. My hair splays out beneath me, and I giggle. "I'll never get this sand out of all my nooks and crevices."

"I'll lick it off you. Or better yet"—he stands and kicks his boots into the grass—"I'll take you for a swim and get you all cleaned up."

As he undoes his belt and fly, I slip the Keds from my feet, stained as they've become. "I've really got to get some other shoes."

He hooks his thumbs in his waistband and winks. "Whatever you want, consider it yours."

I pull the hem of my dress higher, higher, higher. His gaze tracks the movement, heady with desire. When I reach the peak of my thighs, I pause with only the lacy edge of my panties on display. "Does that apply to anything, or just shoes?"

I watch the column of his throat work. He shudders, and it

ripples through every muscle in his abdomen, making me wish he'd rip the pants off already so I could watch that shiver travel south.

"Anything, Temptress. I'm all yours."

Then he gives me everything.

His cock is so hard for me, and I ache for it, feeling suddenly so empty without him inside me. He fists it and squeezes at the base, a groan ripping from his throat. When he kneels before me, I reach out to swipe the bead of cum from his tip and lick it from my finger with a hum of satisfaction.

He blanches, his jaw impossibly taut. "Now is a very bad time to mention I do not have a condom."

A wicked smile tugs at my lips. I slip a hand beneath the lace of my underwear, sampling my wetness, and swirl it over my throbbing clit. "Good thing I've got an IUD and a clear bill of health."

His gaze darkens. "Are you sure, Delilah? I'll run back to the house right now and grab one. Or, better yet, take you with me so we can do it there."

I arch my back just as a cool breeze kisses my breasts and sigh. "No, I like it here. You look good wearing nothing but sunshine."

"Wanna take that dress off so I can say the same?"

I giggle, thumbing the fabric where it's gathered at my waist. My hips roll into my other hand, the one still stroking my clit in slow circles, which only pushes the dress higher. "I mean, it's kinda like sunshine, don't you think?"

"Almost," he says with a wink. "But I'd have to see both to be sure."

"Fair." I reluctantly remove my hand from my panties and grab the hem of the dress, yanking it over my head. I'm just about to toss it aside when Truett plucks it from my grasp and lays it out behind me, giving me a soft place to recline onto, a barrier from the sand. I sprawl on the dress, bathed in the light, as he tugs my panties down my legs and discards them with the pile of his clothes.

"I'm good, too, by the way." His brows lift. "All clear, if you're sure."

I reach for his waist and pull him toward me, lifting my hips to open myself for him. "I'm sure, Tru. I want all of you. Please."

I don't mean for it to come out so high-pitched, so needy, but that evidence of my desire does something to him. Snaps a tether in his spine that held him back. He folds over me, elbow coming down beside my head while his other hand lines his cock up with my entrance. I feel him there, his head sweeping through my slick center, stoking the flame so high I nearly combust from this alone.

"Please, baby," I whine. "I need you."

The hand by my head sweeps my hair behind my ear, and he kisses me there. Our chests are flush, all heat and sweat and heaving breaths. The sky is endless above us, the same gray-blue as his eyes. They find me, so full of a tenderness I've never seen up close.

He rocks into me, stealing my breath. Cinching my heart. My body arches, reaching for him, and he meets me with every thrust.

It's so different from our first time. So sweet and slow and rhythmic. We make music together. A melody all our own.

His tongue flicks against my throat. My jaw. My earlobe. "See? I can be gentle, too." He buries himself to the hilt. Rolls his hips so I feel him everywhere. "I can be everything you need if you'll let me."

"I want you. *All* of you."

I drag my fingernails down his back, and the groan that escapes his throat is guttural. His thrusts falter in their rhythm. His jaw ticks. He's losing this carefully crafted control, and I'm desperate for it. Need it as much as I need the hot summer air filling my lungs.

I dig my heels into his ass and arch, grinding myself against him. His lids flicker shut, his lips part as he holds himself still, letting me take what I need. "Fuck, baby."

"Give it to me," I growl.

When his eyes flash open, they're twin storm clouds, and his voice is the thunder. "Yes, ma'am."

He loses himself in me like I hoped he would. He thrusts wildly; he bites at my flesh. I carve my nails through every inch of him I can reach, when I'm not blindly gasping for air. Every moment without him is too long. Every second he fills me is impossibly short.

"*More. More. More,*" I chant. And more is what he gives me.

"I'm gonna fill you with my cum, Temptress. Is that what you want?"

"Yes," I groan. I spit onto my finger and find my clit throbbing, pulsing with need. I stroke it in time with his thrusts. An orgasm builds in my core, coiling impossibly tight until I'm nothing but the need. The want. The ecstasy. "Fuck!"

"That's right, baby. Now ride my cock."

Tru pauses his thrusts and turns control over to me, and I arch off the ground, doing as he says. I ride him, circling my clit and humming his name in a breathless cry as wave after wave of the orgasm ripples through me. He watches me, utterly rapt, as I take everything I want from his body. And then, when my legs give out, he grabs my ankles and hauls them to his shoulders, tightening them against his neck. His fingers dig into my thighs as he rocks forward, lifting my hips from the ground, and rails into me with everything he's got.

"Fuck. *Fuck.*" His thrusts come undone and so does he. His cock tightens within me, his shoulders going equally taut, and then I feel a warmth I've never known coat my core. He fills me up, eyes closed, head tipped back. When at last he shudders loose and slips from me, I feel his cum dripping from my entrance and coating my thighs. It's a mess. And now that I've had it, I can't imagine it any other way.

Truett collapses onto me, but his weight is a comfort. An anchor. I lace my arms together at the base of his spine and nuzzle into his shoulder, inhaling the scent of him. Fresh air, sweat, and the sweet musk of vetiver all at once.

"If I'm remarkable," I mutter against his skin, "then what does that make you?"

He cranes his neck till there's only a breath between us, then smiles like a new day born. "Yours. I'm yours."

I smile limply, every muscle in me languid after my release. Even the ones responsible for my joy, and joy is what I'm feeling. I glance up at the sky, the same that bore witness to my life splintering apart nine years ago. It feels impossible to be this close to whole again. To have these pieces of my life returned to me, imperfect and all the better for it.

Dad was wrong. Yes, his disease has a cost. He's losing his independence. His career. So many years off his life. But it has not cost him my forgiveness, because he never needed it. What he needed was to be understood for perhaps the first time in his life. For me to see him for who he is, not to me or my mother or even Truett, but to himself, before it is too late.

I hope I've given him that, just as he's given this to me.

Truett laces his fingers through mine and stands, pulling me to my feet and toward the water. The cold steals my breath at first, but soon it is soothing the ache in my trembling thighs, the stinging pink sunburn on my shoulder blades. We submerge ourselves completely, and when I break the surface once more, I feel free for the first time in my life.

His arm loops around my waist and pulls me close. I feel every hard muscle, every soft bit of flesh. I feel his desire for me returning as his gaze finds mine once more.

"What if I forget you one day?" I blurt out. The fear, buried deep in my heart after my initial research, has floated through the doors my confessions have blown open. Try as I might, I can't ignore it any longer.

His brow furrows. "What do you mean?"

"My dad's dementia. It's hereditary." I lick the river water from my lips. Biding my time. "Would you still want to be with me, knowing that's a possibility?"

Add this to the list of things I love about Truett: He doesn't answer right away. Doesn't spew out pretty words to make me feel better. He thinks about it. Really considers what he wants to say. And though I feel like I might vomit with the anxiety of it all, I'm grateful to know he isn't making this decision lightly.

When his lips finally part, a water droplet hangs from his Cupid's bow. It falls to the river below, not lost but forever changed.

I know the feeling.

"Henry once told me that when his mom was near the end, she talked a lot about her childhood. Asked for her siblings, her parents. She forgot everything else but that."

I look up at him, at the face I know as well as my own. He smiles.

"When you think about your childhood, who do you see?"

An odd question. Not *what* do you see, but *who*. I close my eyes and allow myself to drift back through the years. I see my dad, pushing me in the swing that once hung from the live oak out front. I see my mom working on spreadsheets at the breakfast nook when I walked in after school. I see the fields dotted with cattle, their bellows the soundtrack that lulled me to sleep.

And in the background of every memory? There is Truett. He's standing back, waiting for his turn on the swing. He's right behind me, his foot hitting the squeaky floorboard as we tumble into the kitchen in search of after-school snacks. He's running through the fields, chasing down a stubborn steer, a wild grin spread across his face.

A tear streams from my eye. I blink my way back into the present, and when our gazes meet, I'm looking at my past and present and future all in one.

"I see you. Always you."

The pad of his thumb is coarse against my skin. As quickly as the tear appeared, it's gone. "Exactly. I'll be with you till the very end, Delilah. And if ever there's a time where you can't remember, I'll do it for both of us. I promise."

My toes sink into the sandy bottom of the river as I lift up, closing the distance between us. Goose bumps dance on the surface of my skin, and on his in turn. Every touch is electrified by the cold. By the hope. By the beauty and pain of his promise. We embrace each other just as we embrace an uncertain future. Wholeheartedly and without fear.

A breeze filters through the clearing, spurring the leaves on the willow tree to dance. The water ripples around us. Not too far away, a steer lets out a long bellow, reminding us of his presence. Truett's tongue slips between my lips and caresses mine. Our lives shift, changing for the better, even as the world goes on turning around us.

It's a memory worth holding on to, so I tuck it into my heart for safekeeping, knowing that if a day comes when I can no longer recall it, Truett will be there to give it back to me. He'll take care of me.

Always.

Chapter Forty-Two

Henry

December 3rd, 2021

I̲t̲ ̲t̲a̲k̲e̲s̲ weeks to get a complete picture of just how bad "bad" really is. More blood tests, ultrasounds, and finally, a multiphase CT scan that confirms the doctor's suspicions.

Pancreatic cancer. Stage four.

It feels almost laughable how many terrible things one person can be forced to face in their lifetime. If I hadn't witnessed it for myself, I couldn't possibly believe it. Lucy, the most beautiful, tranquil, deserving person I know…diagnosed with a terminal disease. I cry until I laugh. I laugh until I cry again.

Lucy takes the diagnosis on the chin. The night she and Truett share the news, as we gather around their kitchen island with a spread of her favorite desserts between us, her bottom lip barely wobbles. Her eyes gloss over, but no tears fall. Later that night, after Truett has gone to check on the few cows he suspects will be calving soon, Lucy reclines into the couch beside me. We touch, for the first time in years. A rule we created for ourselves that suddenly seems so trivial in light of everything else.

"I'm not scared," she says softly. Her voice is raw. I know

without asking that she cried her tears where no one could see her. That they've ripped her vocal cords apart. When she glances at me, though, there's a smile curving her lips. A peace settling over her features. "Not for me, anyway."

My throat is thick with worry. I haven't been able to take a full breath in weeks. I want to be as strong as she is. But the truth is, I'm absolutely terrified.

"Hey"—she taps my nose—"don't do that."

Her thumb dances over my knuckles, a metronome setting the pace of my thoughts. Back and forth. Here, and then in the future, one impossibly void of Lucy's laughter. Her smile. Her light, in an otherwise bleak world.

"How can I not?" I whisper, not trusting my voice to go higher. A tear slips from my jaw onto the tan suede of their couch, blooming in the fabric.

She shrugs. "Because I said so."

My eyes shutter as a chuckle scrapes my throat. "Not good enough."

"I'm serious."

She reaches up and cups my cheek with her soft palm. I cover it with my own, holding her there. This touch is so precious. So sacred. Why did we deny ourselves of it for so long?

"How can you say you're not scared?"

"Because," she says, shifting so she's facing the muted television rather than me. "All I wanted in life was to be free. And these last six years, that's exactly what I've been. No Waylon. No overbearing father. Just me and Truett. And you, occasionally." She winks, but there's an edge to her voice. A yearning that neither of us dares to acknowledge. Solemnity falls over her face, filling her eyes with a soft reverence. "That's more than a lot of people ever get in their lives. I'm lucky. I know that I am. How could I be scared of dying, when I get the pleasure of leaving on a high note?"

Tears blur my vision. I blink them away, wanting as clear a picture of her as I can get. "How long do we have?"

She rolls her bottom lip, glancing down at our joined hands. "Could be a year. Could be less. Depends on how I respond to treatment."

A sob surges in my chest, begging for release. A year. Such an impossibly short time. A minuscule fraction of everything this life owed her, an insufficient repayment for all that it took.

"Can I ask you something, Henry? And please be completely honest."

"Anything," I manage to choke out.

She swallows hard. When she glances up, her eyes are more blue than gray. Damp with the remnants of her grief. "I know we agreed a long time ago that this would be it. A friendship. A beautiful one, I might add. One that I'm so grateful for. And before you panic, I'm not asking for that to change." She pats my hand, laughing softly. "Turns out, cancer doesn't lend itself to feeling much in the way of desire. And I guess it's not a question so much as a confession." Her lips part as she sucks in a quick breath. "Sorry, I'm rambling."

I bite back a smile. "What else is new?"

That earns me a punch to the bicep. A surprisingly strong one. I rub at the ache, shooting her a glare. She giggles in response, and I smile. For a moment we're not Henry and Lucy, with all the complications that entails. We're just two people talking. Laughing. Grieving, too. All the rest falls away, and I catch a glimpse of who we could've been had circumstances been different for us. Had I made different choices, or the same choices sooner, and changed the entire course of our lives.

Perhaps the problem isn't that I was selfish, but that I waited too long to be. And now it's too late. It's the saddest truth I'll ever have to face.

"I need you to know that I love you, Henry. I really, truly do.

And that love is the greatest gift, the greatest burden, I've ever had the privilege of bearing." Her face crumples, careful stoicism fragmenting. A tear falls against her will, and her tongue meets it on the descent, swiping it from the precipice of her upper lip. "And I guess what I wanted to ask was if you felt it, too. If this big, impossible thing that's taken up so much space in my heart for so long was one-sided all along. Because I don't think it is, but I can't bear to die without knowing for sure."

There's the validation of finding out the truth about a situation after so many years, and there's the pain of finding it out far too late. This is both, and for a moment I'm broken so thoroughly by it that I can't take my next breath, let alone speak.

Then I do, and my confession flows from me with abandon, no longer bound by the ties her words have snapped.

"I think the first time I considered the possibility that I might love you, I was maybe twelve? You were singing in the choir and I was thinking very not-church-appropriate thoughts, and I wondered if that was it. The feeling my parents talked about, or movies I'd seen on TV. Now I realize it was probably hormones, but I digress."

She palms her face, peeking at me from between her fingers. Suddenly I'm seventeen again, and so painfully in love with her I can't form a coherent thought, so I rip the rest of my admission out of thin air.

"It was the moment we played together that very first time that did me in, to be honest. That night I lay in bed with the feeling of that song still vibrating in my fingertips. With the image of you in that sundress, letting loose in front of me for the very first time, replaying in my head on a never-ending loop. I was a goner. So totally confident that I loved you." I smile at the memory. At the phantom tingling creeping its way back into my fingertips. "And I'm sure I did, as much as any kid can love, you know?"

She nods, her gaze distant. "I know."

My throat constricts, holding my next words captive. Their passage from my lips is almost as difficult as the years they recollect were to live. And yet, here I am.

Here we are.

"Losing Dad…it forced me to grow up overnight. Then everything happened with Kimberly, and I told myself I had to forget that feeling we shared. That it was blown out of proportion, bigger in my memory than in reality." My gaze drops, shame coloring my cheeks. "When you and Waylon showed up next door, I'd worked so hard for so long to forget how it felt to be close to you. To convince myself it was a product of teenage hormones rather than anything real. But you were here, right in front of me, and despite the circumstances, those feelings all came rushing back. Just as real. And even more impossible to act upon than when we were kids."

I blink away the image, replacing it with one from the night of Delilah's first volleyball game. "I denied it for years. Forced myself to believe that you were happy, and I was happy, and everything would be okay. But the day you showed up at the school with that bruise on your face, I could've killed Waylon. Do you know that? I wanted to. I've never wanted that before, or since. But knowing he had hurt you. Someone so precious, so perfect. I couldn't bear it. And I knew then that I only felt that way because I loved you. Because I never stopped loving you."

In the silence that follows, the room comes rushing in. The low buzz of the television. The tick of a grandfather clock in the hall. A cow mooing outside, and the engine of an ATV that follows.

We're running out of time together, in more ways than one.

Lucy smiles, her gaze locked on something unseen. "I'm happy we never got to be together."

I startle, one brow raising. "Why?"

"Because," she says, shifting so her knee rests on my thigh, and our joined hands are propped on that tower of limbs. "I'll die without you ever finding out how imperfect I actually am. I'll always be this tidy, beautiful thing in your memory. Never the broken woman I've seen in the mirror my entire life."

Anger pulses in my temples, surprising me. I swallow hard, forcing my words to come out calmly, when the feelings behind them are anything but. "You're forgetting that I know you, Lucy. Not some curated version of you, but *you*. To your core. I've seen you cower for your father. Take more shit from that asshole you married than anyone ever should. I've seen you weak, and I've seen you strong. Brave. Running from your bedroom window at midnight or standing up for yourself and preparing to leave that same man you gave your life to when he didn't deserve it. Leaving him, when the time came to do it. I've seen you lose your cool with Truett, and I've seen you apologize afterward. I've seen every good and awful thing, and I love you anyway. Still. No matter what."

She offers a watery smile that chisels at my heart. Drops a stone in my hollow chest. "It could've been amazing. You and me. We could've had something really special."

That ATV engine grows louder, then cuts off right outside the door. Her gaze flickers to the door, but I'm not done. Not ready to let this moment pass without making her the only promise I can keep.

"We'll get another life, Lucy. Another chance." I lift our joined hands to my lips. "I promise. I'll find you when I get there, and I'll never let you go."

Tru walks in. I don't have to look over my shoulder to know. She finds him, her eyes softening at the edges as soon as she does.

"Maybe we already got our second chance." Her hand pulses in mine, and her words are barely above a whisper as she juts her chin toward her son and adds, "Maybe it's them."

I glance over my shoulder. Truett meets my gaze, a question in his own. He's welcome to search, but he'll find no answers in mine. All I know of the future is hope. And hope is what I want to give Lucy.

"Maybe it is," I reply, letting my thoughts drift to my daughter. I wonder how she's doing. If she's happy. If I'll ever get to see her again.

She loved Lucy, once upon a time. Would she want to know Lucy's dying? Would that knowledge bring her home?

It's unfair and a bit manipulative, but I consider it for a moment.

Then Lucy releases my hand and rises, grimacing in pain as she does, and I'm pulled back from the cliff's edge. I jerk to my feet, reaching for her, but she waves me off. "I'm fine. Not an invalid yet."

She pads over to meet Truett, who's still standing in the doorway with a raised brow and tearstained cheeks. "Everything okay, Mom?"

"More than okay," she muses, reaching up to pinch one of his dirt-smudged shoulders. "Any new babies to name?"

"You know it's not good to name them," he says, a discouraging scowl on his face.

"Amuse me," she replies.

A heavy sigh deflates his chest, but his eyes are warm when they regard his mother. "We've got a new girl. 542 calved sometime during dinner."

"Perfect. We'll call her Rosie."

His expression softens. "Okay, Mama. Rosie it is."

Lucy rises on her tiptoes to kiss her son, and it makes my chest ache with a jealousy I can barely stomach.

"I'm going to head to bed, you two. Big day tomorrow. Lots of needles." She winks even as Truett and I wince. "Relax, y'all. It's not the end of the world. Just of me."

"Mom!"

"Lucy," I groan simultaneously.

"Good night!" she singsongs, ignoring our objections.

We both watch her disappear down the hall toward her bedroom, and when the door shuts, I keep my eyes on it as I say, "Dare I ask, what is tomorrow?"

"More tests. Determining a treatment plan." Truett slips out of his boots and crosses the room, taking the seat beside me that his mother just abandoned. "I know it's a lot to ask, but would you be able to come with us?"

I glance over, finding tears welling in his eyes. He looks so much like his mother that for a moment it steals my breath.

"I don't know how to do this alone," he admits.

I look at him and see myself, twenty-some-odd years ago, facing a funeral I didn't know how to plan. A loss I didn't know how to grieve. A responsibility like no other I'd ever had before.

So I reach out and pat his knee, catching his gaze and holding it tight. "I'll be there every step of the way."

"Thank you," he manages to whisper. "I'm really glad you're here."

My smile is a pathetic, mournful thing. His responding one the same. But we aren't alone in our fear, our uncertainty. For that, I'm eternally grateful.

* * *

May 1st, 2022

Lucy Parker dies on a Sunday morning, with sunlight streaming in her bedroom window, painting her sunken cheeks gold. "You'll Be in My Heart" plays on the radio, and Truett holds her hand, weeping softly. Roberta, her caretaker, sits in the corner, tears streaming down her cheeks. I stand at the foot of her bed, counting each rise and fall of her chest, until there's nothing left to count. Until loss collapses in on us like a demolished house, destroying everything we once knew home to be.

I help Truett plan her funeral. Stand beside him while his grandfather glares from the back row. It's a graveside service, in the hillside cemetery behind their house, where she can rest in the shade of live oaks, kept company by Abel Johnson's family and the birds that sing constantly overhead. The funeral director speaks nothing of salvation, but instead of living life with no regrets. A lesson Lucy and I learned far too late. As I watch the love of my life be lowered into the ground at far too young an age, regrets are all that I have. All that I am. They weigh so heavy on my mind that I wonder if I'll ever be free of them. If this is how I'll feel for the rest of my life.

I stumble home after the last of the attendees have left Lucy's wake and Truett has passed out on their couch, one of her shirts cradled in his clenched fist. The sight of him like that, so large and yet so incredibly small, haunts me when I close my eyes. Is there when I finally drift off to sleep.

In the days that follow Lucy's passing, grief deems me palatable enough to swallow whole. The world grows bleak and dark in a way I've never seen, cutting me off from my own senses. I do not hurt; I do not hunger. I sit on the couch, watching the light paint and repaint my walls with each new day. Another day without her in it.

It consumes me so thoroughly that I miss the calls from the music school. The texts from my coworkers. My students. At one point Truett calls, and it's the first time I feel my hand twitch toward the phone. I cannot make my arm lift. The effort is too monumental. Eventually the screen goes dark. And then it dies altogether.

He resorts to showing up at my door, which I've neglected to lock, and letting himself into the dark mausoleum that is my home. I'm sure I smell. Can't remember the last time I showered. But he doesn't look much better than me. We sit in our numb brokenness and let proximity be enough. Let our shared hurt be the thing that pulls us through.

Months pass, and though I do eventually return to work, my heart is no longer in it. When Lucy left the world, she took music with her. Playing it feels like I'm stealing from the dead. I drop to part-time. Then occasional lessons. My savings dwindle, but I can't bring myself to care.

My brain is filled with fog. I lose hours of the day to it, or sometimes a day in its entirety. I turn on the stovetop but forget until the smell of gas fills the house. Start the shower but never get in. My wallet goes missing. Turns up in a discarded flowerpot. I find my keys after three days in the bottom of a coffee mug. Truett seems to be getting better, while I fall deeper into the hole. I'd be happy for him if I could feel anything at all.

It happens so gradually that I forget to question it. I blame the misplaced words and forgotten tasks on grief, rather than recognizing them for what they are. I go through the motions. Put one foot in front of the other. Disregard Tru's questions as him being overly concerned. Disregard my own confusion as a symptom of entering my forties.

It's not until I'm mowing the lawn on a balmy summer day, and Truett stops me in my tracks that I realize something is wrong. He places a hand over mine, forcing me to meet his gaze, which is filled with genuine concern.

"Henry, the mower isn't running."

"Are you crazy? Of course it is." But when I glance down, the sound of the world comes rushing in, and it's notably absent of the growl of an engine. "Huh. Must've kicked off." I bend over and yank the chain, but the engine doesn't even gurgle. "Did you break this thing? What the hell, Truett?"

He's silent for a long moment. When he swallows, I'm

convinced it's because he's guilty. But his words land on me like a splash of cool water, pulling me out of the fog.

"It's been broken for a week, and you've mowed with it every day regardless." He steps closer but drops his hand from mine to rest on his hip. "Is everything okay, Henry? This goes beyond normal grief. Mom's been gone for months. I'm really concerned about you."

Panic lances my stomach. I try to swallow, but my throat is too dry to work. I feel like I'm suffocating in the open air. Like I'll die if I don't get oxygen, but I can't remember how to for the life of me.

"I think I'm sick," I finally manage to get out. "Fuck, I think I'm really sick, Tru."

Concern flashes in his gaze, but his voice is level when he speaks. "It'll be okay. Do you want me to call your doctor, or do you want me to take you to the hospital? I can do either."

"I— I don't know." I bite at my lip, willing the pain to bring with it an answer, but nothing comes.

"Hospital it is. Come on, then."

"Right now?" I glance down, suddenly aware of the tall grass tickling my calves. I'm in my underwear, socks, and nothing else. How did I let myself go outside like this? "I have to change."

"No worries. I'll help," Truett says, offering me his hand.

I take it, and he guides me forward. Releases my hand to clasp my shoulder, which stings on contact. Sunburnt. I'm sunburnt. How long have I been outside without a shirt?

"I'm so sorry about all this," I mumble.

"Don't be. Let's get you to the doctor and you'll be right as rain."

And I try to believe him, I do. But I know deep down what's happening. I sense it like a cold coming on. A scratch of the throat that will inevitably metastasize into a full-blown illness.

I think of my mother's pearl earrings, how they disappeared

and she accused Kimberly of stealing them. I picture them in the glove compartment of my car, right where my mother had stowed them and then forgotten.

Those earrings were the beginning of the end. Cold dread sends a shiver down my spine.

Truett hands me a shirt and shorts from the laundry basket on the couch. The room is in disarray. Clothes, both clean and dirty, are strewn about every surface. Dishes fill the sink. When did I let it get this way? Where have I been in my brain?

He doesn't say a word, but he doesn't need to. We both know this isn't right.

"Tru, I—"

He glances up from helping tie my shoes. Why is he doing that? Surely I could've.

"What's happening?" I say, not recognizing the desperation in my voice.

"I don't know, but we're going to find out."

"I'm scared," I admit.

He rises in front of me, offering a reassuring smile. "It'll be okay, Henry. I've got your back, remember? You had mine, and now I have yours."

When did he get so grown? I study the man before me, remembering when he was just a little boy, chasing Delilah around my yard.

Delilah.

I don't realize I've said her name aloud until Tru's gaze narrows, an incredulous brow raising. "Do you want me to call her? I didn't...I mean, I thought you two didn't really talk, you know?"

"We don't," I say, my throat constricting around the words. "You have to...to..."

"Anything, Henry." He cups my shoulder, ducking his head to

meet my gaze head-on. "Tell me what you need, and I'll take care of it."

"That," I say, lifting a finger to his chest. "Take care of Delilah. Promise you'll take care of Delilah."

His gaze softens at the edges. A dimple that makes him seem so young hollows out his cheek when he smiles sadly and nods.

"I promise." He draws an X over his heart. "If there ever comes a day when you can't, then I promise I'll take care of our girl. Now let's get you to the hospital and get you feeling better, okay?"

"Okay," I relent. I let him guide me to his truck. Help me up, and buckle me in. I'm lost in another world. Another time, when Delilah was a child, and her grandmother lost so much more than her earrings.

She lost her memories, and now I'm losing mine too.

I know it before we even pull into the doctor. Before the tests that follow, over the course of the next few months. Before the diagnosis lands in my lap, and Truett closes his eyes to hide his devastation. I know that I'm going to forget, and this angry cycle will go on repeating itself if I don't do anything to stop it.

So I take the meds. I do the therapies. And I put the plan in place, so that Delilah never has to choose between her life or mine. So that when I call, when I break the news, the wheels will already be in motion. Her life can go on without a hitch, while mine slowly winds toward the inevitable end.

It may be too late for me, but I'll be damned if I let my daughter follow in my footsteps. I talk to the lawyers. I start to make plans. All of it while I still can, with a little help from Truett. I'm confident I have time, until I find myself in a ditch with the hood of my car caved in. That's when I call Delilah, because the end seems closer than ever.

I listen to the phone ring while Tru sips coffee at my table, a carefully passive look painted on his face.

It goes to voicemail, which I expected. Am grateful for, really, because I don't want her to think I'm asking anything of her. Pressuring her to change her mind and come home. She made her decision, and I'm so proud of her. I want her to put herself first. To truly live a life with no regrets.

To be better than me, in every way. Starting with this one.

The dial tone sounds, and I open my mouth, hoping my love for her laces every word. Hoping I can somehow convey, in the boundaries of a voicemail, just how much I love her. How much I dream for her. That I hope she'll be something that happens to this world, rather than letting this world happen to her, the way I always have.

I picture her listening on the other end of the phone. But in my mind she's fifteen and in the passenger seat of my car, gazing up at me with wide hazel eyes, a quiet demand on her lips.

"Don't call me Delilah, okay? No matter how old I get, I'm sweet pea to you. Promise?"

I promised her then. And I keep my promise now.

"Hi, sweet pea. It's Dad."

Epilogue

Truett

THE DAY OF OUR WEDDING, I climb the hill to visit Mama before the festivities get started.

It won't be a huge affair. That's not Delilah's or my style. Ollie, Jason, and Emmett are coming, towing along their families. Alicia and Destin. Tess and her new boyfriend. Roberta and her husband. Even Delilah's mom made the drive, arriving yesterday with a pinched smile and a passing comment about our choice in florals—wildflowers plucked from the north field—that Delilah nipped right in the bud.

My girl doesn't take that kind of shit from anyone anymore, and I couldn't be prouder.

I place a bundle of white carnations at the base of Mama's headstone. They stand out in stark contrast against the dark granite. I always consider bringing more elaborate, expensive flowers, but these remind me of my mother. And of Delilah. Fragile at first glance, with delicately carved petals, but they can endure almost anything.

It's why I had them tattooed on my ribs, as close to my heart as possible.

"Hey, Mama, do you know what today is?"

I picture her standing in front of me, replacing her solemn stone. She tucks her blonde hair back, smiling brightly at me. *"What day is it, Tru?"*

"My wedding day." Tears prick my eyes. I'd swipe at them, try to hide them the way my dad taught me to, but Mama said it was good to cry. To let it out. So I do. "I wish you could be here."

Her voice travels through the years, from a night when I was at sleepaway camp and called to tell her something similar. She sighs and whispers, *"I am, baby."*

"She's going to be so beautiful. I can't believe I get to marry Delilah. I'm so lucky, Mama. Did you ever think I'd get so lucky?"

A bird calls overhead, and I like to believe it means she's listening. That she is somewhere nearby, just through the trees, dressed in her finest clothes. That she'll be watching when I make my vows to my wife. When I take her in my arms and promise to never let go.

"You be good to her," Mama whispered, the day she closed her eyes for the last time. *"Whoever you marry, you promise me that you will treat her with kindness and respect. That you'll give her space when she needs, and pull her close when she doesn't. That you'll love her the way I've loved you, and then some. And if it's Delilah—"*

"It won't be Delilah, Mom," I'd chastised, because I couldn't let myself hope for such a thing.

"If it is," she repeated, ignoring me, *"you give her an extra hug from me when you get the chance, okay? And tell her I love her. And I'm proud of her."*

And so I did. The day I got down on one knee, with the ring Mama passed down to me, I told Delilah that I love her. That Mama loved her. And that she'd be honored to know we found our way back to each other, back to something beautiful, in the midst of so much ugliness.

"She's wearing your ring, Mama. And it looks beautiful on her."

Not the ring my mother wore when she married my father, but the ring she chose for herself from her grandmother's jewelry case after the divorce was finalized. Her freedom ring, as she called it. Now forever a part of my love story.

"Are you ready, Tru?"

I turn to glance over my shoulder. Delilah's hair cascades in soft curls over her shoulders. A braid holds her bangs back, and it's threaded through with wildflowers. She's wearing a white lace dress that billows in the early summer breeze, brushing the grass at her feet as it dances. There are no secrets between us, not even this one. She dressed in front of me this morning. Asked me to zip her up. Then we went to Edgewood to get her father.

These days his speech is mostly unintelligible, so he tends to remain quiet. But his eyes light up when he sees us, letting us know he still recognizes Delilah and me. I know the day is coming when we will lose even that, but for now I'm grateful.

I cast one last glance at Mama's stone, whisper, "I love you," and blow a kiss her way. Wherever she is, I hope she catches it. Tucks it in her pocket for safekeeping.

"Ready," I say, holding out my hand for my bride. The love of not just this life, but every single one I'll be given. My forever in an existence that promises nothing except this singular moment, and is all the more precious for it.

She takes my hand and squeals as I spin her in, covering her mouth with mine. She is everything soft and warm in this world. My home incarnate. I'll never stop marveling at the fact that she's here and she's mine. That she loves me, despite every reason I've given her not to. That this woman who never stops caring for others, lets herself be cared for by me.

I am the luckiest man alive. I feel it in my soul.

"Everyone's here. They're waiting for us to get started." She smiles against my lips. Nips my bottom one and pulls back. "What do you say we go make an honest woman out of me, huh?"

"But it's been fun knowing we're being bad, don't you think?"

She slaps my chest playfully, her laughter bubbling over.

We've been living together for a few months now. Sold her dad's house to a young family whose kids love to come play in the pasture. The money will help make sure his care continues for as long as needed. That he'll want for nothing for the rest of his life.

And what's left will be donated to research, so that hopefully there comes a day when no one has to suffer like he and his mother did.

We walk hand in hand toward the ceremony site. It's simple enough: a couple rows of chairs in front of an arch I built from a live oak on our property. Everyone's sitting there, waiting for us. As we approach, Roberta helps Henry to his feet. His hair is combed back, the gray so finely woven with the brown that you can barely tell where one ends and the other begins. He's wearing a tweed suit that's slightly too big, with a loosely bound boutonniere of honeysuckle pinned to his lapel.

"Sweet… Pea…" he mumbles, reaching for Delilah. He lets out a bright, happy vocalization and then mutters something that sounds like, "Beautiful."

I don't know who starts crying first, but when I glance at Delilah through tears, her gaze is equally glossed over.

The walk down the aisle is short. As quickly as we part, we are reunited, to the sound of Phil Collins playing on somebody's cell phone. We asked Roberta to marry us, and she was happy to get ordained online for the occasion. She takes us through the traditional vows with careful precision. We are declared husband and wife before the people we love most in the world, and invited to seal the deal. It's the most important moment of my life, and it's over in four and a half minutes.

I take Delilah in my arms and kiss her silly. The girl who became the woman who became my wife. We kiss until the rest of the world falls away, leaving only Delilah and me.

There has only ever been Delilah and me.

I lose myself in her. In the feeling that swells in my chest, an emotion so big I have no words for it. I feel the love of those around us, and those gone before us, like a living thing thrumming beneath my skin. We will never be alone, for as long as we both shall live. And I plan to live a long, long time.

And if ever there comes a day when Delilah cannot remember, when she looks to me for help, for hope, and asks me who she is, I'll tell her this.

You are my love. My life. My heart. You are my oldest friend and the person who knows me best. You are remarkable. And you are mine.

"And you are mine," she says, kissing the remnants of the words from my lips. Words I didn't think I'd spoken aloud but wouldn't doubt she heard straight from my heart.

"To the Parkers!" someone cheers. When I glance at the crowd, Destin is holding up a beer. Alicia smiles brightly beside him, a camera poised in her hand and aimed in our direction.

"The Ridgefield-Parkers," I correct. Out of the corner of my eye, I see Henry smile. Delilah's hand tugs at my lapel, and her bottom lip warbles.

"To the Ridgefield-Parkers!" Ollie adds, and it slowly echoes through the rest of our friends. Even Kimberly joins in, a cordial smile plastered on her face. She's making an effort, and for that I'm grateful. No one deserves it more than Delilah.

I gaze down at my bride. My best friend. My forever love. "To my Temptress," I say, holding up an imaginary glass.

She smiles, grabs my hand, and places it over her heart. There's a spark in her eyes, a delicious curve to her lips, as she says, "And to being tempted."

Hear, hear.

Acknowledgments

No novel is born in a silo, but I'm not kidding when I say this one took a village to raise it.

First of all, to my wonderful husband (!!!) who cheered me on through what felt like the longest self-doubt spiral of my life. Planning a wedding while writing this book was no walk in the park. I couldn't have done it without you. I'm so grateful this story is finally complete, but more importantly, so happy that we're finally married.

To Allie Samberts, if you hadn't come along and offered to be critique partners, I think this book would've died a slow, painful death. You revived my love for it and for writing in general. It has been so fun to walk in tandem through this process with you, always lifting when the other is falling. I can't wait for all the stories and shenanigans to come. I love you dearly.

To Jackie Egan, your endless encouragement has been, and always will be, vital to both my mental health and the quality of my writing. You are my hero and best friend and I love you. To Ronnie Mathews, your critiques and suggestions made this story so much better than I ever could've alone. Thank you for trusting me and for being someone I can always trust in return. I love you times a thousand.

Now, for that village I mentioned. Jennalee, Stephanie, Paige, Sam, Katie: thank you for reading these pages early and rooting for these characters so fiercely. Linda, Chelsea, Stef: your insight as sensitivity readers was so precious to me. Thank you for the honor of sharing your stories with me, and to Linda especially, for letting me borrow your movie night memory. I hope I have done it justice. I hope you all feel seen, and more importantly loved, by this ode to the caretakers who make this world go round.

Thank you as well to Leah, for answering my questions about speech therapy, and to Emma, for your guidance surrounding nursing homes and dementia care. Thank you, Aaron, for the tour of Fly Farms and for answering my incessant questions for months on end. Because of you, I now know the difference between a heifer and a cow, among many other things. I owe you one. Thank you also to Lainey Lawson for answering my early cattle farming questions and for being as hyped about this story as I am about yours. Love you big.

To Lea Ann, editor extraordinaire, I apologize for ruining your entire May with this behemoth. I know you wouldn't read something that makes you cry on the daily for many people, so I consider it a great honor. Your loving touch always wraps up my books in the most perfect bow. I truly couldn't do this author thing without you.

Aunt Lou, I know you've been gone for years, but I still wanted to say thank you. Thank you for loving me. For celebrating me. For always seeking the next adventure. I hope in the end, if you remembered nothing else, you remembered that I love you, just as Henry has always felt Delilah's love through and through.

This list could go on forever and ever, so I'll finish by saying this: if you have read, shared, talked about, or interacted with my books in any way, THANK YOU. This has been the journey of a lifetime, and it's only getting started. I hope you love this one as much as I do. And I hope you forgive me for all the tears.

On to the next one…

About Hannah Bird

Hannah's accolades include a second-grade teacher who said her story about bats had "very good potential" and enough accelerated reading medals to sink a body at sea. Her goals in life are to write novels that will make you cry, and to check everything off the bucket list she wrote at seventeen.

Hannah resides among the rolling hills of Tennessee with her other half and their clingy golden retrievers. When she is not writing, she is trying to outrun her sweet tooth in the gym.

You can travel along with Hannah on her writing journey at her website, hannahbirdauthor.com, and at all the bookish destinations below:

facebook.com/hannahbirdauthor

instagram.com/hannahbirdauthor

amazon.com/author/hannahbird

goodreads.com/hannahbird

tiktok.com/@hannahbirdauthor